STEPHANIE
DENNE

MARK OF THE VASIRIAN

1

BLACKTHORN
SAGA

Published in Canada by Amethyst Corvid Press, Ontario, Canada.

AMETHYST CORVID PRESS

Mark of the Vasirian.
First Edition.
ISBN: 978-1-7387272-0-9
Stephanie Denne.
See more books by Stephanie Denne at https://stephaniedenneauthor.com
Editing by Kelly Schaub
Cover Design by Story Wrappers – storywrappers.com

For my Husband...

I know you don't get the obsession, but thank you for putting up with it, regardless.

A Message from the Author

This book contains content that may be unsuitable for certain readers. To learn more about content warnings in the author's work, please visit her website:

www.stephaniedenneauthor.com/content-warnings

Playlist

Music has always played an important role in my creative process. These are just some of the inspirational tracks that fuelled the creation of Mark of the Vasirian.

Ruelle – Storm
Beth Crowley – I Didn't Ask for This
Beth Crowley – In the End
Halsey – Control
Beth Crowley – Red
Beth Crowley – Savior
Billie Eilish – Hostage
Beth Crowley – Warrior
Nat – Some Say

Instrumentals from YouTube (added exact title so they are searchable):

SYML – I Wanted to Leave
Soundtrack for a Supervillain – Dark and Sinister Music Mix
A (really) Dark Academia Playlist. Vol 1
2 Hours of Dark Music by Adrian von Ziegler
1 Hour of Dark Piano | Dark Piano for Dark Writing
Circles – Ambient Dark Sexy Cinematic Instrumental (NSFW Video)
Invitation – Ambient Dark Sexy Instrumental

Blackthorn Academy Campus

It's easy to lose your way at the mysterious Blackthorn Academy. But with a little luck, and this handy map, I'm sure you'll do just fine… maybe.

1

Trapped

Blaire collected dirty plates and sighed, fighting a headache, and trying to be grateful for the much-needed hours after being cut short the week before. She started wiping down the table but stopped short at the sight of the newcomers taking their seats in the large round corner booth next to the secondary entrance. They were in Charlotte's section, but she must have gone to the back.

The burgundy and black uniforms caught her eye first—Blackthorn Academy students, two girls and a guy. Though uniforms on college-aged students threw her off, a few private Christian colleges had uniforms, so it wasn't unheard of. From the way Blackthorn students accessorized their plaid uniforms, she doubted they were Christian; tattoos, colored hair, fishnet stockings, and certain jewelry choices didn't go over well in the deeply religious South.

The messy table would have to wait. She ducked behind the bar counter to set down the bin of dirty dishes.

The massive compound of the private university sat atop a large, grassy hill at the edge of town, surrounded by mystery. No one Blaire knew had ever been admitted there, not even anyone from Magnolia Heights, the local college prep school populated by Rosebrook Valley's wealthiest elite. Blackthorn's secrecy and exclusivity led to speculation and rumors all over Georgia.

"Hey, sugar, can you top me off?" Bill asked, catching Blaire's attention. A regular in Ricky's Diner, he was a stout man easily in his sixties. His graying mustache curling on the ends emphasized his ear-to-ear smile, making him look like the Cheshire Cat.

"Sure, Bill. How's Maggie?" She retrieved the coffee decanter.

"Same ole, same ole. Still giving me hell whenever I forget to cut the grass, but I love the old gal, so what can you do?" He chuckled. "Thanks, sugar."

Blaire smiled politely as she poured, her gaze drawn back to the students in the corner. Still no sign of Charlotte; Blaire would have to get their initial order.

She pulled out a new notepad from beneath the counter and crossed to their table, laughing to herself about how girls at Magnolia Heights had said students of Blackthorn sold their souls to the Devil to obtain their looks—one of many superstitions still holding strong in the Bible Belt. Tattoos and colored hair aside, the always well-groomed students of Blackthorn Academy were intense looking. Most of them were attractive in some way, and Blaire found their presence overwhelming. She never saw them associate with anyone outside their own circle, other than staff at whatever establishment they were doing business with. But sold their souls to the Devil? The idea was ridiculous, even if she had believed in things like heaven and hell, God, and the Devil.

"Good morning, and welcome to Ricky's Diner. Can I start you off with some coffee?"

A petite Asian girl looked up at Blaire, her features pinched in a way that showed clear disdain. "Juice. Apple." She looked down at the menu in obvious dismissal.

Right. Okay.

Across the table, a throat cleared, and Blaire met the chocolate eyes of a boy with ebony skin and dreadlocks that fell to his jawline. His arm, in a crisp, long-sleeved white Oxford shirt, was wrapped around a girl with dark purple hair and warm, caramel skin who nestled into his side. She wore a more feminine cut of white blouse, as did the Asian girl, and all three wore plaid ties matching the girls' skirts.

"I'd like a sweet tea, loaded hash browns, and eggs," he said in a soft tone, enunciating as if he were choosing his words carefully, for which she was grateful. It made him less intimidating.

Blaire scribbled in her notepad with a nod. "How would you like your eggs?"

"Cheesy and scrambled, please."

The girl with the purple hair spoke up with an accent Blaire couldn't place. "Can I get biscuits and sausage gravy? Same drink." She tapped the menu on the table to point out the item she wanted, exposing a black, swirling tattoo with hatched lines on the back of her hand. While having a tattoo wasn't out of the ordinary anymore, the dark-skinned guy had the same symbol tattooed in the exact same spot on his hand. It seemed a strange thing to have matching tattoos of, but she didn't want to go down the rabbit hole of questioning the lifestyles of the rich and powerful. Their way of doing things never made sense to her.

Blaire cleared her throat and shook her wayward thoughts. "Sure thing. Did you want something to eat as well?" Blaire turned back to the prickly girl.

Looking up at Blaire with her nose wrinkled, the Asian girl gave her a once-over and huffed. "Three sausage links. One egg. Half a grapefruit. One biscuit." She glared, adding quickly, "Over easy."

Blaire's mouth fell open. She could have sworn the girl's brown eyes brightened when she glared. She squeezed her eyes shut to moisten them, then stared into the girl's dark, impatient eyes. Blaire's headache must be worse than she thought. She was seeing things.

"C-certainly. We'll get that right out as soon as possible."

The table fell silent again, none of the students giving her another glance or word of acknowledgment. Their world seemed narrow and self-absorbed if they only spoke to outsiders when it was absolutely necessary to force pleasantries. Blaire couldn't call their interaction pleasant—more like a means to an end. One of the biggest rumors floating around Rosebrook was how Blackthorn was a secret cult society, and none of the students were allowed to socialize with "regular town folk," or they would be expelled.

She crossed to the counter to enter their order into the system, then glanced around wondering where Charlotte had gotten off to. She needed her to take the Blackthorn students' table if she was starting to see things. She didn't need to freak out in front of customers.

After putting everything into the system, Blaire finished clearing the table, giving herself a break from interacting with people. She rounded the bar and pushed through the large, red swinging door to the kitchen, where the greasy magic happened, and then placed the dirty dishes into the bin for the next dishwasher load.

Heading back into the diner to clear one last table in her section, she took a deep breath and plastered on as genuine a smile as she could muster, considering how terrible she felt. Bright sunlight streamed through the large windows of the front wall. Coupled with the large retro lights hanging from the ceiling, the brightness brought pain to her sleep-deprived mind. Add in the fact that she wasn't seeing things clearly, and the clatter of dishes from the kitchen, and she already wanted to call it a day an hour into her shift. Most of the time, she enjoyed the bright lights and delicious smells, but it all overwhelmed her this morning. Coffee permeated the grease in the air, and pie would add to the mix if they got around to stocking the glass-covered dessert stands on the bar counter.

She stopped at a booth along the wall where a woman waved an empty glass at her. This wasn't her section either, but Blaire smiled politely despite the throbbing headache from lack of sleep. "Something I can get for you?" she asked, tucking her tray beneath her arm at her side.

"I'd appreciate it if my tea didn't run out while I'm still chokin' down my breakfast." The woman shook her empty glass at Blaire again to emphasize her point.

The rattling ice made Blaire's eye twitch. Seven more hours to go before she could bury her head under a pillow and hopefully sleep away the awful pain.

"And you call this sweet tea? Honey, your mama clearly didn't teach you the meaning of sweet."

Blaire flinched but didn't apologize; she hadn't made the tea for this shift. She knew how to make it like a proper Southerner should.

The older man at the table offered a sympathetic smile to Blaire, and she returned the smile, but it probably looked more like a grimace. It wasn't his fault that his wife—or at least Blaire assumed the woman with way too much makeup was his wife—was about as charming as cardboard.

"Oh, and while you're at it, you can get more hash browns for my kids 'cause the plate barely held any." The woman gestured with her gaudy, long-nailed manicure toward the three children sitting between her and the man. They happily ate scrambled eggs and drank fresh orange juice, completely oblivious to their mother's behavior.

The small plates with red trim the diner used for orders from the children's menu gave away the woman's ploy to get extra food at no cost. This sort of thing happened all the time with large families, so she didn't know why Ricky bothered with a kid's menu at all at this point.

Blaire forced a smile as the woman loudly tapped her long nails against the table. "I'll be happy to let your server know the portion was not to your liking and get you more tea in the meantime."

The woman rolled her eyes, muttering as Blaire walked away, "More ice wouldn't kill you either."

Going back through the red swinging door, Blaire caught sight of Charlotte coming out of the staff room.

Blaire shot her a pained grimace. "Hey, where've you been?"

Straightening her apron, the petite girl with shoulder-length red curls rushed over. "Ugh, I dumped a bowl of oatmeal all over my uniform and needed to change." She looked up at Blaire's frown. "What's wrong?"

Blaire held her head and explained all about the piece of work in the dining area and her lovely list of complaints.

"Hey, no. Before I deal with any of that… what's wrong with you?" Charlotte craned her neck to accommodate their height difference, as she easily stood four to five inches shorter than Blaire's five-foot-eight.

"Headache… no, migraine. I don't know. It hurts like hell. I didn't sleep worth a flip last night."

Charlotte frowned. "Up late fighting with Caleb again? I've got aspirin in my locker if you want."

"Yeah, thanks." Blaire headed for the staff lockers.

"I've never understood what his fixation on you is all about. He could get any woman he wants with his looks, but he chooses to keep it in the family. Creeeeepy!" Charlotte shook her head and re-entered the diner.

Charlotte was right about Caleb. A piece of work with an ego to match. Yes, he was physically attractive, slender but muscular, with a narrow face and square chin, sporting the typical bad boy haircut. He resembled a model she'd seen in a fashion magazine at the doctor's office, Connor Hill, though she wouldn't feed his ego by saying so. He wasn't her type, and they were stepsiblings, but those facts didn't stop Caleb from wanting to make her his wife.

Blaire sat for ten minutes taking a break, snacking on a bag of chips from the staff room table, giving herself time for the aspirin to take effect. In the meantime, Charlotte could manage her tables.

When her headache ebbed, she got up and put on a white apron over the red, short-sleeved, mini-dress uniform. Adjusting her name tag, she picked up her tray and pushed through the door into the diner to finish cleaning the table she abandoned before the interruption by Mrs. Entitled.

Caleb was late. He never did have courtesy when it came to her or her needs.

She wiped the table, tucking the measly fifty-cent tip into her apron skirt left by yet another "happy" customer. She knew the couple wasn't going to leave much from the looks on their faces when she thanked them as they left the diner.

She groaned inwardly.

At this rate, she was never getting out of this state, much less this town. The idea of spending the rest of her life stuck in Rosebrook, stuck with him, left a bitter taste in her mouth, making an already shitty day worse.

Shuddering, she finished wiping the table. Before she could turn around, a set of toned arms snaked around her waist, and she stiffened.

"Blaire. I've missed you today."

Her stepbrother's voice crept into her ear. She fought the impulse to fling herself away from him and make a scene as he slipped his hand into her apron pocket to deposit the key she forgot that morning—the only reason she even cared for him to be showing his face at the diner.

"Hi Caleb," she said in a clipped tone.

Blaire managed to move from his hold, using the need to take a table's drink order as the perfect excuse. After she finished taking the order, Caleb followed her until she slipped behind the counter to get the drinks.

"So how has your day been, sweetheart?"

"Fine," she said, hoping her curt responses would speed along his departure.

"Good tips?"

"What?" She rounded on him with an incredulous look. "Tips are not the point of my job," she stated, quickly looking around to see if anyone had heard their conversation. One thing about the job of a server in America: the base pay was appalling, and tips meant to fill out the server's pay were based on the customer's subjective judgment of quality. While you expected tips, you didn't make it public knowledge unless you wanted to get stiffed, a bad review, or both.

Caleb shrugged and stuffed his hands in his pockets. "Well, I expect a deposit, or the money left on the counter when you get home. I need to pay my cell phone bill."

"What? I barely get anything, and your salary is huge." She set down the tray holding the customer's drinks and posted her hands on her hips. Frustration twisted her face into a scowl she quickly schooled, biting the inside of her cheek. Caleb made so much money as a mouthpiece and legs for his grandfather he could afford a simple phone bill. He just needed an excuse to take her money.

Caleb narrowed his eyes; this topic was clearly not up for discussion. She'd have to pay at home for her little outburst. "Blaire, baby, we must work together toward our future. I'm saving for our kids."

A passing elderly couple smiled and made an "awing" sound.

Blaire muttered under her breath, "Great. That's just fucking great." Thankfully, that slip-up completely missed Caleb's notice while he hammed it up for the couple, smiling at them like a proud fiancé.

She hated him so much. "Fine, whatever. I've gotta get back to work."

Caleb frowned. "I hate when you speak like that."

Blaire shook her head. When irritated, not only did her Southern accent get thicker, but also her vocabulary became looser. She'd spent only one year at Magnolia Heights, not her entire childhood; she hadn't had etiquette and comportment drilled into her as deeply as had the other well-to-do children of the area. She chose not to contradict him; arguing or apologizing wouldn't make a difference.

"I'll either hit the bank or have it on the counter for you by tonight," she said without emotion.

Another day of no savings to put toward running away.

Another day Caleb marked his territory.

"Good. I won't be home for dinner, so feel free to grab takeout from your tips first at least, sweetheart," Caleb said, as if he did her a favor by allowing her to use her own money. She rolled her eyes as she turned away from him.

As Blaire rounded the counter with the tray of drinks, he kissed her cheek and went for the door.

After he left and she finished serving her table, she went to the back and checked her bank account on the staff computer to see what her pay for the previous week came to, when Ricky had cut her hours in half. She sighed. Only fifty dollars in checking. Caleb must have pulled more money out of her account he still had access to. He had been placed as trustee when their parents died, and when she tried to get it changed after she turned eighteen in October, the bank refused, making up excuses Blaire didn't understand. She wasn't even sure of the legality of it.

Seeking independence, she had opened a separate savings account that he didn't know about at a bank located in Savannah. While the account had been open for nearly five months already, the balance remained meager, as she could only funnel a portion of her tips into it, so she still had something to show at home. She could access the account online and deposit funds using a random ATM in Rosebrook to credit the account. No paper trails. No invested bodies to run to her family.

The influence the Wilcox family held in Rosebrook truly unnerved her.

Upset, and with her migraine threatening to make a repeat appearance, she retreated to the kitchen.

"Hey, Ricky, I need to talk to you about something."

The balding owner looked up from the grill and wiped his hands on the white apron covering his large belly, turning his attention to her. "You gotta make it quick. Soon as these sausages are finished, I gotta start preppin' the kitchen for lunch service."

Blaire nodded. "It'll be a second. I need to ask if it's possible to give me extra hours next week."

He pulled a face and scratched at the salt and pepper scruff on his jaw, shaking his head. "Now, Blaire..." He gave her a reproachful look.

"No, it's because last week you needed me to work half the hours normally scheduled, and I wanted to make up my lost time," she said quickly before he had any opportunity to shoot her down.

Ricky sighed. "Listen… You're a hard worker and all, but I'm gonna have to be cuttin' your hours again."

He turned back to the grill to transfer the sausages onto a platter and walked them over to the window, ringing the bell and yelling out Charlotte's name before turning back to Blaire.

"Again? I need the money, Ricky…"

"I'm sorry, Blaire, but this cut's gonna be a permanent thing, to tell you the truth." He walked back to the grill and scraped the grease and remnants of sausage from the surface to clean it for lunch service.

Upset, she pushed her hand through her bangs, causing loose hairs to fall. Her migraine came back with a vengeance. "Can you tell me why you're doing this? I've worked here for the last two years, never once late or anything. I only missed one week a few months ago."

Ricky shrugged. "It's how it has to be, girlie." He pushed past her to enter the staff room.

Caleb had something to do with this. Caleb paid Ricky to keep tabs on her. She had witnessed not only the exchange of money, but the subsequent conversation detailing everything she had done that week while at work. It wasn't the first time either. It didn't take a rocket scientist to put it together, especially with how Caleb knew details only someone at the diner would know, like with whom she spoke. Ricky clearly kept Caleb in the loop about everything she did and what her pay and tips looked like from the start.

Caleb kept her completely under his thumb.

What had been the point in her going full time after she graduated high school if her hours were going to be cut down to the same hours as a student?

She tipped her head back and squeezed her eyes shut, trying to ward off the tears that threatened to fall. A new job wasn't going to help if Caleb kept stealing her money, and if something didn't change, she would be stuck here forever.

A month after her eighteenth birthday, she tried to run away. She bought a bus ticket and planned to go to Florida, a place her mother always wanted to live. She had barely any money to take with her, but she figured she could find a job fairly quickly when she arrived. Someone working at the bus depot must have been on their payroll because the Wilcox family got wind of what she tried to do and immediately put a stop to it.

She didn't even make it to the bus.

When coming out of the bathroom at the depot, two men in suits stopped her in the hallway and guided her to their car. The gun pointing at her from beneath one man's jacket was enough incentive for her to get into the car without making a scene and allow them to take her to Caleb and his grandparents.

Her last name likely aroused suspicion. She wanted to change it to her mother's maiden name—she didn't benefit from the Wilcox name anyway, but Caleb said there was no point when she was destined to remain a Wilcox. Choosing her battles carefully, she didn't argue. When she finally got away from him, she could change her name. No sense in facing whatever consequence Caleb would bring when it wasn't that big of a deal in the short term.

His grandparents told her if she tried to run away again, Caleb would be the least of her concerns. They made it crystal clear they had no issue making sure no one heard from her again. It would be easier for Caleb to get his proper education and fall in line with a lady of the appropriate pedigree—not opportunistic trash—if Blaire was dead and gone.

After they left the main Wilcox estate, Caleb made sure she couldn't return to work for a week.

When he was twenty, Caleb's grandparents had intended for him to attend Savannah's Christmas Cotillion—the oldest debutante ball in the United States—to meet prospective brides in high society, but with everything that occurred when their parents died that year, and him finally expressing his twisted vision of a future with Blaire, their aspirations for their grandbaby took a hit. As if they needed any more reason to resent her. If it weren't for their indulgence of their spoiled only grandson, she would already be disposed of.

Their attitude didn't stop Blaire from saving up for her freedom. Someday she would find a way to escape, and when she did, returning could be dangerous.

The threat her step-grandparents laid out for her sent chills down her spine. How could they be so cavalier about taking someone's life?

She was truly trapped.

2

Strange Encounter

Stepping out of the diner into the busy walkway of Valley Center Plaza, Blaire breathed in the fresh air, glad to be finished with her unexpectedly long shift brought on by the evening rush.

The day started badly, but by the time the rush rolled out, with the help of additional aspirin, she felt much better.

The bells on the side door jingled as Charlotte stepped out, waving at Blaire.

"I'm so glad that's over! If I dealt with one more pervy dude trying to look down my uniform, I was going to need a lawyer and bail money." She huffed, blowing wayward curls from her face.

Blaire laughed, shaking her head. "You know it's always like that whenever there's a rush. All the crazies like to show up." She adjusted her duffel bag on her shoulder. "I wonder if they host a monthly meeting or something."

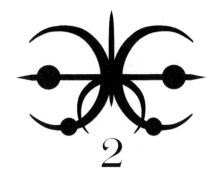

"Yeah, but honestly? I think I want to get a reduction." She gestured toward her chest. Cute and compact, but blessed, Charlotte frequently got unwanted attention in the diner.

The uniforms they wore didn't do much to stop the harassment. In fact, Blaire knew they encouraged it, and Ricky sure didn't care. He figured if the customers were attracted to his staff, they would keep coming back. A real piece of work, that one.

"I wouldn't go that far," Blaire said. "I mean, it's not like you'll be stuck here forever, and there's no point in butchering yourself because scumbags can't act like mature adults." She shook her head. "I can't wrap my mind around the way we're expected to change ourselves to accommodate and cater to those who can't control themselves when they"—she motioned toward the diner with one hand—"are the ones who should be learning how to behave." She sighed in frustration.

Charlotte fidgeted and tugged on her shirt hem. "It's always that way, though. Back in high school, I got sent home all the time because my shirts were 'inappropriate and distracting.' Even this one." She gestured to the lavender tank top with wide straps and a scoop neck that barely revealed her cleavage.

Girls wore shirts like that all the time at the public high school. The straps were wide enough to fit the standard dress codes, so Blaire couldn't understand why Charlotte would be sent home for distracting boys. She shook her head.

"Don't let it get to you. You're perfect the way you are."

Blushing, Charlotte smiled and dug around in her purse before pulling out a wad of cash. "At least one benefit of the rush is I think I made enough in tips this week to finally buy the new PlayStation. Now if only I can find it in stock somewhere."

How lucky she was to only worry about saving for the latest console, not having to worry about someone else laying claim to her wages. Blaire wondered what it would be like to buy things like a car, makeup, clothes, and a cell phone. That wasn't her life, though. It would never be her life with Caleb as long as the Wilcox name hovered over her head.

She made a nice sum in tips during the rush, at least enough to get delicious Chinese takeout on her way home before she gave up the rest. She hadn't been able to save enough through the week for any luxuries, even if it were possible to use it on such things; she opted to put any extra in her savings. Caleb made sure to clean out her account and took her tips nightly, so it was a moot point. She couldn't hide part of her check either, because Ricky always told him exactly how much to expect. Only a portion of her tips that Ricky didn't count escaped detection.

"I'll let you know if I see anything come in stock online, but you'll probably know before I will."

Blaire shook her head. The only time she got on a computer was when Caleb left home, and she didn't have a cell phone with internet access either, severely limiting her internet time. She glanced up at the large clock on a pole in the plaza.

"I need to get going. Caleb said he'd be late today, but I'm sure he'll be in soon. I want to eat and get a shower before he comes in, so I don't have to deal with him."

Charlotte cringed and shook her head. "Blaire… you know you could come stay with me, right? My moms wouldn't mind at all. They love you."

Charlotte had wonderful parents, a same-sex couple who adopted her as a baby from Ireland when her real mother died shortly after her birth. Her American father couldn't be located. One adoptive mother worked at the local vet clinic as a receptionist and assistant, while her other mother ran a clothing boutique in the Valley where she designed her own clothing line.

"I know… but you know Caleb wouldn't allow that."

"You're an adult now. You can do whatever you want. You know that, right?" Charlotte huffed out in exasperation, looking up at Blaire. It was hard for her to be threatening when she was so small, but her heart was in the right place. Charlotte didn't understand that the Wilcox name carried expectations, and any wrong move Blaire made in the Valley always made it back to either Caleb or his grandparents.

"I do… but at the same time, I can't. You know he'd find a way to get me back. You know he'd make my life a living hell if I ran away from him again. His grandparents might even make things difficult for your parents." She didn't dare tell Charlotte what it meant for her if she tried to run away again.

Caleb caught her searching for apartments when she turned eighteen. She forgot to clear the browser history like she normally did, so when closing everything down, her search history remained for him to see. Thinking the compromise would keep her nearby like he wanted, she didn't expect his reaction. He locked her in the basement as punishment and told her to spend the time getting the idea of moving away out of her head. Blaire wasn't going to put up with that kind of thing, so that's when she bought the Florida-bound ticket.

Charlotte sighed and put a hand on Blaire's arm. "I just want to protect you… if you don't get away from him, you're either going to end up married and miserable, or dead." She wiped her teary eyes.

Charlotte was right. Between the beating she received from Caleb after she tried to run, and the threat his grandparents made on her life, she had slipped into compliance for fear of what would happen to her. Even the idea they would discover her savings account and piece together her intentions made her gut roil with anxiety.

"Look, it's going to be okay. I promise. I'm working on getting out of here, but for now, I need to go home. I'll see you tomorrow."

Blaire didn't have the heart to tell Charlotte that Caleb had wiped out her bank account. As long as the other account remained secret, she still held hope.

"Yeah, okay..." Charlotte sniffled and waved as Blaire took off into the busy crowd.

Stopping by Happy Panda, Blaire ordered her usual beef and broccoli with mushroom lo mien, treating herself to crab rangoon for dessert. Little things like that made her day brighter.

Trying to get home before Caleb, Blaire hurried out of the small takeout shop and into the crowd of people as the sun started to set. Valley Center Plaza was extremely busy for a Thursday, probably due to the sunshine after all the rain in Rosebrook Valley last week. It wasn't a surprise to find it crowded; no telling when they'd have another sunny day. Unpredictable weather rolling up from Savannah off the Atlantic directly impacted their small town. Winter, normally the dry season, had been rainy and overcast this year. But spring was well underway, with March coming to an end. Blaire hoped for a longer reprieve from the damp weather before the true wet season arrived in a couple of months. Naturally, she had to work the rest of the weekend.

This evening, the plaza was filled with the laughter and chatter of people milling about, going to the various shops, restaurants, or bars that lined the shopping center. With a movie theater at the end of the plaza adding the delicious scent of popcorn to the air, several restaurants to tempt the senses, and a flashy-looking club on the other end, Valley Center Plaza had everything. The next larger town had a huge three-story mall, but she had to take a bus from Rosebrook to reach it. The plaza contained the important stores from the larger mall, but with the convenience of being within walking distance to the surrounding neighborhoods.

Blaire managed to mostly slip through the bodies moving about in all directions, protecting her delicious treasure as her mouth watered; she coveted her food, especially now that she had to hide when she ate the good stuff to avoid Caleb's criticism.

The life insurance her father left when he died paid for the move to a smaller home and a modest—but comfortable—living alongside her mother's job at the bakery. It also sponsored the gear and camps for the two sports she played throughout her childhood. But eventually, the money ran out. When Blaire was fifteen, her mother married into the Wilcox family. Her stepfather adopted her shortly after they married, and her name legally changed to Wilcox.

Blaire had to change schools to keep up appearances, so she lost her positions on the track and soccer teams. She was prepared to redshirt for Magnolia Heights, but her stepfather wanted her to focus on her studies, so he refused to pay for her to join the teams. Blaire's mom agreed it would be important to focus on academics so Blaire could attend a nice college now that they had the means to make her higher education aspirations a reality. Blaire didn't know what she wanted to be back then, and with money being tight before their marriage, college wasn't her focus. Now, she wanted to help others like her; youth who had suffered loss. With the loss of sports, she had to find other ways to maintain her physique. Walking to and from work daily, swimming when possible, and the rare occasion she could go to the gym helped keep her love of food from showing on her athletic frame. Blaire only became self-conscious and insecure about her body over the last year from enduring her stepbrother's verbal abuse.

She passed several children tossing coins into the large, three-tiered fountain at the center of the plaza. Once past the fountain, she needed to get through one larger crowd, then she had a straight shot home to her reward for surviving another day. Pushing through a group of people, she slammed into a tall, firm body, lost her balance, and fell on her backside.

She rubbed her hip and took in the guy she crashed into. Her gaze traveled slowly from black motorcycle boots, up a pair of tight black jeans with a chain hanging from narrow hips. A black leather jacket draped comfortably on his wide shoulders. He looked muscular, but not bulky.

"Shit. Are you alright?" he asked.

Blaire bit her lower lip as her gaze finally landed on his face, his words snapping her out of her hungry perusal.

When she didn't respond right away, he squatted in front of her to check on her, his brows pinched in concern as he studied her. "Are you hurt?" His deep timbre moved over her like a caress.

He had a squared chin and smooth jawline, full lips contrasting a fair complexion. Long, light brown hair fell just past his shoulders. His eyes were a striking pale green like sea glass, unnatural in their beauty, and deep-set beneath his finely-arched brows. When he ran his tongue over his lips to moisten them—an innocent gesture—something came alive inside Blaire. She wanted to bite his lower lip. He captivated her, the sensation foreign and unnerving.

"Y-yeah, I'm fine. I am so sorry!" She blurted out the last part too loudly when she realized she'd gone mute, taken aback by the absurdly attractive guy in front of her. She never gawked at anyone before, but he looked like he belonged in a fashion magazine for bad boys.

He shook his head. "It's crowded, and the sun was in my eyes. It's not your fault." He picked up the bag of dropped takeout and slowly rose to his feet.

He held his hand out expectantly.

Blaire swallowed hard, reaching out to take the hand offered, and when he grasped her hand in his, she gasped. His touch electrified her.

As soon as he had her steady on her feet, he quickly pulled his hand from hers and ran it through his hair, which settled messily onto his collarbone, the natural highlights catching the rays of the setting sun. She still had to look up to meet his gaze; he was over six feet tall.

"R-really, I wasn't paying attention. I hope I didn't spill anything on you." Blaire pressed her lips together to stop her rambling.

She undid her hair and raked her fingers through the long locks before pulling them into a messy bun on top of her head. It gave her something to do while she waited for his response. She looked up after fixing her hair, only to realize he wasn't looking at her face anymore. His gaze focused on the side of her fully exposed neck, his eyes narrowing further and taking on a hard edge, making a shiver run down her spine. Did she get something on her at the diner? She rubbed her neck to remove whatever had drawn his attention.

He stared at her with a hint of confusion and raw emotion she couldn't read. She took a deep breath, trying to regain her senses, finally breaking away from the hypnotic hold of his eyes. She did not behave this way.

His knuckles were white with the strain of his tight grip on the handle of the bag of her food. She bent down and picked up her duffle, hoisting it onto her shoulder, before turning toward the silent young man.

Uncomfortable, and feeling under a microscope, Blaire pointed with her thumb off to the side, forcing an awkward smile. "Um… so I'm just going to go—"

"Lukas!" another guy called out from the crowd nearby, loud enough to get Blaire's attention.

The guy in front of her shook out of the spell he was under as she turned to look at him again. He moved his intense gaze, which had settled on her neck again, to give her a hard glare, threatening in its intensity as he thrust her takeout bag at her.

Blaire opened her eyes wide, taken aback by the sudden change in his demeanor. She didn't think she had done anything bad, but he looked at her like he wanted to hurt her.

She took a step back, squeezing the strap of her duffle bag as if she'd somehow find protection there, having the sudden urge to run. The atmosphere between them had shifted dramatically. His stare made her feel like a rabbit staring down a predator, and she didn't like it one bit. Under the scrutiny of his piercing gaze, she felt exposed, like he could see through her and read her darkest secrets. The fear of being laid bare to this man outweighed the fear of even her death at the hands of Caleb's grandparents. Something about his eyes reached deep inside her, and the raw feelings that came with that set her off-kilter. When her hands began to shake, she tightened her grip.

He looked down at her tightening hands and then slowly back up to her face before setting the food down at her feet, turning abruptly, and disappearing into the crowd without a word.

She relaxed and released the breath she didn't even realize she held. What the hell was that about?

Blaire looked in the direction he went as the plaza clock began to chime, signaling it was much later than she realized.

She grabbed her food from her feet and took off into the crowd to get home as fast as possible.

Lukas watched the girl until the crowd swallowed her. He couldn't believe what had happened.

He hadn't wanted to come into the valley today. He didn't expect it to be so bright and sunny with all the rain lately. The brightness made his tired eyes hurt and put him in a foul mood after he'd stayed up the night before finishing an essay for his English course.

He hadn't been paying attention to where he stepped, but nothing could have prepared him for the way his body responded when her soft body crashed into him, the sensation like touching a live wire.

Already pissed off from his disinterest in shopping, even with his best friend during the sunniest day since winter, he was now faced with interacting with the locals. Normally, it wouldn't be a problem, but he was running on only a couple of hours of sleep, and the surprise quiz Professor Greene sprang on him had taken all his remaining energy.

When he looked down at her, she took his breath away, and the smell of jasmine lingering in the air where she collided with him sent his heart racing.

Coming to his senses, he asked if she was alright, but she seemed distracted as she rambled apologies.

She finally accepted his hand, and when their skin met, his body lit up. He quickly disengaged from their connection, blaming his lack of sleep for the odd way his body responded. That was until she pulled her blonde, waist-length hair back into a bun on top of her head.

He nearly lost his lunch when his gaze fell on her neck.

A black symbol the size of a child's palm, the significance instinctively striking him, marked the side of her neck like a tattoo, and then faded away as quickly as it appeared.

He couldn't believe it.

He couldn't stop staring at her neck, daring the mark to show itself again. It made no sense for someone like her to have it.

Finally breaking from his focus on her neck, he looked at her face.

The girl was a natural beauty. Her beautiful green eyes stood out on a heart-shaped face with a small, rounded nose set low over full, petal pink lips. But very human.

This couldn't happen.

It couldn't be real.

Lukas needed to send her away and be done with this, so he glared at her and shoved toward her the bag he'd retrieved from the ground.

When her eyes widened in obvious fear, his chest tightened, and his stomach twisted. He didn't mean to scare her; he only wanted to put distance between himself and the strangeness happening in that moment. Even when he softened his glare, a variety of emotions flickered over her face, but the fear radiating off her was palpable.

His lips parted to say something—anything to ease her discomfort—but her hands trembled and tightened around the strap of her bag.

He couldn't fix this.

Why did he want to? He didn't know her.

Lukas set the food down at her feet, as she seemed too afraid to take it directly from him, before turning away from her and disappearing into the crowd. But he watched her departure.

Something was very wrong.

He needed to get home and speak with Professor Velastra to find out what the hell was going on.

3

An Offer She Can't Refuse

Blaire hurried home for nothing; Caleb wasn't home yet.

After dinner, she cleaned up and took a quick shower to rid her hair of the smell of fries. Caleb still wasn't home, so she spent time browsing the internet. After clearing her search history, Blaire called Charlotte from their landline to tell her what Ricky did and how she suspected Caleb was behind it.

Charlotte agreed with her, so Blaire confessed Caleb took her money again, which naturally pissed Charlotte off. She adamantly insisted that Blaire move in with her and her parents. But going to them would paint a huge target on their backs. Charlotte's mother's business would be at stake. Her other mother's job. Charlotte's job. Their lives. Charlotte didn't know murder was on the table. Now that Blaire knew how far her step-grandparents would go, she wouldn't risk harm coming to those important to her, even if it meant remaining trapped in her own personal hell.

While her stepfather lived, she received all the benefits that came with his old money lineage, hence her single school year at Magnolia Heights, but her mother had foolishly signed a prenuptial agreement that left Blaire with nothing after his death except the name. Retaining the Wilcox name required her to meet expectations and not make waves. Keep her head down and obey.

When the door downstairs opened, Blaire cut the conversation short. Once off the phone, she waited until the shower turned on before venturing downstairs to the kitchen to grab yogurt and strawberries. As she bent over in front of the refrigerator to put away the container, Caleb came up behind her and grabbed her backside. She jumped and spilled strawberries everywhere.

"God, you're a mess," he slurred as he leaned against the counter.

Alcohol fumes wafted off him. She wasn't in the mood to deal with it, but Caleb, in a drunken state, didn't take well to backtalk and excuses. Play nice, and he'd go away.

She cleaned up the mess while he watched her with a sneer.

"You know... you really should lay off the midnight snacks," he said as she stood up. "You're starting to get a little chunky around here"—he reached out and put his hands firmly on her sides, squeezing—"and here." He ran his hand across her stomach, sliding it under the hem of her shirt to rest on her bare skin.

Blaire froze as he took the strawberries from her and set them on the counter with his free hand. He leaned down to smell her hair, but she pulled from his hold, walking around the counter to throw away the ruined strawberries.

He smirked and narrowed his eyes. "I think getting takeout wasn't a good idea for you. I mean, the money you left barely covers my phone bill, so you must have bought enough food for a family of four. Did you really eat all of that by yourself?"

She turned sharply and glared at him. To hell with playing nice.

"How much money do you think I make? My paycheck was cut by more than half when Ricky cut my hours." She crossed her arms and sighed. "And today he told me the cut is permanent, so this is going to be the new normal from now on."

She bit back her suspicions he was the reason; she didn't want to deal with his shit when it wouldn't change anything, so she kept her mouth shut on further sass.

He leered at her. "You can make it up to me in other ways, now that I'm essentially the breadwinner. You can start by attending to your wifely duties."

Blaire fought against him, denying his advances when he tried to force her to her knees on the kitchen floor. Then he dragged her by her hair down the hallway to his bedroom, cussing at her. In his drunken rage, Caleb tore off her shirt and fondled her, but she fought with elbows, knees, and nails. When she didn't submit like the good "wife-to-be" and scratched his face, he punched her.

When she came to, Caleb lay passed out next to her on his stomach fully clothed, and she still had her pants on. Other than her throbbing head and bruised face, she detected no pain and concluded nothing more had happened after he knocked her out. She scrambled out of bed like it was on fire, then ran and barricaded herself in her bedroom upstairs. Grateful she had work as an excuse to leave the house, she slipped out the door before Caleb woke up.

Slipping into her uniform at the diner, she looked at herself in the staff bathroom mirror. Sighing, she used the compact of pressed powder to apply additional coverage to her cheekbone where angry bruising threatened to appear.

Last night was the first time Caleb had crossed that line; the memory brought tears to her eyes. She wanted to disappear. She wrapped her arms around herself and took a shuddered breath, looking away from the mirror. She felt so dirty. If he hadn't been drunk, would she have been able to stop what he planned?

Blaire closed her eyes to stop the tears from spilling. Caleb's piercing hazel eyes waited there, haunting her every waking moment.

A loud knock on the bathroom door shook her from her reflection. She quickly wiped her eyes.

"Blaire, you got a guest," Ricky's rough voice boomed.

"Coming!" She stuffed her makeup into her duffel and entered the staff room.

"Morning, B!" Charlotte smiled. "There's someone here for you," she said, gesturing to a table in the corner of the diner where a dark-haired woman sat with her back to them.

"Thanks, Charlotte."

Blaire grabbed her tray and notepad, then approached the slender Asian woman sipping on a latte. She reminded Blaire of an actress from those Korean dramas a friend of hers used to watch in high school.

"Good morning, and welcome to Ricky's Diner. My name is Blaire. They told me you wanted to speak to me. What can I do for you?"

After an awkward silence, the woman gently set down her cup, the cup making no sound as it met the ceramic saucer. She turned her gaze to meet Blaire's eyes, her large chocolate eyes studying Blaire intently.

Her sleek, black hair pulled tight into a low chignon with a small pearl broach as an accent gave her a polished and proper appearance. The broach matched the pearl buttons of her blouse she had tucked into high-waisted navy slacks. She looked sophisticated, aside from the four-inch white stilettos with platform toes, which offset her petite stature evident even in her seated position.

"Yes. I request a few minutes of your time." She dabbed her thin, pink lips with a napkin. "I have already spoken to your boss and paid for the loss of your service for the time I require. He is... rather adamant about his finances."

Blaire cleared her throat and nodded quietly, not sure what to make of any of that.

"Sit, please," the woman stated firmly as she moved to take another sip of her latte. "I have much to discuss with you, if you will grant me the time, and an offer to make if you are receptive."

Blaire slowly lowered herself into the seat across from the woman, placing her tray and notepad on the seat beside her.

After another long pause, the woman asked, looking into her cup, "Have you heard of Blackthorn Academy?"

"Of course, who hasn't?"

The woman met Blaire's gaze again. "Yes, well, I am Professor Soomin Velastra. I manage student admissions and affairs of... special natures," she spoke softly and gestured to a large envelope on the table. "You, Miss Wilcox, are one of those with a special nature I would address if you were a student of the academy."

Everyone assumed the student body to be the entitled offspring of the rich and famous, or politicians; why would they want her? Blaire frowned in confusion. "Wait, what? I don't think I follow."

"In time, Miss Wilcox. I will be happy to go further into detail about your exceptional circumstances once we have the admission forms taken care of." The professor dabbed her lips again, sitting back, and rested her hands in her lap, crossing her ankles.

She reminded Blaire of the girls and women from Magnolia Heights who'd gone through etiquette classes on how to speak, sit, and even eat in a proper manner. She sat up straighter as she realized her posture looked atrocious, the breath gone from her body. Did she miss part of this conversation?

Professor Velastra sighed, noting the blank stare, and motioned again to the envelope. "Blackthorn Academy is willing to grant you a full scholarship to attend through your university years. You show a… unique trait we value above all, and as it stands, we understand your financial situation"—she gestured to the diner and Blaire's uniform—"so we would also cover all fees and living expenses as part of your admission agreement."

"Living expenses?" She didn't have rent or anything like that, so she wouldn't require help with housing, and she had a job.

The professor waved her hand dismissively. "You would have to live on campus like all other students of the academy, so we would furnish housing and food as well as provide you with uniforms and an allowance for clothing and other necessities while you attend Blackthorn, as you simply will not have the time to work while enrolled. The curriculum is rigorous."

Blaire's gaze snapped up to the professor's eyes, her face drained of warmth. "Oh no, that wouldn't be possible. My… family"—she grimaced—"is quite strict about—"

The professor gave her a pointed look, cutting her off. "Miss Wilcox, I'm well aware of the situation regarding your family. I've done my research before coming here. It won't be an issue."

Before Blaire could respond, the door nearby opened and loud laughter pulled her attention as a group of three guys and two girls entered. They were all beautiful and caught the eye of everyone around.

They stopped laughing when their eyes fell on Blaire's table, all eyes on the professor, before she shot them a look Blaire didn't quite understand. Blaire's eyes fell on the young man she ran into the day before.

There was no mistaking his striking green stare, sharp jawline, or beautiful long hair that Blaire had the strange urge to rake her fingers through.

"Miss Wilcox?" the professor said, breaking her focus.

Blaire cleared her throat at the same time the guy moved away to settle into a booth a few tables away, watching her. Everyone else had squeezed into the booth and they all looked uncomfortable trying to fit five people into a four-person booth.

"Oh, I'm sorry… I just… I recognized someone."

Blaire looked up at the professor, but the guy's continued gaze on her caused her entire body to become alight with hyperawareness.

The professor smirked and nodded. "Is that so? Yes, well, as much as I would like to let you speak to your acquaintance, I do need to finalize this with you so we can proceed."

"Huh? Now? Can I think about it?"

She blinked at the professor in confusion, the sensations she felt before dissipating as reality hit. Blaire had been given this information and she hadn't even had a chance to read anything about it. Did they expect her to enroll in a university with no knowledge of her course of study, or anything at all?

"Think about it?" The professor tilted her head, studying Blaire as if she had spoken a foreign language. "Why on Earth would you want to do that? This is an amazing offer, and from my understanding, you have been looking to move from Rosebrook for something new." She gave Blaire a knowing look.

How did she know that? How much research had the woman done?

"Well, yes… but—"

"Miss Wilcox, to put it not so delicately, the offer stands until I walk out that door, and then you remain as a waitress in this diner until you're married to… whomever." She paused, stressing the word "whomever," as if she knew to whom. "And then what's next? Bearing children to a man you resent and growing old as you serve apple pie to Blackthorn Academy students year after year, envying what you might have been able to achieve?"

Blaire shut her eyes as angry tears built behind her eyelids, her breathing quickening on the verge of an anxiety attack. The memories of Caleb crawling over her last night surfaced. Would that be her life forever?

A loud sound on the other side of the diner broke through her panic and she looked up to see the guy from yesterday pass through the exit, his friends staring in her direction.

The professor sighed. "I should go. You need to get back to work selling apple pies, and it seems one of my students may need me." She stood from her chair and dusted nonexistent dirt from her lap before straightening her blouse. "You have a good day, Miss Wilcox."

Blaire's eyes shot up to meet the professor's russet brown eyes. This might be her only chance at freedom; if she didn't take it, she could be stuck here forever.

"Wait!" she called out as the professor stepped away.

The professor paused before turning back to look at her, eyebrows raised.

Blaire swallowed the lump in her throat as she glanced around, licking her lips as she looked toward the window to the kitchen.

"Will I..." She lowered her voice to barely a whisper. "Will I be safe from the Wilcox family there?"

If the woman had done her research, Blaire wouldn't need to elaborate. Her hands bunched in her apron on her lap as she waited for the professor's response.

With a soft sigh, the professor bent forward and set the envelope in front of Blaire once again, before moving around the table and sitting down. "We're familiar with the Wilcox name and their influence in Rosebrook, as well as across Georgia. That being said, I can assure you if you do not wish to continue your association with them, you won't have to. You will find protection from their reach within Blackthorn's walls."

Blaire exhaled, tension leaving her body as she slumped in her seat. The risk that Caleb and his grandparents could still reach her lingered. She didn't know if this woman just told her what she wanted to hear, but something deep within her urged her to act.

She sat up, steeling her resolve, and met the professor's eyes with a determined gaze. "I accept."

"Yes, I knew you would see reason." Professor Velastra reached across the table and placed her hand on the envelope with a smirk. "Inside, you will find all the admission contracts you need to sign. We would like you to start immediately, if possible."

Blaire pulled the stack of papers from the large envelope and looked them over. The pages were filled with legal terms and phrases she didn't understand. She probably should have a lawyer look at them. She glanced up as the professor slid a pen across the table to her.

She didn't have lawyer money, so she took the pen and placed it on the paper, hoping she made the right decision.

"Immediately? How immediate are we talking? I still have work scheduled, and I don't know what I'm going to do about my current home situation." She looked back down at the papers as she added her initials to another form.

Crossing her legs, the professor sat up tall and gestured toward Ricky, who had come out of the kitchen to look at them, getting impatient and nosy. "I will handle the sticky details regarding your departure from your employment. I'm sure I can speak in a language your frugal boss can understand." The professor breathed sharply through her nose and looked as if the entire situation had left an unpleasant taste in her mouth. "As far as your home life is concerned... Do you have someone you need to inform of this situation, or shall we be... discreet?"

Blaire snapped her gaze up to meet the professor's eyes, pausing in her signing of the documents. The professor gave her that same knowing look with a casual smirk, as if she already knew everything about Blaire.

"I... discretion, please." She looked down and quickly finished signing the final document, sliding the papers back into the envelope, and passing it over the table.

The professor stood from her chair and tucked the envelope under her arm. "Yes, I figured as much. I'd like you and your redheaded friend there"—she pointed to Charlotte, who'd been watching from the staff room door—"to figure out the details of getting your belongings here, and I'll meet you in the morning—outside. Only once you're safely within the walls of Blackthorn will I deal with your boss, as I have a feeling there will be opposition should he become aware of your newfound opportunity."

"In the morning? Already?" She looked up at the professor in surprise. This was all happening too fast.

"Yes, Miss Wilcox. When I said immediately, I meant immediately." She gently touched Blaire's shoulder before gracefully walking away.

Blaire sat in stunned silence until Ricky yelled at her to get back to work. She gathered her things and hurried to the staff room to let Charlotte know what happened as the group at the table got up and exited the same side door the man went through.

This was really happening.

4

ESCAPE

As soon as Caleb pulled his car out of the driveway, she grabbed her duffel bag and placed it on her bed.

She didn't intend to bring much when she left the house today. It was supposed to be like any other morning where she carried the single duffel containing her uniform, makeup, and personal items she might need.

She took the opportunity the day before, when Ricky cut her hours, to go home and pack two suitcases of clothes, shoes, and essentials, while Caleb worked. She didn't pack anything that occupied the primary space of her bedroom. Caleb would have noticed.

With time to spare before the end of her usual shift, she called Charlotte to arrange storing her suitcases until tomorrow when Blaire would make her escape. She wouldn't take the chance of someone seeing her bringing them to the diner. She learned from her prior mistake.

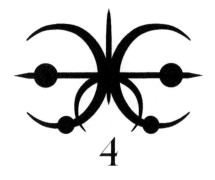

She moved around the room grabbing the last items she wanted to take—a few novels, her favorite jasmine-scented perfume, a photo album, and a small jewelry box that held pieces of jewelry her mother gave her and passed down when she died. The only real things that meant home to her.

Blaire looked around her room and sighed.

This place wasn't her home. When her mother married Caleb's father, they moved here to live, leaving behind the small townhouse they had occupied after her father passed when she was three.

This space had become tainted. The initial happy memories made in the year before their deaths were painted black with the sick and twisted delusions of someone obsessed; marred with actions that would haunt her forever.

Blaire could never call this place home.

She wiped her eyes and stared down at the framed photograph in her hands of her mother and her sitting in a field of sunflowers with huge smiles on their faces.

Blaire's mother had taken her to the mall and purchased matching sundresses specifically for the photo shoot. The pictures happened a month before the car accident, but the prints only came in several months after her death. Aside from the digital proofs, her mother never had the opportunity to see how the prints turned out.

She dropped the picture on top of everything else in her duffel bag with a heavy sigh.

After they returned home the evening of the photo shoot, while they were playing a game of cards in her room, Caleb casually mentioned the dress made her hips look big. She didn't know how to take it—if felt mean, but he presented it as being helpful, so at the time she rationalized the insult. He'd been such a nice guy from the time they met. They spent a lot of time together, and he stepped right into the role of big brother. Her friends with older brothers complained about their meanness as normal, but his criticism affected her more than she wanted to admit. Deprived of a father or sibling most of her life, she longed for his approval. It led to gaslighting herself as his critiques grew more numerous and personal.

She never wore the dress again. It was tainted by a monster's game.

She left it hanging in the back of her closet next to her Magnolia Heights uniform.

Her heart pounded, anticipating how safe she might be behind Blackthorn's gates. During the one year she spent at Magnolia Heights, she learned many of the students' parents tried to get them admission into Blackthorn Academy's university program, but all were rejected. Even the great Wilcox name couldn't get Caleb within their walls when her stepfather tried to get him accepted. No one she knew would be there, and no one she knew would suspect she'd gone there. That fact gave her hope.

Arriving at the diner, Blaire put on a show like it was any other day. If Ricky saw her leaving, or if she didn't show up to work at all, he would immediately call Caleb and she wouldn't make it. She waved at Ricky, who stood at the cash register ringing out an elderly couple. He grunted at her as she made her way to the red door, passing through the kitchen into the staff room.

She didn't see Charlotte in the staff room, or her luggage, so she hoped Charlotte waited for her outside.

Blaire glanced back before moving to the alley door and slipping outside, where she found Charlotte sitting on one of her suitcases.

"I can't believe you're doing this. Blackthorn Academy? Why in the world did they offer a scholarship to go there? I don't know of anyone who's gotten the chance to go there." Charlotte stood quickly, talking fast. "They're so… secretive. Are you sure it's a good idea?"

Blaire shook her head and sighed. "I honestly have no idea. The lady refused to reveal any information to me until I signed a bunch of legal documents, and I won't know anything until I get to the academy, but I need to go… you know I do." She took a deep breath to steel her resolve.

A cold breeze down the alley sent a chill down Blaire's spine.

She glanced up. Professor Velastra waited at the end of the alleyway next to a black sedan sporting tinted windows.

The professor looked as elegant as before in a burgundy chiffon blouse tucked into a black pencil skirt, paired with platform stilettos in black. When she noticed Blaire looking, she lifted her hand in acknowledgment. Blaire nodded before returning her attention back to Charlotte.

"I know you do, but please be careful, and call me as soon as you get settled. We can still get together for a movie, you know. You know Blackthorn students are in the valley all the time… kind of hard to miss them, really," Charlotte said with an awkward laugh.

She wasn't wrong about that.

Blaire expected to feel out of place around them. They stood out.

Nodding, she tied her duffel onto one of her rolling suitcases. Charlotte gasped. Blaire turned around. Charlotte held her hands over her mouth.

"What? What's wrong?"

"Your face! Did he do that to you?" she shouted, pointing at Blaire.

Blaire opened her duffel bag and dug out her compact, holding it up to inspect her face, and groaned.

Sure enough, her makeup had run, and the bruising from the other night was making an appearance. She forgot to touch up her makeup after her crying session in her rush to get out of the house before Caleb returned.

She sighed as she applied powder over the offending eyesore.

"Charlotte... it's fine."

"No, it's not! Blaire! It's not okay that he hits you!" Charlotte's voice was shrill enough to get the professor's attention. She paced down the alley toward them.

"I'm not saying it's alright that he hits me. I'm saying what happened is already done. I can't change what happened, but it's fine because I'm leaving. It won't happen again." She finished applying her makeup and put the compact back in her purse as the professor reached them.

"Girls, is something wrong? I would advise discretion if you want to go undetected, seeing as you are still within a stone's throw of your employer." She gestured toward the alley door they stood next to. With Charlotte screaming, Ricky could come out any moment, and it would all be over.

Charlotte covered her mouth and gasped. "I'm so sorry, Blaire. I wasn't thinking."

Blaire shook her head and held up her hand. "It's fine. I know you were just worried about me. Things got out of hand the other night, and the aftermath was worse than usual, but I'll be okay... now."

That was the understatement of the century. Her body was covered in bruises beneath her clothing from struggling as Caleb forced her into his bed before knocking her out. She swallowed hard and took a deep breath.

"Okay, well... I should go."

"Yes, we should get moving so we can finalize the paperwork and get you into your dorm. We're losing precious daylight hours. Furthermore, I still need to settle things with your boss once you're settled at the academy."

Without another word, the professor turned and walked away to the car where a man built like a house waited by the trunk. The professor motioned toward Blaire, and he walked her direction.

"I'm going to miss you so damn much..." Charlotte threw her arms around Blaire's neck and squeezed tight.

Blaire wrapped her arms around her petite friend and buried her face in her curls. "It's not forever. I'm just going to be across the plaza. I can still visit you, I'm sure. Maybe you can come to visit me at some point."

Charlotte pulled back, wiping her eyes and sniffling. "Yeah, sure. Of course. I'm sorry. I'm just so happy for you, but also worried."

"I know. It'll be alright, I promise. I'll call you as soon as I can and tell you all about it."

A tingling excitement shot through her like something was pulling her to the academy, but an underlying sense of foreboding hung over her like a storm cloud. The heady mixture led her to act on autopilot.

But as the saying went, what goes up must come down. She wondered how far down the fall would be.

She gave Charlotte one last hug and reached to grab the handles of her suitcases, but she paused as she looked up at the man who'd finally reached them.

To look up at the towering man's face, Blaire had to tilt her head back, as he easily stood seven feet tall. Charlotte gawked up at him. Blaire tried to imagine how comically large he looked to her friend, considering Charlotte stood a half foot shorter than she did. He must be a stuntman or wrestler, she mused. He raised an eyebrow at her.

Blaire realized she was blatantly staring at him. "I... Oh wow, I'm sorry. You're just... so big. I've never seen someone as big as you. Not that it's a bad thing, but just... wow, yeah. Sorry."

His loud booming laughter startled her. "Oh, little one, you are quite amusing. It shall be interesting to see how you grow within the academy," he said with a thick Russian accent, before bending to grab her luggage from her, and moving back down the alley to load it into the trunk.

She had never been called "little one" before and found it peculiar.

The professor cleared her throat loudly, motioning to the open back door, and Blaire apologized once more before giving Charlotte one last hug and rushing down the alleyway. She climbed into the car, and the professor slid in behind her.

"It should not be long, little one. Relax. Stop apologizing," the giant of a man called from the front seat before putting up the partition, starting the engine, and beginning the drive toward her future.

5

Truth

Blaire watched out the window at the winding road that led up to Blackthorn Academy flanked by live oaks dripping with Spanish moss. She picked at the hem of her blouse to distract herself from the thoughts running rampant with all the potential ways this could go wrong, working herself up into a ball of anxiety. Things like this didn't happen to people like her.

"Nervous?" the professor asked, breaking through her dark thoughts.

"That obvious?"

"Mm… something like that. It is easy for me to read." She smiled and waved a hand dismissively. "Besides, you're a new student, so trepidation is to be expected."

Blaire shifted in her seat, having trouble keeping still, and she suspected she looked foolish in the eyes of such a proper woman. She swallowed her self-deprecating thoughts.

"How often do you get new students?"

"Close to never, aside from the few stray students who join us from sister locations in other countries. Our students have grown together from a young age at our branch locations across southern Georgia."

Blaire's mouth hung open as she dropped back against the seat. This was much worse than she thought. She assumed other new students might be there, but instead, it would be mostly people who had been together since diapers.

They finally reached a large, black gate with the letters "BA" in ornate script built into the bars. It looked extremely sturdy, like it could keep the entire town at bay if they tried to enter. The driver lowered the partition and informed the professor they had arrived before speaking with someone at the driver's side window.

After a few moments, a security guard appeared at the back window, peering inside. He looked as massive as the driver. The professor nodded to him. Did the school have an entire professional wrestling team at its disposal?

Blaire smirked, and the security guard raised an eyebrow at her.

"Ah. Uh... sorry," she said, looking down.

The driver laughed loudly again. "Oh, little one, what did I say about apologies?"

"Um... sorry?" Blaire blushed, wishing the seat would swallow her up.

The driver laughed again, and the security guard shook his head before walking away as the window rolled back up.

What an amazing first impression she was making.

The professor placed a hand on her leg and smiled reassuringly. "Relax, Miss Wilcox. Everything is going to be alright."

Blaire took a deep breath and looked out the window as they ascended the long, winding road that led to several buildings situated at the top of the hill overlooking Rosebrook Valley.

The road beyond the gate was lined with blossoming fruit trees on each side, flanked by a pristine, manicured lawn. They followed the road straight to a smooth cobblestone courtyard that circled a large marble fountain at its center before branching off to the left and right to buildings on either side.

Azalea hedges in bloom lined the courtyard and side roads in blocks of red, pink, and purple. To the left of the courtyard stood a low hedge maze filled with ominous-looking black marble statues with wings that rose from the labyrinth like demons taking flight.

Blaire assumed it smelled wonderful out there, and she planned to take advantage of the benches near the flowers shaded by palmetto trees to get her reading time.

A wide staircase led up to the massive doors of the main building of Blackthorn Academy. Beautiful stained-glass windows in shades of red decorated each side of the main doors and flanked the stairs on the front of the building, reaching as high as the second floor. Flowering bushes lined the front wall, while intricate vines and lush greenery hanging from the rooftop down the walls and around the windows created a scene worthy of a painting.

Everything looked breathtakingly beautiful, and Blaire tried to get a better look through the tinted window as the car circled the fountain and turned down the right-hand path, pulling around the main building, and stopping twenty yards from a smaller side building.

The driver opened her door, and Blaire stepped out, looking around and breathing in the sweet, magnolia-scented air.

"This place is amazing."

The driver chuckled as he closed the door, then went to the other side to let the professor out.

Blaire made her way to the open trunk and reached for her luggage.

"Miss Wilcox, you need to come with me to my office. Your bags will be delivered to your room for you." She spoke in a sharper tone than before, as if it were an order, and the authoritative tone held a sense of urgency.

Not wanting to break any rules on her first day, Blaire dropped the strap of her duffel bag and crossed to the professor's side. She followed the professor along a small footpath that led to the smaller building.

She took the opportunity as they moved to glance around, taking in everything obscured by the car's tinted windows. Students moved about, but when their attention fell on her, she found it off-putting.

"Miss Wilcox?" the professor called from the door she held open.

"Oh! Sorry!"

Blaire rushed across the drive and up the marble steps into the building. She couldn't make out details in the dark hallway, only that it had a rich, woodsy scent and the carpet she walked across felt plush as her shoes sank into the fibers. The professor led her to another door, opening it and motioning for Blaire to enter ahead of her.

"Please sit. We have much to discuss."

Inside the professor's office, the sounds from the outside completely died out, like she had walked into a soundproof booth.

The smell of old books filled the air from the massive floor-to-ceiling bookshelves that lined three walls. A large window draped in burgundy curtains tied off with black rope, centered behind the professor's desk, allowed natural light to enter. This light reflected from the chandelier in the center of the office, casting the entire room in a warm, amber glow. The professor's massive desk had ornate carvings of thorn-covered vines along the front. A pair of plush, black leather chairs faced the desk.

The professor moved around her desk to sit in her high-back leather chair, folding her arms across her stomach. "We need to discuss why you're here and what the expectations of the academy are of you. Honestly, I don't know how to approach this with you, as I have never in all my years had to explain any of this to an outsider before."

Blaire frowned at her strange choice of words.

The professor didn't look any older than her early thirties, but she spoke as if she had been at this job for decades, like an old woman would. "I feel it best I just say it like it is and we deal with the fallout as it happens."

Blaire took a deep breath and slowly sank down into one of the chairs in front of the professor's desk. The bad feeling from earlier returned in full force.

"Now." The professor sat up in her chair and placed her elbows on her desk, resting her chin on her clasped hands. "What you believe about Blackthorn Academy is true. The students here are all from wealthy families and all start as children at our branch locations. They pass through the same education levels as other students with elementary, middle school, and high school. Some even begin their upbringing with us as babies while their parents oversee affairs outside in the world at large."

She stood and moved to the large window, watching the courtyard, as she let Blaire absorb what she said before continuing. "Blackthorn Academy has been around for centuries in some capacity, and much of the staff has been here since the founding. However, this school differs greatly from conventional Ivy League universities."

Blaire raised her eyebrow, not sure she heard that correctly.

"This is all made possible due to an aspect of the world many humans are unaware of, or at least have little understanding of." She waved her hand dismissively. "Books, movies, and the like, are exaggerations of unexplained encounters humans have had, which they label supernatural."

She turned from the window to study Blaire's face. "Yes, this school is like many other Ivy League colleges in shaping the elite to rule nations, but the similarities stop there."

"Wait… what? I'm not sure I follow or am even hearing you correctly." Blaire drew her brows together.

The professor continued, ignoring Blaire's confusion. "Humans have little understanding that much of their ruling government is heavily influenced by 'supernatural' entities from various academies such as this one." Taking her seat once more, the professor leaned forward and laced her long slender fingers, meeting Blaire with a sharp gaze. "Here at Blackthorn Academy, we raise, and send elite Vasirian out into the world. You are the first human to ever be enrolled here."

"Vass—who? First human?"

The professor let out a scant breath of exasperation. "This is rather difficult to explain. To put it in terms you can understand… You know of the vampire myth, yes?"

Blaire nodded quietly, the hair prickling on her scalp.

"We Vasirian are similar in that we must consume blood to survive. While not human, and we never have been, we are not undead monsters of myth. We are our own species."

Blaire's pulse raced, and her breathing quickened. This couldn't be real. She expected Caleb to come through the door any minute to punish her for thinking she could get away from him. As her anxiety spiked, she wrapped her arms around her waist. She should have known it was too good to be true. "What? You can't be serious right now. I'm being pranked, aren't I?"

The professor shook her head solemnly. "No, Miss Wilcox. No one is playing a joke on you. This is real, and you need to listen and take it seriously. Your family's influence on this town cannot reach these walls, so you need not worry about that."

"They aren't my family," Blaire said firmly.

"Right. Nevertheless, you need to listen to what I'm explaining to you." The professor leaned forward and pressed on. "The reason you find yourself here is because, as fate would have it, through blessing or curse, you possess a Korrena mark, an ancient mark that Vasirian until now only saw in their fated pair, their life mate."

"Wait… you're serious?" Blaire croaked, swallowing the lump in her throat, her mouth bone dry.

"Quite."

"Hold on. Wait a minute. So, you're telling me you're not human, but something like a vampire… am I even safe here? Don't vampires eat humans?" Blaire's voice rose at the end with a near-hysterical laugh. She couldn't believe her ears.

Professor Velastra released a long-suffering sigh. "First, we're not vampires. Second, no one is going to 'eat' you, Miss Wilcox. You are safe within these walls."

Blaire took a deep breath and let it out slowly, her posture wilting.

"As I was saying… Outside these walls, one of my students saw you and claimed to have seen his specific Korrena mark appear briefly on your skin, then disappear." The professor shook her head. "Normally, I would think something this peculiar could only be a mistake, but we all have our own unique mark that is only shared by our Korrena. This mark presents itself once we either find the one, or make a specific connection with them.

"It's not easy to mistake or brush off; it is in our nature to seek out our pair. This particular student is late in finding his pair compared to when most of our kind typically discover their other half. Despite our education system providing opportunity for all Vasirian youth to interact with one another, a sad few are forced to wait their entire lives without finding their pair. That said, if his pair is human, it is perfectly logical why he's yet to find her."

Blaire shifted with unease. Setting aside the strangeness, something didn't make sense to her. "Wait... if these..."—she swallowed hard—"Vasirian... all share a mark with someone, but it doesn't appear until they meet, then how do they know what their mark even is? How can they know it's their... what's the word you said? Cornea?"

"Korrena. You pronounce it core-en-ah," the professor corrected flatly. "That, thankfully, is a simple question to answer." She sat back in her chair. "Along with the appearance of the mark, you will feel a biological reaction."

Blaire shook her head. "I don't understand."

"Often, before there is even a sighting of the mark, the pair can feel one another. Something similar to a pins and needles sensation over the entire body. Warmth, and a bone-deep reaction to each other, are common. Some report being drawn to their scent, and others have a purely lust-driven response. It varies, but at a basic, primal level, if a mark presents itself, and the biological reaction happens, it is quite telling, and hard to deny."

The professor sighed and pulled out a folder filled with papers, pushing it across the desk to Blaire. "I am sorry to have approached the facts in this way, but it is not information you speak of outside of these walls, and honestly, you wouldn't have come if you knew."

Blaire stared at the folder labeled *Blackthorn Academy Rules & Regulations and Korrena Expectations.*

"This sounds too unreal..."

Blaire shook her head quickly to wake herself from this bizarre dream, and then looked up from the folder to find the professor standing above her.

"I can assure you it is real. Very real, Miss Wilcox. You need to read this to understand what I have said to ensure your safety and that you and your pair have the best chance of success." She crossed her arms. "It is imperative that you comply with everything within this text. While this is completely new to me, if you truly are my student's Korrena, I will do everything within my power to help you be successful here, but you must meet me halfway."

Blaire shook her head again. "I just… I can't believe this. It sounds too unreal. I mean, this kind of thing only happens in books and movies." She laughed. "The poor, pitiful human finds herself trapped in a magical world of creatures she must join, or what? What happens to me if I don't stay?"

The professor frowned. "What happens to you if you go?" A dark implication lay under her soft tone.

Blaire didn't want to think of the consequences of turning down the opportunity to get her university education at this beautiful school, complete with freedom from Caleb, but this sounded ridiculous. Supernatural creatures weren't real. Destined pairs sounded silly. What did "destined pair" even mean? So what if she had some kind of mark? That didn't mean she should be someone's mate with no choice in the matter.

The professor leaned forward and used the tip of her index finger to tilt Blaire's chin up in her direction, interrupting her spiraling thoughts. She held Blaire in place with an intense stare, her russet brown eyes edged with the smallest hint of glowing amber. It had to be a trick of the light.

"My dear Miss Wilcox, you would be wise to accept reality before it is too late." The professor smiled at Blaire, allowing the hint of a sharp fang to appear.

The world faded to black.

6

LUKAS

She could hear voices.

Blaire's head felt foggy, and she wanted to sleep. Her hair being moved from her shoulder tickled across the skin of her neck, forcing her to stir.

"Don't touch her," a deep voice said.

There was shuffling on the bed as Blaire's hair fell back down, followed by a loud huff of air and a woman's soft voice. "I just wanted to see if it's there."

"It's not. The bond hasn't been sealed, so just leave her alone."

"Or maybe it's a mistake." Another man's voice held a hypnotic quality to it.

"Dude, no. You know good and damn well the—"

"Shh!" the woman admonished. "She's waking up!"

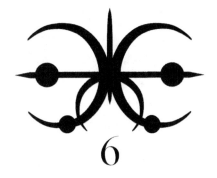

With a soft groan, Blaire slowly opened her eyes, trying to focus on the room around her. She tried to remember how she got here, and more importantly, where she was. Nothing came to mind as her vision came into focus. She gasped when her eyes met a pair of large, smoky blue eyes shadowed heavily in black makeup.

A petite girl with the wildest hair Blaire had ever seen sat uncomfortably close on the bed, leaning toward her. The girl's black hair was shaved on the left side, with the back and right side cut short. The top of her hair was longer, spiked in a pixie style, and dyed a pretty, faded pink. It suited the pale girl's style of goth and punk with a dash of bubble-gum princess.

Blaire closed her eyes as she tried to remember. The image of the professor's fangs came into focus, and she sucked in a breath, her eyes flying open.

She jerked upright, forcing the girl to move out of the way. Blaire scrambled backward until her back met the wall, then she wrapped her arms around her shins, pulling her knees to her chest.

This couldn't be happening, but denial hadn't gotten her anywhere so far; she had to accept reality. The small room with two beds, two desks, and one door out was obviously a dorm room. The girl looked around her age. Maybe. Unless she was immortal.

The girl smiled brightly at her.

No fangs. Had it been a dream?

"So, it's true, right? You're like, totally a human? Or no, wait... are you half-Vasirian or something? Not that I know if that's a thing or not, but yeah, are you, like, a half?"

Not a dream then.

Blaire's mouth opened in frozen shock at how casual this girl... no, this vampire... or whatever she called herself, was being.

Unable to stop her shaking hands as she gripped her legs tightly, she felt like she was having a mental breakdown. The girl continued rambling, but Blaire zoned out, devolving deeper into a state of panic. Were they going to eat her? Drink her blood? Where was the professor?

"Oh yeah!" the girl said, loud enough to cause Blaire to jump, shaken out of her panicked thoughts. "How old are you? Are you, like, going to be commuting to the high school branch? No… you look older than that. I'm in my first year of university, so that would totally make sense, because you look older than me."

"Riley! Shut. Up," the guy with the deep voice said from the other side of the room.

At the foot of the other bed, watching Blaire, sat a guy with inky black hair cut close on the sides and back but long and messy on the top. That just-got-out-of-bed look. His heavy brow narrowed, and he pressed his full lips into a flat line as he studied Blaire with concern in his dark green eyes.

Blaire remembered the two of them from the diner when she spoke to the professor.

"Whaaat? Don't you want to know about her too?" The girl pouted, looking at him.

"Read the damn room. For fuck's sake." The guy speared his fingers through his hair. "It's obvious she's afraid, and you need to calm down and let her process what's happening."

"Afraid? Of what?" The girl genuinely looked confused.

He groaned and rolled his eyes. "Of us, you idiot!"

The girl stared at him in confusion before turning toward Blaire. "Look, I know Lukas might look scary, but he's totally harmless."

The sound of sucking teeth drew Blaire's attention to the long-haired guy she ran into at the plaza. He was just as gorgeous as she remembered him. Without the leather jacket, the definition of the muscles at his shoulders and arms showed through his black t-shirt. She swallowed hard and her heartbeat quickened.

His brows narrowed as he moved his gaze down, giving Blaire the same full-body appraisal she had given him.

If it were physically possible to feel heat from a look alone, Blaire felt it lick along her skin like white-hot flames when his eyes moved over her. Her breath hitched, and his eyebrows shot up as his eyes met hers. They stared at one another in silence until Blaire forgot about the others in the room.

An exasperated sigh came from the dark-haired guy, drawing Blaire's attention. "I doubt it's Lukas she's afraid of, but more the fact that we're all Vasirian."

The girl laughed but jerked her head around to look at Blaire when no one said anything. "Whoa, wait, wait… You're… serious?"

Blaire pulled her knees tighter to her chest, and the girl's gaze fell on Blaire's trembling hands.

The girl threw her hands up animatedly. "Whoa, wait a minute. Like, holy shit. I would never hurt you, or any human, for that matter. I've never even killed a spider before. I actually have to get Aiden to do that for me because I'm totally terrified of the creepy crawlies."

Blaire laughed softly, her body relaxing a fraction, and both guys visibly relaxed in turn.

"I- I'm afraid of spiders t-too…" She wanted to sound brave, but she felt anything but, right now. Too much happened lately, with Caleb, and now this; she wasn't holding up as well as she hoped.

The long-haired guy frowned and looked uncomfortable at her words.

"That's better! You're prettier when you laugh," the girl said, tucking one of her legs underneath herself as she turned on the bed to face Blaire. "So, anyway… my name is Riley Easton, and over there"—she pointed to the dark-haired guy at the foot of the other bed—"that's Aiden, my brother. He's best friends with Lukas."

"Who's Lukas?" Blaire frowned. She didn't remember being

introduced to anyone by that name.

The long-haired guy stiffened, his face morphing into shock and disbelief before he glared at the floor, clearly dissatisfied with her question.

Aiden smirked and gave him a pitying glance. Before Blaire could fix her faux-pas, Riley confirmed her suspicion.

"That grumpy-looking guy over there." She pointed. "That's Lukas. You at least know he's your Korrena, right?"

Blaire thumped her forehead against her knees.

She wished she had more information to prepare for this. Maybe if she stayed conscious, she'd know more, but no, passing out ruined everything. She sighed and shook her head, looking back up at Riley. "No… I wasn't told who that was."

"What have you been told exactly?" Aiden raised an eyebrow at her.

"Um… I know you're not human, and this school is actually a school for your kind." She frowned, hugging her legs close again. "Oh… and Professor Velastra told me about the Korrena. That it's something like a soulmate."

Aiden chuckled. "That's… one way to describe it, sure."

Lukas cut a sharp look at Aiden, glaring at him, before returning his attention to Blaire. Despite the fact he gave her no way inside his shell, he stayed hyper-focused on her every move and sound.

"She told me one of the students had seen their mark on me, but I haven't seen any weird markings anywhere." She lifted her arms and looked about, inspecting herself for the offending mark, causing Aiden to chuckle and Lukas to roll his eyes.

"So, like, yeah, Lukas is your Korrena. Aaaand, he's also your roommate."

The air grew tense again.

Roommate? Blaire had to share a room with a guy? No, not just a guy; a supernatural being whom they all believed to be her soulmate—whom she knew nothing about—and who could potentially suck all the blood from her body the first time alone together. She didn't put it past the guy with the way he stared at her like she was something to eat, with a dash of hatred for the seasoning. Nope, she wasn't on board with that. She shook her head in denial.

"See, all Korrena pairs share rooms because it can get difficult to not be together," Riley said, when Blaire didn't say anything.

Doubting this could get much weirder, Blaire lowered her legs to sit cross-legged on the bed, resting her hands in her lap. "That doesn't make any sense. Do we really have to share a room?" She glanced at Lukas, not wanting to offend the guy, but needing to know if she could get out of this predicament.

"Yeah, it's kind of part of the package when you meet your Korrena," Aiden said.

Blaire tensed, her shoulders drawing up tight, and she wrapped her arms around her stomach. Lukas shifted on the bed as if to come over to her, but he cursed under his breath and sat back, clenching his jaw instead. She thought the reaction strange.

Aiden looked over at him and sighed.

"Hey!" Riley exclaimed, bringing the focus back to her. "It's going to be totally fine. I'll come visit and hang out with you all the time if you want. Because honestly, Lukas is boring as hell, so he probably won't be much fun as a roommate."

Aiden laughed and played it off by running a hand over his mouth when Lukas glared at him.

"What? It's true!" Riley said with a pout. She was certainly funny, and her ease with all three of them helped Blaire relax despite the chaotic mess of her situation.

"Why can't I share a room with another girl?" Blaire said quietly, broaching the subject as delicately as she could. Sharing a bedroom and a bathroom with a guy violated every rule of conduct she'd been raised with. This wasn't the normal in the world she came from. The adults here condoned this? Encouraged it?

Aiden said, "Until we find our Korrena, we either have our own private rooms or share with the same sex, sure. It's just… like Riley said, it can be difficult not being together with your Korrena."

"I don't understand…"

Aiden rubbed the back of his neck. "We're taught that once we find our pair, being physically away from them can sometimes cause distress emotionally, and physically wear on us. Putting us in the same room with our pair soothes those feelings and allows the pair bond to grow without additional stressors."

Blaire didn't entirely understand. Maybe the guidebook would give her insight, or the professor could help her later.

Aiden stood from the bed. "We should get going. Let Blaire settle in and get her things sorted."

Blaire looked up at him in confusion. "How do you know my name?"

He rubbed the back of his neck. "Professor Velastra told us when she brought you in unconscious earlier."

"Why can't we stay longer?" Riley flopped onto her back and whined. "I can help her unpack and stuff."

Aiden raked a hand through his hair again in frustration. "If you get off your ass and come with me, I'll buy you that jacket you've been wanting."

Riley squealed, and jumped from the bed, startling Blaire. She rushed out of the room without even saying goodbye. Blaire ached for the only nice girl she'd met to stay, even for the illusion of security.

Aiden laughed before turning to Blaire. "It was nice to finally meet you, officially."

Lukas shot Aiden another look, his scowl growing.

"Later, man." Aiden rolled his eyes at the attitude Lukas gave, muttering about how this was going to be as fun as a root canal. He exited the dorm, closing the door behind him.

Blaire took the opportunity to inspect the room in more detail, trying to distract herself from the guy who continued to watch her without offering conversation.

The room had bare walls, the design simplistic and plain. From the entrance, a small foyer led to a private ensuite bathroom from what she could see through an open door to the right of the entrance, and then opened into the main area of the shared room. The twin-sized bed she sat on stood against the left wall, dressed in soft black sheets and pillow slips with a burgundy duvet cover accented in ornate, black flourishes along the edges.

Positioned parallel to hers, sat Lukas's bed, with matching linens, just a few feet away against the other wall, with a plush area rug between them. A wide nightstand stood between the beds, divided into six drawers to split between the room's occupants. A small lamp sat on each side. A large window overlooked the courtyard behind the nightstand with a perfect view of the hedge maze and flower beds. Burgundy curtains, with the same ornate design that accented the beds, tied back with black cords to allow light to fill the room.

At the foot of Lukas's bed sat a simple wooden desk and chair with various books on top. Another stack of books sat on the hardwood floor near the foot of his bed, in the middle of the room. His side of the room lacked a personal touch, holding no pictures or decorative accents. She found it strange. Didn't most college students have things like pictures of family and friends, or something like posters… or, well, anything? The barren space seemed sad.

A matching desk abutted her bed at the foot. Beyond that, an open door led into a walk-in closet opposite the bathroom. The right side looked empty, but the left side appeared occupied with what must be Lukas's clothing.

Blaire looked at her suitcases sitting between the closet and foyer. She needed to unpack, but she didn't feel like it. She needed to figure out what was going on; this was all too surreal to be happening.

She got off the bed, and Lukas immediately stiffened. She glanced over at him. It made no sense to her that he acted afraid of her when he was the one who had the ability to drain her of life. She shook her head and crossed to her duffel to retrieve the folder the professor gave her before she passed out. Grabbing it up, she walked back to the bed and plopped down, sitting cross-legged.

She shuffled through the papers, trying to make sense of the information. Points made in the early pages had been explained to her, but as she delved deeper, she started asking questions aloud, talking to herself.

The guidebook confirmed her perception of the Korrena in the Vasirian's world being essentially a soulmate.

> *Each Vasirian born into this world is predestined to be linked with another through this bond.*

She scrunched her nose at that. "So, wait… I was born already bound to this guy?"

> *As long as the Vasirian youth are in proximity to one another, pairs typically manifest themselves by the late teens, generally seventeen to eighteen, but it is possible for a pairing to not discover one another until later. Vasirian are advised to be aware that in rare cases, they may not find their pair at all.*

"Wait… how old is Lukas?" Blaire fit the age bracket, but the professor specifically said Lukas was late in finding his pair. She flopped back on the bed and ran her hands over her face with a heavy sigh.

"I'm nineteen." Lukas's deep timbre broke through her musings.

She grimaced; she'd forgotten he was in the room; he'd been so silent. It was the first time he spoke directly to her since the day they met. She lowered her hands and turned her head on the bed to stare at him. "Excuse me?"

He sighed. "You asked how old I am."

Blaire's cheeks warmed. She didn't realize she'd ask the question aloud. She sat up and turned toward him, twisting the ends of her long hair. "So, you're not a vampire…"

"No."

"But you have fangs?"

"Yes."

Blaire studied him. "How does that work?" Other than the professor at the end of their meeting, she hadn't seen anyone with fangs.

Lukas raked his fingers through his long hair and licked his lips. "They… grow? I dunno."

Blaire blinked at him; her mouth parted as she stared blankly.

"What?" He spoke softly, but the intensity of his unwavering gaze flustered her.

"How do teeth grow? I've never heard of anything like that."

Lukas shifted uncomfortably before sighing. "It's like an itch in your gums. Then it just sort of happens. I don't know how to explain it. I've never had to."

Blaire took a deep breath. "Do you drink blood like vampires do?" A loud swallow followed her question.

"I do… we all do. We need it to survive."

Blaire looked down at her guidebook. She figured as much, seeing the professor's fangs and hearing her explanation, but she had to be sure. She needed to approach this stuff delicately, but her curiosity, and need for information, won over her fear of the unknown.

"Do all Korrena pairs really share rooms? Even the younger ones?"

"From what I know, yes."

"That's not normal…"

Lukas glared at her.

"I mean…" Blaire chewed the inside her cheek. "Isn't it kind of bad to put guys and girls together in a room like that? That's amoral where I come from." She wasn't a prude, but this kind of thing wasn't normal.

Lukas sat back against the head of his bed, resting his hands across his flat stomach, bending one knee up to rest his foot on the bed, leaving his other leg outstretched. "It's all we've ever known. Our world isn't like yours. In some ways, we're much like your kind, but in others, we're not. We're brought up from an early age knowing to expect our pair. To bond with them when we meet. There isn't a taboo around it. We're careful though. We don't procreate young, but we do bond." He glanced over at her. "I mean, you can't tell me you humans don't have sex as teenagers. I've seen enough movies to know better." A faint smile ghosted his lips.

Blaire's heart raced. "Well… yeah, they do, but sharing rooms and all that… what do your parents think?"

Lukas scoffed and shook his head. "It's something we're brought up to expect. It's part of our culture. There's nothing odd about it. Is it really going to be a problem for you?"

"I don't know…" she said quietly. She twisted the ends of her hair around her index finger, looking down, unable to meet his eyes any longer.

Lukas sighed.

"Wait… We're not expected to have sex, are we?" She turned quickly and began thumbing through the guidebook.

Lukas laughed.

She glared at him. "I am not having sex with you."

He stared at her blankly. "Never said you were."

"Good. Not happening. I can't do that. We just met."

A shadow of an emotion she couldn't place crossed his face. Blaire lowered her head and resumed reading. After several minutes of silence, she spoke aloud to the book again, asking questions to the air, debating every point she disagreed with or didn't understand.

"Can you just shut up?" His frustrated voice broke through her studies.

"What?"

"You. Need. To. Shut. Up." He enunciated each word as if she were slow in the head.

Blaire stared at him in shock. What the hell was his problem all of a sudden? His entire demeanor had changed. He'd done a complete one-eighty. She set down the book and glared at him. "I'm just trying to figure this out. It's a lot of information, and this is all new to me."

Lukas clenched his jaw and moved to sit on the edge of his bed, resting his elbows on his knees, leaning forward as he narrowed his eyes at her.

"There's nothing to understand. This is a mistake." He swallowed hard and forced the next words out. "Humans, they don't belong here… and certainly not with me." He dragged a hand through his long hair and closed his eyes, grimacing as if in pain. "Just… pack your shit and go, alright?"

His expression slipped and hurt briefly flashed in his eyes before he schooled his expression. Blaire didn't know what to make of his sudden change in mood, but he wasn't going to run over her. She'd had enough of that from her stepbrother.

"You know what? Fuck off. I don't want to be with a monster, anyway." The waver in her voice betrayed her hurt.

Lukas looked as if she told him his favorite pet died, but then his features shifted from the pained expression to something angrier, and she thought he wanted to throttle her. A chill of unease went up her spine to the back of her neck. Blaire wondered if she made a big mistake and was about to meet her maker. Instead of tearing her apart and making a meal out of her, Lukas moved off his bed, grabbed his leather jacket from his desk chair, and stormed out of the room, slamming the door behind him.

Blaire dropped back on the bed and let out a heavy sigh. Should she leave and go back to Caleb before he realized she left? Maybe she could hitchhike to the next town over before anyone realized she was gone and get a job there; there would be no paper trail, or anyone to tell Caleb's grandparents. She could stay in a women's shelter. They would protect her and not let Caleb know where she went.

The problem was the consequences of running away if anyone found her. She didn't want to die. One misstep and that would be the end of her. The other potential problem was the contract she signed and not knowing the legal repercussions for breaking it, but this situation was beyond reasonable.

She crossed to the closet and stepped inside. Lukas's scent had infused his clothes, a mixture of apple, subtle citrus, and spice. She remembered it vividly from the other day, and it made her lightheaded.

Running her fingers over the uniforms hanging on her side of the closet, she pulled the garments apart to study them. The theme of burgundy and black carried into the uniforms with the short plaid skirt, a tie around the neck of a white button-down blouse, and a lightweight black cardigan with the school insignia embroidered on the chest. A pair of black thigh-high stockings hung over another hanger next to the skirt, and a pair of cute black loafers sat on the floor.

It wasn't a bad outfit, kind of cliché, but it was a prestigious private school. The quality of materials and workmanship shouted "money." The sweater felt like cashmere, and the loafers were Italian leather, polished to a nice shine.

Blaire sighed, and before making any rash decisions, returned to her bed to go over the Korrena guidelines to see what she agreed to when she joined the academy.

> *Sometimes the pair may suspect their connection, if they already know each other prior to their full awakening, due to heightened emotions and other instinctive reactions. A marking will appear on the Korrena's skin, the position and design unique to each pairing, allowing them to recognize one another. They are unable to see the mark on themselves until the pair completes the bonding ritual. No other Vasirian outside the pairing carries this exact mark.*
>
> *The blood of one's Korrena is intoxicating and can be addictive, but there is no cause for alarm, as due to the Vasirian's regenerative nature, they can recover quickly from anemia brought on by the overindulgence of their partner.*

Blaire shuddered and shook her head. "Really? So, what does that mean for humans?"

She frowned; she saw nothing regarding being a human Korrena as she flipped through the pages, scanning the information, until she came to a section about reproduction.

> *Not everyone finds their Korrena pair, but Vasirian, lucky enough to be blessed by the gods, are believed to have a purer continuation of their bloodline when they bring life into the world with their bonded mate. Korrena-born children test higher in intelligence, show sharper reflexes, and develop the power of mental manipulation.*

"Nope. Nope, nope, nope." Done with all of it, Blaire shoved the papers into the envelope and placed them in the top drawer of the nightstand. She needed a break from information overload. She sighed. She had signed a contract, so it was highly unlikely they would let her leave campus so easily.

Lukas still hadn't returned, so she decided to take a shower.

The ensuite bathroom looked sleek and modern. The sink had a large counter with ample space on each side. One side of the sink held Lukas's cologne, bracelets, and a hairbrush that had only a few long hairs in its bristles. Everything was neat and clean, much like the bedroom, so at least she wouldn't have to deal with a messy roommate. On her side of the counter, she found it already stocked with a new hairbrush, dryer, hairbands, facial cleanser, and a blue candle that smelled like coconut. Next to the sink was a two-sided caddy that had toothbrushes and toothpastes. Her toothbrush was still in the packaging on her side.

A stand-up shower sat in the corner of the room and a small table was positioned beside it with fluffy black towels stacked on top. She opened the shower door and peered inside. The fragrance of Lukas's body wash lingered, and she bit her lower lip. At least she liked his taste in shower products.

Reaching out, she grabbed the red bottle from the shelf in the shower and looked down at it. "Bearglove?" Blaire opened the top of the shower gel and took a sniff. She'd found the source of that spicy apple scent that made her insides turn to mush.

Placing the body wash on the shelf, she retrieved her bath products and pajamas from her suitcase, returned to the bathroom, and locked the door behind her. The shower water drumming on her scalp and back helped calm her thoughts.

Once she had finished and dried her hair, she pulled the covers down on the bed, ready for the day to be over. Turning the light off, she tried to relax, nestling into the soft bedding, and closed her eyes.

She hoped for a peaceful sleep to be ready to handle her first day of classes in the morning, but she doubted that, knowing at any moment a Vasirian man would return and occupy the same space as her.

Throwing open the door and flooding the room with light, Lukas charged straight into Aiden's room without knocking.

Aiden shot off the bed and came at him, ready to throw a punch, but pulled up short.

Scowling, he raked a hand over his face. "Have you ever heard of knocking? I almost decked your ass." He adjusted his boxers as he stomped across the floor back to his bed, sitting down and rubbing his tired eyes.

Lukas ran both of his hands through his long hair and looked up at the ceiling, ignoring Aiden's complaints as he paced the room.

"Dude… what happened?" Aiden scratched his chest.

"I fucked up. I already fucked up."

Arching a brow, Aiden stared at Lukas. "What happened? Did

you hurt her or something? You've gotta calm down and tell me what's going on, or I can't help you."

Lukas dragged a hand down his face and stopped pacing. "No! I didn't hurt her. I couldn't hurt her. I almost lost it over the idea of a stupid spider scaring her. Do you honestly think I could hurt her?"

He was spiraling, so he was thankful Aiden approached it delicately.

"Look man, just sit down and tell me exactly what happened."

Lukas slumped onto the empty bed and sighed. "I don't know what I'm going to do… I screwed everything up." He ran a hand through his hair again. "I'm going crazy, and it's been less than a day!"

"Dude, calm down. Explain things to me slowly, because you're not making any sense."

Lukas bared his teeth, feeling like a wild animal that could strike at any moment. He radiated tension, perched on the edge of the bed and jiggling his knee. "I couldn't even stand to look at Blaire when you and Riley were there. I felt this overwhelming urge to protect her when she was scared of us. I nearly went to her and took her in my arms." He sighed. "I know good and damn well neither of you would hurt her, but her fear was so strong."

Aiden shook his head. "You know if you'd done that, it would have made her fear that much worse. You honestly looked at her like you despised her very existence."

"Yeah, I know, and that's why I tried to ignore her, but all that did was create more tension and make it harder." Lukas looked up at Aiden, meeting his eyes with the hopelessness of a broken man. "I… I told her to pack her shit and leave."

"You're a fucking idiot."

Lukas jumped up from the bed. "I know!" He raked his hands through his hair again and squeezed his fists, holding onto the long strands behind his head. He had been screwing things up since the girl first woke up, but he couldn't stop himself.

"She'd been sitting there reading papers and asking questions, but not actually asking me those questions. She was completely ignoring me."

Her disregard worked its way under his skin. He never cared if anyone ignored him before. He preferred keeping to himself, thankful he'd been given a private room at the start of his university term, but he wanted her to talk to him.

Aiden rubbed the back of his neck. "Well, what did you expect? You spent the entire time giving her the cold shoulder. You barely spoke a handful of words, and none of them were directed at her."

Sighing, Lukas dropped his hands in defeat and shook his head. "Everything was fine at first when you left. I even interrupted her and answered what I knew wasn't directed at me. We talked. She asked questions, and I answered. But when we got to talking about sex, it got weird..."

"Sex?" Aiden's brows shot up. "How'd you get on that subject?"

"Yes. We were talking about pairs rooming together. Bonding. I know it's different for her, that humans don't bond like we do, so I didn't take offense when she said she wasn't going to have sex with me."

"As you shouldn't. I wouldn't even take offense if another Vasirian said that if we'd just met. Korrena or not."

"Right. I agree completely, but the way she followed it up by saying she couldn't do it... that it wasn't happening. I dunno... it's stupid, now that I think about it. It wasn't as if she said anything cruel. But something in that moment rubbed me wrong. It felt like she rejected me, not the idea of having sex with me." Lukas put his hand over his face. "I'm so stupid."

"No, you're not. This whole situation is weird. She's human, so it's unfamiliar territory. Hell, having a Korrena is unfamiliar territory no matter how much they try to prepare us. But again, she's human. You need to see things from her perspective. She was terrified of us when she woke up. Not to mention, things work differently in the human world. It was clear the idea of sharing a room with a man made her uneasy. Not you, Lukas. A man. It could have been anyone and she'd likely have responded the same way."

Lukas sighed. "I just… I snapped at her. I told her this was a mistake. I told her a human didn't belong with me, and that's when I told her to leave." He looked back at Aiden again, brows wrinkled in confusion. "I wonder if this honestly isn't all a mistake."

A human and a Vasirian paired sounded so far-fetched that maybe he was seeing things. Maybe it all got to him because of the sun bothering him, and he was in a bad mood that day.

"You're out of your mind if you think she isn't the one. The mark aside, just the way you're acting isn't like you."

"What are you talking about?"

"You're not acting like your usual self," Aiden stated matter-of-factly.

Lukas threw his hands up. "No shit, of course I'm not! Is it all because she's the one, or is it because of all the expectations and drama dropped into my lap? I don't know anything anymore!"

He knew as he said those words, he was lying to himself.

"You're acting like a caged animal that hasn't eaten in a month."

Lukas looked away and muttered under his breath, "She called me a monster…"

Aiden fell silent, his eyes wide. When he regained his composure, he stood from the bed and crossed to Lukas to place a hand on his shoulder.

"Look, it's only the first day. Things just need to process. For now, how about we play Guilty Gear -Strive- so you can work out some of this aggression?"

"Fine... but I don't know what I'm going to do, man."

They played video games for several hours before Lukas decided to face the music and return to his dorm room.

He slid his key into the lock, but it didn't click. He slowly opened the door. Had Blaire forgotten to lock the door, or did she leave it unlocked for him? He walked quietly through the darkened room, enough moonlight filtering in through the window to allow him to see where he was going.

The entire room already smelled of her, and it was driving him crazy.

He stared at the lump on her bed until she moved. He tensed and held his breath as Blaire rolled onto her back, coming into clear view under the moonlight. She looked breathtaking with her blonde hair spread out over her pillow; the moon illuminating her pale skin, casting her face in an ethereal glow.

Lukas stepped toward her. He reached out and gently dragged the tips of his shaking fingers over her cheek. She released a soft sound, causing him to retreat to his side of the room.

The fact that just the touch of her skin could arouse him the way it did spoke volumes when he had never much cared about attraction.

He already felt the call of the bond, and him calling this a mistake was the real mistake.

7

Adaptation

Blaire woke up the next morning alone. She didn't know if Lukas had come back last night. Maybe he wasn't going to return until she moved out, which bothered her, and she couldn't understand why. Like last night, she didn't understand why rejection by someone she didn't know bothered her so much.

Sunlight streamed through the window into her face. She yawned, sitting up and rubbing her eyes. She needed to get ready for class, but she wasn't sure if she wanted to bother.

She heard laughter through the doorway, causing a shudder of uneasiness to pass through her at the prospect of Vasirian on the other side. Real life, blood-sucking predators, and they expected her to walk out there and join them. *Someone ring the dinner bell.*

She put a hand over her face and laughed at her foolish thoughts. "Come on… get your shit together."

Throwing the covers back, she placed her feet onto the plush rug and dug in her toes. The simple, mundane sensation helped calm her.

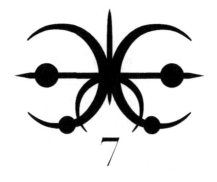

Monsters wouldn't dress their rooms in creature comforts, would they? Padding over to the closet, she pulled out the uniform pieces and retreated to the bathroom to get dressed and groom herself. Once ready, she grabbed the backpack at the foot of her bed and the temporary class schedule the professor provided with a map directing her where to go on campus. Stomach growling, she looked at the map, making a mental note of the canteen location—near the cafeteria on the second floor of the main building—to grab something quick to eat for breakfast before heading into the hall, locking the door behind her.

The first half of the school day went smoothly, other than getting lost once or twice, but other students pointed her the right way. Otherwise, no one spoke to her but her teachers. The students watched her, whether in fascinated curiosity or hunger, she didn't know. Somehow, they avoided turning her into a meal. Maybe she imagined their hunger, but it didn't stop her from being hypervigilant about every lingering glance. She didn't want to tempt fate to discover friend or foe. All in all, she enjoyed her time there so far, if she could get past the students and staff being bloodsucking Vasirian, a fact that hung over her head like a guillotine.

She discovered that after finishing her introductory classes for the university program, she would choose her program focus—her major—and begin those classes tomorrow, along with general education, like all freshmen. It was the start of April, so she'd already missed most of the school year; she would need to play catch up. She honestly didn't see the point with only a few months left. The syllabus of her last class showed courses extending until the first of July. From the looks of it, Blackthorn students only received one month of a summer break before classes began again at the start of August. The school system she was used to had the luxury of taking a longer break.

She walked to the cafeteria for her lunch break, which was at the end of a long corridor. The aroma of rotisserie chicken made her stomach growl loudly. A passing student giggled, and Blaire blushed. The cafeteria was incredibly spacious and large. Floor-to-ceiling windows made up the back walls overlooking the thick forest behind the academy, bathing the entire cafeteria in natural light.

A few students sat at a table eating normal human food, and she raised a brow. What did she expect? She'd been able to get breakfast from the small canteen down the hall, so surely, they ate something besides blood… or humans. A shudder passed through her, and she glanced around her warily. Did she honestly expect to walk into the cafeteria and find tables laid out with human sacrifices on silver platters? An anxious laugh bubbled out of her, drawing the gaze of the student closest to her. She hurried further into the cafeteria.

A full wrap-around buffet sat to the left of the entrance, filled with the selections for the current meal service. Lunch was chicken and roast beef with a variety of prepared vegetables—all familiar—and salads. Another smaller bar sat in the back corner with various desserts and drink choices like juice, coffee, and fountain drinks.

Blaire took stock from the large, empty area between the buffet and seating. Students sat at long, rectangular, wooden tables with well-spaced high-back chairs of the same wood. A few round tables lined the windowed walls of the cafeteria, creating an intimate seating space for students lucky enough to grab one.

The guys' uniforms of pressed black slacks, white button-down Oxford shirts and long ties in the same plaid as her skirt, looked as polished as hers did. Some guys wore the official high-class leather shoes the school provided, while others wore their own unique footwear. She saw everything from Converse sneakers to combat boots, which suited the uniform more than sneakers, in her opinion.

Blaire found the beginning to the main bar and grabbed a tray before moving down the line. She picked up a small garden salad with fresh cucumbers and cherry tomatoes, and a small bowl of cantaloupe. She reached for the delicious-smelling chicken.

"Blaire, right?"

She nearly dropped the plate of the chicken, startled. Setting the plate on her tray, she turned around to face a tall girl with braided, brown hair hanging over her shoulder. Large, hazel eyes looked at Blaire in eager fascination. A shorter guy with slicked-back, blond hair had his arm around her waist. He nodded at Blaire politely.

"Y-yeah. That's right."

"Awesome. I wasn't sure."

Noting Blaire's confused expression, she laughed. "I helped you find the canteen this morning. It's okay if you don't remember me. I'm sure you've had a lot going on. My name is Rueanna, but you can call me Rue."

Blaire blinked. The friendliness took her off guard. "Ah. Yeah, I'm sorry. It's been a lot to take in."

"I'm sure. It has to be weird being a human here, yeah?"

Blaire scuffed the toe of her loafer on the floor, looking down at her tray. "It's different."

Rue reached out and put a hand on Blaire's forearm, causing her to flinch. What was with Vasirian and personal space issues? The professor, Riley, now this girl…

"Oh, crap. I'm sorry. I didn't mean to scare you. I just… wanted to let you know it's gonna be fine. Especially if you'll be joining us."

Blaire tilted her head and her brow furrowed. "Joining you where?"

"Joining us… as in, becoming one of us. A Vasirian."

Blaire's eyes widened.

The guy standing next to her frowned. "I don't think that'll happen."

"Why not?" Rue asked, putting a hand on her hip. "Have you ever seen a human turned?"

He looked around. "No. We shouldn't even be talking about it." His thick accent was unfamiliar; it certainly wasn't local.

Blaire stared at them, frozen to the spot. She didn't know what to make of what they just said, but the guy's discomfort with the topic prompted her to ask. "Do you… is that something you do? Turn humans?"

The guy shook his head. "No. I don't know why exactly, but it's not done. No one talks about it either." He leaned forward and lowered his voice. "I think it is—how do you say? Taboo. As far as I know, there's never been a need to 'make' a Vasirian. We're born this way. We don't need to be created." He flashed her a bracing smile while Rue rolled her eyes.

The casual way they relayed that calmed Blaire. At least she didn't have to think about the possibility of becoming another species altogether.

Rue smiled. "Anyway! I'm sure we'll see each other around—maybe even have some gen ed classes together or whatever major you decide on. They like to get most of them out of the way the first year. You know, English, Math—all the boring stuff."

Blaire relaxed, a small laugh leaving her.

"Well, Liam and I are meeting people in the valley for the afternoon, so we gotta go. It was nice to meet you."

The guy at her side—Liam—offered a smile. "A pleasure," he said,

Blaire watched the couple walk away and exit the cafeteria. So far, the others were friendly; way less snobbish than kids at Magnolia Heights. Maybe it wasn't going to be so bad here after all. She moved to the beverage bar and grabbed a bottle of peach tea, then turned to go find a table but stopped short at spotting a row of refrigerator units with glass fronts.

Filled with medical-grade bags of blood.

She watched in rapt curiosity as a student opened the unit and reached inside to grab the cold blood.

Her breathing quickened as she looked more closely around the room, white-knuckling the sides of her tray to keep from dropping it. A few students glanced up at her as she stood in the middle of the foot traffic, on the edge of a panic attack. When she recoiled at the sight of one of the students drinking blood from a straw, he stopped and looked at her, a wicked look crossing his face. He winked at her and grinned with descended fangs, the blood staining his teeth and tongue.

She wanted to run.

She couldn't run.

Instead, she moved as fast as her legs would take her without drawing attention to herself, but she could still hear the student laughing with their friends behind her.

Blaire dropped into an empty chair at a table in the far back corner of the cafeteria.

Taking a deep breath, she willed her body to stop trembling. Her gaze continuously darted around the room, watching students not only eat actual food, but drink blood from bags. How had she missed that when she first came in? Several minutes passed before she calmed down, finally realizing no one paid her any attention and they weren't going to rush over and trade cold blood for warm, fresh blood.

She sighed and poked at her salad with her fork, lacking the appetite she'd entered with. This was certainly not how she envisioned her week going by when it started. She thought back to Charlotte and wondered if she was doing okay at the diner and if everything got squared away with Ricky. Had Caleb heard the official news of where she went, and was he looking for her? The professor said the Wilcox family couldn't reach her here, but she was still worried.

"Blaire!"

Pulling Blaire from her thoughts, pink-haired pixie Riley rushed to the table, brother Aiden behind her.

A tall, slim man with long, dark hair followed them, holding hands with a pretty, petite, blue-eyed girl with cherry-cola auburn hair hanging long and straight down to her slim waist. The couple looked like they belonged in a goth band, with their dark makeup and uniforms accented with jewelry and lace-up combat boots.

Even Riley gave the academy's uniform a unique twist. She had replaced her stockings with torn fishnets and wore a pair of platform boots with buckles up the sides, adding a few inches to her five-foot-four frame. Riley pulled out the chair next to Blaire and sat, waving at the others to do the same.

While Blaire admired goth fashion and enjoyed the aesthetic, she didn't feel the look suited her. She always wanted to try something new and bold, but her mother didn't have the kind of money for her to play with different fashion styles to find what she liked, so she opted not to step too far outside of the box. Once she became a Wilcox, different was definitely off the table.

Blaire tried to smile politely, but she had lost all desire to deal with the day. She wanted to go home and crawl into bed and not leave the room.

"This is Mera and Kai. They're friends of Lukas's, so by extension, they're your friends," Riley chirped.

Riley had a weird way about her. How did friends with Lukas automatically become friends with her? She wasn't against making friends, but right now, she wanted to leave. Blaire forced another smile and tried to make small talk.

"It's nice to meet you both," she said in the voice she reserved for serving customers.

Kai nodded politely at Blaire, bringing his ankle up to rest on his knee. His long hair swayed across his back with his movements reminding her of raven wings; while black, it reflected the light in iridescent shades of purple, blue, and green. He looked at Riley. "How many logic-bending hoops did you jump to draw that conclusion?"

"Well, see, Blaire and Lukas are totally going to be bonded soon, and that means we'll all be together. Like, a lot. It's only natural everyone would become friends. Right?"

Blaire's face fell and she put down her fork.

Mera chuckled with a hand over her mouth and shook her head, brushing her side-sweeping bang away from her petite face. "I suppose you're right, but you're being quite presumptuous." Her voice held an accent with a melodic lilt that Blaire couldn't place.

Riley turned her attention to Blaire. "See, those two are already a fully bonded pair."

"I don't see any markings on their necks."

"I take it that's where Lukas saw his mark on you, then?" Mera asked softly.

Blaire nodded.

"That's not how it works..."

Mera reached down and started to unbutton her blouse. Blaire opened her eyes wide until Mera stopped, pulling the upper portion of her blouse open, revealing an intricate tattoo of vines with blooming flowers wrapped around a black triangle with a dotted crescent moon in the middle of her sternum.

"All of that is your mark?"

"No, this,"—she touched the triangle symbol—"is mine and Kai's mark, but I had the tattoo done around it because I felt it looked nice, creating one large tattoo rather than a single mark in the center of my chest."

"Wow… it's actually really beautiful," Blaire said as Mera buttoned her shirt.

"Kai also has the same tattoo on his chest, but where I carry flowers, he wields thorns."

Kai reminded Blaire of a stereotypical vampire with his aristocratic features, further emphasized by a long, narrow nose that led down to a cupid's bow above a pair of full lips, accented by a labret piercing. When he made no move to show his tattoo, she turned her attention back to Mera as she spoke again.

"The mark you share with Lukas… when you bond fully, it will manifest itself completely on your necks as clear as the one we carry."

Blaire scrunched her nose as though tasting something sour, and Aiden raised an eyebrow, studying her. She wasn't sure she liked the idea of having a permanent mark like a tattoo on her neck in plain sight. As a point of rebellion against the Wilcox restrictions, she briefly entertained the idea of getting a small one, but to not have a choice in design rubbed her the wrong way. She didn't allow herself to go deeper into what the mark symbolized. She wasn't mentally prepared to face it yet.

Mera continued. "Each Korrena pair holds their own unique mark. The location where it presents itself varies, but there are only so many body parts to go around, so some pairs share the same location for the mark as other pairs."

"A human as a Korrena…" Kai spoke quietly, as if in awe. He pulled Mera to his side with one arm, and she leaned into him. Grey eyes framed in black eyeliner set beneath a deep brow assessed Blaire intently. "It seems unreal, and if I may be so blunt, I'm not sure I entirely believe it. I honestly wonder if Lukas is so enamored with the idea of finding his pair that he is willing to see anything, even if it wasn't there. I mean, he is almost my age and hasn't found his pair."

"Aiden is four months older than Lukas and in the same boat..." Riley gave her brother a sad look.

Aiden tensed in his seat and clenched his jaw.

Blaire tilted her head. "I read pairs are found around seventeen or eighteen on average, meaning later is just as possible. He's only nineteen. How is that so bad?"

Kai shook his head. "Even if only a year or two later than average, it is sad to endure. We grow up learning about the Korrena and eagerly await the time of our awakening. If that doesn't happen—even if only a year or two passes—knowing it could signify centuries of solitude... I can't even begin to fathom how some never find their pair."

"Centuries?" Blaire's eyes widened, and she looked around the group. "Just how old are you? You look so young..."

Riley spoke up first. "We are young. I'm seventeen. Aiden's nineteen. Mera's eighteen, and Kai is the oldest at twenty. He also has a little brother you'll meet later, Seth. He's eighteen. How old are you?"

"I'm eighteen." She took a sip of her peach tea before adding, "I thought most Korrenas found each other by the time they were my age."

Aiden sighed, running his hand through his hair, before sitting back in his chair. "It doesn't always work out like that."

The table remained silent until Kai spoke up again. "Honestly, I couldn't imagine my life without Mera, and let's just say I was immensely relieved when she had her awakening and it clicked for us. I started to worry I wasn't going to find my beloved, as I was already nineteen when she finally connected with that side of herself at seventeen. I felt something for her before, and suspected it was the call of the sacred bond, but with her being younger than I, let's just say I had… difficulties."

Mera put her head on Kai's shoulder and smiled, closing her eyes.

"Sensing the bond before your pair and being around them isn't easy. I even questioned my sanity at one point, thinking I might have been wrong. It wasn't pleasant. Another two years passed before the bond called to her." Kai squeezed Mera's arm as he pulled her close. "All that aside, I couldn't imagine facing the hurdle of a human being my other half, if that's even possible. I can't wrap my mind around the idea of a Vasirian and a human joining. It's nothing against you personally, don't get me wrong. It's just… peculiar."

Riley nodded. "It does seem weird. I don't think I've ever heard of this happening before, but that doesn't mean it's impossible!" She took a bite of her salad.

"Well, of course, nothing is impossible, I suppose," Kai said. "Sure, there's plenty of media out there depicting vampires and other supernatural beings falling for humans, but I've never heard of it as reality. That kind of stuff is only found in books, movies, and the ramblings of human girls going through puberty. The idea of the dark entices them, but they don't understand its reality."

Everyone stayed silent during Kai's long-winded musings before Blaire finally spoke up, changing the subject entirely, not sure she wanted to be talking about bonding; she wasn't sure she wanted to bond with Lukas. No, she had no intentions of "mating" with a Vasirian; she found the idea ridiculous.

"So… I um, notice you eat normal food, except for the…" She motioned to the bag of blood on Riley's tray before biting her lip, not sure how to broach the subject.

Riley rolled her eyes dramatically and grinned. "Of course we do.

We need lifeblood to really sustain ourselves, though. But yeah, we totally eat normal food, just like you do."

Kai laughed. "I suspect there is much you think is true about Vasirian that isn't if you're concluding our eating habits from the myths of other supernatural beings."

"So… like the mirror thing?" Blaire asked, testing the waters of what they were willing to share with her.

"We have reflections, yes. How else would I be able to put on eyeliner every day?" Kai said as Mera giggled softly. "But in all seriousness, we're not vampires. I believe they're the only supernatural being outside of ghosts documented to lack reflections, yes?"

Blaire nodded.

"While we're hematophagous, and do share traits with the mythological creature, we're different from vampires. For starters, we're real."

"Hema—what?"

"We feed on blood."

Blaire shifted uncomfortably and, after a moment of silence, asked, "What about fire?"

"Yes, fire can kill us, but it can kill anyone." Kai shrugged.

"Stake through the heart?"

"Again, ram anything through someone's heart and they die. Same with decapitation, before you ask." Kai winked at her, and she blushed.

Blaire figured her questions bordered on silly if they weren't vampires, but with so much literature out there with myths and legends surrounding the supernatural, it was hard to know the truth, especially when she'd never heard of the Vasirian before. Asking the source seemed like the best possible way to know for sure. She pressed her lips together, pensive for a moment, before asking, "Garlic?"

"Delicious."

Blaire huffed. "Uh… Sunlight?"

"Need I remind you that you were in the sunlight when you met Lukas, and"—he gestured around with two outstretched hands—"we're not exactly underground in this cafeteria that is all windows."

Blaire blushed as she realized that the question had an obvious answer.

Kai muttered under his breath, "…and we sure as hell do not sparkle. That is the most absurd concept ever conceived."

Aiden burst out laughing. Blaire found it contagious and smiled too.

"Hey, having full body glitter all the time sounds hella cool," Riley said cheerfully.

Aiden groaned.

Kai rolled his eyes at her.

Mera ignored them all, looking at Blaire. "Basically, it's like this… other than the effects of the Korrena bond, our long lifespans, being a little stronger than you, and the need to consume blood, we are similar to humans."

"Don't forget healing," Riley said.

Blaire tilted her head. "Healing?"

"So, like, we can still be hurt just like you. Fatally, even. But most scratches, scrapes, and flesh wounds disappear in roughly thirty minutes or so. Sometimes it can take a few hours if it's bad enough."

"Also, severe wounds that are life-threatening can take a day or two, depending on severity," Aiden added.

Blaire ran a hand through her hair, still focused on one thing. "Okay. I need to know…" She looked up at the expectant eyes of her new friends and blew out a heavy breath. "You drink blood."

"We've established that, yes," Kai said.

"Right. So…" Blaire swallowed, her throat suddenly tight. "What does that mean for me?"

Lines formed between Aiden's brows. "Nothing. What do you mean?"

"I'm not going to be…" Blaire looked around nervously.

"Oh, gods no!" Riley exclaimed. "I told you we wouldn't hurt you. And the rest of the students here have access to enough blood"—she held up her bag—"to not need another source."

Blaire looked down. She needed to know, but the question came out in a strangled whisper. "Whose blood is that?"

The group exchanged wary looks among themselves before Kai put his foot on the floor, sitting forward and resting his elbows on his knees, locking his gaze on Blaire, his face turning serious. "We do not attack or feed directly on humans. Not only is it forbidden, but it's also not necessary to our survival, thanks to generous donations."

"Donations?" Blaire asked flatly.

"From what I understand, our administration has connections with blood banks, hospitals, and such, across the Southeast that keep our academy and its branch locations supplied with clean blood."

Blaire stared blankly. Her mouth opened and closed several times before she could form words. "They just… give it to you?"

"Money makes the world go round, Blaire. Between Vasirian on staff, and the exchange of funds to support these clinics and hospitals, it becomes a mutually beneficial transaction," Kai said with a dismissive wave of his hand.

That certainly cleared things up, but a lot still bugged her about the whole situation, and she wasn't sure how to approach the topic without upsetting them. They took this stuff seriously, and if she expressed the desire not to bond with Lukas, they might be angry.

Blaire took a deep breath.

"Is the bonding absolutely required? I mean, I received a booklet that detailed the expectations like sharing a room together and... blood." She shuddered, and Aiden frowned. "I just couldn't read anymore after I hit the section on reproducing, so I'm not sure what else there is, and if it's really mandatory."

Mera frowned. "Bonding with your Korrena isn't exactly required, no, but it's something we find ourselves desiring, so it's never been an issue of whether it's a necessity. That said, if you were brought to Blackthorn because you're Lukas's Korrena, then it's likely you'll need to follow through with bonding with him if you intend to stay here."

Blaire narrowed her eyes and shook her head. She did not like the idea of being forced into anything, especially into something that reshaped the rest of her life. She's spent the last several months trying to get away from that very thing. She didn't want to be like her mother. She loved her, but Blaire watched her walk away from a comfortable life of just the two of them to step into a gilded cage for a man.

Blaire pushed her tray forward, resting her elbows on the table, and put her head in her hands. "I don't think I can do that..." Looking up at Mera, she sighed, her expression tightening. "I don't think I can stay. I know I have a contract, but the idea of being bound against my will..." Her eyes grew hot, and she closed them in an effort to hide.

Blaire had never felt comfortable taking her stepfather's charity without earning it. It was why she insisted he allow her to work at the diner. She couldn't be like her mother and give up her independence to tie herself to a man in a world that wasn't like her own, where strict rules governed her every move. This situation sounded like the same thing. Felt like the same thing. To accept it would make the last several months of planning a waste.

She couldn't get comfortable with the idea that, because a silly mark may have appeared, they expected her to fall in line. Being out of the reach of Caleb and his family was a benefit she couldn't overlook. Professor Velastra promised her safety from them as long as she attended Blackthorn.

Riley frowned. "No one is forcing you… you don't have to be with Lukas. You don't have to stay here, really. I'm sure there's a way out of the contract, but it's not like that. No one is forced into anything. I mean, if it helps… I'd like you to stay."

Blaire looked at Riley. The girl barely knew her, but she had been so warm and welcoming. Comfort in the middle of all the chaos.

"Being bonded with a pair isn't imprisonment. It is freeing," Mera said, setting a bottle of water on the table. "Once you join together with your pair, you will feel a lightness within. They share everything with you and you're not alone. I can't comprehend how someone would reject that. I know you don't understand it but give it time before you reject this. Take the opportunity to learn our kind, what a Korrena bond really is, before you make a rash decision."

"I just don't want to be bonded to some jerk who was forced into being my roommate."

"Jerk?" Mera looked at Blaire, puzzled. "Lukas is rough around the edges, but I'd hardly call him a jerk…" She looked at Kai, and he nodded agreement.

Aiden laughed, then stopped short as he looked up, a strange look crossing his face. He shook his head, returning his attention to Blaire, narrowing his eyes as he focused on her with a serious expression.

"Listen… did you really call Lukas a monster?" Aiden held her gaze. His expression said he wasn't happy.

Kai stiffened in his seat, visibly upset as Mera hung her head and Riley's face held a deep hurt.

Blaire conceded she'd messed up big time, and there wasn't a lot she could say to take it back, but she could be honest. "I… Yes, I did.

I'm so sorry. I said it in anger." She bit down on her thumbnail as she glanced around the table. "I don't think you all are monsters—I mean, I did, but not anymore. The way Lukas acted just really pissed me off, and when he told me to leave, I lashed out. That was the first thing that came to mind in the heat of the moment." She looked down at her tray and whispered again, "I'm sorry..."

Riley sighed. "It's okay... it's just hard to hear."

Kai waved a hand dismissively. "While it does sting to hear the old stigma is still out there, I cannot blame you for thinking we're monsters, considering how the media portrays supernatural beings. Preying on humans and turning them or killing them at will."

Blaire shuddered.

"It's true," Mera said. "It's understandable you'd feel that way. Again, I assure you, as have the others, we have no desire to harm you."

Riley got the strangest look on her face before slamming her hands down on the tabletop, startling everyone. "Wait a minute. Wait just a frickin' minute. Did Lukas really tell you to leave?"

A fresh wave of fury rolled through Blaire, and she threw her hands up, biting out sharply, "Yes! That asshole told me I should pack my shit and leave. His personality sucks! There's no way someone like him could be my soulmate. I don't believe it for a second."

Mera glanced up and cleared her throat. Riley winced, catching sight of someone behind Blaire.

Of course, Blaire thought.

A tray dropped onto the table beside her and her entire body froze as Lukas pulled out the empty chair next to her.

He must have heard everything.

Lukas lowered himself into the seat, his face red with indignation, lips tight, and pulled in.

They sat there for what felt like an eternity. No one dared to say anything. Even Riley held enough sense to not speak up.

Blaire may have messed up again, but she wasn't sorry for it. It was true; she couldn't believe she was destined to be bound to someone who acted this way. She spent the last four months devising a way to escape another fate, only to be told from the moment she was born she was irrevocably tied to someone who acted fine around her one minute but hated her the next. Not only was it confusing; it was downright childish.

Lukas slowly turned his head to look at Blaire. His eyes narrowed, and his face clouded with anger.

"You know…" He breathed deeply through his nose before leaning in and sneering. "I don't want to be bonded either. I've been fine so far without a pair. I don't see a reason to ruin things now."

Mera squeezed Kai's hand and looked at him with a pained expression.

"And you know what else?" His tone was detached, as if he didn't care to even have the conversation, like it didn't affect him. "It absolutely would be better if you packed your stuff, had the professor terminate your contract, and got out of here before someone gets hurt."

"Lukas!" Aiden shouted. "What the hell is wrong with you?"

"That's extremely uncalled for," Kai admonished firmly.

Lukas sat back and raised an eyebrow at Blaire with a smug look, ignoring the others.

He definitely implied she would get hurt if she stayed. Would he hurt her? Last night he didn't seem dangerous. Once she got past what he was, he seemed like an ordinary guy. Until something snapped and he freaked out on her and left her alone. She swallowed hard and glanced down at her lap, unable to look at him. She didn't understand why his words affected her the way they did.

It felt like he reached into her heart and twisted it. It wouldn't normally hurt to be rejected by someone who barely knew her, but this had something more to it than that. The pain in her chest radiated through her, making her feel like she would break into a thousand pieces if someone touched her.

Aiden shot Lukas a look, and Lukas glared back at him.

"Blaire..." Riley whispered.

Lukas returned his attention to Blaire and his smug expression fell, his lips parting as if to say something, but no words came.

Tears filled Blaire's eyes. She didn't want anyone to see her cry, so she stood abruptly, grabbed her bag, and ran from the table as fast as her legs could take her.

Lukas growled under his breath, clenching his fists on the table as everyone stared at him in surprise.

Riley started to get up from the table, but Aiden spoke up, causing her to pause.

"What the fuck is wrong with you? You're doing the exact damn thing you were upset about last night. You're saying the exact same shit."

Lukas ran his hands through his hair and sat back in his chair, crossing his arms over his chest. He didn't know what was happening to him, but he wanted to crawl out of his own skin. His life had been turned upside down, and he couldn't stop the spiral downward.

"I have no clue, okay? She just... she gets me so twisted inside that I can't control what comes out of my mouth." He clenched his jaw and sighed.

"One minute, I want to comfort her for that damn monster comment... like, seriously? Comfort her even though she should feel ashamed for what she said. Just hearing her apologize, feeling the embarrassment radiating from her, I wanted to fix it. And the next minute? I want to shake her until she shuts up."

"But why? Other than that comment, what has she done?" Kai asked.

"She hates me!"

Thinking about earlier, hearing her speak so poorly of his attitude, made his stomach turn. He had acted like an ass, but he couldn't stop himself. Every instinct inside him screamed she was the one, but his head fought it, and not for lack of want of her, no.

He spent many sleepless nights since discovering her, convincing himself the fear of the fallout of taking a human into this world, a human meant for him, was what set him on edge and made him unsure. The idea that her becoming involved in his world would bring her harm made him sick, so he fought it. He fought it with everything he had, but he was no match for the pull of the bond. Last night in their room drove him to a breaking point.

Her resistance and rejection of him prompted another push to protect himself and drive her away. It made him angry, and he never handled his anger in the healthiest ways, lashing out and scaring her.

"That girl doesn't hate you," Kai said. "Get your head out of your ass, Lukas. She's scared. Unsure of her place here. If you'd kept your attitude in check, you'd have been able to get to know her more like we have today. She was open about her concerns." Kai crossed his arms over his chest and stared down at Lukas with disapproving eyes.

"She doesn't understand the bond," Mera added. "You need to help her. Explain to her you're not making her do anything. Right now, she doesn't see it as anything but entrapment."

"I wouldn't make her do anything against her will."

"Then you need to tell her that," Aiden said, narrowing his eyes.

"Look at it from her point of view and set aside your own pride."

He felt attacked. They were right, but that didn't stop his hackles from rising at being put in his place. However, he needed to do exactly what Aiden said—set aside his own pride.

Lukas sighed, putting his elbows on the table, holding his head, and mumbling, "And what's worse than all of it is this gnawing need to take her into my arms and kiss her."

After a brief silence, Lukas lifted his head to catch Kai and Mera exchanging strange glances.

"What? What the hell's that look for?"

Mera frowned. "Ah… it's just that…" She looked over at Kai and then back at Lukas. "Have you and Blaire had any physical contact?"

Lukas furrowed his brow, not following her line of thinking. With so much already swirling around in his head, they couldn't expect him to be able to draw conclusions about anything at this point.

"It's just, the more the physical contact, the closer the bond grows. You already said you felt her embarrassment…"

"Well, other than the day we literally ran into each other the first time we met, and when I helped her to her feet when she fell, I've not laid a—" He stopped himself.

Kai raised an eyebrow at him.

"What? What happened?" Aiden asked.

Lukas ran a hand through his hair. "I mean… when she was sleeping… I—"

"You didn't!" Riley exclaimed too loudly, drawing attention as she spit out the blood she was sipping on. She had waited until Blaire left to drink it, likely out of courtesy, or maybe the monster comment got to her more than she admitted.

"What? No!" He looked at Riley incredulously. "What is wrong with you? I was going to say I touched her face, but only once. Gods,

Riley." Lukas rolled his eyes, groaning, as Riley blushed, clearly embarrassed by her assumption. It wasn't for lack of desire, but no, he hadn't put his hands on her like that. He wasn't an animal.

"Well," Kai spoke up, ignoring Riley's antics. "To have the powerful reaction you're experiencing in relation to the human girl when you normally have your head straight should make it obvious it's true. Even I'm starting to second guess my previous assumptions."

"I told you so," Aiden said with a smug smirk, sitting back and crossing his arms over his chest, to which Lukas rolled his eyes and sucked his teeth in displeasure.

Riley glanced toward the exit of the cafeteria.

"Guys… do you think she's alright? I mean, she was crying when she ran out of here. I'm gonna go find her."

"Shit." Lukas stood from his seat abruptly. "I'm going."

After grabbing his tray, he dumped the contents before heading to the doors. He hoped she hadn't gone back to the dorm to pack her things, but at the same time it would put an end to this torture. He shook away the conflicting thoughts. He needed to check the dorms as soon as possible in case she planned to make a run for it.

"I think we should follow him," Aiden said as he gathered his things.

Kai raised a brow at him. "Why?"

"To ensure he doesn't stick his foot in his mouth again and trigger another meltdown that makes that girl leave this place, destroying his one chance at a bond before she can even understand our world."

8

DANGER

Blaire found her way out to the hedge maze past the main courtyard, where she dropped her backpack and leaned against the base of a large, beautiful black marble replica of *Nike, the Winged Victory of Samothrace*, which stood guard over the entrance to the intricate labyrinth.

She put her head back and closed her eyes as tears poured down her face. With Lukas's rejection, the entire situation finally became too much for her to handle. The urge to run riding her for months reached a fever pitch. To run away from the academy, from Lukas, from her stepbrother, from life. She had never felt so defeated, so resigned to giving up before. She'd always made a plan, focused on the future, endured, and pressed forward, knowing it wouldn't last forever. But the pain she felt in the cafeteria ripped into her and shook her foundation, and this anguish wasn't something she wanted to invest a future in experiencing.

"What the hell am I supposed to do? I don't want to give my

future to someone who hates me so much…" She sniffled, trying to calm down before her afternoon meeting to choose her major. "No, I'm not going to deal with this farce of a pairing. I've had enough."

Blaire would give Lukas one final piece of her mind, and then contract be damned. She was getting out of the academy. No way were they destined to be together; the concept was silly to start with, only written about in books and movies. No one found the one person written in the stars to be their soulmate.

A male voice startled her from her internal war with herself.

"Well, well, well. What do we have here, Phillip? It's the academy's human experiment."

Blaire glanced toward the courtyard. Two male students approached her. The shorter of the two reminded her of a porcelain doll with his pure white skin, pink lips, and the mess of platinum curls atop his head.

The other scared her, grinning like he wanted to eat her. He was roughly Lukas's size and stature, but had short, black hair slicked back on top and shaved on the sides, showing off his multiple ear piercings and tattoos that crawled up his neck and into his hairline at his sideburns.

"It seems the little lamb has lost her way and doesn't want her Korrena." The taller one gave Blaire a faux pitying frown, mocking her and laughing as he stepped toward her.

Blaire pressed herself as close as she could to the statue, looking around for an escape. Before she could consider escape, he got in her face, cupping her cheek with his long, slender fingers.

"Oh, don't be afraid, pet. I can take care of you," he cooed, leaning in.

"Now Aryan, don't play with your food," Phillip, the short one, chastised.

Aryan pulled away and scoffed. "I was serious. She's quite lovely, and while I'm sure she's delicious,"—he licked his lips—"I can also enjoy her in other ways."

Phillip rolled his eyes; he didn't seem like he relished the idea of toying with her like his counterpart, but he came along for the ride.

"Now…" Aryan stepped into Blaire's personal space, wrapping one of his hands around her forearm, moving the hair on her shoulder from her neck with his other hand. He leaned in, pressing her against the base of the statue, squeezing her arm tight enough to cause her to whimper in pain. "Ohh, that is a sweet sound, pet. I wonder what other sounds you'll make as I provide you pleasure to go with your pain."

He moved his hand from her hair, trailing it down her side to the hem of her skirt, where he slid his hand under the edge of her thigh-high stockings, tugging one down to expose more of her bare skin.

"Stop…" she whispered. She wanted to sound brave, but her wavering voice betrayed her fear. Blaire struggled against him, pulling her leg away from his hand in an effort to get away.

"Now, now." He grabbed her face in a firm grip and looked deep into her eyes, his blue irises glowing brightly.

Blaire gasped as the strangest sensation washed over her. She felt like she was floating, but her body remained firmly on the ground.

A diabolical grin crossed Aryan's lips, and he tilted his head as he studied Blaire's face, dropping his hand again. He released her from his hold and looked at her expectantly.

She tried to move, to take the opportunity presented to her to get away, but her brain wasn't sending signals to her body. She couldn't move. Her body remained frozen in place. Her eyes widened as panic seized her chest. She wanted to scream, she wanted to beg him to let her go, but other than her eyes, nothing worked.

Aryan's eyes lit up with glee. He looked like he thoroughly enjoyed her helplessness. "That's better. Now, to the fun part..."

"Aryan... you know it's forbidden," Phillip chastised.

Aryan didn't care. But his friend appeared to have lost his nerve at the reality that Aryan was serious. Aryan opened his mouth and his fangs descended, causing her heart rate to spike. She squeezed her eyes shut as he dipped his head toward her neck.

Suddenly, the air grew colder. The hold on Blaire's body released, and she collapsed forward into a pair of strong arms, unsteady as her control returned to her. She looked up at Lukas. He looked down at her, breathing heavily, his face a mix of concern and anger.

She looked past him to see Aryan in a smaller fountain at the corner of the courtyard, with Kai pulling him up from the water. How did he end up over there? Did Lukas do that? She hadn't asked about things like strength, speed, or other supernatural powers they might possess. She focused on silly things like garlic and sunlight and important stuff like whether she would be a meal, but the rest completely slipped her mind.

She heard scuffling to their left, so she peered around Lukas to see Aiden grappling with the smaller Vasirian, Phillip, who had tried to run as Mera and Riley approached.

Aiden met Blaire's gaze, frowning.

"Come on, let's take this trash to the administration building." Aiden dragged a squirming Phillip away.

Kai climbed out of the fountain, pulling Aryan along as Mera rushed to his side.

Riley started to approach Blaire but stopped, brow wrinkling with indecision, before she finally turned away and followed her brother.

Blaire returned her gaze to Lukas as the group left them alone. He dragged his eyes over her body as if inspecting her for damage. He looked like a spring coiled tight and ready to snap.

Lukas slowly reached up and placed a shaking hand on her face, holding her jawline with his thumb wrapped around her chin, turning her head to examine her neck. He must be checking for a bite mark. She swallowed hard.

He jerked his hand away as if her skin burned him, and where he touched her turned warm and tingly.

"Are you hurt? Please tell me he didn't hurt you." Lukas's voice was tight. His expression shuttered when Blaire stepped back from him.

"No… He didn't hurt me."

They stared at each other in silence. Blaire started to tremble and wrapped her arms around herself. Lukas sucked in a breath and reached for her, but she pulled back, shaking her head. She didn't want to be touched, not after what just happened. She still didn't know what to make of what happened. She needed to feel in control of her own body.

Lowering his hand, he balled it into a fist, looking at her with concern in his eyes. "I thought you said you weren't hurt…"

"I'm not. I—he… I couldn't move." Her voice quavered, her last words cracking as she struggled to explain. A single tear rolled down her cheek. "Why couldn't I move?"

Lukas lifted a hand to reach for her again but stopped. His expression turned pained as he clenched his fist at his side. "What do you mean, you couldn't move?" Lukas spoke softly, as one would speak to a frightened animal.

Blaire took a steadying breath and looked up into his eyes. "I tried to get away from him, but his eyes… they glowed. I didn't imagine it. They got brighter. After that, he let me go, but I couldn't run away. I didn't have control over my body."

Lukas's jaw clenched and he glared over his shoulder in the direction the others had gone.

"Lukas?" Blaire reached a hand out to touch his arm when she thought he might leave her alone there, only to gasp, startled by the anger in his eyes when he snapped his gaze back to her.

He squeezed her hand tightly in a reassuring gesture as his features softened a fraction. She discerned he wasn't angry with her. "Mental manipulation… a form of hypnosis."

Blaire's eyes widened.

"Did anything else happen?" he asked. "Did you do anything against your will?"

She shook her head quickly. "No. After I couldn't move, he tried to…" She swallowed. "Bite me. But you stopped him."

Lukas closed his eyes, a look of relief overtaking the remaining tension in his expression as he exhaled a heavy breath.

She narrowed her eyes. "Are you able to do that to me?"

He opened his eyes and shook his head. "No. Not all Vasirian have that power. Even if I did… I would never do that to you." He let go of Blaire's hand and moved a strand of hair from her face, tucking it behind her ear. "I won't force anything on you. I won't hurt you."

Blaire looked down at her feet.

"You said in the cafeteria…"

"What?"

"You said I should leave before someone gets hurt."

Lukas rubbed his face. "No. I didn't mean I would hurt you." He paced in a circle in front of her. "I meant this world… it's not like yours. You could get hurt. I could—" He stopped in front of her, pushing his hair back from his face. He looked worried.

Blaire frowned. "You could what?"

"Nothing."

"No. Tell me. You just said you wouldn't hurt me."

"I won't," he said firmly, his gaze narrowing on her before his voice lowered to a whisper. "But that doesn't mean you can say the same."

Lukas gave her one last once-over with his eyes and turned sharply to walk away from her.

Oh no, he was not going to act like an ass in the cafeteria, trying to run her off, and then come out here to save the day, only to leave after implying she would hurt him. The idea she could hurt him struck her as ludicrous. She wasn't the one with fangs and a penchant for blood.

"Just what the hell is your problem?" Her composure and confidence returned in her frustration. She pushed off the statue and stood with her hands on her hips, glaring at him.

Lukas stopped mid-stride, his entire body going tense, then he slowly turned around, face pinched in distress.

Lukas stalked toward her, his eyes narrowed and focused solely on her, like a predator cornering his prey. A shiver passed through her, accompanied by the sudden urge to run. In an effort not to provoke him, she backed up slowly as he took slow, deliberate steps toward her until her back met the statue again, and he stood about a foot in front of her.

"I… what are you—"

Blaire closed her eyes and fell silent as he took a step forward, leaning down with his lips close to her ear.

Lukas spoke low, his voice more gravelly than before. He sounded pained, as if holding himself back; it was enough to dissolve her fear, replacing it with cold, spider-like fingers of uncertainty racing up and down her spine. "You… are my problem."

He growled low in his throat as he dragged his nose from the base of her neck up to her ear again. Goose bumps sprouted over her arms, and she shivered.

"Everything about you is my problem." He shuddered a breath, as though maintaining his composure. "You have no idea."

"I don't understand..." she whispered. "Why? I can't hurt you... I'm human."

Lukas dropped his forehead to Blaire's shoulder and sighed.

"You don't have to have fangs to hurt someone." He spoke barely above a whisper, but the waver in his words betrayed powerful emotions.

Blaire hesitated, not sure what else to do, so she spoke the truth. "I'm not going to hurt you..."

She wouldn't. She wasn't the type of person to intentionally hurt others. She'd seen enough pain in the last couple of years to last a lifetime. Being the source of hurt for someone else wasn't in her nature. Regardless, she didn't want to hurt him. Despite his rough edges, something more shone inside when she looked close enough.

Lukas lifted his head and stared into Blaire's eyes, searching. When he found whatever he was looking for, he stepped into her, pressing his body flush against hers. Every place his body connected to hers burned. She could barely breathe as her heart jackhammered in her chest. The scent of apples and spices filled her nose, causing her to melt further into her delirium. He lowered his head to her ear again, his breath stirring the hair at her neck.

Despite her nervousness, desire flooded her system. A desire so strong it stole her words.

"Stay," he whispered. "Don't leave."

Blaire's heart stopped. She bit down on her lower lip softly as he lingered close to her, breathing in her scent.

Lukas suddenly stiffened, as if coming to his senses. He lifted his head.

Pale green eyes swimming with emotion met hers before he turned away and left in the direction of their dorm building without another word.

Blaire released the breath she had been holding, her trembling legs finally giving way as she crumpled to the ground.

9

Secrets Revealed

"Blaire!"

Blaire opened her eyes to find Riley running across the courtyard toward her with a concerned expression on her face. She had no idea how long she sat trapped in her mind going over what happened with Lukas, but the sun had moved across the courtyard and clouds were rolling in.

"Oh gods, are you alright? Where's Lukas?" Riley dropped in front of Blaire and set down her messenger bag.

Blaire released a defeated sigh, her energy depleted. "He's gone." She hung her head and closed her eyes, focusing on the sounds of the nesting birds in a nearby magnolia tree.

After sitting in silence, Riley opened her messenger bag and pulled out a black handkerchief with lace edges, then reached out hesitantly.

"Can I…" Riley motioned toward Blaire's face, and when Blaire shook her head, confused, she added, "Your makeup is a wreck."

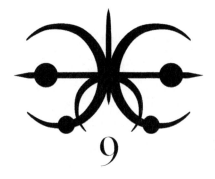

Blaire shrugged, lifting her head so Riley could clean her tear-streaked makeup away.

She didn't want to imagine what she looked like, but she was sure it wasn't pretty. She didn't care in the slightest, but allowed Riley to "mom" her, at least until she probed the tender spot on Blaire's temple.

Blaire winced, pulling back, and Riley opened her eyes wide.

"Shit. You've got a wicked bruise forming."

Blaire shut her eyes tight and leaned her head back against the statue's base. She refrained from laughing. If Riley only knew. She couldn't hide how defeated she felt.

"I don't even know why I'm here…" She turned her face away from Riley to stare into the hedge maze. "I thought Lukas didn't want me here… Why did Professor Velastra even bring me to this place? He saw that… thing on me, but even he thinks it's a mistake. But then he told me to stay. I have no say in any of this. What's the point of my being here?"

Riley clenched the handkerchief in her small hands. "No… I don't think it's entirely like that. I'm positive Lukas is going to warm up to the idea. He just needs time. Things will get better, I promise." She looked up. "Wait. He told you to stay?"

Blaire turned back to Riley, furrowing her brow. "Yes… before he left, he told me to stay. Or maybe he asked. He said not to leave. But I don't want him to 'warm up' to the idea. I don't want someone to be with me because they have to, and I don't like the idea of someone having to get used to the idea of being near me. That's not how it should work. Besides, he's a… well, you know. Why can't I just go to university without all this other stuff?"

Riley frowned.

"Love and being with someone should be instinctive and real," Blaire added.

"Well, with the way Lukas looks at you, despite his grouchy exterior, I'm certain he feels the pull of the bond," Riley said, as usual offering a silver lining to the storm cloud hanging over Blaire's head.

She thought about the way his body pressed against hers, and how he breathed her in. She shivered. His scent did things to her; did he respond the same to hers?

She didn't know if she should take Riley's advice and stick it out, trust it would get better, and do what Lukas asked, or face whatever consequences awaited her if she rejected Lukas and the school's goodwill. These new, conflicting feelings toward Lukas weren't helping her with that decision. He protected her. He made her body react in ways she'd never experienced.

She shook her head. "Everything is just so confusing, you know?"

"Yeah, I know. I understand." Riley said, but her face betrayed her, revealing her own confusion.

They sat in silence before Riley spoke again. "Wow. Those assholes really did a number on you before we got out here. Does it hurt?"

Blaire sighed. "They didn't do this."

"Oh gods, don't tell me Lukas did that? I'll kick his ass." Riley started to get up, her petite face comically red with her newfound anger.

Blaire reached out to stop her, shaking her head quickly. She needed to come clean about everything. She wasn't ready, but she wasn't sure she'd ever be ready for this conversation with anyone.

"He didn't do this either. He told me he wouldn't hurt me, and I believe him… This was the work of my piece of shit stepbrother. I normally keep stuff like this covered with makeup." She shrugged.

Riley's brows knitted together in confusion. "Stuff like this? This happens often?"

Sighing, Blaire looked up at the sky and nodded. "Yeah… it

happens all the time, but mostly when Caleb doesn't get his way." She closed her eyes. "...or when I refuse him."

"What the hell does that mean?"

Riley sounded angry, so Blaire couldn't just leave it at that; she already opened this can of worms, so she might as well see it through.

Opening her eyes and looking back at the mid-afternoon sky above, she watched the cloud cover thicken and become darker, shrouding the courtyard in gloom. She wondered if a storm was coming.

Riley cut into her dissociative thoughts. "Blaire..."

"We lived alone together after my mom and his dad died in a car accident when I was sixteen, and he basically controlled everything."

"Sixteen? So, you had to live alone with him that young?"

Blaire looked from the sky to Riley's confused face.

"Yeah, he was twenty. With no living relatives except my step-grandparents, who wanted nothing to do with me because I wasn't related by blood, Caleb dropped out of Emory University to take care of me. He basically inherited me when he got his father's house."

It sounded messed up when said aloud. She sounded like an heirloom, passed down to the next member of the family. She certainly felt like an object.

Blaire brushed at her plaid skirt. "I wish I'd known at sixteen what I do now. We got along then. He acted like the doting big brother he should have been. When the state suggested foster care, his grandparents petitioned the courts that separating 'two loving siblings' would be 'too tragic' to add on top of the loss of our parents and 'they need one another in this time of grieving.' It was a disgusting farce they all presented until the case closed, and I *naïvely* went along with it. I'm sure money was involved." Blaire snorted. "I hadn't thought about it before, but the Wilcox influence might reach state level."

"That's messed up," Riley said. "But back up. I want to know more about the other stuff."

Blaire sighed, putting her head back, running a hand through her long hair. "Well, if I stepped out of line and didn't give him my tip money, for example, he'd hit me. If he didn't like what I wore, he would discipline me."

Riley raised both eyebrows at that. "What in the hell are you talking about? 'Discipline'? What's that supposed to mean?"

Blaire closed her eyes and a couple of tears rolled down her cheeks. She wasn't sure she could continue this conversation. She could barely tell Charlotte when things went bad. Charlotte grew up with her, so she knew something was wrong before Blaire ever admitted to it. One night when she was seventeen, about two months after Caleb became physical, she couldn't hold it in anymore. She never stopped telling Charlotte after that. But she swore her to secrecy. No one else knew.

Riley put a hand on top of hers. "You don't have to say anything else. I really want to know, but if it's too hard..."

Blaire shook her head quickly, a few more tears escaping when she opened her eyes. "No, I need to finish it. There's no sense starting and not seeing this through." If she didn't get it out now, she would close up tighter than a clam.

Riley nodded quietly, waiting patiently for Blaire to continue.

Taking a steadying breath through her nose and exhaling out of her mouth slowly, she pressed on. "For the first year after our parents passed, he was fine. He treated me like he always did. Sure, a few bullying comments made me uncomfortable, but those grew into controlling behaviors and demands. Once I turned seventeen, he got physical. Not only did he hit me, but he also pushed me, pulled me through the house by my hair, and even locked me in the basement for a 'time-out,' which could last for hours, or even overnight if he felt so inclined, or forgot me."

Riley narrowed her eyes, shaking with anger. "That is beyond screwed up, Blaire! Your stepbrother is a piece of shit. There's no way you're going back to him."

Blaire frowned. "I've been trying to leave the Valley for months now to get away from him, but he keeps taking my money. He always took my tips, and anytime I got anything worth much in the bank, he would clean me out because he had access to the account. I opened a secret account, but with my old boss telling him what my wages were, I could only split my tips to slowly pad the account. It's not like I wanted to be there."

"I didn't think you wanted to go back there or be there…"

"I know, I'm just saying. Caleb didn't know I still tried to leave, because if he knew, I'd probably have suffered something far worse than what I already have. His grandparents made sure I knew that." She shrugged. "I mean, when he discovered I had looked at apartments a few months ago, I spent the weekend in a dark basement with no food or light. Well… except for the lightning through a tiny window after the power went out."

Riley sat with her mouth hanging open, no doubt surprised she could talk about something traumatic so casually, but here they were.

"I honestly wouldn't be surprised if he doesn't try to get to me here and pull me out of the school, even though I'm of legal age." She sighed and shook her head. "He's controlled my life for years, and he knows people in town… he's got connections. And if he does run into opposition? Well, Mollie and Richard are there to save the day."

"Mollie and Richard?"

"His grandparents. Mollie and Richard Wilcox. Old money. They helped him claim me when our parents died. They've helped him obtain anything else he needed or wanted, knowing how sick and twisted his mind is. He was born with a silver spoon in his mouth. Expectations and entitlement were ingrained into him early on. Richard owns over half of the shops in Rosebrook. He's made a career leasing and micromanaging the business owners there. Much of the town itself has been in the Wilcox's family possession for several generations. I honestly believe there's more than just real estate involved in their high dollar dealings."

Blaire shifted her position, her skirt riding up slightly. Riley gasped.

Following Riley's line of sight, Blaire bit hard onto her lower lip. That bastard Aryan had pulled down her stocking enough to expose the bruising on her inner thigh.

If she didn't put up a fight every time Caleb tried something, and just let him have his way, she wouldn't have bruises like this, but she wasn't that type of person. She would fight him until it killed her. She wouldn't belong to him.

She pulled her stocking higher and tugged down on her uniform skirt, looking away.

"Shit, Blaire… just how much did he beat you?"

That was enough to break her.

Blaire sobbed, wrapping her arms around herself. The shame overwhelmed her, and she trembled.

Riley was taken aback and then, as if something dawned on her, she opened her eyes wide. "No way… he didn't. Did he?"

Blaire shook her head rapidly, her tears not ceasing. She knew what Riley meant. No, Caleb had never raped her, but based on what happened the other day, it was only a matter of time. He manhandled her in so many other ways. Sexual violation was inevitable. She'd be damned if she allowed that monster to take everything from her.

Choking down her sobs, she whispered, her voice raw, and throat dry, "No… but he's come close recently."

Riley's forehead wrinkled. "Has he tried before?"

"No, but he touched me before. Mostly outside of my clothes, but there have been a few times where he…" She bit hard on her lip, surprised she didn't draw blood.

"He what?" Riley's voice rose.

"He has touched me under my clothes on occasion, but never… penetrated me in any way." Blaire swallowed. "This is so humiliating," she murmured under her breath.

Blaire shook all over. She had never sat down and shared her trauma with anyone but Charlotte, and not all in one go like this. Only Charlotte knew everything Caleb had done, except what happened the other night. She remembered the first time she told her friend when she slept over at her house. Blaire tackled her to the floor to stop her from going to both her mothers and telling them everything. Blaire wouldn't risk her friend's or her family's lives.

At the time, Charlotte had gotten as wound up as Riley appeared to be right now, and that was before Caleb started pushing the boundaries further because of her age. Which was stupid, since by touching her body outside of her clothes in inappropriate ways, he basically committed the crime anyway.

Blaire laughed bitterly. "You know, he says it's his right. Can you believe that?"

"Seriously? What right is it of his to molest his stepsister?" She stood abruptly, not waiting to hear any more. She turned and looked down at Blaire, pointing at her. "You will never ever have to face that again, you hear me? I'll make sure of it."

Smiling weakly up at her, Blaire got to her feet slowly, still shuddering with the aftereffects of her panic attack. "The sick thing? His grandparents know what he wants from me, and they still financially backed him until he settled into his new job position."

"What does he want from you? Sex?"

"No. Well, yes. I guess he wants that too… but—"

Surprising her, Riley pulled her into a tight embrace, cutting her words off. "You'll never be alone again."

Blaire fell silent and wrapped her arms around Riley. She closed her eyes, comfortable with the small girl.

She didn't know what to think of Riley's statement. She'd been alone for quite some time, except for Charlotte, and even then, she was still alone, because Charlotte couldn't help her without risking herself. Blaire wouldn't allow that. Could Riley help her? Could being here with Riley provide the safety and security she so desperately craved? Did the Wilcox family truly have no reach here? The Vasirian said she didn't have to stay, that she could leave if she needed to.

"There's no way you can leave and go back to that trash. Even if Lukas acts like an ass about everything, I'm not letting you go, my damn self. Even if you don't stay here, you can't go back to that." Riley shivered as she pulled from the hug.

Blaire wiped her cheeks to get rid of any residual wetness and knelt, digging through her backpack, pulling out her compact.

Riley sighed.

"I'm not ready for anyone to see anything like this, and besides, it should fade soon. It's already been a few days." Blaire shrugged as she began the process of covering her bruise. She didn't tell Riley it would last longer than that.

"You really need to talk to someone about this…"

"What do you mean?"

"A therapist. The university has an entire department dedicated to psychology, and the majority of the staff are licensed. It couldn't hurt to talk to them. I can go with you if you want…"

Blaire looked at Riley with apprehension. "I'll… think about it."

After vocalizing the trauma she'd been through, she realized one thing above all others.

Riley was right. No way could she leave, because if she did run away, Caleb would find her, and she might not survive the punishment.

Besides, did she even want to run away anymore?

No. She wanted to stay.

If the events of today were any representation of the future, she had at last found protection in a school full of bloodsucking monsters.

10

A Dark Stranger

Heavy rain pelted the windows of the cafeteria, echoing through the enormous space.

There weren't many students around after breakfast, most in classes, and since Blaire hadn't made it to her advisor meeting yesterday, they rescheduled to mid-morning. She sat at the same table they used before, reading one of the vampire romance novels she brought from her old home. A small laugh bubbled up from Blaire as she read a passage. The author clearly didn't do her proper research. She quickly discovered the real supernatural world was nothing like fiction.

Blaire stretched, glancing at the windows, watching the storm clouds nervously. The sun was nowhere to be seen, and the entire cafeteria dimmed with softer ambient lighting filling the space. The staff turned the lights down when there wasn't a meal service in progress, but there was still enough light to read, and with the rain, she found it relaxing and peaceful.

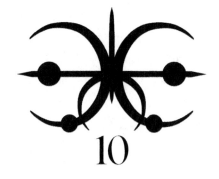

She took a sip from the bottle of peach tea she got from the twenty-four-hour canteen and lifted her book, picking up where she left off. She read in silence, snacking on a package of yogurt raisins for another ten minutes before a pair of legs in black slacks with polished men's shoes walked into her peripheral vision.

"Is this seat taken?"

Blaire raised her head, tensing when her eyes landed on the student towering over her. He had to be as tall as Kai, if not taller, and much bigger. Not like the wrestler security guard and driver, but definitely built. Despite the aristocratic air in his appearance and aesthetic, his physique awed her.

She was already on edge from what happened yesterday with Aryan and Phillip, so she wasn't receptive to making a new friend, or small talk with a stranger, at least not a Vasirian. However, she'd been raised with Southern manners; she couldn't find it in her to be rude to someone she didn't know, so she shook her head quietly as she returned her attention to her book.

The man took that as an invitation to sit across the table from her. Grateful for the distance, she wasn't going to complain. She'd had enough of Vasirian getting all in her personal bubble lately.

Blaire tried to get back into her book but kept sneaking glances at the man who sat staring at her with arms folded across his chest. His scrutiny made her uncomfortable.

His facial features appeared refined, from his sharp jawline to his long, narrow nose over full lips. These features softened only slightly when their eyes met, and he smiled.

"What?" Blaire finally snapped in frustration. She'd had enough of being stared at like a prized pig.

A black brow lifted a fraction as his ice-blue eyes, lined with black eyeliner, widened in surprise. "Nothing," he said with amusement in his tone. "I'm simply admiring our newest addition."

"Well, please stop."

"Apologies." The man raked a hand through long hair the same shade as Kai's, the soft cafeteria lights bringing out the iridescent shades off the deep black.

As Blaire tried to return to reading, a flash of lightning lit the room, followed by loud thunder echoing through the space. She jumped.

"Afraid?" He tilted his head with a slight grin.

She looked up at him from her book again, drawing her brows together in confusion.

"Are you afraid of the storm?"

Blaire frowned and shook her head.

"I've just had a rough few days..." She tried to explain away her reaction, then grew irritated with herself for oversharing. Was a storm closing in? She looked warily at the large windows, wondering how sturdy they were. The forest behind the school looked black and foreboding through the sheets of rain. She hoped it would only rain. Today wasn't going to give her a break, either.

She set her book down on the table after earmarking the page she stopped on. She hated to do that to her books, but she lost her favorite bookmark, and didn't have any paper with her to make a temporary substitute.

He motioned to the book. "Might I ask what you're reading?"

Blaire blushed and shook her head. She wasn't about to tell a Vasirian she was reading a vampire romance; talk about embarrassing. She should have left the book in her room, but she wanted to finish it soon. "It's nothing."

"Mmm... I don't think so."

He gave her a charming smile as he reached forward, the tungsten band on his index finger glinting in the ambient light. He tapped a single, manicured black fingernail on the cover of her novel, which depicted a man in black with a woman in his embrace, his face buried in her neck. "This certainly doesn't look like nothing, my dear."

"It's silly."

"I highly doubt that."

Blaire's face warmed from the embarrassment lighting up her face, and she looked down at the book in question as he withdrew his hand, sitting back and folding his arms over his chest.

"It's a love story. A dark love story, where a human woman is given to a vampire lord as payment for her father's gambling debts."

The man waved a lazy hand, motioning for her to continue.

"Um… well, the woman is afraid of the vampire, but from the looks of it—from where I'm at in the story so far—it seems like she's gradually growing to love him." Blaire laughed. "Honestly, it sounds more like Stockholm Syndrome than genuine love, but it's what the author thinks is supposed to be romantic."

After a beat of silence, the man nodded. "Do you think it's possible to fall in love in that sort of situation?" He clearly didn't find it as amusing as Blaire did, as though they were discussing classic literature.

She shook her head. "I really don't know. I mean, it wasn't the vampire's fault her father was heartless and sold her, but at the same time, he could have set her free."

"I see the logic in that, yes; he could have let her go." The man nodded. "But perhaps he became enthralled by the woman and couldn't let her go?"

Blaire bit on her lower lip in thought, and the man's eyes lit up as he studied her before she shrugged lightly. "It could be something like that, but it's only a fantasy. It's not like reality. Real women don't fall in love just because they're trapped." A fact she sorely wished her stepbrother would have accepted long ago.

Things didn't happen this way. It was silly to entertain the idea.

He smiled and nodded at her. "There could be truth found there. I personally do not see it as far-fetched for a vampire to fall in love with a beautiful human girl,"—he waved a hand—"or vice versa."

Blaire shook her head as Lukas crossed her mind. No way did she love him, so why in the world did he cross her mind? Sure, he was gorgeous and set her body on fire with a single touch. And his voice… she could be lulled to sleep nightly by the timbre of his speech if the words that came out of his perfect mouth weren't so confusing. But none of that equaled love. That was basic attraction.

The man continued to watch Blaire, studying her as she sat lost in thought.

"Vincent!"

Blaire spun around upon hearing Lukas's voice ring out through the cafeteria. He strode toward them, followed by Riley and Aiden. Speak of the Devil and he shall appear. Her face warmed, and she turned away when she met his eyes.

He clenched his jaw as Vincent gave him an amused grin.

Lukas stepped up behind Blaire's chair, pressed against her back as he glared down at Vincent. Riley and Aiden took seats on either side of Blaire, watching closely.

Aiden smiled at Blaire, which relaxed her, distracting her from the hostility hovering over her head.

"Oh… so is this the chosen one?" Vincent said, sitting up in his chair, clearly entertained by the new arrivals. "The lucky vampire who fell for the beautiful human girl. Ah, I mean Vasirian." He winked at Blaire, which in turn caused her blush to deepen.

"What the fuck do you want with her?" Lukas all but growled out.

Vincent lifted his hands in the air as if they had pulled a gun on him. "Now, now. No need to be defensive. I only wanted to meet the rare jewel who has become a part of our world."

Lukas glared at him. "Yeah, you and every other Vasirian on campus."

Vincent slowly stood from his seat. "She's quite interesting, though. You can't blame us." He moved around to the side of the table and took Blaire's hand, bringing it to his lips. "It was a pleasure meeting you, my dear. Hopefully, we will see each other again so you can tell me more about what happens between our fanged friend and his human lover. I'm intrigued to see how it plays out."

Lukas growled and put his hands on Blaire's shoulders, pulling her back so her hand slipped from Vincent's grip.

Vincent chuckled and walked toward the exit as Lukas watched him, glaring.

Another loud rumble filled the cafeteria, and Blaire jerked in Lukas's grip slightly. Aiden raised an eyebrow at her before moving from the chair beside Blaire into the seat Vincent had vacated to allow Lukas to sit next to Blaire instead.

"Did he do anything to you?" Lukas looked her over as if he expected to see bite marks.

If she had been bitten, everyone would know it, because she sure wouldn't be sitting calmly in the cafeteria. No, she'd be running from this place as fast as her legs could carry her, contract be damned.

Blaire frowned and shook her head. "No. He was nice. I just didn't know him."

Riley said, "He's Kai and Seth's older cousin, Vincent Brandt. He's in his last two years, and then he'll be leaving Blackthorn."

"Who's Seth?"

Riley blushed. "Oh, remember? He's Kai's little brother I

mentioned yesterday. You'll probably meet him soon; he practically lives with Aiden." She laughed, and Aiden rolled his eyes.

Lukas stared at Blaire, agitation on his face, but she tried to ignore it. She wasn't sure if he was irritated with her or not. Sometimes she could breathe wrong, and he'd be pissed off, but in the same breath, he'd assure her she was safe, show her she was safe. Even running off Vincent came across as a misguided act of protection rather than just being a jerk.

Aiden looked at Blaire. "So, what did Vincent mean by wanting to hear about what happens between 'our fanged friend and his human lover' exactly?"

Lukas tensed up, and he looked at Aiden as if thankful Aiden asked the question. She didn't understand him at all.

Blaire's cheeks turned hot again, and she snatched up her novel from the table to stuff it into the backpack on the floor, but Lukas was faster. He grabbed the book from her hand before she could stop him. He stared at the cover and then looked back up at her with an expression she couldn't decipher. Like he'd lost his breath. He held the book up so Aiden could see the cover and title, *Eternal Claiming*.

Aiden raised a brow.

"Oh, I know that book!" Riley said as Lukas turned the book over in his hand. "I read paranormal romances too, and this one is like really popular among human women who love the fantasy of vampires but like something more mature than *Twilight*."

Riley reached for the book, but he pulled it back from her, forcing her to lean forward over him. What was this, a game of keep away?

Riley got it away from him, and then opened to the page Blaire left off on.

"You're about to get to the good parts where Garrick and Vivian finally have sex for the first time." Riley grinned. "Garrick is soooo primal in the scene. You're going to absolutely love it. It's mind-blowing."

"Riley!" Blaire turned wide eyes on Riley, shocked.

Riley looked up from the book. "Oh right, spoilers. Whoops. My bad."

Aiden rolled his eyes.

Lightning crashed again, and thunder shook the windows, the storm growing more intense outside. Blaire squealed and threw her hands up to protect her face. Lukas was beside her in an instant and pulled her into his arms, flush to his chest.

She froze in his hold, unsure if she did from fear of the storm or the proximity to him. Probably both.

"Are you afraid of the storm?" he whispered softly, staring into her eyes.

Lukas had never spoken to her so tenderly before, even when concerned for her; an underlying tension always echoed in his tone. Her nerves, tightened by the thunder, melted as she relaxed against him.

"So, you… like this sort of book?" Lukas asked, swallowing hard, a hopeful look in his eyes, which returned the tension and resistance to her body and confused the hell out of her.

Blaire frowned and pressed her hands against his chest to gain distance, his question distracting her from the storm outside. "I find it enjoyable. What of it?" She closed her eyes, wishing the floor would open up. She whispered, "Let go." She didn't even sound convincing to her own ears.

Lukas was wound tighter than a drum, his breathing shallow, and his gaze locked on her as she returned her attention to his face. He tightened his arms around her.

"Lukas?" Blaire asked nervously as he leaned in. Her breathing quickened. The urge to run tingled in her spine.

"Please…" she whispered, as Lukas got close to her face. His unsteady breathing against her skin made her body betray her by shivering. When he was within mere inches of her lips, she whispered where only he could hear, "…don't."

Lukas pulled his head back like he'd been slapped. He stared at Blaire with a pained expression, as if letting her go posed a challenge. But she wasn't ready for this. He made her feel safe, her attraction to him aside. But she wasn't ready for physical intimacy with anyone. He closed his eyes and slowly released her, giving her space.

Blaire licked her lips as she stepped back, overcome with a swarm of butterflies in her stomach.

She stuffed her things into her backpack. "I-I need to get to my advisor meeting. I'm gonna be late." She hurried toward the exit and left the cafeteria, passing Vincent, who stared at her as she made her way to the stairs.

Lukas hit the table. "I lost my composure. Just the mention of Blaire and sex." He raked a hand through his hair. "The very idea she could be okay with a lover like our kind." He clenched his jaw, releasing a self-deprecating laugh. "It's just a damn fantasy book. She thinks I'm a monster, nothing more. Why did I think kissing her was a good idea?" Lukas closed his eyes as Aiden placed a hand on his shoulder in silent support.

Riley sighed. "She's probably afraid…"

Lukas scoffed. "Of course she's afraid of the monster with fangs who could suck her dry." He ran a hand through his hair again.

"No." Riley glared at him. "Blaire went through something brutal and tragic before coming here, Lukas. Something I could never imagine in all my wildest dreams experiencing and still be as good as she is."

"Tell me. Now," Lukas all but growled out at her.

11

DISCOVERY

Lukas took a deep breath to steady his nerves before knocking on the door to Professor Velastra's office. After a few beats of silence, the door opened, and the professor waved him in.

"I'm surprised it took you this long to come see me, Mr. Virtanen."

Lukas raised a brow at the professor as he passed her to drop into the leather seat in front of her desk with a heavy sigh. "I saw you the other day."

"Yes, but after Miss Wilcox's placement, I expected you'd seek me out right away."

Lukas shrugged.

Professor Velastra stepped around the desk, her stilettos tapping lightly against the hardwood floor. Lowering herself into the desk chair, she looked at Lukas expectantly.

"I'm confused," he finally admitted.

She chuckled, then shook her head when Lukas didn't elaborate further.

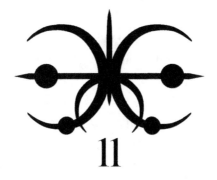

"You have to give me more than that, Lukas."

He ran a hand through his long hair. "Just… this whole thing with Blaire doesn't make sense to me."

"Okay. That's more information. What exactly about this 'thing' has you confused? Are you uncertain of your initial finding? Is she not the one?"

"No!" He sat up quickly and shook his head. "I mean, I thought it was a mistake at first… but now I'm not so sure."

The professor hummed and sat back in her chair, crossing her legs, and resting her hands on her knee. "What changed? Why did you question it to start with?"

Lukas sighed. "I thought when we found our Korrena it was supposed to be easy. I thought things just… I dunno. Clicked into place and the pairs just knew. Mom and Dad make it look so natural."

The professor laughed, and then cleared her throat when Lukas shot her a glare. Nothing about this was funny. His life was turned upside down and he was at a loss for what to do. He needed help.

"I apologize. It would seem the curriculum needs to change a bit if that is the general consensus as to what happens." She gave Lukas a pitying glance. "You should speak to your parents. They have been bonded for a very long time. You don't see them enough to get the full picture. I'm sure they could help with this as well. I suspect they'd like to know you've found your pair."

Lukas grimaced. The last time he saw his parents was the Christmas before last, when they came to visit. They normally came for that holiday and rarely, on occasions, when their business brought them to the Southeast. Last Christmas, they had been caught up with dealings in Hong Kong and didn't make it in time. They spoke briefly on the phone then, but he hadn't bothered calling in the last year. Something about hearing their voices made the distance harder, and it wasn't like they reached out to him, so why should he be the one to make the effort?

Shaking from his depressing thoughts, he looked at the professor. "Blaire rejected me anyway."

"Pardon?"

"I…" He chewed at the corner of his mouth. "I may have tried to kiss her. She stopped me."

The professor didn't hide her laugh this time. "I'm not surprised. Miss Wilcox just met you. Why did you think it was a good idea to kiss her?"

"I dunno… I've felt the urge since we met. I could have sworn she felt it, too. She looked like she wanted the same. I guess I misread the signs."

She gave him another pitying look. "It takes more than just attraction for some people to accept an act of physical intimacy. Especially one of this nature. That isn't a trait exclusive to humans. I certainly wouldn't have allowed my husband—may the gods rest his soul—to kiss me within a week of discovering our bond. Not everyone is comfortable with acting on lust without emotional intimacy. This is why you need to learn about Miss Wilcox."

Lukas shifted uncomfortably. He hadn't been intimate in any way with anyone before. He found it hard to even connect with his friends sometimes, so opening himself enough to allow the kind of connection he'd need to have with a girlfriend had never been something he allowed.

"Establishing boundaries between the two of you would help with this. Despite the biological connection, the bond that pulls from within, you still have to work for your relationship just like any other. The bond only makes it easier to establish a connection. Feelings of intimacy are heightened, and the empathy found in a pairing can make navigating the process simpler. But you don't magically just know the other person if you've never interacted before. And with Miss Wilcox, you need to approach things differently than Vasirian pairs would."

"What do you mean?"

"Miss Wilcox doesn't understand our world, Lukas. She isn't going to be ready to exchange blood and speed the process along when she doesn't understand what a Korrena is, outside of the basic textbook definition we've provided her. She will need to experience the natural growth of the bond between you both, feel its effects, before accepting it. We've watched our family and friends bond and grow throughout the years, and you've had classes on this since childhood, so it's only natural we know more than what the textbook teaches."

Lukas clasped his hands together and looked down at the floor. "Okay… so tell me about her. Give me something to go on, because I feel like I'm losing it."

Professor Velastra's lips turned up slightly, and she pulled a folder from the middle of a stack at the side of her desk, opened it, and scanned the pages within. "I can help you, but I can't give you all the answers. I can give you information to get you started so you have a foundation to strengthen your approach, but you must put in the work yourself to get to know her. You need to learn her organically, not be spoon-fed information like cramming for one of your exams. Your bond will not grow this way."

Lukas sighed. He knew he had his work cut out for him, but something about Blaire called to him. Maybe it was the bond already, but he felt drawn to her. Not only did he feel the need to protect her, but he needed to know more about her—what made her tick.

The strength he saw in her eyes, despite being thrown into this supernatural world unprepared, warmed him and made him want to try. She'd been through a lot, according to Riley. To face not only the loss of her parents, but also her stepbrother's assault. To experience Vasirian hypnosis and still look at him not as a monster, but as someone who had the answers she needed—to trust him—made him want to step up and do right by her.

The professor looked up from her paperwork. "Do you know anything about her at all?"

"I know about her stepbrother…" Lukas clenched his jaw, grinding his teeth. Just thinking about what happened to her made his blood boil. He wondered if Riley told him everything, or if Blaire had even told Riley everything.

"That's it?" The professor's brows pulled together, and she stared at him incredulously. "Lukas, I've done extensive research on Miss Wilcox and her family. I have obtained records regarding her history and even have gone so far as learning a few of her basic preferences in the days leading up to her joining Blackthorn. You've been with her exclusively, and the bond is there. How have you not tried to form a connection? Have you not spoken in greater depth about yourselves at all?"

"No. Not really. I tried to run her off when she first got here."

Shame warred in his gut, and he put a hand over his face, resting his elbow on the arm of the chair.

"Why did you do that?"

"At first, because I thought it was a mistake. Then, I just wanted to protect her. Protect myself. She's a human. I don't see how this can work…"

The professor frowned. "That aspect is certainly going to make this more difficult, but it doesn't mean it's impossible. You can protect her without sending her away. From what I gathered from the report your friends provided the Order when Aryan and Phillip were brought in for attacking Miss Wilcox, you did a fine job of that."

"But that wouldn't have happened if she weren't here. She'd have been safe."

"No. She most certainly wouldn't."

Lukas looked up and creased his brow. "What are you talking about?"

"Lukas… Blaire has been trying to escape Rosebrook for months, unsuccessfully."

"Escape? Her stepbrother? Why hasn't she been able to leave?"

"Yes. Bigger things are holding her to Rosebrook than an unstable twenty-two-year-old." She closed the folder and sat back in her chair. "The Wilcox family holds a lot of power locally. When Blaire recently tried to run away from her stepbrother, they threatened her life. The poor girl has been living in fear for her life for months, saving every penny she can spare for a time when she can run and not look back. I assured her in exchange for her joining Blackthorn Academy that she would be safe from their reach."

Lukas slumped back in his seat and ran a hand through his hair. He vaguely remembered Riley saying something about her stepbrother's family's influence in Georgia, but he didn't think they would go so far as to kill someone—especially not family. Riley's assumption had been right.

They hated Blaire.

Blaire shifted in the chair, the leather upholstery sticking to her thighs above her stockings. The air conditioning did nothing to alleviate the sweat that beaded her forehead.

The door she sat directly across from opened. A student exited the room, followed by a tall woman with copper hair in a tight bun atop her head. Her salmon-toned pantsuit complimented her pale complexion. It was the boldest color Blaire had seen anyone around the academy wear. The woman said her goodbyes to the boy and turned her attention to Blaire with a warm and reassuring smile.

"Miss Wilcox?"

Blaire rubbed her clammy palms on her skirt. "Blaire."

The woman nodded and kept her smile. "Please. Come in."

Blaire stood and took a deep breath before stepping past the woman into the office on the other side of the door. The space felt inviting. Filled with various houseplants and a few flower arrangements, the room held the scents of nature, which relaxed her.

"I'm Professor Isla Sinclair. You may call me Isla, Professor Isla, Professor Sinclair… whatever you'd like. But please, do not call me doctor. While I have a Ph.D., I never liked being called doctor. It's pretentious." She chuckled.

Blaire stared at the professor, not quite sure how to respond as she stood in the middle of the room. The woman certainly didn't talk like any psychologist she'd heard of. Of course, her only experience with that was what she'd seen in movies and television series, and the therapist she saw growing up was elderly, and reserved.

"Have a seat." Professor Sinclair gestured toward a plush, burgundy armchair and a black leather chaise lounge.

Blaire took the plush armchair.

"So, tell me what brings you here today." The professor moved to a mini-fridge and retrieved two bottles of water before taking a seat across from Blaire in front of a low coffee table that had a box of tissues, setting the bottles on top. "I had hoped to meet you soon after seeing your request for enrollment in our department. Have you settled on an area of study in psychology?"

Blaire gripped the hem of her plaid skirt as she perched on the edge of the chair and licked her lips.

"I want to be a grief counselor... specifically for children, if possible."

Professor Sinclair crossed her legs and tapped her chin.

"An undergraduate bachelor's degree in psychology is plenty to enter into that field. No need to go full doctorate. Is there a reason you've chosen a focus on children and grief and not counseling services as a whole?"

Blaire shifted and looked up at the professor.

"I like kids, and I know what it's like to experience loss young."

"I see."

"My parents. Not long after I turned sixteen, my mom died in a car accident. My stepfather too."

The professor nodded quietly, not pushing as Blaire volunteered the information freely. However, when Blaire didn't add anything more, she asked, "Where is your birth father?"

"He died when I was a toddler."

"I'm sorry to hear that."

Blaire shifted in her seat and looked out the window behind a desk on the back wall, watching the dogwood trees sway in the wind. After several minutes of silence, when it became apparent Blaire wasn't providing any additional details, the professor cleared her throat.

"I think taking a career path you can relate to is a wonderful thing, but if only you have dealt with your own grief. How does one help others if one doesn't know how to help oneself?"

Blaire shifted her focus back to the professor and began twirling the ends of her long hair around her finger. "Mom put me in counseling when I was a little older, when I started asking questions about my dad she had difficulty dealing with. I went for a couple of years."

"Have you spoken with a therapist since your mother and stepfather's passing?"

Blaire looked down at her lap. "No."

"Why is that? It appears to me as if you have no reservations about therapy."

"My..." She took a deep breath and exhaled. "My stepbrother would never allow it. It would be shameful for his family to need therapy."

Professor Sinclair sat back in her chair, surprise flickering across her face before she schooled her expression. "Allow it? I apologize, but I'm not following."

Blaire gnawed on her lower lip before standing up from the chair and walking to the window. Quiet filled the room as the professor watched her intently. Breaking the awkward silence, Blaire began to share her story with the professor. When she finished, she dropped back into the chair. At some point in her rambling, she had made her way back over to the middle of the room. She waited with suspended breath for the professor to respond.

"That is... quite the story, Blaire. Thank you for sharing with me. That took a lot of strength and bravery. Again, I thank you."

Blaire breathed out. She didn't think it brave to explain what happened to her, but she wasn't going to argue. She was finally in a place she could deal with it. Splitting-hairs over something basic, like what was or wasn't brave, held no purpose.

"I would like to work with you on this. Help you develop coping mechanisms for dealing with what happened to you. Give you a safe space to talk about that, and about the loss of your family. Would you accept this?"

Blaire nodded. "I'd like that." She could trust the professor. While a Vasirian, she was a licensed professional, and Blaire had experience with this sort of thing before. She found comfort in something that seemed normal in the weird world she'd found herself in.

"Wonderful. I believe we should approach this slowly. I want you to be able to trust me before we get into triggering subject matter. Let's start with more basic things."

"Sure." Blaire finally settled back into the chair.

Noting her relaxed posture, the professor motioned to the bottle of water and Blaire picked it up, taking a long drink of the cold liquid.

"So, as I understand it, you're here at Blackthorn because you share a Korrena bond with another student. Is this correct?"

"Well… that's what they tell me. I don't really know. I don't fully understand what it means."

Nodding, the professor tapped her chin. "From my experience, I feel like it is something that needs to be experienced more than read about. The nuances of a bond and natural connection between two individuals vary wildly from person to person."

Blaire took another drink.

"Can you tell me about your pair?"

"Lukas?" Blaire choked on her water and her face warmed.

The professor smiled and lifted her own bottle for a drink. "Is that his name?"

"Yes… he's… different."

"Different how?"

"Well, he's an asshole."

The professor laughed, then held up a hand, apologizing.

"He is. But not always. He's confusing. One minute he's trying to run me off, and the next he's asking me to stay. Or telling me. Or… I don't know."

"That does sound confusing. You're not sure if he told you or asked you to stay after trying to send you away?"

"These two guys attacked me—they got in trouble for it with administration, so it's handled—and after that, we… talked. He seemed to think I would hurt him. I don't know how I could do that. He doesn't know me."

"People often hurt those they don't know."

"I know, but I couldn't hurt him."

The professor tilted her head, studying Blaire, and she looked away from the assessing gaze.

"Why?" It was a simple question, but so complicated.

Blaire looked back to the window. "He seemed afraid. He might have protected me from those students, but he seemed afraid. He seemed hurt. I wanted to protect him." She looked back at the professor. "I wouldn't want to hurt him if I want to protect him, right?"

"No. I don't suppose you would. But you mentioned you weren't sure if he told you or asked you to stay. There's quite a difference between the two."

"I don't understand."

"When someone makes a request of you, they give you agency to choose what is best for you. When someone tells you what to do, they take that away and make the choice for you."

Blaire tried to remember Lukas's exact words but shook her head. "I really can't remember how he said it."

"Then let us focus on something else. In the future, try to look at the things he says this way. It's part of setting healthy boundaries. I'm sure in the time since your family's passing, your stepbrother has blurred those boundaries in a way that may have stolen your voice."

Blaire looked down; shame was heavy in her heart.

"It's not your fault. You've done nothing wrong. You didn't ask for what he did. You were denied the safety and security that was necessary for your growth. I can't give that to you, but I can give you the tools to reclaim that for yourself."

"Okay…" Blaire took another sip of her drink and looked up again at the professor. She set boundaries. She'd forged hard lines she didn't allow Caleb to cross, even to the detriment of her own safety. With Lukas, her boundaries were there. Loose. But she still told him no when he tried to kiss her.

"I… I stopped him from kissing me."

A slender, copper brow arched as the professor eyed Blaire.

"I got spooked by the storm the other day, and he comforted me. We were so close he leaned in to kiss me… or at least that's what I thought he wanted."

"Did you want to kiss him? That's the important part."

"Yes… no… I did, but I wasn't ready for it."

"That's okay. That's a perfectly reasonable answer. It's completely normal to feel attraction and want to act on those feelings. It's healthy that you acknowledge your own boundaries within yourself. What happened?"

"I asked him not to. I stopped him."

"How did he handle it?"

"He looked hurt, but he let me go."

"Good. Not that he was hurt, but that he respected your wishes. Your boundaries."

"Yeah… but now he's avoiding me."

"Perhaps he doesn't know how to approach you after rejection. How does that make you feel?"

"I didn't reject him." She squeezed the bottle in her hand. "But I don't know how I feel about him avoiding me. I mean, it avoids conflict, but…" She didn't know how to express how she wanted to know him more. Something about the look in his eyes when he thought she would hurt him stuck with her.

"While you may not have rejected him as a person, rejecting his advances is still rejection."

Blaire looked down.

"Blaire, you set a healthy boundary. He respected it. This is ideal. What needs to happen now is you both need to talk about things. He needs to understand you weren't distancing yourself from him as a person. He doesn't know your limits. It is up to you to make him aware. You are in control."

Blaire set down her bottle.

"It's okay to not completely understand your feelings. If we always knew exactly what we felt and why, life would certainly be simpler, but sometimes the path of discovery can be exciting—scary, but exciting, and very rewarding."

An intercom on the professor's desk buzzed, and a man's voice came over the speaker. *"Olivia Whitmire is on Line 3 for you."*

Professor Sinclair looked at Blaire with apologetic eyes. "I wish we had more time to discuss this, but we will get to everything eventually. I'd like to see you every Wednesday after classes, if that works for you?"

"Sure. My classes end early those days, so I can be here at one o'clock."

"Perfect. I'll pencil you in as a reoccurring appointment."

Blaire stood and straightened her skirt.

"In the meantime, I'd like you to work on trying to talk with Lukas. Building your Korrena bond together is the perfect opportunity for you to exercise boundaries."

The phone buzzed again, and the professor sighed.

"I'll see you on Wednesday."

12

Movie Night

A couple of weeks passed, and Blaire finally started adapting to her life in the academy. Lukas sometimes avoided her, which disappointed her. After she pushed him away when she could have sworn he tried to kiss her in the cafeteria, he hesitated to get too close to her. It allowed her to get to know his friends better, but she wanted to know him too. She wanted to try, like her counselor had been encouraging her to do.

She spent a lot of time with Aiden after the incident in the courtyard; he adopted a protector role in Lukas's place while Lukas kept his distance. Aiden never left her alone, and when they didn't have a class together—which was rare, considering most of the classes were general education courses most everyone had to take—he'd be waiting outside when she left. If he were human, she'd call it stalkerish, but here she accepted the protective friend gesture on face value. His presence comforted her and gave her an anchor in unfamiliar territory.

Everyone planned to meet at Aiden's dorm after dinner service, where they often got together for movie night to relax and unwind.

Aiden's room held the same layout as her dorm, with the same color scheme and linens, but instead of a single bed on each side wall, one bed sat angled along the side of the window with its foot facing a second bed along the right wall.

A shelf hung on the wall above the headboard of the bed under the window that, on closer inspection, held a framed photo of Aiden and Riley and additional photographs of Aiden and Riley with other people of various ages, likely their family, Blaire assumed.

Beside the bed, a single wooden nightstand sat with a simple lamp on top and a stereo system standing beside it. A flat-screen TV sat on a stand against the wall next to the foyer, with various video games and consoles. Charlotte would have a field day with his collection.

The bed on the right was neatly made and looked untouched, with bare walls and an empty desk sitting at the foot of the bed against the wall. It was easy to see this room lacked a second occupant.

"Dude, get off my bed," Aiden said to another guy who lay on Aiden's bed going through a stack of movies.

The guy rolled over on his side before sitting up and climbing off the bed. "What's the problem? It's not like you're using it."

Aiden gestured toward the young guy, "Blaire, this is Seth. Seth, you know about Blaire already. Be nice."

"Piss off, I'm always nice."

Aiden rolled his eyes.

Aside from the same cupid's bow above a thin upper lip with a fuller lower lip, Seth didn't look anything like Kai. He stood shorter than his older brother, standing around six feet with a medium build, but he looked stronger than Kai.

His brown hair was cut similarly to Aiden's and styled as if he didn't care, but the cut was tighter on the sides and back and longer on top than Aiden's hair. The most notable feature about him was his piercing smoky-colored eyes set beneath a heavy brow, making him look as if he were capable of staring into someone's soul.

"You're way too comfortable here," Kai said as he stepped around everyone and moved to sit down on the spare bed, Mera following him.

Seth huffed. "Whatever." He carried the stack of movies and put them on top of the desk next to a laptop.

"It's true. He practically lives here. He should just petition to get transferred into this room," Riley said to Blaire as she took a seat on the floor in front of Aiden's bed and Seth rolled his eyes. "He spends most of his free time here since Aiden doesn't have a pair and lives on his own for now."

"Actually, I planned to do that next term, so shut it," Seth said.

As Blaire sat down next to a laughing Riley, leaning back against the bed, Aiden watched her with a peculiar look on his face before spearing his fingers through his hair, messing it up. He gave her looks like that often lately, and he seemed to be growing tense around her, which disappointed her because she liked being around him. She didn't have the opportunity to give it too much thought before a knock at the door drew everyone's attention.

"That's probably Lukas," Mera said, getting off the bed and moving to the door. "He said he'd be late."

Riley nudged Blaire. "Don't worry. If he's an ass, I'll throw him out."

Aiden climbed behind Blaire and sat against the wall, hanging his leg off the edge of the bed next to her shoulder.

Blaire laughed and shook her head. "It's fine. He's not really an ass. I mean, not all the time… and besides, he's been keeping his distance."

"Really?"

"Yeah, I don't mind though, honestly. It's given me the chance to settle in and get to know you guys without dealing with attitude." Blaire offered a smile, causing Riley to laugh as Lukas walked into the room. But she did mind. At least a little. Beneath Lukas's prickly surface, she'd glimpsed something more, and she wanted to break through and discover what that something more was.

Lukas's long hair hung slightly damp over his shoulders as if he had just taken a shower. He wore his usual black jeans with a chain on his hip attached to a corded leather belt. It seemed to be his staple wardrobe, along with black t-shirts, and sometimes a leather jacket when not in his uniform. Rarely did she see him in anything but black, but it looked good on him. He looked like a classic bad boy.

His eyes found Blaire and he stared at her. She cleared her throat and he looked away. That same unfamiliar tingle ran through her. She felt exposed under his gaze.

Lukas sighed and crossed to the only remaining spot available beside Aiden on the bed behind Riley.

"How are you holding up?" Aiden asked him, leaning over to talk quietly.

Lukas grunted in response and stared at the back of Blaire's head.

"That well, huh?" Aiden chuckled.

Blaire turned to look back at Lukas and noticed him staring again. "What?" she snapped at him, growing tired of how he stared and brooded all the time lately.

Lukas glared and turned his gaze away from her, watching Seth put the movie in. He looked uncomfortable and like he wanted to say something but didn't, so Blaire turned away. She lifted her hair, twisted it, and dropped it back onto the bed behind her in front of Aiden.

If he wanted to snub her, she could play the same game.

She didn't relish in the idea of playing stupid games with people, but something about the way he pulled away from her the past couple of weeks before she even had the chance to know him rubbed her the wrong way. Ever since the near kiss, things had become strained. Part of her deeply regretted stopping him. Her mind replayed that moment many times as she lay in bed at night. She didn't know how to fix things.

Mera climbed onto the bed with Kai, sitting between his legs as he leaned against the wall.

Riley got to her feet. "I'm going to go grab snacks. Don't wait for me. I've already seen this movie, so it's alright if I miss some."

"Wasn't gonna."

Riley flipped Seth her middle finger and stalked to the door in frustration, turning the lights off as she left.

It was extremely dark in the room; even the moon wasn't shining through the window, the room only lit by the TV on the other side of the room.

Leaning against the bed, Blaire felt something tugging on her hair. She glanced over her shoulder and found Aiden running his fingers through the long strands, untangling the twist she made. When he realized she noticed him, he stopped and let the strands fall through his grasp as he stared at her with the same hard expression he'd given for the past couple of days.

The air had grown suffocating. Blaire never experienced someone act like this around her before without ill intentions behind it, and it confused her; it caused a knot in her stomach.

She bit softly on her lower lip, not knowing how to act, but she didn't look away, and neither did he. He started to reach out to touch her hair again, but the bed shifted as Lukas moved.

Blaire jerked her head around to look back at the movie and took a deep breath as Lukas slowly lowered himself onto the floor beside her. His apple and spice scent filled her nose as he stirred the air around her. Blaire closed her eyes to focus on steadying her breathing. Was he finally going to try to connect with her again?

The door opened and Riley entered, carrying a mesh bag filled with treats.

"What the hell, Lukas?" Riley stomped over and looked down at him with her hands on her hips, the bag hanging at her side. "That's my spot!"

Lukas shrugged. "You snooze, you lose."

"You are such a child."

Blaire giggled, and Lukas tilted his head at her, meeting her eyes and raising an eyebrow. She promptly shut up and looked back at the TV screen, yawning as Riley passed out the snacks to everyone.

Riley climbed onto the bed next to Aiden, took Lukas's old spot, and started eating her jellybeans.

Ten or fifteen minutes passed with only the sound of the TV in the darkness of the room.

Lukas shifted and felt a soft impact on his shoulder. He glanced down to find Blaire turned toward him, asleep on his shoulder, her hair falling in a blonde curtain over her face. A half-eaten package of jellybeans was limply held in her hand.

He'd missed being near her, but after she rejected him in the cafeteria when he could have sworn he read the signals right, his pride was wounded. He wanted to respect her boundaries and give her space, but he didn't know how to do that without completely distancing himself from her because of the powerful urge to touch her every time he got near her. But he couldn't do it. He couldn't stay away. He wanted to know more about her. What Professor Velastra had been giving him wasn't nearly enough.

Lukas gently removed the jellybeans and set them aside before slowly reaching up and moving Blaire's hair from her face, tucking the strands behind her ear before caressing a hand down her jawline. His movements caused her to stir and turn more to snuggle into his side, breathing in deeply against him as if she were smelling him. Faintly, Blaire whispered his name with a contented sigh.

Lukas tensed and quickly glanced around the room. No one seemed to have heard her or paid them any attention, until he glanced behind him and met Riley's eyes. She grinned.

Riley leaned forward, whispering, "I wonder what Blaire's dreaming about."

"Shut up." He glared at her.

She started laughing, which prompted Aiden to glance over and follow her line of sight. He looked at Blaire's head on Lukas's shoulder, then up at Lukas. They looked at each other for a moment, and Lukas didn't understand the discomfort he saw in Aiden's eyes. He didn't have time to focus on his friend, not with Blaire's hand falling onto his leg as she shifted. He couldn't take it anymore.

Thankfully, the movie ended, so he slowly moved Blaire's hand from his lap before Seth turned on the lights.

Mera stretched and sat up. "I don't think I can manage another movie tonight." She smiled at Lukas. "I don't think Blaire can either."

Kai chuckled. "She does look pretty comfortable, though."

Lukas rolled his eyes. He could only imagine how they would behave if they heard her.

They remained on the floor as everyone started leaving. He wasn't ready to disturb Blaire.

"You're not going to wake her up?" Riley asked as she stood.

Lukas shook his head. "I'm not going to just leave her, but no, I'll carry her home."

He moved Blaire's head from his shoulder and rested it gently against Aiden's bed. She shifted and her head fell over to rest against Aiden's leg. He clenched his jaw, staring at her.

Mera and Kai said their goodbyes and exited the room, Riley following behind. Seth moved to go through Aiden's video games; it seemed he wasn't leaving anytime soon.

Lukas stretched and bent down, putting one arm under Blaire's knees and the other around her shoulders to pick her up, princess style. She turned her head into his chest and took a deep breath through her nose before snuggling in and sighing. That was the second time tonight she had smelled him. He didn't know what to think of it.

Lukas wanted things to be different between them. In keeping his distance, he tried to observe and learn anything he could about her. He spent time with Professor Velastra to learn about Blaire's history, her family's impact on Rosebrook Valley, her preferences, and dislikes the professor had researched about her. He soaked up all the information like a sponge and found the more he discovered, the more he liked her as a person and wanted to connect with her directly, and not just because she was his Korrena.

The bond's pull only added to the fascination and physical desire for her. She looked beautiful, and he wanted her without their biological connection, but it amplified everything. It made him more determined to make this work. The problem with trying to connect with her directly stemmed from the fear of rejection for what he was. He didn't know if he could handle being called a monster again.

He pulled her close as he left Aiden's dorm.

Entering the darkened dorm room, Lukas walked to Blaire's bed and gently laid her down. He stared down at her for the longest before sitting next to her on the edge of the bed.

He caressed the fading bruise on her face that started to show through her worn makeup, recalling the information Riley shared the day before about Blaire's stepbrother. It made him angry to hear what she'd been through, and he vowed not to make her suffer through anything like that again. The insight was a big reason why he kept his distance after she rejected him. He didn't want her to label him another creep like her stepbrother seeking to take advantage of her. Why was she still bruised like this? He knew humans didn't heal like Vasirian, but shouldn't something like this already be gone?

His movements caused Blaire to shift and open her eyes.

Startled, she pressed her head into the pillow to move away from him. He shot off the bed, away from her.

"Sorry! I..." He looked around the room nervously. "Sorry," he muttered again and stalked across the room to sit on his bed, removing his boots before pausing with a heavy sigh. "I didn't scare you, did I?"

Blaire sat up and rubbed her eyes. "No... just surprised me. Where am I?"

Lukas switched on the lamp and the room filled with light.

"Home. You fell asleep, and I had to carry you."

"Why didn't you wake me up? I could have walked."

He ran a hand through his hair. "It wasn't a big deal. Don't overthink it." He cringed at how harsh he sounded and cursed himself internally. He stood and pulled his shirt off over his head. Why did he say it like that? He tossed his shirt in front of the desk at the foot of his bed. "I'm sorry. I just thought you looked comfort—"

He stopped short as he turned around, noticing the way Blaire stared at him. No, not at his face; her eyes were focused on his exposed torso.

Lukas shivered with pride at the appreciative look on her face as her eyes raked over his shoulders and bare pecs. He licked his lips and swallowed hard, enduring her silent appraisal of his body. Her eyes moved down to his abs and the faint trail of hair leading from his navel into his jeans. He tensed as his body stirred with arousal. He didn't want to scare her.

Lukas cleared his throat. Face turning scarlet, she snapped her gaze up to meet his.

When he turned away, she jumped up quickly and ran into the closet, returning with pajamas in her arms. She didn't even look at him as she rushed into the bathroom.

Moments later, the shower turned on. He finished changing into black sweatpants and climbed into bed, turning his back to where she would sleep near him, knowing he wouldn't be able to look at her once she returned, not after everything that happened tonight. He wanted her more than words could say.

Lukas thought back to earlier in the night, to the way she snuggled into his body and smelled him. Blaire's responses to him told him she felt the bond, even if she didn't know what it was. As he listened to the shower, he wondered if the bond was the only reason she responded. He doubted it. He could tell from the first day she felt attraction toward him, and he couldn't deny he wanted her too. He needed to do something to reach her so she wouldn't be afraid.

The bathroom door opened, and Lukas closed his eyes as Blaire padded quietly across to her side of the room. He listened to the rustle of her covers as she turned down her bed and climbed inside. The lamp clicked and cast the room into darkness as he opened his eyes again.

It was going to be another long night.

13

Revelations

The next morning, Blaire stood with Riley in the hall before the start of their shared class. Blaire had relaxed, but this morning Lukas acted weird around her. He didn't say anything rude or ignore her outright, but he didn't speak to her either, although that was normal.

The weird part was the trivial things he did, like handing her a towel after she washed her face and couldn't see, or when he passed her backpack to her before they left. Simple stuff, but he interacted with her in a civil manner. It seemed as if he was trying to find ways to interact with her after keeping his distance for the past couple of weeks.

"So..." Riley said hesitantly. "Has it happened yet?"

Blaire raised a brow at her. "Has what happened yet?"

"Um... have you shared blood with Lukas yet?"

A wave of panic washed over Blaire as her eyes went wide. She had to will the visceral reaction away before she could respond.

"I have absolutely zero intentions of sharing my blood with anyone!" Her voice rose in pitch as she ended her sentence, drawing the attention of several students. Considering she was supposed to be with a Vasirian, she wasn't surprised some snickered at her.

Riley winced and shook her head. "You know, the only way to complete the bond is through both the sharing of blood… and body."

Blood rushed to Blaire's cheeks. She fidgeted with the strands of her long hair, twisting them around her fingers.

Riley's eyes went wide. "Wait… have you guys already done it?"

"No!" Blaire yelled, drawing attention again as she shook her head rapidly.

"Methinks the lady doth protest too much," Riley said with a posh accent before bursting into giggles.

"It's true! Lukas and I have never had sex!" She ran a hand through her hair in frustration and lowered her voice as she tried to calm down. "I've never had sex with anyone, for that matter. I'm a virgin."

"Well, so am I, but still… You've found your Korren—" Riley paused, looking over Blaire's head. "Hooo-lyyy shit."

Blaire turned at the sound of a throat clearing to find Lukas and Aiden standing behind her. "You've got to be kidding me."

Lukas looked ready to tear the head off something as he stared at Blaire. She didn't know what his problem was, but he would grind his molars into dust with the way he worked his jaw. Was he angry? No, she recognized the look in his eyes. She'd seen it before in the cafeteria when he tried to kiss her. But he didn't want to kiss her now, right? That would be weird. She didn't understand at all. Blaire looked away from his intense stare.

At least Aiden had the decency to look embarrassed about eavesdropping as he rubbed the back of his neck, looking away from Blaire, not meeting her eyes.

Blaire looked down at her loafers. So they heard her proclamation about her sex life. Well, lack of one. Not that she felt embarrassed about it or saved it for marriage. She'd just never felt that urge before. She felt proud she managed to fend off Caleb as long as she had to keep her virginity, and it wasn't like she ever had a boyfriend to share that with if she did have the urge. Either way, she didn't want to make it a big deal by broadcasting that personal struggle to everyone who knew her.

"They didn't hear anyyything," Riley said while glaring at the two guys. "Right?"

"I have no idea what you're talking about," Aiden said, taking Lukas's arm. "We, uh… need to get to class." He pulled Lukas—who still hadn't moved—toward the classroom and disappeared inside.

"My brother can do good things sometimes."

The hallway began to empty in anticipation of the bell. Riley bent down to pick up her messenger bag when Blaire slumped against the lockers, exhaling.

"So, speaking of sex… I've been having these weird dreams."

"Dreams?" Riley immediately dropped her bag.

"Yeah… sex dreams. About Lukas. It's been happening every single night since those guys attacked and he saved me." She blushed and looked toward the classroom door. She needed to talk to someone about it because she didn't know how to handle the intensity.

Riley put a hand over her mouth to hide her large smile and obvious excitement. "It could be the bond beginning to take." She sounded way too giddy.

Blaire opened her mouth to respond, but the bell interrupted. Sighing, she grabbed her backpack from the floor and walked with Riley into class.

Once inside, they sat in their assigned seating, which put Blaire between Aiden and Riley and in front of Lukas. She didn't dare look back at him.

Riley spoke up. "So, Blaire, I was thinking maybe we could go into the valley to catch a movie after school tomorrow. You haven't been out since you started here, right?"

"No, I didn't know I could leave."

Aiden chuckled. "Of course you can. You're not a prisoner here. You can leave whenever you want."

The academy didn't feel like a prison. She knew what it felt like to live in a prison. Not a real one, but it may as well have been. She shuddered. She wanted to put the past behind her so badly, but the entire world outside Blackthorn felt like a jungle full of man-eating tigers. She'd been assured she would be safe here, but no guarantee had been given for her security outside the academy grounds in Wilcox territory. Was it safe to go out? She needed to know.

"He doesn't mean to move away, though," Riley added in a rush. "I don't think any of us want you to go." She glanced back at Lukas briefly. "So yeah, movie. Wanna go?"

"Will it just be us?" Blaire twisted her hair up and clipped it.

Riley motioned in Aiden's direction. "Aiden can come."

He rolled his eyes. "Oh, thank you so much for allowing me into your special girls club."

Blaire giggled and he winked at her. She blushed.

"So, you in?"

"Um… sure? I guess." Blaire opened her English book. It would be nice to get away and have the chance to forget about the fact she now attended a school full of Vasirian, expected to bond with one of them. She still hadn't fully wrapped her mind around the meaning of that. She leaned toward Riley and whispered so the others couldn't hear her, "Will it be safe?" She gave Riley a pointed look.

"Oh... well..."

Riley turned in her chair and faced Lukas.

"You're coming too, right?" She tried to make it sound like an afterthought, but Blaire knew better. She had come to realize, in the brief time she'd known the girl, that Riley was very crafty and knew how to get things to go her way.

Lukas shrugged, muttering his agreement as he stared at the back of Blaire's head, his arms crossed.

"There. With Lukas there to protect you, it'll be fine. I mean, Aiden and I will be there too. We're stronger than humans, so... yeah."

Blaire huffed an exasperated sigh. What was the point of whispering if Riley was just going to blurt out the answer? Strangely, neither Lukas nor Aiden questioned her response.

"I wondered about that," Blaire finally said, tilting her head. "After that guy ended up in the fountain, I wondered just how strong you are."

"Stronger than humans, but we can't, like, lift buses or rip trees out of the ground. That's Hulk-level strong," Riley said.

Aiden chuckled.

"So, yay! Movie night!" Riley bounced in her seat and looked at Blaire.

The professor at the front of the room shot a glare in their direction. "Miss Easton, I see you're going with the method of drawing upon personal experiences. Care to tell the rest of the class how you plan to use movie night to develop the skills of structure and exposition in your response essay?" He crossed his arms and gave her a disapproving stare.

Several students turned their attention in their direction.

"Sorry, Professor Rutledge..." Riley smiled sheepishly before looking at Blaire and muttering, "I just thought it'd be romantic."

Blaire's face heated.

"Oooo, it looks like Blaire is excited about the date!" Riley exclaimed loudly, giggling at her own ridiculous humor.

"Miss Easton!"

"Sorry!"

Lukas raised an eyebrow, leaning over and resting his cheek against his fist, sticking his leg out under Blaire's chair, which caused her to turn and look at him when her chair jerked, exposing how red she was for him to see. He smirked. That smirk did things to her insides. The deep sound vibrated through her as if he had done it right next to her ear.

She turned away quickly, feeling exposed. "It's not a date."

"Aw, it's okay to admit you're excited about going on a date with him. You're becoming a serious bonded pair, after all."

Blaire shook her head quickly, her face still flushed. "Nothing is happening between us," she whispered.

Lukas lifted both brows, leaning to where he could see Blaire better, staring at her intently without speaking. Riley frowned as she looked between the two.

"You know, it would make for a pretty awkward date," Aiden spoke up, breaking the tension starting to surface.

Riley looked at him in confusion. "What are you talking about?"

"Well, think about it. Do you think anyone would want to go on a double date with a brother and sister? The incest thing is creepy, don't you think?"

"Ew, gross! Just because we're close doesn't mean we're 'close.' Who would even think I'd be with you? I much prefer—Nope. Never mind."

"Seth?" Aiden grinned at his little sister.

"Shut up. No. You need to leave that train of thought back at the station."

Lukas laughed.

Blaire squeezed her fists on top of her desk. She knew Aiden didn't mean anything by those words; he didn't know her past. Besides, she wasn't blood-related to Caleb, but she still couldn't help but be reminded of her stepbrother and his unhealthy attraction to her.

"Oh shit," Aiden said when he noticed Blaire and frowned.

Blaire looked over at him in confusion. "What?"

"Ah… nothing. I was just thinking I needed to tell Seth I won't be in that night. He's been crashing a lot at my place, and I don't know the movie times, so it's better just to tell him not to show up," Aiden said, floundering for something to say. He rubbed the back of his neck and looked away as Riley glared at him. Something was weird about that.

Riley bit her lip. "Why isn't he in this class, anyway? I didn't think he'd be on a different time because he's in my other general ed classes."

Aiden shook his head. "He's in the advanced English course with Professor Dupont. Back in high school, he was in honors, so he didn't have to start with basic courses."

Riley whistled. "Why so advanced?"

"His major is Creative Writing. How do you not know this?"

"It's not like I keep up with him!" Riley snapped and glanced at the front of the room as the professor looked up from his paperwork to give her a reproachful look. She ducked her head with another sheepish smile and the professor rolled his eyes.

"Huh," Aiden said, sitting back and crossing his arms.

"What?"

"Nothing. Nothing at all."

Riley started going through her cell phone, and after a few taps, she looked up. "So, I'll come over about five o'clock tomorrow and we can get ready then. The movie starts at seven, but we can get there a little early to grab snacks and make sure we get good seats. Last time, Aiden was late, and we ended up in the back row. The view was terrible."

"At least it wasn't the front row. I prefer the middle," Lukas said.

"Hey, how was I supposed to know the theater would be packed?" Aiden said, narrowing his eyes at her.

"Dude. It was opening weekend for the final installment of the best dinosaur movie saga ever. Of course it's going to be packed!"

Aiden rolled his eyes. "You know it won't be the last one. They always say it's the last one, it does amazingly, and then three years later they release a new one. I'll still go see it, but it's what they do."

Blaire laughed softly at the brother-sister back and forth. It helped her forget the earlier upset.

This wasn't good.

Blaire stared at her bloody underwear and sighed. She looked over at the bathroom door, thankful for the lock on the inside.

"Great. Can I ever catch a break?"

In all the chaos of settling into the academy, she never once thought to ask about what happened when her menstrual cycle started. She scrubbed out the blood under cold water in the sink, pinching a washcloth between her legs, but now she stood trapped in the bathroom without a change of clothes or reachable supplies. She could dry the underwear with the hair dryer, but a knock on the door startled her.

Blaire backed up quickly until she stood as far away from the door as possible. Thankful in that moment that the bathroom was nearly the size of the main space of their dorm room. "Go away!"

Lukas's muffled voice came through the door. "Are you okay? You've been in there a really long time."

Blaire looked at the small clock on the counter. She hadn't realized how much time had passed in her panic.

Another knock.

"Go away!" She looked down at the wet fabric in her hand. She couldn't leave the room like this. "No! Wait! Call Riley!"

A pause. "Riley?" Lukas sounded uncertain.

"Yes! Call her and tell her to come here!"

Lukas said something on the other side of the door, but she couldn't make it out as he moved away from the door. After another minute, he spoke through the door.

"She said she's on her way. What's going on?"

"Nothing!"

"You're scaring me, Blaire."

She didn't want to worry him, but she didn't want to tell him she was bleeding either.

"I'm fine. Just… I'm fine."

Blaire opened the cabinet under the sink and grabbed one of the small trash bags they kept stored there to put her wet panties in for the proper laundry. She had just finished tying off the bag when a knock sounded on the door again.

"Lukas! I told you I'm f—"

"It's me," Riley said before jiggling the door handle.

"Oh, thank God."

Blaire dropped the bag and shuffled to the door, unlocking it. She cracked the door enough to reach out and pull Riley inside. Her eyes met Lukas's and she could see the concern there. She frowned. "I'm fine," she said quickly before closing the door and locking it again.

"So, what in the world is going on? Lukas is freaking out. Says you've been in here for ages and keep screaming at him anytime he comes to the door."

Blaire ran a hand through her hair and closed her eyes.

"Can you smell it?"

"Smell what?"

"Blood."

Riley's eyes widened. "Blood? What? Are you okay?"

Several hard knocks on the door echoed in the bathroom. Lukas heard Riley.

"Shh. Keep it down. I'm fine… but I started my period."

Riley's mouth opened in an O shape, and she gaped at Blaire before bursting into a fit of laughter.

"What? I'm serious. I'm bleeding. I don't know what to do."

Riley wiped her watering eyes. "You've never had your period before?" She looked confused. "You're eighteen…"

Blaire blinked and frowned, frustrated. "Yes, of course I have. I mean… what am I going to do about bleeding around…" She motioned at Riley and then the door.

"Oh, Gods. Blaire. It's not a big deal."

"How can you say that? I basically now have a dinner bell ringing between my legs!"

Riley held her stomach and doubled over in another fit of laughter.

"I'm glad you find this funny."

"I'm sorry." She held a hand up as she struggled to get her giggles under control. "It's just… Vasirian menstruate too."

"You do?"

"Yes. We have the same biological functions you do. How do you think we can reproduce? We don't just sprout up from the ground."

"But how do you not want to… eat… drink… whenever you smell it?"

"First, we're not so bloodthirsty that we'd stoop to attacking each other like that." Her nose wrinkled. "Second, because it's not as detectable, I guess. I mean, unless it's fresh and in the air like on your arm, we don't smell such a minor amount. Unless it was all over you."

Blaire shifted uncomfortably on her feet. "Like starting without supplies and getting it on your clothes…and a towel?"

"Yeah, that could be a problem. But we can wash them."

"It really doesn't affect you?"

"Nope. I've had a packet recently, anyway." She shrugged. "Typically, unless someone is bleeding out all over the place, we're unaffected because we feed throughout the day. Some of us have difficulties with large amounts of blood, but even then, some Vasirian have no issue. Usually, they work in the health sector. Like Mera. She's working toward a bachelor's in Health Science."

It made sense when she stopped to think about it. If the Vasirian walked around humans every day in town, how would they handle blood lust every time they passed a woman on her cycle, or a kid with a knee injury from a bike accident?

"I need tampons. I have a box in the top of my closet. I didn't know how to get there from here when Lukas wouldn't leave."

"Why didn't you ask him to grab you the box?"

The flush of humiliation heated her face. "In my world, we don't tell guys when it's going on. We just don't."

Riley nodded dubiously and went to the door. "I'll be right back." She unlocked the door and left the bathroom. Lukas started questioning her as soon as she opened the door.

After several minutes, the door opened again and Riley stepped inside, calling back to Lukas, "I told you she's fine. No, you can't come in."

"Does he know?"

"No. But he's really worried."

Riley set the box on the counter. Blaire picked it up and looked at her.

"I'll just…" Riley motioned toward the door. "I'll get you fresh clothes." She left the bathroom.

When Blaire finished cleaning up and sorting herself, she called Riley back into the bathroom. She came in carrying a pair of blue plaid cotton pants and a loose white t-shirt. Blaire made quick work of removing her stockings and her uniform shirt and tie, pulling the t-shirt over her head before slipping on a pair of fresh panties under her skirt.

She had just dropped her skirt when she froze as Lukas stepped through the doorway.

"Oh, come on. I told you not to come in," Riley said, heading toward Lukas to push him out of the room.

"I couldn't hear anything. I need to know she's alright."

"She told you alrea—Hey!"

Lukas shoved past Riley and stared at Blaire. "What the fuck is that?" The concern on his face when he first entered the bathroom contorted into a mask of fury.

Blaire followed his gaze to her thighs, then snatched the pants off the counter and pulled them on.

"Did he do that to you?" Lukas spat, his jaw tightening, the vein at his temple on display.

"What?"

"Did your stepbrother do that?" Lukas flung his hands toward her bruises, exasperated.

Blaire's gaze snapped to Riley, who looked away. *She told Lukas.*

Blaire narrowed her eyes. "How could you tell him? I told you that in confidence." Her voice shook. She didn't know if anger or hurt fueled her questions. Likely both.

Lukas stepped away from them to pace the corner of the bathroom, both hands on the back of his head as he muttered under his breath. She hoped he was trying to calm down.

"I'm sorry… I thought I was helping," Riley whispered, bringing Blaire's attention back to her.

"How does that help?" Blaire crossed her arms over her chest and pressed her lips flat.

"He's your pair… Aiden's your friend… I thought—"

"Aiden knows?"

Riley flinched.

"God, Riley. Who else have you told? Kai? Mera?"

"No one."

Lukas stepped toward Blaire, but she held up her hand.

"Stop. I'm too pissed off to deal with whatever you're going to say right now."

Lukas stepped back and leaned against the bathroom wall, shutting his eyes.

Riley looked back at Blaire, and her eyes watered. "I'm sorry, Blaire. I really didn't mean to hurt you. I thought if they knew, it would help them understand you… protect you."

The rational part of Blaire understood Riley's intentions, but it still didn't soothe the upset of having her trust betrayed. Charlotte hadn't told her mothers when Blaire asked her not to; at least, they never indicated they knew.

"I trusted you."

"You can trust me. It won't happen again. I messed up. I should have let you tell them in your own time. Again, I really thought I was helping."

Blaire sighed. "I know…"

"Please forgive me." Riley sniffled.

Lukas stared at her legs, saying nothing.

Blaire shook her head. "It's over now. And yes, Lukas... my stepbrother did this."

He growled.

"Why are you still so bruised?" Riley asked, her voice wobbly.

"I don't know. It's always been this way. I bruise easily, and when it happens, the bruises last for a really long time. My mom had me examined periodically as a child, but even after lots of tests they couldn't figure out what exactly causes it. I don't have any diseases or anything like hemophilia, so your guess is as good as mine."

Lukas stepped forward again until Blaire looked at him. He stopped, as if waiting for approval to approach. It made sense he'd hesitate; she had stopped him moments earlier. She stepped toward him and Riley.

"Does it hurt?" he whispered.

"Not really. Not unless you press on it."

"Can I see them?" Lukas asked softly, meeting her eyes.

Blaire averted her gaze. She wasn't sure what good would come of him seeing the evidence more than he already had. Her response came out small and uncertain as she looked back at him. "Why?"

"I just want to know... what you went through."

Blaire's brow furrowed, but she stepped back. If it helped ease Lukas's mind, then it couldn't hurt to show him. Riley had already seen them close up, anyway. She rolled up the loose pant legs to expose her inner thighs.

Riley turned away.

Lukas knelt in front of Blaire and held out a hand, looking up at Blaire, waiting. Blaire nodded. He growled as he looked at the bruising, resting his fingertips over the finger-pattern bruises. His eyes momentarily flared wide as he made the connection as to what caused that pattern.

Blaire bit down hard on her lower lip, shame bubbling in her stomach and threatening to surface. She had hoped the bruises would be gone before anyone saw her bare legs, since her uniform stockings hid them so well.

Lukas pulled his hand away as he studied the larger bruise on her other leg.

"I'm sorry this happened to you." He met Blaire's gaze.

Blaire shrugged.

"Don't do that."

"What?"

"Act like it isn't a problem."

"It's over now." Blaire rolled the legs of her pants back down, feeling overexposed.

"It shouldn't have happened. It won't happen again." Lukas stood. "You don't have to go back to that. Ever. Stay here."

Riley turned back around to face them, tilting her head. "I thought we'd established Blaire wasn't leaving."

"I just… need to hear her say she's staying."

Blaire pursed her lips and looked down for a moment, recalling her meeting with Professor Sinclair, before looking back up to meet his eyes. "Are you asking me or telling me?"

"What?" Lukas wrinkled his forehead in confusion.

"Are you asking me to stay… or are you telling me to stay?"

"What's the difference?"

Blaire sighed. She couldn't be frustrated with him. She had her own confusion about the difference before too. "Are you telling me what to do?"

"No!" His brows shot up and his eyes opened wide.

"Then you're giving me a choice." She moved a hand to her hip.

"Well, yeah. Of course. But I hope you'll make the choice to stay."

Blaire smiled and looked at Riley, who was beaming.

"Yeah… I'm staying. But first, I need chocolate."

14

Nightmare

Fierce winds blew the trees and flowering bushes in the dark courtyard. The moon hid from view behind ominous clouds that moved quickly through the sky. The landscape maintenance team would have a lot to do tomorrow when the storm finally passed.

Lightning flashed across the sky in a sideways streak, and despite anticipating it, Blaire jumped with a yelp as loud thunder echoed through the deserted courtyard.

She didn't remember coming outside, or why she came.

"It's time to come home, Blaire," Caleb said from behind her.

Blaire froze. How did Caleb get on the academy grounds? She slowly turned to face him, and he stood with his hands in his pockets, grinning at her like he always did before something went his way. A full-body shudder passed through her.

"What are you doing here?" she whispered.

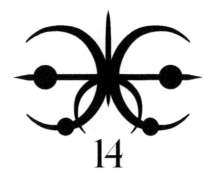

"Oh, sweetheart. Aren't you happy to see me? I came all this way to take you home. I heard how awful things turned out for you here." He looked at her with pity before waving his hand. "I mean, attacked by vampires, Blaire… vampires. Bloodthirsty monsters! You can't stay here."

"They're not vampires," Blaire whispered.

Caleb started walking toward her, and she couldn't move. Her feet felt glued to the cobblestone. How did he know they weren't human?

"Besides, that thing doesn't want you, anyway. Come home where I can take care of you." He grinned again, and she shivered. "I promise things will be different."

"H-how?" Blaire stammered as he finally closed the distance and stood in front of her, looking down at her face.

"Well, for starters…"

He grabbed her, his grip tight on her upper arms as he pulled her against his body. She gasped and struggled in his hold, but he was stronger than she ever remembered him being.

"For starters, you won't be going anywhere. You won't be leaving the house again. No diner. No Charlotte. No academy. Only me. Only us," he hissed through gritted teeth.

"No…" She struggled to get away.

"Oh yes, my love."

Lightning split the sky again and thunder cracked immediately after, signaling the storm's arrival as the sky opened, releasing a torrent of rain, soaking them within seconds.

Caleb lay his head back and cackled maniacally. "It's time you experienced a real man, Blaire. No more playing with your silly little monsters."

He wrapped an arm around her in a vice-like grip, running a hand up her thigh beneath the edge of her skirt, making his way higher.

She thrashed in his hold, but he was solid and unmoving. "No!

Please!" she begged, as his hand slipped beneath her skirt entirely.

Lightning illuminated his sinister grin as thunder crashed again.

"No!" she screamed. "No, don't do this!" She couldn't fight him as she had before. He was too strong.

"Blaire..."

"Please don't do this!"

"Blaire!"

"Please!"

"BLAIRE!"

"No!"

Blaire bolted upright, screaming, and fighting against the hands that gripped her upper arms. "No! Let me go! Please don't do this!"

"Stop it, Blaire!"

Suddenly, she was hauled into a hard body, and the scent of spices, apples, and citrus met her nose. She immediately went limp, trembling in Lukas's hold as her brain caught up to reality.

"For fuck's sake... what happened?"

Blaire shook her head against his chest rapidly before reaching out and wrapping her arms around his back, clutching onto his body for dear life. "Please don't leave me," she whispered.

He stiffened for a moment before he clicked on her bedside lamp. Then he held her tighter, putting a hand on the back of her head as he cradled her in his arms.

"I'm not going anywhere. It's okay... it's over. Whatever it was, it's over."

Blaire was still trembling when thunder rumbled through their room and she gasped, her nails digging into his back.

He shifted and pulled her with him to lean against the wall, pulling her halfway into his lap. He buried his face in her hair as she clung to him.

She was a mess. Caleb had come for her. Only, he hadn't. Her dream had felt so real she couldn't calm down. Another flash and clap of thunder. The storm must have influenced her dream. She yelped and dug her nails into Lukas's flesh as she squeezed her eyes shut.

The only thing grounding her was Lukas's scent. Something about his scent comforted her. She turned her head into his chest and took a deep breath in through her nose.

Lukas cleared his throat. "Did you… did you just smell me?"

Gasping, Blaire pulled away, but he locked his arms tighter around her, refusing to release her.

"I-I-I'm sorry… I just…"

He stared at her, his eyes softening, but his face strained as he waited for her answer.

"You smell nice. I'm sorry."

Lukas closed his eyes and let out a quiet sigh before nodding and pulling her in close again. His heart thundered in her ear beneath his chest. His bare chest. Her face heated as she realized he only wore a pair of boxers.

The temperature of the room rose to scorching heights.

He whispered against her hair, "Do you want to talk about it?"

Blaire shook her head against his chest, her hands moving down his back slowly over his skin before slipping away as she shifted in his arms and put her hands in her lap. He didn't release her, but allowed her to sit sideways in his arms, resting her head against his chest. Despite his hard muscle, his skin was incredibly soft.

"Alright. You don't have to tell me anything…"

He acted so differently from how he'd been since she arrived. She didn't know what to make of the situation. She felt so much comfort with him like this.

"D-do you have any siblings?" she asked softly, hoping to take her mind off her dream, but still managed to focus on the sibling dynamic.

"No. Only me," he spoke against her hair. "What about you?"

"I…"

The question was stupid of her to ask, given it kept Caleb at the forefront of her mind.

"Just the stepbrother."

Lukas growled low in his throat, and she shivered.

"He wasn't always like this…"

"Don't make excuses for him."

"I'm not. He's horrible. I just… want to explain."

Lukas nodded tightly.

"When our parents married, he was a kind older brother. He was already attending Emory University in Atlanta at the time, but he always came home on the weekends and holidays. I guess without him being there all the time, it was easy for him to keep the mask on."

She shifted and Lukas stroked over her hair.

"When our parents died in a car accident shortly after I turned sixteen, he dropped out to take care of me. He had to finish college remotely. He inherited his job position, placing him in a cushy six-figure job before he was even finished with his degree, but I think he might have still resented me for taking away his life at school. Why else would he act like this?"

"Any other family? he asked, his voice strained and agitated sounding.

Blaire sighed against his skin. "Ah, no…"

"What about your real dad?"

She cleared her throat. "He died of a heart attack, but I was only three then, so I don't remember him."

"What about the rest of your family? Not your stepfamily…" He said the word as if it repulsed him. "…but your mother's and father's families?"

"Mom's parents died before I was born, and she didn't have any siblings, so there wasn't anyone. And Dad's family… well, when he married Mom, they disowned him."

"What? Why?"

"Apparently, they were extremely religious, and to them, Mom being agnostic was just as bad as waving a banner saying she worshiped Satan. They forbade their marriage. Dad chose Mom though, and they moved from North Carolina to Georgia before they had me."

Her parents wanted to start fresh, a new family tree. Now only Blaire remained. She didn't make for a convincing tree. No roots.

"The state tried to contact them when Mom died, but they wanted nothing to do with me. Called me the 'child of an unholy union,' like I was tainted. Can you believe that?"

"I'm sorry."

"Don't be. Everything happens for a reason, or whatever positive nonsense you're supposed to believe in."

Lukas's chuckle vibrated through his chest into her ear. She smiled. It was the first time she heard him laugh, and she liked the sound. It soothed her. She unconsciously shifted further into his hold. He tightened his arms around her.

She closed her eyes, focusing on his calm breathing and the slowing beat of rain against the window. "You?"

"What?"

"Family… do you have any family?"

"Oh… yeah, I do, but I never see them," he said, a note of discomfort in his voice.

"What do you mean?"

"My parents, Helena and Jyrki, travel a lot for business. I don't even know what they do; they have their hands in so many things.

They brought me to the academy when I was five, so I've basically grown up here. Aiden and Riley are my family."

She lifted her head and looked up at his face. "Yurrkey?" She frowned when she couldn't roll the r's the way Lukas had when he said the name. "I've never heard a name like that before."

"It's Finnish. I was born in Finland. My parents are Finnish, but I don't have the accent they do because I was raised here in America at the academy. Whatever accent I did have is gone."

"Wow, that's so cool. I couldn't imagine what it would be like to go to another country. My friend Charlotte is similar. She was adopted as a baby from Ireland."

She finally started to relax, and with relaxing came rambling, anything to distract her from the warm body holding her close and the low rumble of the passing storm outside.

The room stayed silent for a while. Anytime Blaire tried to move, Lukas subtly pulled her in further. He wasn't done holding her, protecting her again. She enjoyed getting to know him like this, enjoyed his company. Was this the something more beneath his prickly surface she'd seen glimpses of? If only he could stay this way; she could see herself really liking him.

He cleared his throat. "Favorite food."

"Huh?"

"I said, favorite food. What is it?"

She looked up at him. His cheeks looked a little red. He reached up and put his hand on her head, tucking her back against his chest to hide his embarrassment. She assumed he wasn't used to this sort of thing, so she couldn't leave him wavering. Not when he was trying to be nice.

"Oh, that's a hard one. I like a lot of things. I guess top contenders would be anything with shrimp, stuffed mushrooms, and different melons. What do you like?"

"Chicken and dumplings."

"Really?" Blaire giggled and shook her head.

He tensed. "What? What's wrong with that?"

"Oh, nothing at all. I just figured you'd give a 'guy' answer. Like steak or pork chops, not something specific. My mom used to make the best homemade chicken and dumplings when I was sick."

She missed her mom and wished she were here to guide her through the situation she found herself in. Though, if her mom were here, she wouldn't be in the situation. Caleb might've stayed a normal big brother figure. But then she wouldn't have met Lukas. Anxiety stirred inside at that realization, and her chest felt tight. It confused her.

Lukas nodded against her head. He still hadn't moved away.

"Favorite color," he whispered.

"Shades of blue to teal. You?"

"Black."

She snorted, and he leaned back, raising an eyebrow at her. She burst into laughter. "What? I'm sorry! That was totally a guy answer."

He sucked his teeth and rolled his eyes at her. "Whatever. Biggest fear?"

Blaire shook her head. He was trying to get to know her in a weird sort of way. She smiled to herself. "Spiders. And um… thunderstorms."

Lukas shifted again. "Yeah, I gathered that one."

"Your turn."

"No."

"Oh, that's not fair."

"Yeah, I know."

Blaire laughed and poked his chest with her finger. "That's not cool, not even a little bit. Why do I have to be vulnerable and not you?"

He tensed and grabbed her hand where her finger remained pressed against his chest. He held her hand for what felt like forever as he stared down into her eyes, until she turned her gaze away in embarrassment, her heart racing.

"Being alone forever."

Blaire snapped her eyes back to meet his as he released her hand, the unnatural green of his eyes glowing in the dim lamplight. Did he really say that? He feared being alone. She didn't know what to say, so she looked down at her hands in her lap.

Lukas cleared his throat and took a breath through his nose. "Alright, that's enough. I'm tired. You okay now?"

"Um, yeah… I'm okay," she whispered.

He finally released her from his arms and got up with a serious look on his face.

She shouldn't have tried to force him to answer that. They barely knew each other. She expected something silly like clowns, or spiders, or anything other than that heavy-weight answer. His retreat after sharing something that deep with her implied he wasn't being manipulative by saying it; it was a genuine fear. Her heart followed as he climbed under the covers of his bed with his back to her.

She crawled back up to the top of her bed, turned out the lamp, and pulled the covers over her body, hoping she didn't dream of Caleb again.

Thunder rumbled in the distance.

Blaire had gained ground with Lukas, and she wanted to know more. This moment, wrapped in a bubble all their own, left her warm and happy—secure. She hadn't felt that in a very long time. Maybe things would be different going forward.

15

CONFUSION

The next afternoon after classes, Blaire was sitting on her bed going through her guidebook when a knock sounded on the dorm door. She got up and walked across the floor as quietly as possible to not disturb Lukas, who lay fast asleep on his bed.

Opening the door, she found Riley waiting. "Hey! You almost ready?"

"Shh."

Blaire put a finger over her lips and motioned to where Lukas lay on his stomach, his face half buried in the pillow, his hair fanned out and covering part of his face.

Riley stepped inside, whispering, "What's wrong with him?"

"Nothing. I don't think, at least. He doesn't exactly tell me things, you know." Blaire shrugged. "He's just been doing a lot of sleeping lately during the day."

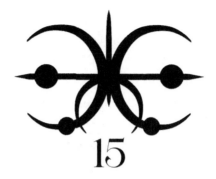

"Huh. Well, he didn't have a roommate before, so he might have napped like this before, and we never knew. Who knows?" Riley said with a half-shrug.

"After last night, I'm not surprised he's tired." Blaire sighed.

Riley perked up and looked at her. "Why? What happened? Oh, please tell me it's good."

"Oh, well, I just... had a nightmare... he helped me. That's all."

Riley frowned and looked at Blaire suspiciously.

"That's all, huh? Suuuure." She started laughing before marching over to the bed and shaking Lukas's back.

Lukas spun and grabbed Riley's arm.

"Hey!" she shouted, pulling away from him.

He let go and rolled over onto his back, rubbing a hand down his face. "Ugh. Don't do that."

"Me? How about you don't grab people who try to wake you up?" Riley narrowed her eyes at him.

He sat up and huffed a breath. "Sorry. I wasn't fully awake. I didn't mean anything by it. I'm just... tired."

Blaire sat on the edge of her bed, watching Lukas. His eyes held faint traces of darkness beneath them, and his movements had been dragging lately. The contrast worried her.

"What's wrong?" Riley said, sitting on Lukas's bed at his feet.

"Nothing."

"Dude. You know no one believes that, right?" Riley motioned to Blaire. "Right, Blaire?"

"Ah... um... yeah. You do look exhausted," Blaire said, looking down.

She wasn't sure commenting on his appearance or anything about him would be a smart move. She did her best not to provoke him. Since things had been going smoothly, and given his temper, it could be like flipping a light switch. Cold Lukas would come out to play. She figured the best strategy was to avoid pushing him and let him come to her, even if she didn't exactly want to at the same time. Professor Sinclair told her to give it time, but after last night, she longed for more.

Blaire worried about his fatigue, and she didn't know how to handle it; much like everything else related to Lukas. She itched to know more about him and desired him physically. Her dreams were not helping.

Lukas looked at Blaire, studying her. "I'm fine. I'll be fine." He swung his legs off the bed and put his socks and boots on before standing up. "Meet you for the movie later."

Saying nothing more, Lukas went to the door, and with one last glance in Blaire's direction, he exited the room.

"That was weird." Riley frowned at the door.

Blaire shrugged. "Seemed pretty normal to me."

Riley shook her head. "No, he's been acting all sorts of weird since you got here." She rushed to add, "It's not your fault or anything. I think he's probably struggling with the bond thing."

Blaire sighed and twirled the ends of her hair absentmindedly. She didn't know Lukas before, so she didn't know what he had been like. Before the school dumped her into his life, he was a different person. It made her curious how he was before. She wondered if her presence made things difficult. He ran hot and cold constantly. He was certainly different last night. She liked him like that. She wished he had stayed like that. But she'd only gotten bits of that before.

"So! We need to hurry up and get ready. The movie starts soon, and you're still in your uniform."

Riley had changed before arriving and sported a schoolgirl-style skirt in solid black with safety pins attached to the front. She wore a short-sleeved black t-shirt with the arrow cross logo for the band The

Pretty Reckless on the front, paired with a long-sleeved fishnet shirt worn underneath that she accented with several black and pink rubber bracelets. She still wore the same ripped fishnet stockings and buckled boots from earlier in the day.

Blaire went to her closet and grabbed a pair of slim-fitting jeans and a sheer, long-sleeved teal blouse with a tank top of the same color to wear underneath. As Blaire unzipped her skirt, Riley spoke to her from outside the closet.

"You know, you guys are really lucky..."

Blaire tossed her skirt into the small hamper in her closet. "What? Who's lucky?"

"You and Lukas." The 'duh' she didn't say came through clearly.

Yeah, Blaire didn't know where on Earth she would be considered lucky, and she was sure Lukas probably agreed with her. Sure, it was easy to tell they were attracted to each other, but neither of them was having an easy time with whatever this was between them.

"I mean, you guys are lucky to have found each other. I'd give anything to find my pair."

Blaire left the closet, pulled her long hair free from her shirt, and sat on the bed. "But you're only just the age where you might find your pair, right?"

"True... but it still doesn't mean I don't want it to happen already." Riley kicked her feet dangling above the floor. "Then there's Aiden. He doesn't have his pair either. He's in the same situation as Lukas... almost twenty and still without a life mate."

Blaire sighed as she slipped on her socks. "Yeah, I know... I feel bad for him because he seems like such a good guy. He shouldn't be alone." She got up and grabbed her brush off the nightstand to brush out her hair.

Riley watched her, her brows knitting together in confusion.

"How do you know about my brother?"

"Well, you mentioned it before the first time we had a movie night in his room, but we do share a lot of classes together, so we've had a chance to get closer, I guess." Blaire shrugged. "We've gotten to know each other."

Riley stared at Blaire like she'd grown a second head.

Blaire sighed and set the brush down before turning to face Riley. "Why can't we just have relationships the way we want, with who we want? Why does it need to be this fantastical 'soulmate' kind of deal?" She huffed out a breath, frustrated by the whole thing and the mixed-up emotions warring inside her.

Riley blinked, her mouth hanging open in shock. "How could you not want a soul—Wait a minute!" Riley shouted. "Do you like Aiden?"

Blaire winced and looked away. She was attracted to Aiden. But "like" in the way Riley implied felt like too strong a word to describe her feelings for him. Lukas, on the other hand…

"Holy…"

"He's a nice guy, but I barely know him." Blaire shrugged and tried to play it off. It wasn't a matter of liking him. Of course she would like him; he was a good guy. Kind, funny, and he protected her. He didn't make her feel inferior for being human, like she wondered if some students thought of her. He didn't look at her like something to eat. That didn't necessarily mean she wanted him as a romantic partner.

Blaire sat on the bed and pulled her knee-high boots over her jeans, zipping the sides.

"If I'm being totally honest, I had a feeling Aiden liked you from the start." Riley sighed. "But dude… I had no idea you might feel the same. Poor Lukas."

Blaire shook her head. "What? No. It's not that serious for either of us."

Riley laughed awkwardly. "Well… of course it's acceptable to form a relationship with a compatible partner, but it's never the same as finding your Korrena. Being paired is unlike any regular relationship someone could have. Most Vasirian don't go the route of a compatible partner because they hold out hope for their Korrena. Unless they really have strong feelings for someone, that is." She got a dreamy look on her face as she sat down again. "Once fully bonded, you can feel each other's emotions. Up until then, you can usually pick up on their feelings and sense things about them. Some have even been able to share thoughts. And the sex? It's amazing. Or… so I've been told. I don't have any experience with any of this." Riley shrugged. "Oh! And the blood of your Korrena? Well, that supposedly tastes like the best thing ever."

Blaire cringed at the mention of drinking blood. Then she crinkled her eyebrows at Riley. "Wait… Vasirian drink each other's blood?"

"Yeah." Riley's tone indicated this ought to be obvious.

Blaire rolled her eyes. "Me, human. You, Vasirian. I don't know this stuff, so don't 'duh' me."

"I didn't 'duh' you."

"You were thinking it."

Riley rolled her eyes. "Point. But yes, pairs exchange blood. But we don't just randomly drink each other's blood. Same with humans. We don't drink their blood aside from the medic packets supplied by clinics. Never from the source."

Blaire shuddered.

Riley got a serious look on her face, her features sad. "Do you feel anything at all for Lukas? I mean, it sounds like you want to be with my brother instead."

Blaire sighed.

"I… I am attracted to Lukas. A lot. Like, I can't describe how he makes me feel all over, and even my heart has started to respond to him when he's not running cold. When his actions say he cares. He just keeps doing things that confuse me. He stirs up my heart and then he turns around and throws me back into hell the next minute when he distances himself like he doesn't want me." She looked down at the floor. "Nothing makes sense."

Riley shook her head. "You told me yourself you haven't been able to be with anyone before. It's confusing. No one expects you to have the answers. I'm sure Lukas doesn't have the answers either. It's not like he's ever had a girlfriend."

Blaire blinked. That would explain a lot.

Riley cringed. "Forget I said that."

Blaire looked at Riley with confusion. "It feels like it's moving way too fast because any connection we've established is weak, but at the same time there's this… pull… I feel toward him deep within myself, and I'm not sure if I like it, because it feels like I'm not even in control of my own feelings anymore."

Riley sat with a hand over her mouth, staring at Blaire with widened eyes. She lowered her hand and shook her head. "It has to be the bond forming."

"I don't get how that's possible, considering we haven't done anything."

Riley shrugged. "I don't know how it all works, but something is there, and it seems like you both are fighting it, which honestly doesn't make a lick of sense when, if you guys would just let go, you'd be happy."

Blaire put a hand over her face, resting her elbow on her knee, mumbling quietly, "Is it even real?"

"What do you mean?"

"I mean, if we're both fighting it, then clearly these are not our true feelings." She frowned at Riley. "Lukas doesn't even know me. I don't know him." At least not enough to be in a relationship. But she didn't know. How much did you need to know someone to be with them if you liked them?

Riley looked down and sighed. "Just give it time… it'll work out. Somehow."

"Yeah, I don't see what you're seeing, apparently." Blaire stood to get ready to leave.

Riley shrugged. "It's not for me to say… but I wonder if he's fighting it because he feels resistance from you. I think you're fighting it because he's kept his distance. You both need to talk through this."

Blaire's forehead wrinkled as she looked at her in question.

Riley added as she crossed to the door and took hold of the handle, "And I think your trauma and humanity hold you back from accepting him."

Blaire stood still. Riley's bluntness surprised her. She didn't know if any of it was true, but it made sense. The idea of being with a Vasirian made her keep her distance, but that was the least of the concerns.

After everything she'd been through, she didn't allow herself to get close to people for worry about their connection to the Wilcox family, outside of Charlotte and her mothers, and definitely not the opposite sex in a way that broached the lines of friendship. Even before her mom died, before being forced to go to Magnolia Heights, she was too focused on sports to really pay attention to boys. And now, faced with a guy—a guy to whom she felt a growing attraction both mentally and physically—she didn't know what to do. Lukas hadn't hurt her or demanded things of her the way Caleb had, but it still didn't stop the intrusive thoughts from creeping in that he wouldn't do it if they got together. Caleb wasn't always a monster. Only when he had Blaire where he wanted her did his true colors come out. Would Lukas be the same? She needed to talk to Professor Sinclair about this at their next meeting.

"You coming?"

"Ah, yeah." Blaire went out the door with Riley following behind her.

She had a lot to consider. Her new friend's words replayed in her mind as they hurried to meet Aiden and Lukas.

16

Tension

The dampness from the rain that blanketed the area for the past two days left a chill in the air. Blaire regretted her outfit choice as they stood in the long ticket line at the theater in the cool breeze of the night. She couldn't remember the last time she had the opportunity to see a movie outside of the home, but it was nice. It gave her a sense of freedom she didn't have before starting at Blackthorn, but she still felt nervous. Could they really keep her safe outside of the academy walls?

"Hey… I'm going inside to use the bathroom before the movie starts," Aiden said, looking at Blaire. "Do you want me to get you anything from concession? I'm going to go ahead and get mine, and figured I could grab yours, too." He rubbed a hand over the back of his neck.

Riley shot Aiden a look as Blaire shook her head and put a hand on her forehead. "Dammit, I got distracted before leaving and forgot my purse. I'm not even going to be able to get a ticket."

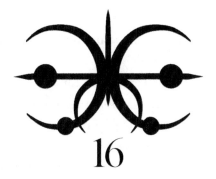

"I can take care of it, and your ticket. It's no problem. That's what I meant, anyway."

"Oh… um, I don't really want anything, but thanks," Blaire said with a smile.

Riley sighed and shook her head as Lukas glanced over at her.

"Alright, I'll meet you guys inside. I gotta piss. Can you grab my ticket for me?" Aiden asked Lukas, slipping him a handful of bills.

Lukas shrugged. "Yeah, I got it."

"Not the visual I wanted, bro…" Riley scrunched her nose up in disgust at her brother as Blaire laughed.

Aiden went into the theater as the line moved forward.

Blaire glanced back toward Valley Center Plaza, in the direction of the academy. She wasn't going to let Aiden pay for her ticket. "I don't have time to go back to get my purse, do I?" It would probably be ten minutes if she ran, another ten back. Not counting the time to get into the dorm to get her purse. No way she would make it.

Lukas stepped up behind Blaire. He stood so close to her that his body heat radiated through the sheer fabric of her shirt on her chilled skin. Leaning his head over her shoulder, he whispered into her ear, "I've got you too." His deep timbre reached deep inside her.

Blaire tensed, swallowing hard when his breath brushed against her cheek. Four simple words sent her stomach into a free fall. She let out a stuttered breath, closing her eyes. She had to calm down, but with his unique scent invading her senses, it proved a difficult task.

Riley nudged Blaire, snapping her out of her daze, oblivious to the swarm of murder hornets Lukas released inside her belly.

"I'm really excited about this movie. I've heard a lot of good things."

"How good can a slasher movie really be? Especially one so old," Lukas interjected, as he brushed past Blaire and stepped up to the counter to pay for their tickets.

Riley pouted and handed Lukas the money for hers. "Really good if they're doing a special feature on a busy night like tonight, thank you very much." She crossed her arms over her chest and stomped like a petulant child.

Lukas turned back with tickets in hand and rolled his eyes. "Right. Let's go."

Blaire tugged at the ends of her long hair as she followed them into the theater lobby as Aiden came back from the concession counter. Blaire hesitantly reached out and pulled on the sleeve of Lukas's leather jacket. He stopped and turned toward her, raising an eyebrow.

"You didn't have to do that."

"I know." He shrugged.

Blaire bit her lip. "Well… thanks."

Before Lukas could respond, Riley spoke up.

"I want to get some candy."

Lukas turned from Blaire. "Yeah, I want to grab a drink, too. Let's go." Lukas passed Aiden two tickets. "Here, we'll meet you both in the theater."

"Sure, man. We'll save your seats. C'mon." Aiden tipped his head toward the hallway leading to all the different theater rooms.

Blaire followed Aiden into the theater. The lights were turned down low, so it was difficult to see where to go, but she managed for the most part. Aiden found an empty row midway up and walked to the middle, sat down, and put his drink in the holder. Blaire took the seat beside him as she glanced around the theater, her nerves getting the better of her again now that she was away from Lukas. It wasn't very crowded, but she still wasn't going to risk separating herself from someone who could protect her.

"So, how terrible do you think this movie is going to be?" Aiden smiled at Blaire, oblivious to her apprehension.

Blaire rolled her eyes. "Come on… give it a chance, at least for Riley. Not big on horror movies?"

"Actually, I love them. I'm just not into hack-and-slash, gory murder fests. That's not real horror. The real horror is psychological stuff. You know, it's what you can't see in the shadows. That's the real terror. The creepy sounds. The implied monster, so you're left to imagine it."

Blaire sat back and thought for a moment. "Yeah, maybe."

"What? What's your favorite kind of movie?"

"I don't think I have a favorite. Never had the opportunity to see a lot of movies over the last couple of years, so I'm just happy to watch anything."

Aiden fell silent and clenched his jaw as the previews started to play. Blaire didn't know what she had said wrong. Before she got the chance to ask, Riley came up the aisle, rambling on and on about the nuances of how they got blood to look realistic in old cinema.

Riley plopped down in the seat next to Blaire before Lukas shook his head at her.

"Move."

"Oh, come on."

Lukas crossed his arms over his chest and stared down at her.

"Fiiiine. Grumpy pants." Riley got up and pushed past Lukas to take the next seat over.

Lukas sat next to Blaire and glanced over at her before putting his feet up on the back of the empty seat in front of him, lowering into his seat further, and said nothing as the previews continued.

Blaire clasped her hands together, annoyed at Lukas and grateful at the same time. She would have liked to sit by Riley and felt weird being next to Aiden now that Riley pointed out her attraction. But once Lukas claimed the seat next to her, she had stopped looking over her shoulder for Caleb's spies. At last, the lights went down further and plunged the theater into darkness.

Aiden leaned over and whispered, "Hey, if you decide you want something to drink, you can have some of mine. You don't have to ask."

Blaire nodded before relaxing back into her seat as the movie started.

The movie didn't hold Blaire's interest as much as she hoped, and she shifted restlessly. Maybe Riley didn't have the best choices in film, she thought to herself as the sound of squelching blood and breaking bones filled the theater. When one of the girls on screen got her leg crushed by the killer's trap, Blaire cringed and reached to grab Aiden's drink.

After taking a sip, she looked over to place the cup back and caught Aiden watching her lick the wetness from her lips, his face only half-lit by the screen. He visibly swallowed and the look on his face in the high contrast made Blaire nervous. He shifted in his seat and sat with his leg pressed against her thigh.

She tensed when Aiden made no move to shift away from her, realizing it wasn't accidental. He couldn't be serious. Blaire jerked her head back to look at the screen as she moved her leg away, rubbing her palm on her thigh. She couldn't see the movie, but she did her best to pretend.

Another woman screamed on the screen as the killer found her hiding in her closet and Blaire jumped, her heart beating fast in surprise. She then felt a gentle graze across her hand—a comforting gesture—and her heart rate kicked into overdrive. Aiden had his hand on hers. Willing herself to calm down, she bit down on her lower lip as Aiden slowly moved his hand away after dragging his fingertips to her wrist. The actions were simple, but her inexperience made her nervous and unsure of how to handle the situation.

Blaire glanced at Aiden, who stared at her with a hard expression before his eyes flickered past her. She tensed and slowly turned her gaze to meet Lukas's eyes. His brows were narrowed and his gaze searching, the muscle in his jaw jumping as he stared at her. The plastic water bottle crinkled in his hands from the tight grip he had on it. Her chest hurt from how hard her heart raced. The tightness made it hard to breathe.

Lukas opened his mouth to say something, but Blaire cut him off.

"I… I need to go to the bathroom," Blaire blurted as she stood abruptly and squeezed past Lukas and Riley, not daring to look back as she moved down the stairs of the theater.

Blaire splashed water on her face, putting her hands on the sink as she tried to calm down. She didn't understand what happened in the theater. Aiden wasn't just being friendly in there. Riley was right, or at least Blaire began to think so. Aiden sure acted as if he liked her. Had he shown the signs before, and she missed it? She had no idea if the time they spent together had meant more to him than friendship.

Sighing, she dried her face with a paper towel before heading out of the bathroom and stopping short with a gasp. Lukas stood across the hall, leaning on the wall with his foot propped on it, his arms folded over his chest. His eyes were cold as he glared at her. He hadn't looked at her that way since the first day when he tried to make her leave. She didn't like it.

Blaire looked around at the empty hall, and backed up into the bathroom, hoping that would be enough for her to avoid Lukas for the moment, because he looked pissed, and she wanted to give him the opportunity to calm down so she could talk to him. Apparently not, because he shook his head at her as if to tell her no and pushed off the wall, advancing toward her as she backed into the bathroom. He wasn't going to let her get away so easily. Whatever he was mad about clearly had to do with her, and she wasn't sure she was prepared to deal with it.

Looking from side to side, she backed inside the bathroom as he came toward her like a predator stalking its prey. The way he came toward her reminded her of the night Caleb took her to his bed. So much anger in his eyes. Her mouth went dry.

She quickly backed into a stall, and her hands shook as she grabbed for the door to shut it and lock him out, but Lukas moved faster than she did. He pushed his way inside the stall before she could engage the lock, forcing her into the back corner next to the toilet. He latched the stall door behind him.

Before she could figure out how to slip past him, he stepped to her, moving to press his body to hers the same way he had done in the courtyard, his intoxicating scent hijacking her senses, warring with her fear. Fear of what this Vasirian, who seemed thoroughly pissed at her, might do while they were alone. He didn't seem like the Lukas of the past few days. Even at his worst when they first met, he wasn't like this.

It wasn't just his body language or the look he gave her that spoke of his anger. On some level, she felt his anger. It wasn't something she could put into words; tension that wasn't there before she left the theater vibrated through her.

Blaire slowly put her shaking hands up against Lukas's chest to try to keep at least some distance between them.

Lukas stared down at her. "What the fuck was that all about in there?"

"W-what are you talking about?"

He scoffed. "Don't. I could feel the tension rolling off you in waves. I could hear your heart beating wildly."

Lukas clenched his jaw as he obviously struggled to keep his composure. What the hell was he talking about? Feel her? Hear her?

"Nothing was going on," Blaire blurted, desperate not to say the wrong thing.

"Don't lie to me."

"I'm not… I wasn't doing anything."

Lukas licked his lips, and she could have sworn she saw fangs when his lip pulled back.

"Then why were you so wound up?"

Blaire looked everywhere but at Lukas directly. "I don't know…" She didn't want to tell him about Aiden and cause a scene, or worse, ruin their fragile friendship.

Lukas hit the stall wall above Blaire's head with the side of his fist. She jumped and dropped her arms from his chest, pressing them against the wall at her sides. The sound was loud in the empty bathroom. Lukas covered her mouth with his hand as a woman entered the bathroom, stifling Blaire's yelp. She stared up at him with wide eyes.

Lukas placed a finger over his lips in a silent command.

The minutes stretched as they stared into each other's eyes. The tension between them ebbed gradually, and Lukas's facial muscles relaxed as he focused on her eyes. How was she able to feel him like this?

The woman's heels clicked on the floor further away as she exited the bathroom. Would Lukas get angry again? She began to tremble again.

He gently removed his hand from her mouth.

"Please don't hurt me…"

Lukas's eyes widened, and he stepped back, stricken.

"I would never hurt you," he whispered.

Blaire looked away from him.

"Please believe me." He reached toward her, but she flinched. Dropping his hand to his side, he clenched his fist. "I don't know what came over me… At first, I was confused by what I felt from you in the theater, but I saw the way he looked at you. I got jealous. It made me angry."

Blaire swallowed hard. "I didn't do anything wrong."

"No… you didn't. I messed up."

Blaire looked up into his eyes, and he ran a hand through his hair.

"You scared me."

"I know. I'm sorry… I wouldn't hurt you. I need you to know that."

Blaire sighed. "I…" Something in the emotions bleeding from him left no room for doubt that he spoke the truth. "You can't do that again. I can't handle that."

"I'm sorry."

Lukas stepped forward and Blaire didn't make a move to stop him. He stopped directly in front of her, and she looked up into his eyes. He caressed her face and she leaned into the touch. She needed the physical reassurance as much as he did. Another step and his body pressed against hers, and she didn't push him away.

After several minutes in each other's space, the tension faded away, and she shifted against him. Lukas closed his eyes. Her eyes widened as something hard pressed against her abdomen when she moved. She looked up into Lukas's eyes locked on her face, her breathing becoming heavier as her heart hammered in her chest. This nervousness wasn't like what she felt in the theater. Blaire tingled all over.

He leaned forward, pressing his forehead against hers. He lingered so close his labored breathing brushed her lips, the sweet smell of theater candy on his breath.

Lukas lifted his head and looked down into her eyes before leaning in to close the distance. He was going to kiss her, and she wouldn't stop him this time. She didn't want to stop him. Her heart raced. Her entire body screamed for him, every place where he pressed against her on fire.

Just as his lips were about to connect with hers, Riley's voice rang out in the bathroom as she entered. "Yo, Blaire! You okay in here?"

Lukas quickly stepped back, the look in his eyes strained. He mouthed for her to "Go" before unlatching the door, stepping to the side, and allowing Blaire to leave.

Disappointment settled heavily in her stomach, and how easily she responded to him embarrassed her. She tripped over herself as she rushed from the stall to get away before she embarrassed herself further by mauling Lukas in a bathroom stall.

Blaire had never felt anything like that before for a man, and it scared her. The intense longing for his touch, drowning in the spicy apple scent that drove her senses mad. Was this what it felt like to desire a man? Like, physically desire a real man and not some book boyfriend she could conjure up fake scenarios for in her head? It certainly felt different from her dreams of Lukas, as much frightening as it was exhilarating.

"What's wrong? Everything okay?" Riley said when she rounded the corner.

"Oh no, I'm fine. I just had to pee really badly."

"Are you sure? You're really red."

"Yeah…" Blaire cleared her throat. "I'm just a little hot."

Riley shrugged. "Alright. You were just gone for a while and Lukas also left, and now the movie's over. You guys totally missed the ending."

"It's okay. Honestly, the blood and guts were a little too much for me." Blaire cringed as they exited the bathroom.

"You're as bad as my brother. Can't handle a little gore. I wonder where Lukas went…"

Blaire shrugged as they stopped in the hallway.

"Maybe he's in the bathroom too," Riley said. "Aiden said he'd meet us outside, so let's go wait there. Lukas will figure out where we are."

Blaire glanced back at the woman's bathroom as they walked away. Lukas stepped to the doorway before they rounded the corner to the lobby, and a shiver went through her body when their eyes met. His eyes were glowing dimly.

They exited the theater to find Aiden standing out past the ticket line. A few minutes later, Lukas stepped out to join them. They walked back toward campus in silence. Blaire kept her focus on the ground, not wanting to make eye contact with Aiden or Lukas. She didn't know if she could handle it. She felt confused and her heart hurt when she thought about it.

Stretching, Riley said, "That movie was actually a lot better than I expected." No one said anything, so she pouted. "Oh, come on, you all didn't see the way that security guard at the camp was acting from the start?"

"Y-yeah… he did seem suspicious," Blaire said with a forced laugh.

She honestly hadn't paid much attention to the movie, so she had no idea. With the way things happened in that theater, and the way Lukas responded, she suspected neither Lukas nor Aiden watched much of the movie either. The entire night had been a failure. She would have done better to stay at the academy than have this night of "freedom."

The walk back to the academy cleared her mind. One of the perks of being only a few minutes away from the plaza was being able to walk and take in the scenery, but at night, it became peaceful and quiet. The scent of magnolias as they approached the main courtyard calmed her.

Lukas didn't speak to anyone, just continued to walk toward the dorm.

"What's Grumpy McGrump Pants's problem?" Riley watched Lukas leave.

Aiden shrugged. "He's always grumpy." His phone dinged, and he checked it.

Riley peeked over his shoulder. "Seth?"

"Yeah, I texted him on the walk over. He's gonna come and play video games."

"Well, whatever." Riley yawned. "I'm wiped. I'll see you tomorrow, Blaire." She waved, before skipping off in the direction of her dorm building. She literally skipped.

Blaire turned and looked at Aiden standing with a hand in his pocket, running the other through his messy hair, watching her. He ran his tongue over his lower lip.

"So… goodnight then," Blaire said, trying to ignore the look he gave her.

"Yeah… goodnight." Aiden cleared his throat and rubbed the back of his neck. "Sweet dreams."

They both turned away toward their separate dorm buildings. She had no idea how to deal with this recent development between them. She needed to tell Aiden she had feelings for Lukas, but Aiden was such a good guy. He wasn't running hot and cold like one particular Vasirian she knew. She liked him as a friend, but she felt guilty, even upset, at even entertaining the idea of something more with Aiden.

She found the door to their room locked, and since she forgot her purse, she didn't have her key with her. Great. She tried knocking and calling out to Lukas, but he didn't answer. She didn't have a cell phone, and if she did, she didn't have his number, anyway. She sighed and sank to the floor next to the door. Maybe he hadn't come back yet. Maybe he went to the canteen first for a late-night snack …or blood bag. She wrinkled her nose.

When ten minutes passed and she still hadn't seen or heard a sound, she decided to give up. He locked her out. He was probably still pissed about their confrontation earlier and was taking it out on her. Had everything he said after he calmed down been a lie? It hadn't felt that way.

She decided to visit the administration building to see if someone was around to give her a spare key.

This night just kept getting better.

17

AIDEN

Blaire stalked out of the dorm building, cursing Lukas.

The audacity in him getting angry with her at the movies over whatever nonsense about what he claimed he could feel, or hear, made absolutely no sense to her. Sure, she felt something too, but none of it made sense. Regardless, what reason did he have to be angry over that, anyway? Was it because of Aiden? There wasn't anything going on between them. Well, no. There was something there, but it wasn't like they were together or anything. She didn't do anything to encourage it.

Blaire glanced around nervously. The courtyard was so dark with the moon barely peeking out from behind the cloud cover, and none of the outside lights lit the area she passed through. Crickets chirped in the surrounding flower beds as she hurried along. The wind whipped her hair around her face, and a chill went down her spine as she recalled her nightmare.

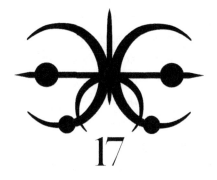

She stopped short as she stared at the statue that guarded the entrance to the hedge maze. The gaping black maw of the entryway looked so ominous at night when she couldn't see anything beyond the statue. She gulped and took off, sprinting across the main courtyard to get as far away from that place as possible, the memories of Aryan's teeth coming toward her flashing in her mind.

Not paying attention to where she was going, she collided with someone small and soft. She screamed at the same time as a high-pitched yelp came from the other person. Reflexively, she reached out to catch them and saw it was Riley as she stumbled backward.

"Ouch. What are you doing out here?"

"Lukas. What are you doing here?"

Riley tilted her head and lifted the mesh bag in her hand. "Snacks! But hold up. What's going on with Lukas?"

"That asshole locked me out of the dorm because, like usual, he's pissed at me. I need a key from administration." Blaire crossed her arms to ward off the chill from the wind.

Riley shifted from foot to foot, her pink fuzzy slippers drawing Blaire's attention. She stood dressed in black pajama pants with little skulls with pink bows on their heads all over them and a solid black pullover.

"I thought he stopped with the asshole moves?"

"Yeah, me too..."

"But I'm sorry. You're outta luck. The administration and staff building, where the housing department is located, are both closed for the night."

Blaire stared at her, dumbfounded, and sighed in frustration. "Well, that's just peachy. What am I going to do now?"

This night kept getting better and better.

"Well duh. You're going to stay with me." Riley smiled brightly. "Actually... let's go bug my brother."

Blaire squinted at Riley. "You just want to see Seth."

Riley looked affronted.

Blaire laughed, her mood lightening. "Sure… I mean, what else can I do?"

Once they reached Aiden's room, Riley banged on the door and the door swung open. Seth stood in the doorway in a pair of black sweatpants and a white t-shirt.

"Not going to sleep already, are you?" Riley said, pushing her way inside.

Seth stepped back and narrowed his eyes at her. "No… why are you here?"

"Can't a little sister visit her big brother? Oh. And I brought Blaire."

Blaire stepped into the room. Aiden jumped up from the bed.

"I thought you were going to bed," he said quietly.

"Lukas locked her out."

"What?" Aiden and Seth said in unison, looking at Riley.

Aiden crossed his arms, moving his gaze back to Blaire. "Why did he do that?"

Blaire shrugged. "He's pissed at me."

Riley flopped down on the spare bed and began digging through her bag of snacks. "We figured since she couldn't get a key from the staff building, we'd come hang out with you for a while before going back to my room."

"Is that so?" Aiden lifted a black brow at Riley. He glanced at Seth, who stood there staring at Riley, and then he chuckled. "Whatever. We were just playing video games, anyway."

"Awesome. I'll watch," Riley said.

Blaire moved to sit on the spare bed, and Riley held a pack of gummy bears out to her. Blaire shook her head. She had lost her appetite.

They sat watching Seth and Aiden battle it out on the flat screen, throwing insults and laughing for an hour before the sound of soft snoring grabbed Blaire's attention. Riley had fallen asleep next to her on the bed.

Seth looked over and snorted a laugh. "Yeah, I'm tired too." He stood and stretched. "I'll catch you later, man."

Once he left the room, Aiden looked over at Blaire.

"I'll wake her up and we'll go."

Before Blaire could shake Riley awake, Aiden stopped her. "Want to just crash here? You guys can take that bed."

Blaire already felt like she was inconveniencing Riley. Waking her up and making her go to her room half asleep would just make her feel worse. She nodded.

"Yeah, that's fine."

Aiden rubbed the back of his neck. "Want to play some games before I put everything away?"

"Sure."

"Let me get you something to sleep in first."

Blaire stood up and watched as Aiden went into his closet. A few video games and sleeping with Riley seemed innocent enough. This steered things back into friendship, and it felt right. This was where their relationship should be. Aiden returned with a folded t-shirt and boxers.

"They'll at least fit better than anything else I have," he said with a sheepish grin, rubbing at the back of his neck. He did that a lot. Her conditioning to interpret body language wondered what it was a tell for.

"It's okay. This will work fine. Thank you."

Blaire retreated into the bathroom to change into the clothes which still swallowed her up. She came out to find Aiden sitting on the edge of his bed, already changed into a pair of basketball shorts and a t-shirt.

Blaire had to roll down the waist of the boxers a few times, so they stayed up easier. This, in turn, exposed the large, still fairly dark bruise on her thigh. The other spots were nearly healed, but the large bruise was still an ugly sight. She glanced up and caught Aiden staring at her legs and froze.

She'd forgotten all about the bruises when she agreed to wear the boxers. She'd become relaxed about them since Lukas had already seen them and Riley knew. She knew Aiden knew about Caleb, but he hadn't seen the evidence. It likely would take a while for the larger bruise to heal. At least the finger marks were fading. Caleb messed her up that night.

Blaire shifted uncomfortably under his hard stare.

"Your brother did this, didn't he?" Aiden asked before she could say anything.

Blaire sighed.

"*Step*brother, but yeah, it's his doing."

He bit the side of his lip before getting up and moving over to Blaire, lowering to his knees in front of her. She tensed. She'd only let Lukas get this close to her bruises. Having Aiden scrutinizing her legs made her want to step away. She knew he wouldn't hurt her, but she didn't enjoy being this exposed to him. She didn't feel this way with Lukas.

"I'm sorry this happened to you..."

She folded her arms and lifted her chin. "I'm not. It's proof I fought back."

Aiden blinked up at her. He wouldn't understand.

In a twisted way, the bruises were battle scars that symbolized survival. She couldn't allow herself to fall prey to a helpless victim's mentality, becoming someone who gave in and accepted something she didn't want. She accepted she was a victim of cruel circumstances, but she wasn't going to accept it as the end all be all for her life. That mindset didn't stop the shame and anguish from creeping in when she least expected it.

"It still shouldn't have happened..."

Aiden slowly reached out toward her thigh, making contact with the larger bruise before lightly touching over the smaller ones, shifting his attention to the finger marks. His light touch and gaze raked over the offending marks as if he were in awe of the wounds her body carried. His soft touch lulled her into relaxing. The familiarity of being around him when he'd always looked out for her made it easier to let go of the tension she felt.

Aiden brushed his fingertips over the large bruise once more with a little too much pressure, and she gasped, snapping out of the relaxed state she'd been in.

Now she backed away from him. She didn't want to be seen like this. She spent months keeping this dirty secret, and now it was all out in the open for yet another person to see. The shame washed over her, and she began to cry.

"No..." Aiden whispered as he stood up from the floor.

He took her hand and guided her over to his bed, where he sat down and patted the bed beside him. "Sit with me. Please?"

She hesitated only a moment before sitting next to him. He slid back until his back met the wall and he held an arm out. Blaire moved back until she sat against him, and he put his arm around her shoulder. Aiden reached over and turned the lamp off. She was thankful for the discretion the darkness gave her. Being in the dark calmed her. Her bruises weren't on display any longer. Her shame was hidden.

They sat in silence in the dark. The only sound in the warm space was Blaire's soft sobbing as everything building within her lately came pouring out.

After a while, her cries tapered off and she quietened completely, only the sounds of her uneven breathing remained. She tensed when she realized how close to Aiden she sat. His embrace had been innocent, but something didn't feel right about it. Knowing he liked her made cuddling feel wrong.

Pulling herself from his arms, Blaire sat up and pulled her knees to her chest.

"Listen…" Aiden cleared his throat. "If you and Lukas really don't want to be together… that's, well, that's okay. Like we told you… No one is going to force either of you to complete the pairing."

Blaire bit her lower lip as she stared across the room at Riley sleeping on the spare bed as a sliver of moonlight passed through the window. She wasn't sure where he was going with this, and she was too tired to decipher it.

Sighing, he said, "I mean, Lukas is my best friend and all, so I would never dream of interfering if you both wanted to be together, but with him locking you out, and the weird tension… Well, I just can't seem to feel guilty in saying I have feelings for you."

Blaire jerked her head around to stare at him in the moonlight, her eyes widening only a fraction. It wasn't as if she didn't know he liked her, but at the same time, hearing confirmation of it straight from the source shocked her.

"Blaire… I want to be with you," he whispered.

She swallowed hard, remaining silent. Her heart skipped and pounded.

Aiden leaned forward, reaching up with his hand to lightly cup her jaw, then he pressed his lips against hers in a soft kiss, before going in once more for something deeper.

Blaire had been kissed before when she was younger. This felt different. The tingles she expected to feel when someone kissed her were there, but she felt something much more intense earlier tonight with someone she had never kissed. The contrast intrigued her.

When she didn't push him away, he slowly guided her down until she lay on her back. He hovered over her body as he continued to kiss her deeply. A soft sound left her throat as she returned his kiss, testing how it felt to allow herself to be kissed by someone she felt attracted to. She wouldn't lie to herself; it felt nice. When his tongue slid across her lips, she turned her head away. She wasn't ready for that.

Despite how good his kisses felt, something was missing, something important. Her thoughts warred inside, and dread washed over her.

Aiden kissed along her jawline when she turned her head, undeterred, and she sucked in a breath as he pressed his body against hers, allowing her to feel the physical evidence of his interest.

This was too much, way too much, and with the wrong person.

Blaire's mind became a jumbled mess, but one alarm bell clanged clearly inside; this was wrong, and she had to stop it before it got out of hand.

Aiden moved to her neck, where his lips parted, but before he could do anything more, she placed her hands against his chest and shoved against him. She didn't want to hurt him, but she needed to be clear about her refusal. He was much stronger than her, but she had put enough force into the push to make him take notice and sit back. He hung his head back, face aimed at the ceiling, and closed his eyes.

Blaire couldn't do this to Lukas. She felt guilty at the idea of leaving him and being with Aiden.

After taking a moment, when he seemed to finally have himself together, Aiden opened his eyes to stare down at Blaire. He found what he was looking for in her eyes and nodded in confirmation at her resolve, acknowledging the wall she had erected.

"I'm sorry… I thought you…"

Blaire shook her head. "I did… but I can't. Lukas…"

He moved across the bed and sat on the edge, whispering, "It's alright, just sleep now. I understand. I'm not going to try anything again if you don't have feelings for me. I'll back off."

Blaire hung her head and twirled the ends of her hair. "It's… It's not that. It's complicated." She didn't say anything more as she climbed off his bed and crossed the room to get into the bed with Riley.

Aiden clenched his jaw. "Of course it's complicated. He's my best friend. He's your Korrena." He sighed and then whispered, though Blaire could still hear him from her place next to Riley, "I knew it wasn't going to be easy if you chose me, but at the same time, I was willing to try."

She could say nothing to that. Apologizing would be insulting when an attraction existed between them. He knew it, she knew it. But she couldn't stop how she felt overall.

She couldn't help that something was missing.

Someone was missing.

That was the problem. She couldn't shake how guilty she felt about even considering Aiden's proposal with her growing feelings toward Lukas. But she didn't understand what had happened with him tonight. She needed to talk to Lukas.

18

CONFRONTATION

After saying her goodbyes to Riley, Blaire went to the floor where she shared a dorm room with Lukas. She didn't look forward to confronting him about locking her out after she thought they'd come to an understanding last night, but he needed to know that move wasn't okay. At least she'd had the opportunity to calm down and wasn't going into the conversation angry anymore. But she still didn't want to deal with fighting with Lukas right now with her feelings all over the place.

Blaire tried the handle, and it opened without resistance. Lukas must have left it unlocked for her when he left for breakfast. Maybe this was a good sign he'd also calmed down.

Entering the dorm, Blaire found the main room empty. A small rush of relief swept through her. Sighing, she gathered a change of clothes and headed to the bathroom to take a much-needed shower.

As she reached for the doorknob, the bathroom door opened, and Lukas stood in the doorway. Blaire recoiled, stepping back a couple of steps.

Lukas glared at her and stepped forward as she clutched her clothes to her chest tightly.

"Where have you been all night?" he demanded.

Blaire backed away further. He hadn't calmed down at all. In fact, he loomed, sounding as upset as he had at the theater. Even without the physical cues—narrowed eyes, clenching fists, tight jaw—she could sense his tension rising. Is this what he meant when he said he could feel her? She hugged the clothes tightly, as if they could protect her.

Lukas looked exhausted. The heavy dark circles beneath his eyes made it clear he didn't sleep last night. He didn't stop coming toward her despite the fear sweeping over her. If he really could feel her, then he would know, right? Why would he still be like this?

Maybe he didn't care, after all. She snapped at him, "If you hadn't locked me out, I would've been right here in the dorm!"

Lukas clenched his teeth and stepped forward, backing her until her legs bumped the side of his bed as she clutched the clothes in her arms like a shield.

"I didn't lock you out," Lukas grated out through clenched teeth.

"B-but… the door was locked, and you didn't answer!"

He sighed and fisted a hand through his hair, studying her before speaking in a calmer tone. "Where were you?"

Blaire turned her head away to stare at the window in a clear refusal to answer. She could tell him, but why should she roll over and tell him what he wanted when he behaved this way?

Fed up, and clearly not in control of himself, Lukas grabbed her upper arms. She gasped. Instead of hurting her, as she feared for a brief moment, he surprised her by pulling her down to sit on the edge of the bed, falling to his knees between her legs. He looked up into her eyes with clear desperation on his face. He looked tired.

Her chest tightened in a way she couldn't explain, and she didn't like it. The look on Lukas's face made it hurt worse. Could this be his feelings? He wasn't angry, but this feeling she could only describe as uncertainty and anxiety felt so much worse. She had this overwhelming urge to soothe it.

She sighed and looked down at her lap. "Because no one was around in administration to give me a key, I stayed in Aiden's room."

Lukas's grip tightened on her arms as he growled under his breath, forcing his next words out. "Why did you go to him for help and not someone like Riley?"

Blaire sucked in a breath. "I ran into Riley in the courtyard, and she offered me a place to stay. She wanted to go see Aiden and Seth first, though. She ended up falling asleep, and instead of waking her, I joined her on Aiden's spare bed after Seth left."

Lukas stood abruptly and paced the room before stopping and turning to her quickly. "I'm really starting to think you want him."

Blaire tensed, clutching the clothes in her arms. Where had that come from? How did he get that from what she said?

"I've seen the way he looks at you. I can feel the way you respond to him, and it needs to stop right now." He growled out the last word.

Oh no, no way was she going to be bossed around like this. She didn't escape her stepbrother and his control, only to find herself in another controlling situation with someone else she was supposed to be with. Not happening. This was exactly the kind of thing Professor Sinclair worked with her to get past. If she was ever going to consider anything with Lukas, she had to make her boundaries crystal clear, because he obviously didn't see them if he thought acting this way was okay.

Blaire stood, tossed her clothes aside, and put her hands on her hips. "Where do you get the nerve to tell me who I can or can't be with?"

Lukas glared at her. "Seriously?" He marched right up to her, getting in her face. "You are my Korrena. You're only here because of me, and no one else!"

Blaire scoffed and rolled her eyes, which made Lukas turn and resume pacing, his agitation rising more. His alpha behavior was really pissing her off.

"You know, Riley told me relationships can be formed outside of the pairing," she said matter-of-factly, crossing her arms. She waved a hand. "Even Aiden said it was okay for us not to be together if we didn't want to be."

Lukas stopped, turning abruptly to stare at her with his mouth hanging open in disbelief.

Blaire didn't pay him any attention as she added, "And since you clearly don't want me, and Aiden has made it clear he does, you can just stay the hell out of my life!"

Lukas raised his voice to shout at her. "Just because your precious Aiden says it's okay, doesn't mean it fucking is, and you are mine, so you can get the idea of being with Aiden out of your pretty little head."

Blaire blinked at him in momentary shock. "Well, what if I've already been with him? What then, huh?" Lost in the heat of the moment, she winced the second the words left her mouth. She shouldn't have said that. Instead of helping the situation, it only served to provoke Lukas.

He lunged at her, putting his hands on her shoulders, taking her down onto his bed. He straddled her waist, staring down at her, breathing heavily.

Blaire stared up at him with wide eyes. Waves of anger rolled off him.

"Tell me what you meant by that." His cold tone matched the daggers he stared at her.

Blaire looked away from him, turning her head to the side on his pillow, and muttered, "I'm done with this..."

She was exhausted. So fed up with his hot and cold attitude. Sure, she couldn't accept Aiden, but that didn't mean she should accept this. This wasn't what a relationship should be. This was abusive. Controlling. She had never seen Lukas like this, but if this was a prelude to his real self now that she grew closer to him? She didn't want it. She closed her eyes.

Lukas leaned down into her hair behind her ear, breathing in her scent, then growled low under his breath. She could tell he fought to keep himself together, but she couldn't bring herself to help him. She was too tired.

"I smell him on you... he's all over you."

Blaire tensed beneath him, and he growled again.

"I only thought it was because you were in his room, but... I'm starting to think otherwise. Your responses, your heart... tells me another story."

He buried his nose in her hair, breathing her in once more, before lifting his head to stare down at her again.

"Now tell me, what did you two do?" he asked, his voice eerily calm.

Blaire's cheeks heated, which sent the anger radiating from Lukas even higher. In the same moment, he jerked her back to face him with a hand on her chin, not enough to hurt, but with force.

"Did you allow him to drink your blood?" he said through clenched teeth.

"Absolutely not! I'm a human! I don't want anyone drinking my blood." She shivered. "It's weird… and the idea honestly scares the shit out of me."

Lukas took a steadying breath. He calmed when she mentioned fear.

He stared down at her, a look of pain in his eyes. "Did you… did you have sex with him?"

"No… we didn't," Blaire whispered.

Lukas gripped the pillow beside her head tightly, his impatience apparent the longer he went without finding the answers he sought. Clearly, he suspected something happened, but she didn't understand how she gave that away.

"Fuck. Did he touch you in any way, Blaire?"

She pulled her face away from him, unable to look at him any longer. She couldn't tell him what had happened. They weren't together, but she still felt guilty. She also didn't want to get in the middle of their friendship. They'd been friends since they were children.

"We just… he comforted me because I was upset," she said quietly, figuring that while it wasn't the whole truth, it was still the truth.

"Oh, really?" Lukas looked at her incredulously. "He just happened to be a shoulder to cry on?"

"Exactly. He put his arm around me and let me cry."

"Is that all that happened between you two? And why were you upset?" A flicker of concern crossed his face.

Blaire stared at the wall.

Lukas gritted his teeth. "Did he see your body… or did he touch your body?"

"Nothing sexual happened," she whispered.

"Tell me what the fuck happened then, because I'm getting really tired of this run-around game you're playing."

She remained silent, not knowing how to deal with this anymore, just wanting to check out and go somewhere else. He was giving her the third degree the way Caleb did anytime Ricky let him know some guy at the diner had tried to get to know her. This was getting ridiculous.

Lukas put his hand on her chin and pulled her gently to look at him again. He slowly caressed his fingers over her jaw and down the side of her throat, stopping to trace his thumb over the pulse point that beat erratically before pulling his hand away, staring at her lips. He clenched his jaw and then he asked the one question she had hoped he wouldn't ask.

"Did he kiss you?"

Blaire's eyes widened for only a fraction of a second, but it was all the confirmation Lukas needed.

He growled and pinned her hands on each side of her head, leaning toward her.

"You said you wouldn't hurt me," she reminded him quickly.

Lukas froze, released her hands, and then dragged a hand through his hair, though he didn't get off her. "And I meant that."

"What do you think this is? Do you think acting like this makes me feel safe?"

They stared at one another in silence and several emotions passed over Lukas's face before he exhaled heavily.

"You are safe." His conviction stared back at her in his pale green eyes. "I just..." He stared at her mouth. "I need to erase it..."

Lukas leaned down again, his movements slow, and Blaire could have pushed him away if she wanted to. He gently brushed his lips over hers, hesitant and uncertain. When she didn't stop him, he pressed into the kiss.

Blaire saw stars.

This. This was what had been missing from Aiden's kiss.

Her body melted beneath his as she returned his kiss eagerly, whimpering against his soft lips. Lukas shuddered against her body, taking what he wanted from her and leaving no question that this was a kiss meant to claim, to show her who she truly belonged to. She did belong to him. She'd felt it building for a while, and with each layer she peeled back, she found she only wanted more of him.

Her body sparked instantly alive with Lukas's spicy apple scent filling her nose, creating an intoxicating haze in her mind. She had no idea kissing Lukas could feel this good. His kisses tasted like honey, and she didn't want to stop tasting him.

He reached up and interlaced his fingers through her hands that still rested on the pillow. She squeezed his hands as he pressed into her, his arousal evident as it pressed against her thigh, and instead of feeling uneasy like before with Aiden, desire pooled at her core. The feeling was scary, but maddening.

Lukas licked over her lips slowly in a silent request for access, and she opened to him without hesitation. He slipped his tongue into her mouth, caressing hers as he explored, laying his claim, groaning into her mouth. A thirst she didn't know she suffered was quenched, and she moaned into the feeling.

He broke the kiss and stared down at her panting face, his pupils blown wide with desire.

"You're mine, Blaire. I will never let you go."

Blaire stared up at him, trying to catch her breath. She had never wanted anyone this badly in her life. A wildfire raged deep inside her body that she couldn't put out. He spoke the truth. This single kiss confirmed everything for her.

After staring down at her in silence for an eternity, an eternity where her eyes begged him to kiss her again, he climbed off her and left the room, slamming the door behind him.

Blaire lay there as her breathing began to relax and she put her hands over her face, trying to get her body to calm down. She didn't know if she wanted to laugh, cry, or scream. What was she going to do? There was no way she could ignore this thing between them, but his attitude made it so hard. They hadn't even talked about what happened. He said he didn't lock her out, so why couldn't she get into the room?

She turned over and buried her face into the pillow, which smelled strongly of Lukas; his scent started to relax her. She sighed.

Lukas didn't have to say any of that. She already knew she belonged to him.

19

Want

After thirty minutes spent roaming the academy grounds trying to cool off the intense urge to claim Blaire, Lukas returned to the dorm room and opened the door, not sure if he could handle another confrontation. He felt certain if Blaire looked at him with those same lust-filled eyes, he would take her then and there and nothing would be able to stop him. He would not take her like that. He wanted Blaire to give herself to him when she wanted him completely, without being clouded only with physical urges. He wanted it to be real in the way he wanted her. He needed her heart, not just her body, but if she had kissed Aiden, then he didn't know how much of her heart belonged to him, and it made him uneasy.

Lukas barely made it out of the room earlier when she was pinned beneath him, her desire raging around them, her heart beating rapidly. He shuddered as he stepped into the room and stopped.

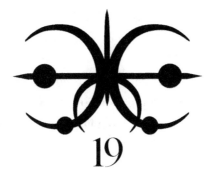

Blaire was lying on his bed on her side, clutching his pillow in her arms, her face buried in it. He had no idea what that meant, but he didn't dare disturb her. He sat on the floor at the foot of the bed, running a hand over his face before there was a knock on the door.

"Come in," he muttered quietly, only loud enough that whoever was there could hear him.

The door opened. Mera entered the room before Riley shoved past her as Lukas looked up from his position on the floor.

"What the hell happened last night? Why did you lock Blaire out?" Riley demanded loudly.

He clenched his teeth and glared at her. "Either get out, shut the hell up, or lower your voice."

Riley noticed Blaire lying on his bed and raised her eyebrow. "What's she doing on your bed?"

Lukas rubbed his face again and sighed. "I got upset with how close Aiden and Blaire have become..."

Mera asked, "What's that have to do w—"

Riley cut her off, mocking playfully, "Aw, are you jealous?"

Lukas growled at her. "It's so much more than that. Aiden said he wanted to be with Blaire and I... I can tell Blaire has had a physical response to him."

Mera leaned against the wall, observing the conversation in silence as Riley argued with him.

"Why don't you just let her go, then? Isn't that what you wanted?"

Lukas squeezed his fists tightly as he shook his head. He couldn't understand why everyone was convinced he didn't want Blaire. Sure, he had been an asshole and tried to run her off at first, but they had connected since then, he thought. If only everyone knew what was happening inside him. She was tearing him apart. Blaire came into his life and caught him completely off guard, and he didn't know how to handle it constructively at all. Professor Velastra had been trying to help him. Trying to explain to him why his emotions were all over the place because of the bond, but it still didn't help him know how to deal with it.

He closed his eyes and put his head in his hands, muttering, "I'm losing her… I don't want to lose her… It's all just so confusing. It's not like that at all. It's not what I wanted at all." He looked up at Riley. "I can't let her go. I feel connected to her in ways I can't explain, and the mere idea of losing her causes me physical pain, and I don't understand any of it."

Mera spoke up quietly, "It's your bond taking root. It's the reason you feel these things, and it's only going to get worse."

Lukas raked a hand through his hair. He didn't know if he could handle more. He barely held on as it was and if his control snapped, then what?

"If you don't complete the bond, it is only going to continue to negatively impact you, and it's likely causing the same issues for Blaire," Mera said, motioning to Blaire, who clung tightly to his pillow but looked to be asleep.

That got his attention, and Lukas looked up at Mera with a furrowed brow. He didn't like the idea that Blaire could be experiencing even half of what he did. This wasn't something he would wish on anyone, especially her. It was bad enough he sensed her emotions at times. Whenever he sensed her fear, like earlier, and at the movies, it broke him inside. This was why he needed her heart to be in it. He couldn't claim her in a moment of fear just because their bodies were ready. He wouldn't do that to her. To himself. He wanted that moment to be something special.

"Do you not remember anything from the Korrena education classes? If you don't get a grip on this, you're going to hurt her. One way or another," Mera said calmly.

Lukas shrugged lightly.

Every year, from the age of ten through the end of high school, students took a mandatory course in learning about what the Korrena was. How the bond worked. The marking. Everything. But all the textbook information and lectures could never have prepared him for the emotional and physical experience.

"I don't want to hurt her..."

Riley rolled her eyes. "Well, duh. We all know that. But you're going around acting like you're withdrawing from some sort of drug."

He glared at her before hanging his head back against the bed, staring at the ceiling.

"Does she know you won't hurt her?" Mera asked.

"I told her I wouldn't... but I... I put my hands on her," he admitted quietly.

Riley stomped her foot in protest and before she could lash out at him like he could see coming, he raised a hand to stop her, sitting up and assuring her, "I have never hit Blaire or anything like that... it's just that I've been more forceful in the way I've touched her. Moved her. She just... has this way of getting under my skin, and I lose all reason."

Lukas ran a hand through his hair again and chewed the inside of his cheek for a moment before shaking his head. "I don't want it to be that way. It's not who I am."

Both Mera and Riley nodded before Riley said, "We know that, but she doesn't." She pointed at Blaire.

He hung his head back against the bed again and stared at the ceiling. "None of it matters, anyway. Blaire doesn't want me. She wants Aiden."

"The only reason Blaire isn't with you is because of you, and no one else," Riley said, raising her voice again. "You've done nothing but push her away since she arrived, despite telling everyone you acknowledged her as your Korrena. You're an idiot if you haven't noticed the way Blaire looks at you. I'm not even bonded to her, and I can tell something is there."

Lukas stared at her, not sure what to even say to any of that. They didn't know what went on between him and Blaire. They could only go on what they saw when they were all together, and most of those times Lukas had kept his distance from Blaire and kept the conversation short. Feeling utterly defeated and uncertain, he could only go on what little scraps Blaire gave him, or the words his friends shared, but it wasn't enough. He was tired of holding back. It apparently pushed Blaire away, anyway.

"Sure," Riley continued. "Blaire might be attracted to my brother, but any attachment there is likely from her seeking comfort because of feeling rejected by you. It's not a surprise, honestly, considering how much time they've spent together."

"They do share several general education classes," Mera added.

Lukas frowned and added, sounding childish to his own ears, "I do too, though."

Riley glared at him. "Yeah, and you spend the entire time sulking and never bothering to engage with her unless it's to be a smartass or scare the living daylights out of her. Besides, Aiden also spends time with Blaire in the cafeteria and on campus, even when they don't have to be together. Do you, Lukas? Do you go out of your way to be around her, or are you going out of your way to avoid her?"

Lukas opened his mouth to respond, but Riley held her hand up.

"No, I already know the answer. Blaire already told me you avoid her."

He looked down at the floor, surprised to hear Blaire had complained about him avoiding her. He didn't think she cared to be around him because of what he was. Though thinking about it, it was a stupid thought to have if she was willing to be near Aiden and the others, and they were the same as him. But he had stopped avoiding her a while back. When had she told Riley that?

"Oh, and let's not forget, Aiden also looks out for her. And before you say you do too, know when he does it, he doesn't treat her like an eyesore, or like it's a chore to do anything for her or with her," Riley added, staring Lukas down. "He respects her."

Mera reached out and touched Riley's arm. "I think he's had enough."

"No. No, he hasn't. It's about time he hears this, because the way he's going, he really is going to lose Blaire, and I for one don't want to see her go. I like her, and want her to be happy, even if it's not with him," Riley said with tears in her eyes. "You either need to truly walk away and let Blaire be happy, even if it's with someone else—"

Lukas growled.

She rolled her eyes. "—or grow a backbone and man up, because that poor girl has gone through hell, and she doesn't deserve this." She huffed out a breath after her rant and crossed her arms.

Mera put a hand on her shoulder. "Lukas…" she said calmly. "Have you ever been intimate in any way with Blaire? I'm very curious about how your bond is progressing the way it is despite the distance you so clearly place between the two of you."

Lukas glanced away with a grimace, which caused both girls to quickly sit down on Blaire's bed, Riley bouncing out of her skin with excitement, forgetting all her frustration as she exclaimed loudly, "Details! Like, yesterday!"

Lukas rolled his eyes and sighed.

Before he could say anything, Blaire shifted in response to Riley's loud exclamation, her brows pinching together. He watched as she took a deep inhale of his pillow, her features instantly relaxing as she settled with a soft breath. When he turned his gaze back to Mera and Riley, they were staring at him. Mera had a hint of a smile on her face.

Not about to get into the details about Blaire smelling him and his things all the time, he said, "We haven't been together, but I have kissed her… but that didn't happen until today. I held her the night before last, after she had a nightmare during the thunderstorm." He shrugged. "There's also that time I touched her bruises."

Mera shook her head. "No… something more has to have happened between you two, because the only way to progress the bond is for the pair to both become emotionally connected, which you obviously have not with the way you argue—or at least you haven't grown enough emotionally for the kind of raw reactions we are witnessing, so clearly the only logical conclusion would be that you both are growing in physical intimacy."

"Do you mean sex?" Riley asked, sounding way too interested.

Mera nodded. "If not intercourse, then some other form of sexual contact to bring about this strong of a change."

Lukas ran a hand down his face. "No. Nothing like that."

Riley had been right. Lukas had made an effort to get to know Blaire, but it wasn't enough. He didn't seek her out; he only connected with her if the opportunity presented itself. He needed to make more of an effort. It wasn't that he didn't want to. He wanted to spend all his time with her. But if he were honest with himself, he still felt afraid. Afraid of being hurt. Of rejection.

The only constant over the years had been Aiden and Riley. His parents were never around. Business came first. He was an afterthought. He faced the same rejection from Blaire. So far, she was only near him because she had to be because of their Korrena bond. He wanted her to want him for him. No, he needed that desperately.

Mera shook her head. "Then I don't know. Perhaps her being

human is playing into the strengthening bond, but it's clear it's still unstable."

Blaire stirred again on the bed, getting his attention.

Blaire sat up and looked around, confused for a moment, before realizing she was still in Lukas's bed. She blushed before stammering, deflecting from her current situation, "W-what are you two doing here?"

Riley glared at Lukas. "I wanted to see how you were doing today. See if you were able to get back into your room."

Lukas growled. Blaire stared at him.

"I didn't lock her out on purpose," he grated out. "The latch was probably still turned, and it must have slid into place when I closed the door last night before I went to take a shower and didn't hear her try to get in."

Riley rolled her eyes, clearly not convinced, but he told the truth, so he wasn't about to argue the point. What's done is done.

"Anyway, we're all going to the diner in town if you guys want to join us for dinner," Riley said.

Blaire immediately perked up. "I've only had some chips since before we went to the movies yesterday, and I'm starving."

Lukas frowned. He didn't know she had skipped dinner.

Riley smiled at Blaire. "You seem happy."

"Oh... um..." Blaire blushed. "I'm just excited about the idea of seeing my friend Charlotte and letting her know how things are going for me. I haven't contacted her since I got here like I told her I would. I mean, all things considered... I didn't know what to say to her. She's probably worried sick."

Riley looked at Lukas, still with a slightly sour look on her face. "So, you coming too?"

He sighed. "Yeah, I'm going." He couldn't reject something that would make Blaire happy.

Blaire climbed off the bed. "I still have to get ready because I haven't had a shower or changed clothes since yesterday, and I feel gross."

Riley laughed as Blaire rushed to the bathroom.

"We'll just be over at Aiden's dorm, waiting. Meet us when you both are ready," Riley said as she and Mera left the room.

Lukas went to the closet and tossed his t-shirt into the clothes hamper, pulling a black long-sleeved Henley over his head, before pushing the sleeves halfway up his forearms. He raked his hands through his hair, finger-combing the strands down before going to the nightstand, grabbing his leather bracelets, and putting them on.

The bathroom door opened as he turned around and his heart stopped. Blaire stepped out of the bathroom wrapped in a fluffy towel, beads of water still running over her shoulders from her wet hair.

She startled and started to stammer. "I-I didn't know you were still here. I thought you left with the girls."

Lukas didn't say anything, just stared at her until she rushed to the side of the bed where her change of clothes lay discarded to grab them up. He moved out of her way as she brushed past him, retreating inside the bathroom and re-engaging the lock. He sighed.

When she came out of the bathroom dressed in a pair of jeans and a black tank top, he took a step toward her.

"Have I scared you away?" he asked in a gentle tone. The vulnerability in his question made him uncomfortable.

Blaire paused in the process of pulling on a short-sleeved cardigan and stared at him.

"No… but you did scare me."

"I messed up," he whispered.

"You said that before."

"I know. It needs repeating... I was jealous. I am jealous. I can tell how much Aiden wants you, and I... do you really want to be with him?"

Lukas swallowed around the tightness in his throat. If Blaire told him she wanted to be with Aiden, he'd let her go. It would kill him, but he would do whatever was necessary for her to be happy and secure. If she didn't feel that with him, he wouldn't force her into the bond. He would face his biggest fear head on and accept reality.

Blaire gaped at him, her mouth opening and closing before she exhaled sharply. "No, Lukas. I don't want to be with him. I'm attracted to him."

Lukas growled until she frowned at him.

"But he's not who I want."

Lukas couldn't stop the smile that overtook his face. If her words implied what he thought they did, he had a chance after all.

Blaire stared at him, surprise in her widened eyes. "You're smiling..."

"I smile."

"Not like *that*." Blaire waved a hand at his face as if he could see his own expression.

Lukas shrugged and picked up another bracelet from the nightstand.

Blaire entered the closet and grabbed her shoes. When she returned, her expression clouded with an emotion Lukas didn't recognize, and an unfamiliar sensation passed through him. She didn't meet his eyes, and her lips were pressed into a tight line.

"Blaire?"

She sighed. "I kissed him back."

Lukas dropped the bracelet he'd been holding.

"Before you get all growly..." Blaire held a hand up. "I haven't had a boyfriend before. I've only been kissed once in my life during a game of Truth or Dare when I was twelve. Hardly something to write home about. I needed to know."

"Know what?" Lukas's voice sounded weak to his own ears. He didn't enjoy listening to her admission, but she needed this.

"I needed to know if it was just physical attraction, and if I would feel anything more."

"And?" He couldn't keep the hope from bleeding into his tone.

"And nothing. The kiss felt nice. But that's it. It wasn't right. It wasn't like…"

Lukas tensed when her gaze fell to his mouth.

He crossed the room in a few steps and reached out, wrapping his arms around her, pulling her close. She relaxed into his hold. They fit together perfectly. The smell of her shampoo filled his nose, and he closed his eyes, resting his forehead against hers.

"Blaire…" he whispered her name, his breath fanning over her face.

She shivered, and his heart insisted that no way could he let her go.

Lukas tightened his hold around her waist with one arm and trailed his fingertips up her arm with the other, watching goose bumps rise on her pale skin. He took a stuttered breath as his fangs descended in response to her rapid heartbeat, knowing she responded to him too, that she preferred his kiss. He hadn't lost her completely. The urge to taste her railed strongly inside him, the beast inside wanting free. He'd never wanted to bite anyone before.

He willed himself to calm down before Blaire spotted his fangs.

When she looked up into his eyes, she gasped, and he closed his eyes, knowing what she saw.

"I won't hurt you…"

"Then why?"

"I don't know. It's not conscious. I just feel this need." He pulled away from her and crossed the room to put distance between them. "I won't act on it. You don't have to be afraid."

"I'm not," Blaire whispered softly.

Lukas took a breath to steady himself and grabbed his leather jacket off the back of the desk chair.

He needed to get out of this room filled with her scent.

20

CALEB

Lukas decided not to confront Aiden about things yet. He wasn't in the mood for any more conflict after everything that happened with Blaire. With Riley raking him over the coals, he was glad to get off campus, and Blaire's excitement about seeing her friend again eased his heart. They walked into town together. Riley chattering away between Blaire and Aiden, while Mera and Kai walked behind them holding hands. Lukas trailed them as he tried to sort his thoughts.

Riley rubbed her flat stomach. "I'm staaaarving. I'm going to throw down on some cheese fries and a milkshake."

Lukas wondered where she put all the food she consumed.

"Oh yeah," Riley said as they entered the diner. "There's this new store that opened up in the Valley Center Plaza this week I wanna check out. I want you to go with me."

"Sure, I—" Blaire started.

"Blaire!" A small red-headed girl ran and collided with Blaire, taking her into a tight hug and looking up at her. "Why haven't you called me? I've been so worried!" Her voice broke at the end.

"Whoa, dude…" Riley laughed in surprise.

Blaire smiled down at her friend and shook her head. "I'm sorry. I've just been so busy. I don't have a phone still, and I haven't had the opportunity to call from the office. Things have been kind of chaotic."

Lukas could feel the guilt bubble inside her as she made excuses. He couldn't blame her for not reaching out. What would she tell the girl? She couldn't exactly tell her what they were. It wouldn't be easy to explain how chaotic her life had become; he had a hard time explaining it to himself, and he was part of it.

"Charlotte, this is Riley, Mera, Kai, Aiden, and…" Blaire glanced at Lukas, their eyes meeting before she bit her lower lip. Lukas's eyes tracked the movement. She released her lip and snapped her gaze back to Charlotte. "Lukas," she said quickly.

"Hi! I looove your earrings." Riley reached out and flicked the bat earrings dangling from Charlotte's ears.

Charlotte smiled. "Thanks." She tucked a red curl that had fallen from her pinned-up hair behind her ear. "I can show you to your table, but I assume it'll be the usual one?"

"Usual one?" Blaire asked.

"Yeah, we come all the time and sit in the big booth in the corner," Riley said.

Wouldn't Blaire have seen them before? Lukas didn't remember her working when they came to the diner in the past except that one day, which he found strange, since Professor Velastra told him Blaire worked as much as she could to save money to leave the Valley.

Charlotte said, "They're usually here on the later shifts when you're not working, oddly enough."

"Yeah… I've seen Blackthorn students before during the day, but unless Ricky needed me for a double, I always made sure to be home not long after school." Blaire glanced at Riley.

"Well, isn't that interesting?" Kai leered at Lukas. "So many opportunities to meet, and it never worked out until the right moment."

Lukas rolled his eyes as Charlotte looked at Kai, her brows drawing together, clearly not understanding. Thankfully, she didn't question him as she led the group to their table.

The cook gave Blaire the stink eye from behind the counter before disappearing into the back. Apparently, her boss wasn't happy about her leaving.

Mera and Kai slid into the booth on the right side, far enough to where Aiden could sit on the outside, while Riley climbed into the left side, moving to sit next to Mera in the middle. Blaire scooted in next to Riley, and Lukas sat on the outside across from Aiden. Charlotte took their drink order and went back to the counter.

"Hey, have we ever met her before?" Aiden asked as he glanced toward the counter with a serious expression.

Mera glanced Charlotte's way and shook her head. "She's served us before, but we've never met formally, no."

Aiden's brows knitted together as if in deep contemplation.

"What's wrong?" Blaire asked.

Aiden returned his attention to the table and smiled at Blaire. "Nothing. She just seems familiar. I probably just remember her from another time we've been here."

Lukas cleared his throat, and Aiden glanced at his irritated expression, his smile fading. Before anything could be said, Charlotte returned, setting the tray on the table, and passed out everyone's drinks.

She smiled. "So, Blaire, tell me what it's like."

Blaire blinked at her. "What what's like?"

Charlotte passed a strawberry milkshake to Riley. "You know, the academy. Don't hold out on me. Is it as amazing as it looks?"

"It's..." Blaire glanced around at everyone at the table. "It's beautiful there. They have a lot of sweet-smelling trees and flower beds. A hedge maze. It's a peaceful-looking environment, but it's like most universities with dorms."

"Do you have a roommate in your dorm, or is it private?" Charlotte asked, passing Aiden a Cherry Coke.

Riley choked on her milkshake.

Blaire blushed, glancing at Lukas briefly before clearing her throat. "I do..."

Lukas could tell she had trouble addressing it, but he didn't understand why. There wasn't anything wrong with them sharing a room. Before Blaire could say more, the owner called from across the diner, ordering Charlotte back to work.

Charlotte rolled her eyes. "So, what would you guys like to eat?" She held up her notepad and pen to show Ricky she was doing her job as she muttered, "Hard ass."

Aiden chuckled and Kai grinned as everyone gave her their food orders, and then she disappeared back into the kitchen.

"She seems nice," Riley said as she devoured her milkshake.

Blaire sighed. "I'm really sorry. I didn't know what I was allowed to say or not say."

"Don't worry about it." Lukas sipped his water. "It's fine if she knows it's coed dorms."

Riley shrugged. "Yeah, it's not a big deal. There are coed dorms in plenty of human universities. ...I think?"

"No... it's definitely weird." Blaire chuckled.

"How so?" Kai asked.

Blaire looked at him. "Well, even coed dorms aren't shared. Men and women don't share dorm rooms or bathrooms. Actually, while they might be in the same building, some universities don't even allow them to share the same floor."

Riley gaped at her. "That's weird. I mean, if you're not a pair, sure... but it's not like we have to be separate. I'm sure we could request to room with a friend."

Blaire laughed. "Well, it's not like humans have this weird magical marking and a fated mates sort of thing. That sort of thing is weird to us. And if you can just put in a request like that, your rules are definitely looser than ours. Human parents and administration tend to frown on that sort of thing. They think we'll be in each other's pants the moment they leave us alone together."

Kai cleared his throat.

Mera asked with a serious expression, "There's nothing wrong with that, but don't you humans have any self-control?"

Blaire stared at her. "You're serious?"

"Of course."

Blaire laughed again, and the sound warmed Lukas's heart.

"We have self-control, sure. Some less than others, but generally human parents—especially in the South—frown upon premarital sex."

"What a strange culture..." Kai mused.

The gang chatted amongst themselves until the bells above the front door on the other end of the diner jingled, and Blaire glanced up.

Aiden looked concerned. "Blaire? Hey, Blaire."

She didn't respond but moved closer to Lukas, catching him off-guard until he picked up on her racing heart and the fear radiating off her. It made his stomach turn. Her face had lost all color.

"Blaire..." Lukas whispered as he placed a hand on top of her trembling hands on the table, but he still didn't get a response. She didn't even pull away from him. He followed her gaze to the newcomer in the diner.

Riley waved a hand in front of Blaire's face. "Hey, Blaire… you're scaring me." When Blaire didn't respond to her concern, Riley looked over at Mera and Kai. "What's wrong with her?"

"I don't know," Mera said softly.

"She's shak—" Kai's words were cut off by a low growl coming from Lukas.

Everyone stopped and followed Lukas's line of sight to the entrance of the diner, where a man in a suit, who looked not much older than they did, stood watching them with a grin on his face.

"Caleb!" Charlotte called as she rushed over to him. "What are you doing here this time of evening? Aren't you usually at work?" Caleb turned his attention to her, and Lukas couldn't hear what he said.

Riley turned back to look at Blaire. "Oh gods, is that Caleb the stepbrother?"

Aiden whipped his head back around to look at Riley and then Blaire.

Blaire burrowed closer to Lukas and buried her face in his hair. He wrapped his arms around her shaking body to comfort her. She took a deep breath, smelling him again like she had after her nightmare. Grounding herself.

Holding her tightly, Lukas whispered against the top of Blaire's head so only she could hear, "I've got you… you're safe. I won't let him hurt you."

She relaxed further into his body at his words, which soothed his heart.

Riley jerked in her seat and pushed up. "Move," she barked.

Aiden shook his head and gave Riley a reprimanding look. "Sit down. You can't cause a scene here."

"I just want to talk to him."

Her face twisted into an angry sneer Lukas had never seen on her before. He didn't blame her. If it weren't for the overwhelming need to comfort Blaire, he'd have already dragged the piece of trash out the door and disposed of him.

Lukas returned his attention to the stepbrother at the same moment Caleb finished talking to Charlotte and looked back at the group again, glaring when his eyes landed on Blaire in Lukas's arms. He headed their way and Aiden abruptly stood, ready to intercept him, but before Caleb could even take a few steps, his cell phone rang, and he answered it.

"Wilcox, here. Yeah, yeah. I'll be there shortly."

Caleb turned to leave, then paused, glancing back over his shoulder.

"I'll see you later, Blaire. You need to come home soon. My bed is awfully cold without you." He laughed as he left the diner, the bells banging against the door signaling his departure.

Suddenly, Lukas choked as the force of Blaire's fear ramped up tenfold and slammed into him. She gripped his shirt, her nails digging into his stomach as her body shook. Caleb's words had sent her into a deeper panic, and Lukas could barely breathe.

He put his lips against the top of her head and held her close. "Shh, he's gone. I promise I won't let him hurt you." He had to stay calm and collected for her sake when all he wanted to do was go and rip her stepbrother's head off.

Aiden jumped up and started to chase after him, but Kai pulled him back to sit down.

"Stop. You just told your sister to not make a scene. Blaire clearly needs us right now. We need to figure out what's going on and why she's so upset."

Kai and Mera didn't know. They weren't there when Riley told Lukas and Aiden what happened to Blaire at the hands of her stepbrother. Lukas didn't even know the stepbrother's name until now.

"Fuck!" Aiden slammed his fist on the table and Blaire jumped.

Lukas tightened his hold on her body to anchor her. "It's okay…" he whispered before glaring at Aiden.

Aiden ran a hand through his hair. "Sorry…"

They sat in silence until Charlotte showed up with their food.

"I am so, so sorry, Blaire. I didn't know he was coming. If I'd noticed him sooner, I would have warned you. Ricky must have called him."

Blaire turned her head against Lukas's chest, calmer, before sitting up enough to reach out and distract herself by playing with her fries. She stayed plastered to Lukas's side, and he kept an arm securely around her waist.

He sensed on a deep level she needed him, but even if she didn't, he would still be there.

"It's not your fault," she said softly, finally acknowledging everyone for the first time since Caleb had arrived. "I'm not surprised Ricky called him. He always tracked me through Ricky."

Riley asked, "Why would he show up here like that? Is he really that obsessed?"

"Oh, he's obsessed alright," Charlotte said, her words dripping with disgust. Ricky called her name, and she sighed, giving Blaire another apologetic look before moving to another table.

Kai glanced over his shoulder, and then back to the table. "Who is this Caleb even?"

Riley sighed. "Blaire's stepbrother. A piece of trash who beats Blaire up when she doesn't give him her money, act the way he wants her to, dress the way he wants, or basically anything he deems 'unacceptable.'" She air-quoted the last word with a sneer. "He's a disgusting pig of a molester, and I want to rip his throat out." She stabbed her fries into ketchup.

Lukas hit the table, causing Blaire to jump again and pull away from him. He pulled her back into his body as he glared at Riley. "What the fuck do you mean 'molester'? You sure as shit didn't mention that before."

Blaire's eyes watered, and she tried to pull away from Lukas again, but he wouldn't let her go, so she stayed silent, looking down at the table.

"Shit. He hasn't like… raped her." Riley looked around awkwardly, clearing her throat. "But he's… he's done other—"

"Stop!" Aiden said loudly. "We get the picture."

"I… fought back. I didn't let him." Blaire met Riley's eyes with determination on her face. "I couldn't just let him." She swallowed audibly. "Maybe that's why he'd never gone that far…"

Lukas looked ready to commit murder as he spoke harshly, glaring at Riley. "Maybe some of that shit should have been kept to yourself."

Blaire shook her head quickly. "It's alright at this point… you're all my friends."

Mera smiled at Blaire and Kai cleared his throat, looking like he wasn't sure how to respond to something like that.

Blaire spoke up softly. "He's… wanted us to be more than siblings from the start."

"Wait, he touched you as a small child?" Kai said, looking horrified. It was a strange expression to see on his face, as he usually maintained such a calm and collected demeanor.

Blaire immediately shook her head. "No, we didn't meet until I was fifteen, and I didn't know about his feelings for me until later, after our parents died when I was sixteen. He was a normal stepbrother before then. He never touched me that way until a few months before I came to Blackthorn, but he told me he had always wanted me to be his. That's why he spent the last couple of years trying to mold me into what he wanted, he said."

Blaire swallowed hard and twirled a fry in her ketchup, not picking it up to eat it, just occupying her trembling hands.

"He criticized how I dressed, the way I acted… who I talked to…" She sighed. "When I turned seventeen, he became physically abusive… I had to start wearing makeup to cover what he left on my face if I stepped out of line." Blaire glanced over at Lukas, her eyes filling with tears again before she looked away. "On really bad days… the days I would refuse his…"—she swallowed hard—"advances… he would lock me in the basement. That's why I hate storms."

"What does that have to do with storms?" Kai said, arching a brow.

"The first time he locked me in the basement, was the first time I refused to sleep with him. He left me there all weekend while he went out of town on business. A string of severe thunderstorms came through the Valley that weekend and it stormed all weekend long. The power eventually went out and the lightning flashes were my only source of light for two days through a tiny window near the ceiling of the basement." She shrugged lightly. "Even during the day, it was too dark because of the storm to get much light in the basement." She sighed. "Caleb believes I was brought into the family for him to eventually marry and have children with."

That gem dropped a bomb into the pit of Lukas's soul. He pulled Blaire tightly against his body, afraid that if he let go, she would float away. She didn't fight him this time, settling in against him for comfort.

"I will kill him if he ever touches you again," Lukas said through gritted teeth.

"I'm sorry..." Riley shook her head. "I meant what I said. You won't ever be alone again. Whatever it takes. You won't have to be with him again." She sat back in her seat with a heavy sigh. "Gods. You must think this is the same thing."

Blaire looked up at Riley. "What do you mean?"

"Well... you were technically brought to the academy to be bonded to Lukas. It's similar...don't you think?"

Lukas flinched and loosened his grip on Blaire. She sat up and stared at the table in silence. No one said anything for the longest time until Blaire cleared her throat and looked up to meet Riley's eyes.

"It's different. I mean, you all have said I have a choice. I don't have to be with Lukas. If I really wanted, I could go talk to Professor Velastra about my contract. But I want to be at Blackthorn. Maybe the reason I ended up there was underhanded, but I've moved past that. I have friends. I have..." She glanced at Lukas and his heart raced. "It's different," she whispered as she looked back at Riley. She finally dropped the fry she had been playing with. "I just... I want to go home." Blaire stared up at Lukas as if asking him for permission.

Lukas swallowed and nodded at her. The feeling she needed him was something he had to get used to. While exhilarating, it made him nervous. Could he be what she needed? His heart hurt to know the cause of it.

Mera said quietly, "We should get out of here in case her stepbrother ends his business early and returns to finish whatever he intended from the start."

Aiden stood and pulled his wallet out of his back pocket. "I've got the bill."

Riley glared back at the front door. "Let the bastard come back. I'll rip his throat out."

Blaire tensed against Lukas, and he immediately stood, pulling her up from the booth into his arms as Riley slid out behind them.

Charlotte came over, and Blaire hugged her before wiping her eyes.

"I'm sorry, Blaire…" Charlotte whispered.

Blaire shook her head. "Stop. It's fine. It's not your fault. You know he does whatever he wants. If anyone is to blame for him being here, it's Ricky."

She glared at the kitchen as Ricky stared at her with his arms crossed over his chest. He snorted in disgust in their direction.

"I promise I'll try to keep in touch, but maybe we'll have to meet elsewhere, because I can't risk seeing Caleb again. I just can't come back here, okay?"

Charlotte nodded quickly. "Yeah, of course. I don't blame you."

Lukas took Blaire's hand and led her from the diner as Aiden paid. The group walked in silence back to the academy.

21

Bonding

The next afternoon, the dorm room door flew open, then Blaire slammed the door behind her and stepped into the room. Lukas sat up on his bed, alert, taking in his roommate's wide eyes and heavy breathing.

"What happened?"

Blaire's wild gaze darted to the door, then back to him. "I know Riley said it happens, but seeing it was something else entirely."

Lukas slid to the edge of the bed and raised his brow. "What are you talking about?"

Blaire dropped a small bulky bag on the bed and let out a heavy breath. "They were drinking each other's blood."

Lukas had no idea what Blaire was talking about, but sensing her panic made him uneasy, and he needed to do something to help her. "Who was drinking blood?"

"I don't know!" She threw up her hands. "I was coming back from the canteen after a meeting about switching my math courses with

Professor Hidaka, and I saw two students in the hall making out."

"Okaaay..."

Blaire dug around beneath her bed and pulled out a thick leather binder with worn edges and dropped it on her bed.

"So, that's not really that strange. People kiss."

She glanced at him briefly, and her cheeks were tinged pink. "But when they heard me approaching, this girl lifted her head, and she had blood running down her chin."

Lukas hummed knowingly. "A pair, then."

"I guess. Riley said pairs drink each other's blood."

"They do..."

Blaire's full body shuddered, and he sighed. He hated how difficult it was going to be to get past that hurdle with her. But with Blaire being human, he accepted the long road ahead.

She kicked off her loafers and dropped down on the bed, crossing her feet beneath her as she sat on the comforter and dug through her bag. She pulled out a couple of chocolate bars, a package of M&M's, and a bottle of peach tea.

"Sweet tooth?" Lukas said with a smirk.

Blaire looked over at him and shrugged. "I dunno. I haven't eaten much recently, and I'm craving chocolate." She opened the worn binder in front of her, revealing several photographs on the pages.

He shrugged. "Nothing wrong with that."

After a brief pause, Blaire held up one of the chocolate bars. "Want some?"

Lukas stood from the bed and crossed to her side of the room, taking the chocolate bar from her outstretched hand. Their fingers grazed as he took it from her. He opened the wrapper and took a bite, looking down at the photos absorbing Blaire's attention.

"Who's that?"

Blaire looked up at him and swallowed the mouthful of M&M's. "Who?"

Lukas leaned down and pointed to a group of three girls in soccer uniforms. It was obvious the girl in the middle was a younger version of Blaire, probably a preteen. He smiled; she was cute with lopsided pigtails and stickers on her cheeks.

"Oh. Just some old friends from middle school."

She slid over on the bed, and he took it as an invitation to sit down next to her.

"And this one?" Lukas sat down beside her and pointed to a picture with Blaire holding a small trophy, standing between a man and a woman he already knew was her mother from the picture she kept by her bed. She'd told him as much before. But he didn't know the man. It couldn't be her real father; she was a teenager in the photo. Stepfather, maybe?

"My old track coach, Mr. Cooper, and Mom. I won second place in the eight-hundred-meter middle-distance competition."

"Impressive." He didn't know much about track and field but placing in a sports competition was worthy of praise.

Blaire smiled and looked back at the photo.

Her pulse had calmed from the hallway incident, but when she flipped the page, the tension in the room increased. He looked down at the photos on the new page, searching for what could make her react that way.

"What's wrong?" he asked quietly.

Blaire sighed. "I don't know how I'd never seen it before…"

Blaire tapped a photo of her and a younger version of her stepbrother. Lukas growled under his breath. They stood together, and she was smiling brightly at the camera. Caleb's arm was tight around her shoulders, and he looked down at her. He also smiled, but it was obvious he wasn't looking at her in a way a brother would look at a sister. Aiden never looked at Riley the way Caleb looked at Blaire in that photo.

"You said you're an only child… had you not had the chance to be around others with siblings?"

"No. Not as a teenager. I lost most of my friends when I transferred to Magnolia Heights my senior year, except Charlotte, because we worked together, and she's an only child."

"That explains a lot."

Blaire leaned toward Lukas the way she had at the diner yesterday, and he put his arm around her shoulder. She sighed and turned her face into his long hair that lay over his shoulder and took a deep breath. She'd done that on several occasions at this point. Curiosity won out.

"Why do you smell me?" Lukas asked hesitantly. He didn't want to embarrass her by calling attention to it, but he wanted to know.

"I dunno… I've always been drawn to your scent. Is it too weird?"

Lukas squeezed her shoulder. "Not weird. It's the same for me. They explain it in our Korrena classes back in high school. I think it involves pheromones."

Blaire looked up at him, and the proximity allowed him to take notice of her features better. She had the smallest triangle of freckles to the left of her eye.

"They say the scent of your pair is supposed to be stronger. Comforting."

Blaire looked back at the photo album. "My counselor told me I subconsciously use your scent as a grounding tactic when I get upset and scared."

"Counselor?"

"Yeah… in the psychology department. I've been seeing Professor Sinclair since not long after I arrived, to help me get past what happened with my stepbrother, and to understand my feelings about… all this."

"All this?"

"The Korrena thing… you."

Lukas pulled her closer, and she relaxed into him. They sat together in companionable silence, junk food forgotten. Eventually, Blaire pulled away from him and peeled back the clear film that covered the photo page and removed the photograph of her stepbrother and her. She held it out and then looked back at Lukas. She smiled, ripped the photo in half, and passed the pieces to him.

Lukas looked at the two pieces in his hands and closed his eyes.

If he could help her move past that ugly chapter of her life, he would certainly try.

22

Dreaming

Blaire startled awake in the night to find Lukas kneeling beside her on the bed.

She sucked in a sharp breath as he met her eyes in the moonlit room. He looked hungry, and she wasn't sure exactly what for, but her body tingled in anticipation as she slid her eyes from his shoulders down his naked torso to his black boxers.

Lukas placed a hand beside her head, slowly pulling her covers down her body with the other as he leaned into her neck, breathing in her scent, making her shiver.

His torturously slow movements did nothing but ramp up the anticipation of whatever he planned. Blaire didn't want to stop him; she wanted him to devour her. Done fighting whatever this was between them, she didn't care. They didn't yet know each other on a deep and profound level. This wasn't about a relationship. This wasn't about love. She wanted him. Needed him. The truth of that made her shiver.

Once the cover was down far enough, he glided a hand over her thigh before moving to the inner side and gently spreading her legs apart.

Moving his face down her body, Lukas leaned in, and kissed lightly over the bruises that remained, before dragging his tongue over the abused flesh, bringing a moan from Blaire from deep in her throat. She quickly put a hand over her mouth to silence herself in embarrassment, and partly, because she wasn't sure she wanted to let him know what he did to her with such a simple action.

Lukas lifted his head, narrowing his gaze as he reached up to remove her hand from her mouth, pinning both of her hands in one of his.

They stared at one another as he hovered over her, in no rush. Blaire's breathing grew uneven and heavy in the silence of the room; his eyes were unmistakably filled with need.

He slipped his tongue over his lips as he watched her, listened to her, and she swallowed hard.

Lukas drew his hand down the front of her t-shirt, between her breasts, and over her stomach, moving it away before reaching where she wanted him. Blaire let out a soft whine in wordless protest, and he grinned at her with his dark gaze fixed on her face.

He lifted her shirt enough to drag his fingers over the front of her panties, causing her to whimper and press her lips together to stifle the sound. His soft caresses over her body tickled and drove her mad.

Lukas's face remained hard as he leaned down to her neck, his breathing deep and raspy. Releasing her hand and dragging in her scent through his nose, he worked his way down her body until his head lingered between her thighs.

He gently moved her panties to the side and stared at her for what felt like forever. Her cheeks heated in embarrassment, and she tried to close her knees together, but he growled, causing her to freeze and let her knees fall apart again.

Taking a deeper inhale, he reached out and dragged the tip of his index finger down her slit. She sucked in a breath. She was soaking wet for him, so when he ran two fingers over her sensitive bundle of nerves, her back arched and she moaned, her hands reaching out to grasp the covers. She was so sensitive.

The room fell away. Nothing mattered. Nothing existed. Not the fact that her life had been turned upside down, that she was in a school filled with Vasirian, or that her stepbrother still pursued her… none of it mattered. Her mind was lost to the pleasure Lukas brought upon her body.

She never felt anything like it before. The sounds her body made as he rubbed his fingers over her at a faster pace aroused every nerve ending in her body.

Blaire closed her eyes tightly and tried to stifle her moans by biting into her lower lip again, but it was no use. If she tried to silence herself, Lukas increased the pressure. She allowed herself to relax, giving in to the pleasure his touch brought her, her lip slipping from its bondage as once again a breathless moan filled the air without restraint.

Lukas's breathing became ragged, and his composure slipped.

He didn't stop, but he slowed down, moving his finger in languid strokes over her swollen folds as he raked his teeth over the thigh that didn't have bruising. Kissing her skin, he moved his tongue over her warmed flesh before sucking gently, not enough to mark her, but enough to cause her legs to tremble.

Blaire didn't mind if he did leave behind evidence of his lust—a mark she would proudly wear, a bruise she welcomed.

Lukas kissed over the spot on her thigh where he had been

sucking as he worked his fingers further down, not yet breaching the entrance. The way he played her body, teasing her, was agony. Her heart played a staccato rhythm she wasn't sure would ever calm, but she should have known.

As he ran his tongue up her inner thigh toward her warm center, his fangs grazed her skin. She gasped, her fear spiking and her thighs tensing up.

Lukas sank his teeth into her flesh at the same time as he slipped two fingers completely into her body in one quick thrust. She cried out as she fell over the edge of the orgasmic abyss she had been teetering on for so long. All the while, he drank from her greedily.

"Lukas…" she whispered as she came down from her high, as he continued to take from her. And then everything went dark.

Blaire suddenly woke, bolting upright in her bed, panting heavily and completely covered in sweat. She held onto her head as it spun, a sharp cramp in her stomach.

Confused, she glanced over at Lukas, who lay with his back to her in the same position as when they went to bed. Did she have another dream? Did she seriously just have another sex dream where Lukas bit her this time? She couldn't wrap her mind around her conflicting impressions. She didn't want to be bitten, but it felt so good. It felt too real to be a dream.

Shaking her head quickly, another wave of dizziness moved over her. She threw the covers down and examined her thigh.

Huh. No bite marks, blood… not even a hickey. But she felt so dizzy it made no sense it hadn't been real. But she had gone two days without any real nutrition. She hadn't eaten a lot since before they went to the movies, except for the couple of fries she managed to choke down at the diner and the junk food she shared with Lukas that evening. She heard an echo of her mother in her mind, "M&M's

aren't a meal, Blaire."

Between that, and the intensity of the dream, she shouldn't be surprised she felt disoriented and dizzy. She shifted, and realized her panties were damp beneath her shorts. Glancing over at Lukas's bare back, she blushed. He had been so perfect with his slow torture of her body. She wanted so much more. A shame it wasn't real. She always woke feeling disappointed the fantasy world didn't line up with reality.

She slowly climbed out of bed and stumbled to the bathroom, only to discover that once again her cycle had come. Changing her panties, she bagged them for laundering later, and cleaned up the mess before returning to her bed and crawling under the covers, feeling way too dizzy and barely able to stay awake.

23

Anemia

Lukas returned from breakfast to find Blaire still asleep. A faint scent of blood wafted in the air and his stomach clenched.

"Blaire?" he called to her as he stepped further into the room.

A groan came from under the covers, and Lukas moved to sit on the edge of her bed. When he placed a hand on the lump of covers, she groaned again. She sounded like she was in pain.

"Tell me what's going on."

"My stomach hurts."

"Did you eat too much chocolate?" He didn't think she ate more than usual when they had snacks yesterday afternoon, but he didn't know how a human's body worked entirely. He knew she liked to eat a lot. She was always snacking on something. Maybe having too much of the same thing made her sick.

"No." Another groan. "Cramps."

The smell of blood wasn't severe, but it was enough to make him concerned.

"Are you bleeding?"

The lump on the bed tensed.

"Blaire?"

"Go away."

Lukas raised an eyebrow. "Why? What's wrong?"

Blaire threw the covers off and looked up at him. She looked incredibly pale. "I'm on my period, okay?" She looked over at the wall and pulled the covers back over her head. From beneath the comforter came a muffled, "Just let me rest. It's worse than usual."

Lukas couldn't leave it alone. He hadn't smelled her blood the last time. If it was worse, what if something was wrong with her?

He stood from the bed and left the room without another word, locking the door behind him.

Thirty minutes later, he came back with the head of the student health department trailing him.

"I'm sure it's fine, Mr. Virtanen. Menstrual cycles are different for each woman."

"No. She's pale. She's in pain. I couldn't wake her this morning." He looked at the lump on the bed that wasn't moving. "I can smell her blood."

"I don't smell anything." The woman stepped further into the room toward Blaire's bed.

Lukas sat on the edge of his bed and watched as the woman lightly shook Blaire's shoulder. "Miss Wilcox?"

Blaire moaned uncomfortably and rolled over, pushing the covers off her head. She looked paler than before, and she looked up at the nurse with unfocused eyes.

"I'm Eloise Montgomery, the head of the nursing staff from the student health department. Your pair here says you're having a difficult cycle?"

Blaire covered her face with her hand and nodded drowsily.

"Can you tell me about it? Is there anything you need? Does this happen frequently?"

"No… it hasn't happened like this in over a year, but when it does, it makes me sick." She looked over at Lukas, who kept his gaze steady on her and sighed. "It's really heavy, and I sometimes get anemic."

Pursing her lips, the nurse nodded before asking, "Menorrhagia?"

Blaire shook her head against the pillow. "My doctor checked me for that. It's not that severe."

"And what do you usually do in these situations?"

"Sleep. When it's like this, it only lasts for a few days."

The nurse nodded. "You need to make sure you eat something to keep your strength up and drink plenty of fluids." She turned to Lukas, "Otherwise, she's correct, Mr. Virtanen. She needs to rest. Her body knows what it needs during times like this."

Lukas ran a hand through his hair. "What can I do?"

A warm smile crossed the nurse's face. "Make sure she gets something to eat and drink. Green leafy vegetables and meat will help with iron levels. Let her sleep. You likely smell her blood because her scent is stronger to you. Are you having difficulty?"

Lukas shook his head. No more difficult than just being around her brought on.

"Well then, you take care of our newest addition to the student body. If you need it, the health department is always open. I will inform Professor Velastra of student affairs that your pair is unwell."

The nurse got up from the bed and strode to the door. She gently closed the door behind her, and Lukas returned his attention to Blaire, who had her eyes closed. He crossed to her and touched her forehead. She had a clammy sheen of sweat on her brow. She groaned and leaned into his touch.

"Sleep. I'll get you something to eat from the canteen later."

Blaire turned in the bed and he pulled the covers up over her shoulder.

Later that evening, Lukas sat back on his bed and stared at his cell phone.

He'd made sure Blaire drank plenty of fluids and helped her to the bathroom when she needed to change. He stopped short of going in with her when she insisted she was fine, but it didn't stop his worry. She'd barely eaten any of the food he brought, and he wasn't going to force-feed her if she didn't want to eat.

Lukas sighed and scrolled through his contacts, stopping at an entry that made his chest tighten.

Pressing the button, he lifted the phone to his ear and waited for the call to connect. With each ring he got increasingly anxious, shifting on the bed until his back met the wall and he could focus on Blaire's sleeping face across the room. Was he really going to tell them?

"Poika?"

His mother's Finnish accent drifted over the line into his ear, and he closed his eyes. She knew he didn't understand the language, but he knew the word for son, and he felt a lightness in his chest as nostalgia settled in.

Lukas cleared his throat.

"Hi, Mom."

"What brought this on?" She sounded worried. "Is everything okay?"

"No… yes, I'm fine. How are you? Where are you?" He hoped he hadn't called at some weird hour, but he wasn't sure what country they were in.

"We're in New Zealand. We just finished having lunch with your father's associate. How are you, *poikani*? I haven't heard from you in so long. I miss you."

Their relationship was complicated. He knew they cared about him, but their business came first. Why else would they have dropped him at the Blackthorn Academy's primary school and barely returned to visit each year? It always felt weird to hear things like they loved him or missed him. It rang hollow in his ears, but he craved the affection, nonetheless.

"I dunno, Mom. I…" He took a deep breath, eyes taking in Blaire's sleeping form. She still looked pale, but the sheen of sweat had finally gone away. He hoped the pain pills the nurse had given him for her were helping. "I found my Korrena," he whispered.

"Poika! Onko se totta?" Her voice came out loud and fast as she spoke in Finnish.

"What? I don't understand you."

"My boy… is it true? Have you found her?"

Lukas closed his eyes at the sound of relief and contentment in her tone.

"I'm sure of it. I've found her."

"Jyrki! It's Lukas! It's happened!"

Lukas smirked to himself as he could hear his mother shuffling on the other end of the line and muffled speaking before a deep voice came over the speaker.

"Lukas?"

"Hi, Dad."

"Your mother tells me you've found your pair."

"I have."

"Congratulations. I knew it was only a matter of time. When do we get to meet her?"

Lukas looked at Blaire and sighed. "I don't know... we're not fully bonded yet."

"No?" The confusion was evident in his voice. "Why is this?"

His mother asked questions in the background. "No, no, they've not bonded," his father spoke to her. He heard more shuffling, and then his mother's voice came over the line again.

"Why have you not bonded with this girl? *Poika*, you mustn't wait!"

Lukas bit at the side of his lip. "It's complicated."

"There is nothing complicated about bonding. You just need to—"

"I know how it works." He cut her off before she went into a long-winded spiel about the claiming process.

"Then what is the problem?"

A long pause stretched.

"She's human."

His mother's gasp and quick rambling to his father in Finnish made his gut roil with anxiety. Was she upset? Angry?

His father asked, "How is that possible? Are you sure? You haven't claimed her. How can you be certain?"

Lukas thunked his head against the wall. "I saw my mark. I've seen it. I... feel things. Not just for her, but I feel her emotions sometimes. It's everything they describe, but so much more."

"Oh."

"Dad?"

"Yes, Lukas?"

"Is it... are you okay?"

"Of course! I'm very happy for you. Surprised. Good surprised, but surprised. Does she accept the bond? I assume she knows what we are, yes?"

"Yeah, she knows. She's a student at Blackthorn now."

His father hummed on the other end of the line.

"I think she accepts the bond, but sometimes I don't know. Things have been difficult. I feel like I'm losing my mind."

"This is understandable. It can be hard in the beginning. I imagine with a human it is harder. Here. Speak with your mother. Maybe she can help you."

The line went quiet, and after a moment, his mother's voice came over the line again.

"*Poika*. A human... That is very peculiar, but the gods make no mistakes. This girl has a reason to be with you. She is chosen for you."

Lukas smiled and relaxed against the wall. He didn't realize how wound tight he had been, not knowing if his parents would accept his Korrena. He didn't realize how happy it would make him that they did.

"I keep messing up, though. I tried to run her off. And then tried to get her to stay. Then I got angry with her when Aiden—" He stopped himself from bringing it up. It made him upset to think about it. He hadn't even talked to Aiden about what happened yet.

"What did Aiden do?"

"He likes her."

"Oh, my... and does she like him also?"

"I don't think so. She rejected him."

"Good. This is good. So, what is the problem?"

"I got angry with her. I lashed out when he got too close to her. I acted like a jealous, possessive idiot. I scared her. We've been fighting the bond from the start... and I'm starting to question why I even tried to fight it."

"Oh *poika*... Your father and I had the same issues when we first met until we completed our joining. Your father was even violent toward people who showed even the smallest attention to me. He even scared me as well. Lashing out like a barbarian at me. Harrowing stuff." She huffed. "We don't really talk about it. It was a difficult time."

"I would never hurt Blaire," Lukas said with conviction.

"No, no. Your father didn't hurt me either, but he was rough with me. We weren't even fighting the bond, and he still was rough, and there were times when he acted negatively toward me, and I thought he didn't like me at all! Can you believe that?" Her soft laugh filtered through the phone and calmed Lukas's heart. "The pull of the Korrena is primal. It makes people act like they normally wouldn't. Makes them violent and aggressive."

Lukas never remembered that as part of the lessons taught growing up.

"Wait a minute... were you aggressive?" He stifled a laugh. He couldn't picture his mother lashing out in any way. "I can't see it. You're so..."

"Calm? Sweet and cuddly?" They both laughed. "I'm calm, yes. That's my true nature. But you must know, *poika*, the bond in its early stages is weak and is missing a solid foundation. Until there is security, it's unpredictable, which makes the Korrena unpredictable. I wasn't as bad as your father, but I had my moments."

Lukas sighed. "I definitely have been more aggressive..."

"Then you must work on that. It is hard, I know. But it will be worth it. I promise."

Blaire rolled over onto her side to face him. He knew what he wanted. He needed to convince her he was worth the effort. Worth the unknown.

"I must go now, *poika*. Please, call me more. Your father and I miss you so much."

He heard his father grunt in the background and call out, "I want to meet her soon!"

Lukas laughed softly. "Sure. Soon."

Monday morning, Blaire and Lukas went to class together, not having talked much since she ripped up the picture of her and Caleb. She had stayed in bed most of Sunday after the nurse visited.

She felt awful. Lukas had brought her a sandwich on Sunday, since she hadn't eaten anything but a bunch of chocolate since Friday, but she couldn't eat more than a bite or two. Her cycle kept her nauseous. Not eating made it worse. But eating also made it worse. It was a double-edged sword. He grumbled about her stubbornness, but she did manage to drink the teas and juice he kept bringing her. He wasn't angry, he was concerned for her. They didn't get much opportunity to talk, so he didn't know what was wrong. All she wanted to do was sleep. She was ready for it to be over with already. It had been a long time since it had been this bad, but the nurse assured her no one could smell it except Lukas, and he said that was only if she had an accident. She visited the bathroom often.

Lukas carried Blaire's backpack for her as he walked with her to class, resting his hand on her back gently in case she had trouble with balance at any point. His caring and attentive behavior made her heart flutter. The big problem was she couldn't look at him. Every single time their eyes met, she had to look away due to the blush overtaking her features. She couldn't stop thinking about the dream from Saturday night.

Something in the way Lukas had changed since he confronted her about Aiden had Blaire looking at him differently. He seemed softer, the lingering edges disappearing. She thought back to how he acted in the diner when Caleb came. She felt so safe in his arms, and his reassuring words calmed her even in the face of her trauma. Then, on her bed, sharing chocolate, and his attentiveness to her need for physical closeness. His understanding of her seeing a counselor without judgment.

Blaire opened the classroom door and stepped inside with Lukas following, shutting the door behind them, and ran a hand through his hair.

"Blaire!" Riley shouted from her desk, causing Aiden to swing his gaze toward the door and furrow his brow when he saw Blaire's face.

Blaire lowered herself into her seat as Lukas set her backpack down, before taking his seat behind her. Aiden raised a brow at him, nodding toward the backpack. Lukas shrugged.

"I heard you weren't feeling well..." Aiden said, frowning as he gave Blaire a once-over with his eyes.

Blaire looked at him in confusion. "Where'd you hear that?"

"Riley came to see you yesterday, and Lukas said you weren't feeling well."

"Yeah," Riley said. "You were asleep, so I didn't want to wake you. ...not that he would have let me, anyway. He didn't even let me in the room." Riley glared at Lukas.

Blaire looked over her shoulder at Lukas, but he just stared at her quietly. She felt thankful he didn't blab to everyone she was on her period. It wasn't anyone's business.

"But for real... you look pale. Like, really, really, pale. Are you sure you're okay to be in class?" Riley said, studying Blaire's face.

"I'm fine..." Blaire sighed and rubbed her eyes with her hand. "I just haven't been feeling all that good since I woke up Sunday, so I spent most of the time in bed trying to sleep it off. I haven't eaten much of anything."

Blaire put a hand on her lower abdomen as it cramped, her face twisting in discomfort. She should have taken more pain pills. Riley looked at her and her brows lifted. Blaire wondered if she figured it out.

"I mean, Lukas tried to get me to eat yesterday, but I just didn't feel like it. I've only had those few fries at the diner and some chocolate with Lukas on Saturday—aside from those couple bites of sandwich Lukas made me eat. That's probably why I'm pale."

Riley frowned at her.

Lukas shifted in his seat again behind her and Aiden glanced in his direction, asking, "What is it?"

Blaire followed his gaze to Lukas, who looked stressed. "Are you okay?" she whispered.

Lukas nodded. "Just wondering if you need pain medicine..."

Before Blaire could tell him she would love some, wondering if he could feel her pain, Vincent approached the aisle and stopped next to her desk. She hadn't seen him since the day they met in the cafeteria. He wasn't in uniform today, instead wearing a pair of tight black slacks, a button-down black shirt with the sleeves rolled up his corded forearms, accented by a black vest buttoned over the top. Aside from the bracelets, rings, and nail polish, he looked aristocratic but with a dark and gothic edge. While the polished and refined look wasn't what she found attractive in a man, she could appreciate his masculine beauty.

Vincent stopped at her desk and tilted his head to the side, studying her face. "Are you alright, Blaire?"

Lukas snapped at him. "What the hell are you doing in our class?"

Blaire stared at Lukas, and Aiden raised an eyebrow.

"What is your problem? He's only worried like the rest of us," Riley said, turning in her seat.

Lukas shrugged and looked away from everyone, his face clouded with discontent.

"I am the teacher's assistant for this course for the remainder of the year, as it will apply to my employment after my time here at Blackthorn is finished." He flicked his gaze back at Lukas. "If that is okay with you, of course."

Lukas sucked his teeth and leaned back in his seat, crossing his arms over his chest. Blaire didn't like the sudden change in attitude; he was acting like an asshole.

Vincent crouched down next to Blaire's desk, intently studying her face. "Are you sure you're alright, beautiful? Do you need anything?" He gently placed his hand on top of hers. "Do you perhaps need to go to the student health department? You look awfully pale."

Blaire shook her head and then put her forehead in her hand as a dizzy spell set in from the movement. She rested her elbow on the desk.

Riley reached out and touched her arm. "Blaire..."

Lukas jerked upright in his seat, and Riley glanced back at him, raising an eyebrow.

"Dude. Calm down."

He dropped back into his seat with a huff, his expression pained. Aiden narrowed his eyes at him.

"I'm fine..." Blaire breathed. "Everyone just needs to stop worrying. I'm just a little dizzy, that's all. I didn't eat breakfast, and not much before that. I'll be alright."

Aiden stood abruptly, glaring at Lukas, before quickly leaving the classroom. Blaire glanced at the door in confusion. She wondered what was wrong with him too. Everyone was in a foul mood today.

Vincent stood and gently patted her hand. "If you need to go to the nurse at any point, please let me know, and I will be happy to escort you." He turned away, not giving Lukas the opportunity to say anything.

Lukas had sat up abruptly, ready to strike, but dropped back in his seat again and closed his eyes, sighing. Blaire's condition wasn't improving with the way tension and distress radiated from Lukas. She had no idea why she suddenly could feel him this strongly, but it was almost suffocating at times.

"Listen... if you do need to go, I'll go and stay with you." Riley removed her hand from Blaire's arm and sat back in her seat.

Aiden returned shortly after and set a small package of peanuts on Blaire's desk. "Eat these." He set down a small bottle of orange juice. "And drink this."

"Why do I need these?" She raised an eyebrow at the odd combination.

"The juice will raise your blood sugar, and the peanuts... well, they're rich in protein and iron." Aiden shot Lukas a hard look.

Blaire raised an eyebrow. "Iron? Why do you think I need that?"

"You could be anemic, since you're this pale and dizzy." Aiden rubbed the back of his neck. "Or it might just be low blood sugar from not eating." He took his seat.

She looked at the peanuts and juice on her desk. She knew she was suffering from anemia already, but why would Aiden make the connection?

Lukas sighed and nudged the back of Blaire's chair with his boot when she hadn't touched the items in front of her. She turned to look at him. His face looked strained and tired. He tried to speak calmly, but an edge of discomfort bled into his tone. "Just eat it. You might feel better, alright?"

Blaire turned around and looked down at her desk. She opened the packet of peanuts and ate a few before putting the straw into the bottle and taking a drink.

During class, her vitality returned some; the things Aiden brought did take the edge off. She glanced over, prepared to thank Aiden for the smart idea, but she decided against it at the look of pure anger on his face as he wrote furiously in his notebook. Yeah, she wasn't touching that even a little bit. What happened while she slept yesterday? Everyone except Riley was on edge.

Blaire twisted her hair and sat back in her seat, dropping it back. The strands fell over Lukas's desk. She shifted to sit forward, but paused when she felt a tug, and light movement, as Lukas began to play with her hair. She closed her eyes and lowered into her seat, trying to relax and feel better while Lukas's soothing touches gently pulled at her scalp.

She had almost fallen asleep in her seat when movement to her left got her attention as Aiden turned and tossed a paper onto Lukas's desk. Other than Aiden's expression, nothing seemed out of the ordinary. She shrugged it off, returning her attention to the front of the class again, but she wouldn't be able to concentrate. All the equations on the board bled together into a jumble of numbers. She'd get notes from Riley later.

When class dismissed, Blaire stood too quickly and lost her footing. Lukas jumped up and reached for her, but Aiden moved faster, taking her arm.

"It's okay, I've got you."

Blaire smiled up at Aiden. "Sorry… Thank you. I just got up too fast."

Nodding with a clenched jaw, Aiden placed his other hand on her lower back to steady her.

Lukas growled low in his throat as he stood from his desk, causing both Riley and Aiden to turn and look at him. Aiden raised a brow at him in question.

"Stop being a jealous asshole, Lukas," Riley admonished. "He was just making sure Blaire didn't fall."

Lukas slumped against the edge of his desk and ran a hand through his hair as Riley grabbed Blaire's backpack. Both Aiden and Lukas continued staring each other down before Riley rolled her eyes and finally spoke.

"I have her. I'll walk with her." She reached out to take Blaire's arm gently from Aiden, who still hadn't let go. He turned his attention back to them.

"I'm fine. Really," Blaire mumbled with a sigh.

"The testosterone is getting too thick in here, so I'd rather get the hell out of here as quickly as possible, so it's easier this way." Riley shot both Lukas and Aiden another glare.

Blaire didn't understand what was going on between them. They were best friends. Was this all because Lukas found out about how Aiden felt? How Blaire had been attracted to him? The kiss? She bit her lower lip softly. She wanted Lukas to understand she didn't want Aiden; she was only drawn to him. Nothing could compare to the way Lukas made her feel, both good and bad.

Shortly after Riley and Blaire left the class and were standing by the bathrooms out front, Aiden came out of the classroom, passing them without saying a word, not even giving them a second glance. Lukas stormed out right behind him, a scowl shadowing his face.

"Wow… I think Lukas is pissed," Riley whispered.

Blaire laughed. "Lukas always looks pissed," she joked, trying to lighten the mood, but something was wrong with Lukas. She just didn't know what.

Riley laughed. "I'm glad to see you've got your sense of humor back. I was starting to worry…"

“Listen, I said it before… I’m fine. The juice and nuts made me feel much better.”

While she wasn’t completely fine, she was better. That wasn’t a lie. The main thing bothering her at that moment centered on Lukas, and whatever upset him.

She wanted to fix it.

24

Intentions

The door of the hallway flew open as Aiden shoved his way out, Lukas hot on his heels as they made their way toward the tree line along the dark forest that spanned the back of the academy.

"You need to back the fuck off," Lukas growled out, breaking the quiet as he came to a stop.

Aiden spun around, staring at Lukas in confusion. "What the hell are you talking about?"

Lukas dragged both his hands through his hair in frustration, gripping the mid-shaft at the back of his neck as he glared at his best friend.

"Blaire is my Korrena and doesn't need you to bring her snacks or take care of her."

He hadn't paid it attention before, but Riley had been right. Aiden was there for her. Aiden was always by her side and quick to support her. Aiden received her smile. Aiden wanted her. Aiden,

Aiden, Aiden. Lukas dropped his hands and clenched them at his side. Never in all their years around one another had he wanted to hit his friend until that moment. What was happening to him? Was this what his mother talked about?

Aiden stared at him, momentarily stunned. "That's what you have to say?" He glared at Lukas. "I wouldn't need to take care of her if you did a better job of looking out for her yourself."

Lukas sucked his teeth, looking away from Aiden. He had been looking out for Blaire. He spent the weekend making sure she didn't… bleed out or whatever. He didn't know what would have happened if she didn't have fluids, food, and sleep. The whole female system struck him as weird, but he took care of her. That's all that mattered. He had been there for her several times. He didn't need Aiden to see it to make it a reality. It wasn't any of his business what happened between him and Blaire.

"I mean seriously… did you really bite her?" Aiden finally asked the thought Lukas knew he suspected in class.

Between the looks, the anemic comments, and giving him a letter demanding that they talk, he knew this had been coming. Lukas still wasn't prepared for it, though. He felt sick to his stomach at the idea his best friend would think him capable of doing something like that to Blaire when they all knew she wasn't ready for it.

Lukas growled. "It's none of your fucking business what we do together." He narrowed his eyes at Aiden. "And you really need to get it out of your fucking head that you two have a chance of being together."

He didn't care this guy was his best friend. The fact that they had been so close since they were children didn't matter one bit when it came to Blaire. He was not about to just hand her over for the sake of their friendship. She was something so much more. Worth so much more.

Aiden clenched his jaw and looked away, caught out on what he did.

Lukas didn't have to tell Aiden he knew what happened; from his guilty expression, Aiden knew he was aware of it.

Aiden threw his hands up in a placating gesture. "I have absolutely no intention of interfering if you both are bonding and want to be together." Aiden raked a hand through his hair. "The only reason I even considered pursuing Blaire is because I thought you didn't want to be with her." He sighed and looked at Lukas with sincerity in his eyes. "You're my best friend, Lukas. I'd never take something like that away from you, or even try to."

Lukas finally relaxed, but he paced around the grass before turning toward Aiden with a glare. "Blaire is mine, and I'm not going to let her go. Not for you, not for anyone."

He turned and stomped toward the building, done with the conversation, and not wanting to address the real reason he knew Aiden dragged him out there.

Aiden patted him on the back as they went back through the doors into the empty hallway where Riley and Blaire were waiting at the lockers. "You know, I'm happy to hear you both are finally beginning to bond. I am. I want you to be happy, but you need to be more careful with her if she's left that weak from sharing blood while she's still a human. They're fragile."

Blaire whirled around abruptly, obviously overhearing what Aiden said. Her mouth hung open in shock.

Lukas groaned and ran his hand down his face. He did not want this confrontation. He knew this was what Aiden wanted to talk about.

"We have not shared blood, and I never plan to… ever," Blaire said emphatically, putting her hands on her hips and glaring at Aiden. "And if you must know, I'm on my period. It's bad. Thank you for helping with my anemia, but can we please move on now?"

Aiden rubbed his neck.

"Oh, and for the record, I have no intentions of being anything other than a human. I mean, 'still a human'? Always a human, thank ya very much," Blaire huffed, her dialect slipping into a thicker Southern accent.

Lukas had come to realize that only happened when she was angry or out of sorts.

"Shit. I read the whole situation wrong…" Aiden said, spearing his fingers through his messy hair.

Lukas said nothing, staring at Blaire. His entire body screamed at him, but he couldn't say anything. He wouldn't demand she sacrifice her humanity, but it hurt that she would outright reject him this way when the only way they could become one as a bonded pair involved the exchange of blood.

He swallowed hard and closed his eyes tight before opening them to glare at Blaire, pushing past her and storming down the hall.

Blaire winced as the door slammed at the end of the hallway.

"What is with him today?" she asked quietly.

Riley put her hand on Blaire's arm with a serious look on her face. "If you are even remotely considering being bonded to Lukas, you do know that sharing blood is part of it, right? The longer you go without bonding, the harder it will be." She sighed. "Do you feel it yet?"

"What do you mean?"

"Have you felt the physical ache to be near him yet? I asked my mom about it... I didn't tell her anything about you personally. I'm not making that mistake again. I just told her I'd made friends with the human student at the university, and you were having trouble with your pairing."

Blaire smiled. Riley felt remorse for spilling her guts to both Aiden and Lukas about what she'd been through, and Blaire appreciated she was trying to help without overstepping.

"She told me about some of the negative effects pairs experience when they haven't sealed their bond."

Aiden slumped back against the locker and rubbed the back of his neck, looking uncomfortable as he muttered, "Lukas must be dying inside..."

Riley raised her eyebrow at him.

"Considering how I feel, and I'm not even her pair..." He cut his eyes at Riley. "I'm sure you already know; everyone else seems to." he said with a sigh.

She looked down and nodded.

Blaire lowered her head and sighed. "Yeah... something is different. I find myself wanting to be closer to him, to touch him more. I want him to touch me... and when he has,"—she blushed—"it's like someone lights a wildfire inside me."

Aiden closed his eyes and shifted uncomfortably.

Blaire felt bad admitting it in front of him, knowing how he felt, but she couldn't lie to him. She couldn't lie to herself. Her body completely belonged to Lukas, and it began to feel like her heart was in danger of belonging to him too, between the comfort he brought her and how much she ached to soothe his discomfort today.

"Well, for Vasirian, it's apparently even worse because we also have to fend off our thirst because we naturally crave blood, right?

And supposedly, the blood of our Korrena is potent to our senses and it can cause us to physically feel pain from the cravings. You won't feel anything like that, obviously, because you're a human." Riley paused and looked upward in thought before adding, "…welll, other than the taste of the Korrena blood."

Aiden raised his brow. "What do you mean by that?"

"Well, Mom told me it's possible Lukas's blood will be appealing to Blaire on taste, but because she lacks the basic need of a Vasirian, she won't crave it the way we do. But there's a strong possibility if she were to taste his blood, she would want to consume it and feed on him in the same way we crave our own Korrena's blood. That she too, could possibly become addicted. She said she wasn't sure, but that was her suspicion."

"I don't think anyone will really have the answer to that until it happens, since Blaire's the first human in this situation," Aiden said.

Blaire made a disgusted face. "Yeah, I doubt I'll ever be on board the 'blood tastes delicious' train. Sorry, but just… no."

Aiden chuckled, and then Riley turned serious again.

"Listen, Blaire, I can say with complete certainty that Lukas is probably suffering…" She sighed. "He was completely within his rights to be angry by your outburst. You basically told him you'll never do what's required to be his pair the way it's meant to be."

Blaire glanced at Aiden, and he looked down.

"I'm sorry, but she's right," he mumbled.

"Dude. Say that again." Riley giggled. "It's not often you tell your little sister she's right, so I have to milk it while I can."

Aiden rolled his eyes before looking at Blaire seriously. "I couldn't imagine hearing my Korrena say she had no intentions of bonding with me if I wanted her the way it seems Lukas wants you."

"I'm sorry…" she whispered softly. She didn't mean to hurt Lukas. "I just… I can't imagine sharing my blood with anyone, much less drinking blood mysel—" She paused and covered her mouth with her hand.

Aiden stepped forward in concern. "Are you okay? What is it?"

"Nothing."

"Oh, no way. Spill," Riley demanded.

Blaire glanced away and fidgeted nervously, twirling the ends of her hair around her fingers. There was no way she could tell them about the last dream she had.

Riley frowned at Blaire. "Come on. It can't be any worse than some of the other things you've shared with us… we're friends. We just want to help."

Blaire swallowed hard and tugged on the ends of hair that she wrapped around her fingers. She didn't want it to get back to Lukas. She wasn't prepared to admit it to him.

"Remember the dreams I told you about?" Blaire gave Aiden a sidelong glance. His brows knitted in confusion, but she didn't elaborate. She wasn't about to tell him how she dreamed nightly of being taken by Lukas in the dark. Talk about twisting the knife.

Riley glanced at her brother briefly and then nodded at Blaire. "Yeah, what about them?"

"I had one where I was…" Blaire ran a hand through her hair, the blonde locks falling over her shoulders in a messy cascade. "…where I was… bitten." She took a breath, finally able to get the words out.

"Lukas bit you?" Riley shouted.

"No!" She looked at Aiden and sighed. "I dreamed he bit me…"

"What does that have to do with anything, though? It's just a dream," Aiden questioned.

Blaire swallowed hard. "...I liked it. I woke up wanting him to bite me. I wanted to give my blood to him willingly."

"Holy shit... that's... that's awesome!" Riley jumped up and down in excitement, the buckles on her boots jangling and echoing in the empty hall.

"How is that awesome? I don't wanna share my blood with anyone!"

Riley shrugged. "Clearly your body is on board and your mind needs to catch up," she said, as if it was the most obvious solution to all of Blaire's problems.

Aiden added, "It does sound like on some level you do know he's your Korrena and you're responding to him on a base level. Raw instinct."

Riley nodded.

"Has anything else been different?"

So many things had changed in their dynamic, and a lot of it happened quickly once they lowered their walls with each other. She didn't know what to address first, or if she should mention anything.

"So... Lukas says he can feel me, hear my heartbeat, things like that."

"Yeah, he mentioned it before when Mera and I spoke to him while you were sleeping the other day after we stayed over at Aiden's," Riley said.

"He told you about what happened then..."

"Yeah, well," Riley glanced over at Aiden. "He told us how he could feel how you responded to Aiden."

Blaire blushed, not meeting Aiden's eyes. "Yeah..."

She felt thankful Lukas hadn't spilled everything that happened at the movies or in the bedroom before she slept, even if it was embarrassing for Aiden to hear she had responded to him when she did her best to hide it in the moment.

"Well, the thing is, I'm starting to sense his feelings, too. I can't hear his heartbeat or anything like that, but whenever his emotions are strong, I feel it. It messes with my head. Like today, he was in so much turmoil from the moment we got to class. He was upset, and then angry. All I wanted to do was to make it better. It was like my body was screaming at me to fix it for him."

"Shit, Blaire," Aiden said.

Riley stared at her with her mouth open.

"What? What's wrong?"

"Something is really pushing your bond together, and if you two aren't doing anything more than what we know and have seen, then something weird is going on," Riley said. "Mera said without a strong emotional connection, there has to be physical intimacy for that to happen."

"But... other than kiss me, and put his arms around me, we haven't done anything for real," Blaire mumbled.

Aiden raised a brow. "What do you mean 'for real'?"

"I mean, other than... dreams." Blaire's face warmed, and she looked at the floor. Thankfully, Aiden didn't ask her to elaborate. He was a smart guy; he should be able to put two and two together, and judging by the sigh he let out, he did.

"This is intense. Something weird is definitely going on," Riley said.

"Yeah, but we don't have time to look too deep into it. We're already late for class..." Aiden pointed at the clock on the wall.

"Shit!" Riley took off running down the hall.

Aiden chuckled. "So much for helping you get to your next class."

"I'll be fine. I said I was better."

"Yeah, no. I'm not hearing it. Let me walk with you?"

Blaire looked down. She wasn't going to argue with him. She had probably hurt him with some of the things she said, even if it was honesty. Leading someone on didn't sit right with her. Hurting someone didn't either, but if it must happen to maintain honesty and friendship, then so be it. "Fine."

Aiden picked up her backpack from the floor and put his hand on her back as he guided her down the hallway in silence.

25

Concern

Everyone sat waiting at the table in the cafeteria's corner that had become their regular spot as Riley and Blaire walked up, carrying their trays.

Blaire managed to get two portions of teriyaki chicken with her vegetables and soba noodles when Riley told the lady in the line Blaire hadn't eaten in two days. The woman looked appalled and scolded Blaire, telling her that around here that just won't do, and she wouldn't be doing her job if her students weren't well fed. She said humans needed to keep their strength up. Blaire cringed at the implication of those words, thinking back on the shared blood conversation from earlier.

"Hey, everyone!" Riley said cheerfully, plopping down in the seat between Seth and Mera across the table from Lukas. She immediately stuck a straw into her blood packet and began to drink.

"I just don't get it..." Blaire said, pausing in front of the table and staring at Riley with a pinched expression. She chewed the inside of her cheek.

"Get what?" Kai asked, as he cut the noodles on his plate into smaller bites.

"You realize you're drinking someone's blood? A human?" She sat her tray down at the only empty spot left.

While Blaire had gotten used to seeing them all drink blood, it still came as a shock to her when it first happened. She had never seen Lukas drink; she assumed he had blood when she wasn't around. There was no way he was some sort of blood vegetarian.

"Well, yes. But what else do we do? Die? Because that is exactly what will happen if we don't drink blood. At least this way we're not acting like the uncivilized monsters from your fairy tale books," Kai said derisively. "I do not mean any ill-will toward you, but it has always bothered me the way species similar to ours are depicted in the media."

Blaire nodded quietly and shook the thoughts from her head. As she moved to sit in the seat next to Lukas, he reached out and grabbed her around the waist, startling her as he pulled her into his lap.

She landed with a gasp, and he buried his face into her hair at the side of her neck, closing his eyes as his breathing came out unsteadily. Her stomach roiled with the overwhelming feelings of distress radiating off him. She squirmed in his lap as she tried to get back up, unable to handle the onslaught of his emotions, hoping if she put distance between them, it would stop.

"Let me go."

Lukas tightened his arms briefly around her and whispered, "Just… let me have a moment." He shifted her in his lap, pulling her as tightly to his body as he could. "Please…"

Blaire stilled, swallowing hard as she looked at everyone at the table who stared at her as if she had grown an extra head. She picked at the hem of her stockings in embarrassment.

"You did look really bad this morning… I'm not surprised he's unsettled," Aiden said quietly.

Blaire had no idea he would act like this considering how angry he seemed with her this morning in the hallway the last time she saw him, but it was stifling. The same tension from this morning. She took a deep breath, and his unique apple, citrus, and spice scent eased the discomfort his emotions brought her. She could let him have this.

She relaxed back against his body as they sat in silence until his breathing evened out. He dragged his hands up and down her arms as if to self-soothe.

This was the Lukas he had been for days now, the same Lukas she remembered from when she had the nightmare about Caleb. The Lukas her heart was about to leap out of her chest for. If he stayed like this, then she would try to get to know him more, to connect with him on a deeper level, to see what this might be. There was still the hurdle of the whole Vasirian and human thing. She still didn't think she could let him drink her blood, and she sure as hell wasn't going to drink his. She shuddered.

Lukas slowly lifted his head, glancing up toward Blaire's face.

"Are you feeling better?" he whispered.

They were so close to each other that if she moved forward, even a couple of inches, their lips would meet. Goose bumps rose on her skin as she recalled the kiss they shared when he confronted her about Aiden. His eyes dropped to her lips and his nostrils flared as she pulled her bottom lip between her teeth.

"I… yeah, I'm doing much better now. I'm just tired…"

Lukas dropped his head against her shoulder once more and sighed in apparent relief, taking one last inhale of her hair before finally loosening and releasing her from the cage of his arms.

"You need to eat," Lukas said before dragging his hand through his hair, leaning back in his chair, and letting out a long exhale. He hung his head back as if utterly exhausted.

Blaire moved into her seat and opened a bottle of peach tea, taking a long pull from it before she poked at her chicken with a fork.

"Your mood swings are starting to give me whiplash," Riley quipped, but Lukas didn't even entertain her with a response as he closed his eyes, remaining still.

Blaire twirled noodles onto her fork, before stabbing a piece of chicken, and taking a large bite, moaning as she closed her eyes. The food was either really amazing or she was definitely starving. This was the most delicious thing she'd ever had.

At a clatter next to her, she opened her eyes to find Lukas sitting up, staring at her with his jaw clenched.

She swallowed down the bite and stammered out, "W-what?"

"I think it's…" Aiden rubbed the back of his neck. "You didn't hear yourself." A forced laugh slipped out of him. "You must be pretty damn hungry." He cleared his throat.

Kai let out a loud laugh, and Blaire's face burned. She had no idea she sounded any different.

Lukas turned his gaze from her quickly, snatching up the blood pack from his tray and stabbing a straw into it before taking a long drink.

Blaire stared at him with wide eyes. She had no idea what to make of his sudden change in behavior.

Mera spoke up, noticing Blaire's confusion. "He's just a bit hungry, that's all." She cleared her throat, and her cheeks tinged pink. "Just not in the way you'd think."

"What?" Blaire looked at Mera in confusion.

Kai sighed. "The sounds you made as you enjoyed your meal…

you likely stirred him up. Please don't make me spell it out for you. I gather you are naïve, but not that naïve."

Blaire thought for a moment before her eyes went wide again. Kai laughed at her reaction.

"There she goes. She gets it now," Seth said with a smirk.

Mera frowned. "To her credit, she has been malnourished. She likely has brain fog."

Blaire jerked her gaze over to find Lukas staring at her intensely, draining his blood packet. She swallowed hard as he finished, slowly licking the blood from his lips as her heart kicked into overdrive, her breath hitching. There was that feeling again. That deep desire to have him consume her entirely.

"Oh boy…" Riley muttered, looking down. "He's not the only one hungry."

Mera chuckled at Riley and shook her head. "Oh, come on, I think it's a beautiful thing to watch a pair begin to truly connect."

"If this is what having a Korrena is like, then I'm not sure if I want one after all. They're giving me major heartburn from the stress." Riley laughed.

Seth muttered, "This is what I've been saying all along. Not having control over yourself all because of some biological pull is like being a damn slave. It's not real."

Lukas glanced over as Seth motioned toward him and Blaire.

"They are a prime example of a situation where only the biological connection is at play. They wouldn't even be friends if Blaire wasn't his Korrena."

Blaire quietly ate her noodles as she listened to Seth pick apart whatever was happening between them. She didn't know what to say, because she didn't understand it either. Yes, she had been attracted to Lukas from the start, but his personality bothered her then. She wouldn't have given him a chance in hell. They wouldn't have been friends. But it was different now. It had been for a while. Was it only the bond's pull that made her want him and receptive to the things growing between them, or was it because he had changed, and she was learning more about him? Seth's assessment made her more confused than ever.

"Blaire wouldn't even be at the school, so we would never know, so it's basically a moot point," Kai said, giving his little brother a look.

"No, if they didn't have that weird connection, then they wouldn't even want to be with each other. It's disgusting that our kind is forced into being with someone, especially if we don't want them."

"I don't think that's true at all." Aiden sighed as he looked over at Blaire. "You haven't been around enough to know everything that's been going on with them, and I'm convinced there's more to it than just the biological aspect they were born with."

Lukas glared at Seth, and Blaire stiffened in her seat, dropping her fork as she stared at the table. Lukas swung his gaze back to her in concern.

"Blaire?" Mera spoke softly. "Are you alright?"

Blaire glanced over at Lukas with a pained expression, then back down to her plate. Seth was wrong. Hearing Seth say she didn't want Lukas burrowed deep inside her and made her sick. She wanted Lukas. She had never desired anything more. She did nothing but think of him, but she was only confused now about the true motivation behind it. Was it this mystical bond, or were her feelings real? Could the bond make her want to be with him against her will? She needed to know for sure what she felt was real and not hormones.

Blaire looked at Mera. "Can the bond force me to want to be with Lukas?"

"The bond doesn't hypnotize or compel you," Kai answered

instead, after swallowing a bite of chicken. "The bond stirs a pull toward your pair to get your attention, but everything you feel beyond that is organic. The bond allows you to feel these things stronger than you normally would, but that is all. At least from my experience."

Seth threw his hands up in obvious frustration and exasperation. "Then why the hell have they been acting like they hate each other and want to get away from one another all the time?"

"I believe there is a lot of confusion surrounding this pairing because Blaire's human." Mera addressed Seth calmly, meeting his chaos with her mellow energy. "I believe Lukas was resistant at first because of how it's unfamiliar and not well understood, thinking perhaps it might have been a mistake."

Lukas clenched his jaw but said nothing, which was as much of a confirmation as anything.

Kai sighed and motioned toward Lukas. "It's clear he doesn't think that now." He looked at Lukas with a single arched brow in question.

"No, no I don't," Lukas said quietly before glancing over at Blaire.

Her breath caught. She continued to stare at him as his green eyes bored into hers with so much conviction her heart raced in response.

"Well fuck," Seth said as he stared at them.

Riley punched him in the arm. "If you were around more, you'd see the way they look at each other more often. There's no way you can miss how much they want one another."

Blaire quickly looked down at her tray, her face heating as she avoided Lukas's eyes.

Lukas sat up and reached toward her. "Do you really want—"

Feedback over the PA interrupted him before a woman's voice summoning Blaire to the student affairs office echoed in the cafeteria.

He dropped back into his seat and ran a hand through his hair, a look of disappointment crossing his face.

What in the world could they be calling her for now? Were there more things they expected her to do? Did she break a rule? She shifted in her chair uncomfortably and pulled on the ends of her hair as she glanced toward the doors.

"Want me to go with you?" Riley asked.

Blaire shook her head. "I'm feeling fine now that I've eaten." She motioned down to her tray, where three-quarters of her large meal was gone. "I'll be fine to go on my own."

She rose from her seat, and Lukas immediately stood. Blaire shook her head at him. "You shouldn't miss class. It's fine."

Blaire scooped up her tray and headed for the door before he could protest.

26

Trust

Blaire knocked on the door to Professor Velastra's office, glancing around the empty corridor only lit with candlelight. It looked vastly different from the rest of the academy, where modern lighting and more open-concept spaces showed remodeling over the years. The student affairs building hadn't changed in many years.

"Enter," the professor called from behind the door in her stern voice.

As she stepped into the office, the smell of books filled Blaire's nose, instantly relaxing her from the nervous tension she felt regarding the reason she may have been called to the office.

"Welcome, Miss Wilcox. Please, sit," the professor said as she motioned to one of the black leather seats in front of her desk.

Blaire lowered herself into the seat and glanced around.

"So, tell me, how is school going for you? Are you enjoying your time here at Blackthorn?" She sat across from Blaire as she went through papers in a folder on her desk. "Oh yes, I also wanted to apologize for the previous… unruly students. I assure you they have been dealt with. They won't be a problem again."

"Thank you… and school is fine. The classes aren't hard, and the academy is beautiful."

The professor smiled for only a moment before her face turned serious. "Now, for the real reason I called you here into my office today."

Here it was. Despite the relaxed feeling she had just moments ago, the expression on the professor's face unnerved her. She tensed in her seat, gripping the hem of her skirt tightly. She was sure something bad was going to happen or had happened. Had Caleb's grandparents come demanding her withdrawal and Blackthorn decided it wasn't worth the hassle? Was she going to have to go back to Caleb? She shifted nervously, panic threatening to grip her.

"Calm yourself," the professor said in an authoritative voice. How did she know Blaire was panicking?

She swallowed hard, nodding.

"Let's try this again, shall we? Have you, or have you not, completed your bonding as per the handbook with Lukas Virtanen?"

"I… ah… no," Blaire looked down at her lap. "We haven't, no."

The professor lifted one slender eyebrow in Blaire's direction. "Pray tell me why has there been a delay? I was certain you both would have quickly sealed the bond by the way Lukas behaved."

Blaire looked up at the professor in confusion. How did she know how Lukas acted? She hadn't been around them.

"I don't know… I used to think Lukas didn't want me here, but I know better now. But I just can't come to terms with it. His moods shift so much I don't know if he'll fall back on how he was in the beginning again and try to get me to leave."

The professor shook her head. "Oh, my dear girl… I can assure you he definitely wants you here. Lukas has met me on several occasions since your arrival. He is confused and is struggling with the strong connection because he has spent so long on his own."

She closed the folder and placed her hands on top of it. "His parents left him at the academy when he was only five and probably see him maybe once a year, if that. Couple that with the fact he didn't discover his fated one until later than most… He's used to being alone, and now here you are… a human. You must understand this has thrown his world into disarray."

Blaire frowned, remembering when Lukas told her his biggest fear. No wonder the idea of being alone forever scared him. He hadn't found his pair before her, obviously, but she didn't know his family had abandoned him to the state like that. She thought he exaggerated, and they visited him often. She hadn't grasped how alone he'd been. He hadn't had a girlfriend either. She didn't like the idea of him with another woman, but it made her sad to think he'd been alone for so long.

"Do you have feelings for him, Miss Wilcox?"

Blaire looked down and nodded.

The professor smiled. "Then I'm sure everything will work out. I need you to trust the process, because the gods do not make mistakes in choosing the fated pairs of Their children."

"Why was I chosen even though I'm a human, though?"

"I honestly cannot tell you that. Not because I do not desire to, but because I simply do not have the answer you seek. I have been researching since before you arrived to try to discover how a human could carry the Korrena mark to no avail, but I can only assure you it is no mistake." The professor gave her a resolute nod. "I honestly was not sure myself when Lukas first visited me and told me of the human girl with his mark, but after speaking with him, it is clear to me you are truly a fated pair."

Professor Velastra stood and walked over to the window, looking out toward the large building on the edge of the academy grounds.

"I can at least say with certainty it would be wise to seal your bond soon, as it is the reason you were accepted into Blackthorn Academy in the first place. While unbonded Vasirian attend the school, the Order will see no need for a human to remain here if they have no purpose in being here."

Blaire gave the professor a quizzical look. "The Order?"

"The school's administration." Professor Velastra opened her mouth as if to say more but stopped, simply shaking her head, and returning her gaze to Blaire. "That is all I had to say. You are free to return to class now."

Blaire slowly got up without saying anything and left the professor's office, uncertain about her future at the academy.

Lukas met Blaire outside Professor Velastra's office when she exited.

"Everything okay?"

She didn't know how to explain to Lukas that if she didn't bond with him, she was going to have to leave. She still struggled with the whole idea of it.

"Yeah…"

Before they could say much else, Vincent approached on the cobblestone pathway.

"Blaire, how are you feeling?"

Lukas glared at him, and Vincent rolled his eyes. "Settle down. I'm not here to take your toy away."

Blaire's eyes widened. "I'm not his toy, or anyone's for that matter," she huffed and put her hands on her hips. Her expression soured, affronted by being referred to as an object.

Lukas growled. "Fuck off, Vincent."

"I'm here to check on Blaire, considering her condition in class earlier." He turned his attention back to Blaire. "I apologize. I meant no disrespect to you. He's just behaving like a petulant child who doesn't like to share."

Blaire didn't like how Vincent was talking about Lukas, but Lukas wasn't acting much better with his attitude out of nowhere. His mood swings were really starting to wear on her.

"She's fine. Now get out of here," Lukas spat.

Blaire shot a look at Lukas, narrowing her eyes. "I can speak for myself." She looked back at Vincent. "I'm fine now that I've eaten. Just a little under the weather."

Vincent nodded quietly.

After several beats of awkward silence, he spoke. "Do take care of yourself, Blaire. We don't want our jewel to lose her shine." He chuckled as he walked away.

Lukas cursed under his breath, then snapped, "What is his problem?"

Blaire rounded on him once Vincent was out of earshot. "What is your problem?" she demanded, pointing at him.

Lukas looked at her in confusion and she sighed in exasperation, turning and walking through the main courtyard, Lukas hot on her heels.

"Wait up!"

Blaire stopped once she entered into the hallway of their dorm building and turned to face him. "What?"

"What did I do?" He looked like a lost puppy, and it pulled at

Blaire. If he wasn't going to act like an ass anymore, she could at least explain things to him. Maybe he didn't see what he was even doing. The only way she would know is if she talked to him.

She sighed heavily. "I might like that you're demanding, and possessive at times..." She held a finger up. "But only when we're alone." She cleared her throat as her cheeks flushed. Talking about this sort of thing felt awkward, but she needed to be honest, or he wouldn't know where she stood—and while she found the dominant part of his personality exciting on a gut level, she needed to set limits or he would become insufferable. Like today, nothing about the way he lashed out at Vincent was attractive. "I especially don't like what you just did. But what I might like in private... I don't like it around others. They'll think you don't respect me."

"But I do respect you."

"What you just did says otherwise."

"I don't understand."

Blaire crossed her arms. "When you get all growly, answering for me, and trying to drive away someone who only showed concern for me, you make it seem like I'm not allowed to do things, or speak to certain people. I'm not just some pet you can call to heel."

Lukas raked a hand through his hair, the muscle in his jaw twitching. "You're mine though."

"You've said that. But the thing is, I'm not a possession, Lukas. I'm a person. A person with my own thoughts, desires, and feelings. Feelings you disregard when you go all alphahole on me."

"Alphahole?" Lukas's brows drew together.

"Yes. I won't deny it can be exciting when you get a little jealous or even possessive, claiming me as yours—but not if you truly believe I'm not my own person capable of making my own choices. You take it to extremes. I've already lived long enough with one person who thought he owned me"—she rolled her eyes when Lukas growled—"I don't need it from you. If you can't accept that, then there's no future here. Predestined fates or not."

Lukas slumped back against the wall and sighed. "Look, I'm sorry. I just… this whole thing is new to me. They tell us all about the bond and what to expect, but hearing about it and experiencing it, are two completely different things. I wasn't prepared for this. Sometimes I feel like I'm losing my mind, and when assholes like Vincent come sniffing around what's mine—"

Blaire gave him a look.

Lukas rubbed the side of his neck, his expression tense, brows drawn down. "I mean… sniffing around you, and I can see the attraction. It's difficult not to respond. I see red—I don't think. It's not an excuse, just explaining… Something about Vincent in particular rubs me the wrong way. The way he looks at you…" Lukas looked weary, defeated, struggling.

She softened her expression but kept her firm tone. "While I don't see what you do with Vincent, I can't say your feelings don't make sense. Anyone would be bothered if someone flirted with or tried to hook up with their partner, but that's where you need to trust me. I mean, we're not fully partners yet… but we'll never be anything if you can't respect my choices and trust that just because I talk to someone you don't 'approve' of, it doesn't mean I want them."

Lukas clenched his fists. "Yeah… I'm sorry. I'm trying. I really am." He met her eyes, his sincerity obvious. "I need you to know that."

Blaire nodded quietly. Lukas had been making an effort. His outbursts had diminished significantly, and he shared more with her. When she heard he reached out to his parents and told them about her being his Korrena, it surprised her. Knowing how estranged he was from his family made it feel even more impactful that he reached out to them. Knowing he cared enough about whatever this was between them to reach out felt important to her.

"I know, Lukas…"

27

Caught In The Act

Blaire lay on her bed, trying to read, but thinking about Lukas's behavior earlier in the week kept distracting her. She wondered what he had planned to say to her before she was called to the professor's office. The confrontation after they ran into Vincent still bothered her; she hoped her words reached him.

A cell phone rang on Lukas's nightstand. He must have forgotten it when he went to his evening advisor's meeting. She wasn't going to mess with it, but as soon as it stopped ringing, it immediately started again. She sat up on the bed and put her book down as the ringing stopped again.

If it was important, they could leave voice mail, but repeated callings made her think it was urgent. The third time it started ringing again, she walked closer and saw Riley's name on the screen.

Blaire picked up the call, keeping her voice low as if someone might hear her in the empty room. "Hello?"

"Hey, Blaire? It's me, Riley."

"Yeah, I know… your name was on the screen." Blaire smirked. "Is everything okay?"

Riley laughed. "Yeah, of course. I was just calling to check on you to make sure you were feeling better. I figured I would have had to make Lukas give you the phone."

"No, he's not here right now. He's in a meeting with his advisor. He said he finally decided on his major. But he forgot his phone."

"Oh, yeah? What's he going to do?"

"He said he wanted to study Modern Languages and Cultural Studies with a focus on languages to start with, maybe taking on another degree later. Something about better understanding his family."

"But is that going to work with your major?"

"What do you mean?"

"Well, if you bond and get married in the future…"

Blaire wasn't sure how to respond to that. Marriage wasn't even on her radar at her age. She was only now trying to come to terms with bonding, which appeared to be a permanent commitment, like marriage, anyway. Her head hurt just thinking about it.

"I don't know. But he did say the degree opens up a variety of different job paths for him, so who knows?"

"Oh. Well, how are you feeling?"

Thankful for the change of subject, Blaire walked back across the room. "I told you, I'm fine. I've been eating regularly, and my cycle is finally gone. It usually passes quickly when it's heavy like this." She shrugged at no one in the room and sat on the edge of her bed. "I've just got a lot on my mind at this point."

"What's wrong?"

Blaire sighed. "Well, when I met with the professor, she told me Lukas had visited her several times. I don't know what about, but whatever it was, it was enough to convince her we really are a fated pair."

"See, I told you!" Riley laughed.

"Yeah, well, she also told me I need to bond with him soon, otherwise there's no reason for me to be here if I don't. And you know what that means… I'd have to return to the life I had before Blackthorn. Caleb. The diner. All of it." Blaire closed her eyes and tried to force away the swelling anxiety, her eyes burning behind her eyelids.

"Then do it."

"What?" Blaire opened her eyes and furrowed her brows in confusion. Had she missed something?

Riley sighed in exasperation. "Bond with him. You both want each other. Stop fighting it."

Blaire sighed and ran a hand through her hair.

Riley clucked her tongue. "Look, I gotta go. I just wanted to check on you. I'll see you tomorrow, okay? It's gonna be alright. Goodnight, Blaire."

"Yeah… I guess. Goodnight." She ended the call and set the phone back where she found it.

She lay back on her bed and grabbed her book again, trying to read once more, but her thoughts drifted again. This time she recalled the dream where Lukas bit her, which made her body stir. Sighing, she set the book aside, giving up on the idea of getting anywhere in that fantasy world.

Reaching over, she turned off the bedside lamp, plunging the room into total darkness. Even the moon hid away from what she was about to do. She settled back onto her bed, nervousness washing over her despite knowing Lukas wouldn't be back for a while. Contemplating what she hadn't done in a long time, in the room she shared with him, in the same room where she dreamed of him so many times, heightened the ache of need in her body.

Blaire slipped her hand beneath her pajama shorts and under her panties, dragging her fingertips over her already damp crease. She was so pent up, having not taken the chance to do anything since she came to the academy, that she whimpered at first touch. With Lukas invading her senses daily, it didn't take much to get her going.

The room was heady with the scent of Lukas, and Blaire moaned low in her throat as she worked her clit with her fingers, her hips grinding and seeking something to fill her that wasn't there for her to take. Her body chased the orgasm she longed for.

She froze when the lock on the door clicked, and then the room filled with light from the hallway. Closing the door, Lukas flipped on the overhead light and Blaire stared at him with wide eyes.

"Lukas…" she whispered; her voice strained.

As his eyes fell on where her hand rested, he tripped over the books at the foot of his bed.

In her shock, she hadn't removed her hand from her shorts. While he recovered his balance, Blaire whipped her hand from beneath her clothes, but her fingers were shiny with the evidence of her silky arousal.

Lukas growled low in his throat, eyes widening before a smile curled his lips and his gaze heated. Blaire bit her lower lip. Her heart pounded loudly in her ears. Her desire for him overrode her embarrassment of being caught in a moment of self-care.

Walking toward her, Lukas kept his eyes locked on hers. Laid bare under his gaze, a delicious shiver passed over her. He stopped next to her bed and leaned his knee on the mattress.

"You are so beautiful…" he whispered.

Her face and neck warmed.

Lukas moved farther onto the bed and leaned over her. Drunk on the scent of that perfect blend of apple and spice, she lay her head back against the pillow and let out a sigh of contentment as the weight of his body pressed against her. The physical connection lit up her nerve endings and tingles passed over her body.

Her heart beat in an uneven rhythm she was sure wasn't healthy.

Lukas brushed her hair away from her neck, trailing his fingers over the pulse point that beat erratically. A shiver of anticipation passed over her body. His face looked tortured, as if he was doing everything possible to maintain self-control, his desire more than evident in his intense green stare that bore into her. His breathing came as ragged as hers.

"Lukas…" she whispered, breaking the spell.

He leaned in, never taking his eyes from hers, and captured her lips with his in a demanding kiss. Blaire moaned into his mouth as they fought for dominance of the kiss that had her body trembling beneath his. She didn't want it to end. She wanted to get lost forever in the kiss. Lost forever in him.

Lukas stopped the kiss abruptly.

She whimpered at the loss. "Please…"

He shuddered at her plea.

He took the hand she had used to pleasure herself, bringing it to his face and inhaling. He shook, then opened his eyes, locking his gaze on hers. His eyes glowed the way they had at the theater, and she sucked in a breath. He languidly ran his tongue over her fingers before taking them into his mouth, groaning the moment her flavor hit his tongue. In a reflexive move, she pushed her hips up toward him, seeking friction to end the ache between her thighs.

Lukas let her wrist free as he pulled her fingers from the heat of his mouth. He reached down and gripped the covers on each side of her head, then took her mouth again in a bruising kiss. His moans mingled with hers, swallowed by her mouth as he pressed his obvious arousal against her core, giving her what she asked for without words.

She felt like kindling that had been doused in gasoline, and all Lukas needed to do was light the match and she would go up in flames.

Blaire wrapped her arms around his neck, entangling her fingers in his hair. When she grazed her nails across his scalp, he shuddered, groaning into her mouth. She loved that she could arouse him with the simplest touch.

Lukas bit gently onto her lower lip, before dragging his tongue to soothe the tenderness left behind. He pulled back and whispered, his voice strained, as he forced his words out.

"Do you have any idea how much I want you?"

He put his hands on each side of her waist to hold her still and pushed forward with his hips, rolling them against her center to emphasize his point.

Blaire gasped, and her eyes fluttered closed as her lips parted on an exhaled sigh, his name slipping free.

"Say it again."

She opened her eyes to look up at him, not understanding what he asked of her. What did she say? In a state of arousal-induced fogginess, she didn't remember saying anything.

Lukas leaned down again, dragging his nose up the side of her neck to her ear, and whispered, "Say my name again, Blaire…"

While he said the words in such a low and unsteady whisper, she could not mistake the command. Her name sounded just as sweet on his lips.

Wrapping her arms again around his neck, she buried her face in his shoulder, and he pressed his hips forward again, causing her to moan his name.

Lukas shifted, and in fear of losing that beautiful feeling, Blaire lifted her legs and wrapped them around his waist. She rocked her body against the significant bulge straining to be free. Lukas closed his eyes, and groaned against her neck, before lifting his head and taking her lips again.

This was everything. It was the aftermath of so much built-up tension. She could get lost in the pleasure he pulled from her body. He hadn't even removed her clothing, or his, and she was already at a breaking point.

He worked her body like a symphony, hitting the right spots over her clothes. Blaire could only imagine what it would be like if he truly took her. She didn't want to imagine it. She didn't want to dream of it. She wanted the reality.

Blaire's moans became louder in the room as Lukas broke away from the kiss, burying his face into her neck once again as he moved against her, the friction of his jeans against the thin material of her sleep shorts increasing the pleasure. The heat of his body against hers drove her toward that edge. That sweet, dangerous edge over which lay euphoria.

She ground herself against his body shamelessly, panting his name over and over like a mantra, her inhibitions thrown out the window in the face of the overwhelming desire and intoxicated feelings washing over her in his presence.

"Mine..." he whispered, kissing down the side of her neck inch by inch. "Only mine." He sucked gently in random spots, not lingering too long in one place, as she turned her head to give him better access.

Lost in the moment, Blaire didn't care if he claimed her body or if he was her first. She wanted him to be her first. She wanted everything Lukas. She wanted to give him everything her. The connection between them burned through her veins like fire.

But as his fangs scraped over the pulse point of her neck, that beautiful moment crashed. She froze. Unlike in her dream, he didn't bite her. He stopped, holding himself rigid, his breathing labored against her skin as if he had just run up several flights of stairs.

Lukas cursed under his breath and lifted his head to stare down at her, panting heavily, his fangs visible.

"Lukas?" she questioned nervously as her legs dropped from his waist. She felt like someone had dumped a bucket of ice water on her.

He shut his eyes tight, arms shaking. "I'm sorry…" he whispered before climbing off her.

She felt abandoned and cold, despite the desire warring inside her. No, he couldn't do this. He couldn't stop now when she was ready to give him everything. She didn't know if she would have the perfect storm of emotions, and whatever else this was, to allow it to happen again.

Lukas stood with his back to her, not saying anything as he caught his breath. He reached down and picked up his cell phone from the nightstand and held it up.

"I forgot this…"

Slowly, he turned to face Blaire on the bed as she wrapped her arms around her torso in a self-soothing gesture, bringing her knees tightly together. He looked at her legs and then back to her face, his expression pained, before he whispered once more, "I'm so sorry…"

Blaire had no idea what he apologized for. Was it for his fangs? For nearly bringing her to the best orgasm of her life just by pressing against her body? While she didn't have the experience to draw from, she'd never been able to wrench those sensations from her body by herself. She felt so confused, so hurt by his rejection. No, she wasn't ready for him to bite her, but did he have such little control he couldn't be with her that way without biting her? The questions swirled around her head and her stomach turned sour.

Lukas finally looked away from her toward the door as the emotionless tone found its way back to his voice. She'd lost him.

"I'll be stopping by Aiden's after my meeting… so I won't be back until much later tonight. Get some sleep."

Not the words she wanted to hear. Not the tone she wanted him to use. She didn't want him to leave. She thought his meeting was done. She wanted to figure this out and, most importantly, she wanted to ease this strangling desire for him.

Lukas turned without saying another word, not daring to look back at her again. Not giving her the chance to respond.

All he left her with were questions. So many questions she didn't even know where to begin in a bid to find answers. Her head hurt to even try after what had just taken place between them.

Blaire curled up into a ball, wrapping her arms around her lower legs, drawing her knees to her chest. She was unsure what would have happened if Lukas hadn't stopped himself.

28

Bloody Night

In the wee hours, exhausted both mentally and physically, Lukas walked down the corridors leading toward the wing housing the dorm room he shared with Blaire.

Despite the way she begged him with both her mouth and body, her trepidation when his fangs touched her skin turned him off. He wouldn't take her in a moment of fear. Until she wasn't afraid of what he was, he couldn't cross that line. The sting of rejection for what he was made pain lance through his tight chest. He couldn't control how he was born.

Lukas shuddered, as if Blaire's fingers were still scraping over his scalp. He wanted it again. He wanted more. He prayed to whichever god watched over him that she would be asleep when he got back to their room, because he wasn't sure he would stop himself a second time if she tried to engage with him again. He only had so much patience, and he walked a fine line that was beginning to fray.

As Lukas walked down the quiet hallway, he felt off. With each step he took toward his door, the feeling of physical exhaustion grew. The overwhelming lethargy was crippling; he posted one hand on the wall as he moved. Something was wrong, but he wasn't sure what. Maybe with what happened earlier, stress was overwhelming his body.

Opening the door to their room, ready to crash into a deep sleep, he froze as the scent of blood assaulted his nose. Fresh blood. Blaire's blood. A lot of it. The smell threatened to bring him to his knees.

Lukas shut the door quickly before the smell could enter the hallway and alert the other students. He didn't have the physical strength at that moment to fend off hungry Vasirian.

Reaching out, he slapped the wall, feeling frantically for the light switch. His heart pounded wildly in his ears in a deafening beat, his breathing labored as he fought against the intoxicating smell. The entire room suffocated him in the rich scent of Blaire's sweet blood.

His gums throbbed as his fangs readied to descend. He was so incredibly thirsty.

When he found the switch and flipped it to bathe the room in bright light, the scene that greeted him caused him to double over, clutching his stomach, and taking in a deep lungful of air as if he'd been underwater and just resurfaced.

Blaire lay on her bed on her back, the covers pushed down to her feet. The sheets she lay on were saturated with blood. Most of her left forearm was stained red with the dark liquid; her t-shirt on her left side and upper arm no longer held any trace of the crisp white color it once had.

"Blaire!" Lukas shouted in a choked cry as he rushed toward her, stumbling over the pile of books he'd tripped over earlier in the night.

He dropped to his knees beside Blaire's bed. Putting his shaking hand on her face, he tapped at her cheek. She didn't stir even a little.

"Blaire, please... please wake up," he begged as he stared at her deathly pale face, listening to her shallow breathing.

Taking a steadying breath, he laid his head against her chest and listened. Her heartbeat was there, but slow. This couldn't be happening. He squeezed his eyes shut tightly as he willed her heart to beat faster.

He fought his hunger. She was dying, and he couldn't avoid his basic instincts to take what his body knew was his birthright.

In that moment, he did feel like a monster, and he hated himself.

Lukas lifted his head and stared down at her, gaze moving down to her bloody arm. His fangs descended as he licked over his lips, the ache of his gums subsiding. He couldn't see past the haze of bloodlust to help her in the way she needed. No. This could not happen.

Throwing himself back in panic, he crawled across the floor and fumbled for his cell phone in his jeans pocket. Pulling it out, he tried to access Aiden's number, but his fingers were slippery with the blood that coated his hands. He was covered in her blood. It was smeared on his face and his hair from listening to her heart, his hands from touching her. He finally managed to open his contacts and hit the button, silently begging his best friend to answer faster.

"Hello?" Aiden answered.

"Hurry..." Lukas rasped. "She's dying... blood... so much blood..." He grasped at words, unable to form coherent sentences, and he didn't know if he made any sense.

"Wait. What's going on? Lukas?"

"B-Blaire," he stammered, and then inhaled sharply and groaned. "...blood everywhere..."

"What?"

He choked on a sob. "She's going to die..."

"Calm down." Shuffling sounded and someone spoke in the background. "What's happening?"

"I'm so… thirsty," Lukas whispered hoarsely as he stared at Blaire from across the room. His throat burned.

"Lukas… what the hell is going on?"

There was silence as Lukas sat staring over at his destined pair. Blaire was supposed to be his forever, not just for this brief time she had been in the academy. He was only just now starting to feel he had a chance of truly making her his. He hadn't even begun to have her, and now she was leaving him by neither of their choosing.

"Lukas!" Aiden yelled through the phone, snapping Lukas out of his spiraling thoughts.

Lukas groaned again, slightly drunk from the smell thickening the air, increasing his need to have her.

"Lukas… by the gods, tell me what the fuck is happening!"

Suddenly, the sound of Blaire's heart breaking through his haze slowed even further. He gripped the phone tightly, almost breaking it in his grasp.

"Hurry!" Lukas screamed into the phone, his voice cracking, before dropping it to clatter on the floor as he raced back to Blaire, kneeling beside her bed.

Aiden called out to him on the phone before the line went dead. Lukas hoped his friend came because he was barely able to function. He covered his face with his bloody hands as he tried to keep his composure, the scent of her blood filling his senses as he panted, hyperventilating.

Lukas barely registered Aiden busting through the door, then immediately staggering back, recoiling at the scent of blood saturating the air.

"What did you do?" Aiden yelled as he stepped into the room with his arm over his face, followed by Seth, who pulled his shirt over his face.

"What the fuck?" Seth choked.

Lukas growled out, yelling at Aiden, "I didn't do this! I would never do this!" He took a stuttered breath. "I found her like this when I came back from your room."

He looked up from his hands at his two friends in the doorway, tears streaming down his face through the blood. He was lost.

"Please..." Lukas choked on his cries. "Please tell me what to do..."

Riley entered the room. "What's going on? I can smell blood down the hall and students are filling the hallway." She shut the door, not seeing Blaire or Lukas yet.

"Why didn't you close the door?" Aiden snapped at Seth.

"I wasn't thinking, okay? How can anyone think with that smell everywhere?"

Lukas placed his shaking hand once more on Blaire's face, needing to feel her. His thirst be damned.

"Wait, what's going on?" Riley moved around Aiden and Seth and screamed. "Oh gods, Blaire!" She ran over and dropped next to Lukas, pulling the sheets up to press over Blaire's arm, applying pressure to where the most blood was concentrated. "What happened?"

Aiden ran a hand through his hair and dropped his arm from his nose as he clenched his jaw. "I don't know. Is she still bleeding?"

Lukas lowered his hand and looked at Aiden, his face weary. "I don't know."

"You didn't check?" Aiden shouted, incredulous.

Lukas bared his teeth. It wasn't that he didn't understand basic first aid, but in his panic and fight against the thirst, he barely managed to keep his composure. Thinking clearly wasn't exactly his strong suit at the moment.

Riley held Blaire's arm tightly and shook her head. "I can't tell, but I'm not taking any chances."

"We need to contact the health branch to get help," Aiden said. "It's too dangerous to move Blaire in her condition with a hallway full of Vasirian. We don't know what we're dealing with, anyway." He pulled his cell phone from his pocket and cracked the door, slipping outside to make the call.

Lukas slowly lifted himself from the floor and bent over the bed, lifting Blaire's limp form, avoiding disrupting Riley's efforts to keep Blaire from bleeding out. He slipped behind Blaire on the bed and pulled her into his arms. He buried his face against her shoulder, rocking her. "Please don't leave me... oh gods... please don't leave me." His shoulders shook as he sobbed into her hair.

"Who could have done this?" Seth murmured, still holding the shirt over his face.

Aiden came back into the room and shut the door. "I told Professor Velastra the situation. She's on her way and said to make sure we keep the door closed to anyone but her." He gripped his hair. "Fuck. The hallway's filled with students. They can smell her."

After several minutes of anguished silence, a knock sounded on the door. Aiden peeked out, before opening the door, and allowing the professor to step inside. Two staff members, one man and one woman dressed in scrubs, followed her carrying a large case that looked like a cooler and a tote bag, rolling a metal stand behind them as they entered.

"By the gods!" Professor Velastra exclaimed, her usual prim and stoic demeanor slipping as she rushed over to Blaire.

"Did things get out of hand between you two?" she asked, checking Blaire's pulse at her throat.

Lukas lifted his bloody face, his narrowed eyes meeting the professor's over Blaire's shoulder.

"I… did… not… do this," he reiterated through gritted teeth. "I found her like this."

He struggled desperately with his thirst and hadn't done a single thing to Blaire in this situation. What made anyone think he could have gotten her to this state if he was resisting now? He didn't understand it. The anger helped him keep his senses now that he wasn't alone with Blaire. He wasn't sure what he would have done to her if Aiden and Seth hadn't arrived when they did.

The professor lowered herself to her knees and motioned for Riley to move. Riley stood on shaky legs and moved toward Aiden and Seth. When she reached them, she slumped to the floor, unable to stay on her legs any longer.

Professor Velastra reached out for Blaire as the two members of staff began sorting through the items they'd brought into the room. Lukas growled at her, pulling Blaire tightly to his body. He didn't want anyone else to touch her. It had been hard enough having Riley so close, but a rational part of him knew she would never hurt Blaire. He wasn't letting Blaire out of his sight again if this was what happened when he did.

"I won't hurt her, Lukas. I only wish to help," she whispered softly, enunciating her words slowly as if trying to calm a feral animal, as one of the staff members passed her a pair of latex gloves that she snapped on her hands.

Lukas squeezed his eyes shut as he clung to the limp body in his arms, the faint heartbeat his only grounding point.

The professor sighed. "Lukas… Blaire needs blood; she's lost too much. The nursing staff and I are only here to help." She glanced over at the others in the room. "Can you please gather towels and a wet washcloth so we can clean her up and assess the situation? We need to see if she's still bleeding."

Seth rushed to the bathroom to get the supplies needed. He returned moments later and approached the bed, his shirt held high over his face as he handed everything to the professor.

Reaching out and taking Blaire's arm, the professor began cleaning away the blood despite Lukas's growls of protest as he stayed wrapped around Blaire's body, lost to the hunger and worry clawing at his insides.

The professor gasped. "She wasn't bitten."

The large male nurse moved over, putting on latex gloves, and knelt beside her, examining Blaire's arm.

Lukas snapped his head up, his head clearing at the professor's words, taking in the grim look on the nurse's face.

"What do you mean?" Aiden demanded, helping his sister to her feet.

The nurse's calm baritone was impervious to the severity of the situation. "While she's no longer actively bleeding, she's missing a chunk of skin from the inside of her forearm."

The professor pressed her lips into a firm line and stared down at Blaire's forearm.

"And it's obvious by the marking here"—the nurse pointed out a spot on the crook of Blaire's arm to the professor—"that someone used a needle, and they did a pretty poor job with it." He frowned as the professor cleaned the blood from Blaire's arm. He then secured a tight binding around the area where the chunk was missing to staunch the bleeding.

Riley glanced over toward the professor, swallowing hard. "W-what do you mean?"

"Based on Blaire's medical history, we're aware she has some sort of condition that makes it difficult to heal, and she bruises easily, so the bruising that has spread over her forearm hidden by the blood is quite bad, but it likely wouldn't have been this severe if whoever did this knew what they were doing."

The professor moved aside so the nurse could get a better look at her arm.

"But why is there so much blood? Why would someone take her skin?" Aiden asked, stepping out of the way of the other nurse as she rolled up the soiled rug and moved across the floor with a towel to clean up the blood Lukas had trailed from the bed when he crawled away from Blaire.

"Generally, skin is taken for testing, or I also suppose for consumption," the male nurse said matter-of-factly.

Riley recoiled. "What? Why would someone want to eat her?"

He gave Riley a flat look as Lukas tightened his hold around Blaire.

"I doubt that is the purpose, considering the small amount and the wound's shape. It appears as if someone merely wanted a sample, but I can't see why someone would need it. No one in the medical department has requested any tests, and we would have had her come to us so a proper biopsy could be done in a controlled, sterile environment. We would have made a formal request to both the Order, explaining our need for such a procedure, and to her."

He lowered Blaire's arm to the bed and looked at Riley again.

"A skin biopsy doesn't bleed in this manner. Yes, they bleed a little… but this doesn't appear to be the same thing. Whoever took her skin had no training and cut deep, causing excessive venous bleeding—which is why she is in the state she is in. She's lucky her radial artery wasn't severed."

Seth asked, "Why would a student use needles and not bite her? Why cut her skin?"

"A student didn't do this," the professor said quietly, staring at

Blaire's arm.

Lukas stared at the professor, his brows drawing together in confusion.

Aiden speared his fingers through his hair, gripping the top. "Just fucking tell us what you're talking about!"

Riley gasped and looked at her brother.

"I'm sorry, it's just…" Aiden squeezed his eyes shut. His struggle was obvious.

The professor frowned and shook from her thoughts, nodding. "You need not apologize. You're concerned, and I understand. I am happy to know that Miss Wilcox—"

"Blaire," Lukas growled.

"Yes, Blaire. My apologies," she said, giving Lukas a pitying glance. "I am happy to know Blaire has found people who care about her within these walls. She has suffered for a long time, from what I gathered from our background checks, and it would be beneficial to her to find her place here. I also understand it is likely difficult for all of you to be around this much human blood."

Seth turned his head away and Riley bit her lip, her fang catching the flesh there.

Turning serious, the professor looked at Lukas. "You need to let her go."

The nurse placed his fingers on Blaire's wrist to check her pulse. He reported it was weak, something Lukas already knew. It had been weak for way too long.

"You need to lay her down and get off the bed so I can hook her up to an IV line. Our time is running out." He sighed in frustration. "I would much prefer to do this in a sterile environment, but the situation outside is dangerous for the human, and we don't have much time. While there is pressure applied to avoid excess bleeding, she is still in a critical state. We need to get her replenished, and the wound stitched as soon as possible. There is no telling how long it would take us to transfer her to the medical department while dealing with what's outside that door."

Lukas tightened his hold on Blaire and Aiden stomped over to tower over them on the bed.

"If you don't get up, I am going to beat your ass, man… because if you don't get up, Blaire is going to die. Do you understand? She's going to die." His voice cracked. "Snap out of it."

That got Lukas's attention as he stiffened in fear. Not fear of his friend's threats, but the reminder that Blaire was dying in his arms.

Lukas slid from the bed and gently laid Blaire down before he stood and backed away. He ran his bloody hands through his hair, streaking it red.

The big male nurse stood and got to work right away, the female nurse moving the drip stand over next to Blaire's bed. She opened the chest, which wasn't a cooler, but a blood warmer. She removed a blood bag and prepared the Y-tubing, readying the blood in an infusion pump.

"When Miss"—the professor paused and shook her head, correcting herself as she watched the nurses work—"When Blaire first came to Blackthorn, we tested her blood type and obtained a reserve of blood that we kept on hand in case something ever happened to her."

The female nurse tested Blaire's vitals, and after she finished setting Blaire's transfusion to begin, she motioned toward Lukas's desk. "Please give me the chair."

Aiden grabbed the desk chair and took it over to her. She sat down beside the bed.

"I need to keep a close eye on her for about fifteen minutes to ensure there is no negative reaction to the donor blood."

Riley's brows pinched together. "Negative reaction?"

"Yes, it is possible for humans to have reactions to a donor's blood if it doesn't agree with them. This usually will manifest itself in the first fifteen minutes, and I need to be prepared to stop the transfusion and produce another solution should her body reject the blood," the nurse said.

"Wait… she might not be able to take the blood?" Riley exclaimed loudly.

The male nurse looked over from where he was writing in a notebook he'd taken from his bag. "It's a possibility, but I believe she will be fine. Once the fifteen-minute window passes, then we only have to assess her vitals each hour."

The professor sighed. "I had hoped never to have to need this blood, but I am immensely glad I took the precaution."

"Yeah, me too," Lukas muttered under his breath as he paced the room. "Is she going to be okay or not?" All the talk of a potential negative reaction had done nothing to calm his panicked state. He looked at the professor with a desperate plea in his eyes.

"She should be fine in a few hours, but I will stay and monitor her with one of the nurses," the professor said, looking Lukas over, assessing his bloodied state. He still breathed heavily. "You, however, should stay elsewhere tonight."

"What?" Lukas stiffened his arms and loomed over the diminutive professor, who looked undaunted.

The female nurse looked at him with sadness in her eyes. "It is probably more difficult for you than anyone else with this much of the girl's blood in the air."

That was a simple way of putting it. He was so unbelievably thirsty, and he just wanted. He craved. He didn't even know what he wanted anymore. He ached for Blaire, and it ripped him apart inside. He was so scared, but he wanted to taste her, glut himself until nothing was left.

Shuddering, he bit down on his lower lip and one of his fangs pierced the skin there, blood running down his chin, his eyes focused on Blaire with intense heat.

The professor nodded and gestured toward Lukas. "See?"

Aiden placed a firm hand on Lukas's shoulder, shaking him from his trance as Aiden steered him toward the door, whispering, "I've got you."

"I'll get his clothes and stuff," Riley said as she rushed to the closet.

Stepping out into the hall, Lukas released a shaking breath, trying to ignore the burn in his throat.

Aiden glared at the students nearby. "Get the fuck out of here," he growled at them.

Several students disappeared into their rooms while others farther down the hall stared at Lukas covered in Blaire's blood.

"This is not good," Aiden said under his breath.

Riley and Seth finally came out of the room, and they ushered Lukas and Aiden out of the building and over to Aiden's dorm.

29

Breakdown

As soon as they stepped into Aiden's dorm, Lukas collapsed to the floor, his body finally giving out on him as he held his head, sobbing like a child.

Aiden rushed to his side, dropping to his knees, grabbing onto Lukas, and pulling him into his arms.

"I've got you. I'm with you, man… it's going to be alright," Aiden whispered. "I've got you."

Seth looked down at Lukas in Aiden's arms with a tense expression.

"I can't do this. I can't stay here. The smell of her blood all over him is too much for me to handle." Seth looked over at Riley, who shook all over. "I'm sorry. I just can't."

Aiden swallowed thickly and looked at Seth with a nod. "I don't blame you. I'm honestly on autopilot here. I had a packet not long ago… I'm… managing."

With one last glance at Riley, Seth rushed out the door as Mera and Kai came in.

"What happened?" Mera took in the state of Lukas.

Kai narrowed his brows in confusion before adding, "The entire school is talking about Blaire being attacked."

"Shit. How did it get around so damn fast?" Aiden muttered under his breath.

"The smell was everywhere… it's not a surprise." Riley shuddered and sat down on Aiden's bed.

Lukas squeezed his hair in his fists as he cried against his best friend's chest. He was losing it. This was finally it for him. All the fighting he had done to drive Blaire away, and the subsequent fall as he could no longer resist his desire to be with her, was all coming to a head. He was going to lose her. He couldn't lose her. He barely registered what happened around him. What was being said, and by who.

Riley was at least explaining what happened, so he didn't have to relive it until she broke down in tears, Mera sitting next to her to console her.

The small room was crowded, and he was suffocating. But in that moment of his collapse, his best friend, with whom he'd been irrationally angry for so long, was the only thing holding his sanity in check.

Kai sat next to Mera, and the room fell silent. The only sounds in the small space were Lukas's anguished cries and the occasional sniffle from Riley as she calmed down.

"I'm going to lose her… I'm losing her. I can't lose her," Lukas chanted as he clung to Aiden in a desperate bid to soothe his agony, barely hanging onto himself, Aiden his only anchor.

Riley shut her eyes, no longer able to look at Lukas and keep her own self together.

"That's not going to happen," Aiden gritted out through a

clenched jaw. "The transfusion is going to make everything alright again, okay?"

Lukas looked up at Aiden, his face streaked from the tears running through Blaire's smeared blood on his cheeks. He swallowed hard.

"It hurts… It fucking hurts," he croaked. He had to force himself to speak, and it felt like swallowing razors. His throat ached so badly.

He took in another large swallow of air, giving his best effort to push away the panic attack. "I feel physical pain, and I don't know if it's hers or mine."

Mera sighed softly and looked at Lukas.

"I'm not surprised you would be hurting physically from this level of distress, but it is highly probable you also feel the pain Blaire is currently experiencing, since nothing happened to you physically tonight."

"I'm going to kill whoever did this when I find them," Lukas growled out, his voice strained, hoarse from his crying.

Riley wrapped her arms around her middle and shook her head.

Aiden said, "I understand how you feel, but you need to stay calm and strong for Blaire. Going after whoever did this right now isn't wise."

Lukas sat back from Aiden's hold.

"Who fucking cares! I want them dead!" He held his head in his hands, resting his elbows on his knees.

"Who would have done something like this?" Kai asked.

Mera shrugged lightly. "I don't know, but I have to agree with the professor's assessment that a student would have just bitten Blaire."

"Perhaps they wanted to save some for later? If so, they could easily have done that by using a needle, but that still doesn't explain the missing flesh."

Lukas jumped up from the floor, no longer able to listen, and paced around the room. He couldn't stand how casually they talked about it. In a sudden fit, he threw a punch in frustration and knocked a hole in the closet door. "Fuck!"

"Hey!" Aiden got to his feet. "Take a shower, Lukas. The smell of Blaire's blood isn't helping you to maintain your composure."

Lukas ran both hands through his hair, fingers catching on the dried blood that had matted the strands together, and grimaced.

Aiden gripped Lukas' shoulder. "Besides… it's difficult for me to smell it and I've drank recently, not to mention she's not my Korrena, so I'm damn sure you're suffering."

Lukas wandered toward the bathroom door. He wasn't thirsty anymore, just agitated. The blood kept him agitated, but he wouldn't be able to rest until Blaire was safe again in his arms. Blood, or no blood.

He stepped into the ensuite bathroom and slid down the closed door, closing his eyes as he tried to calm himself, listening to the others talking through the thin door. He wrestled with the idea of washing away the blood, the only thing that kept him connected to Blaire in this moment of hell.

Riley's voice came muffled through the bathroom door. "I've never seen him this upset before. It's like he's a different person."

"I've never seen him cry." Aiden sighed heavily. "Even when we were children."

Mera's gentle calm came next. "It's the bond. Whenever something happens to your Korrena, it can cause a wide range of things to take place. The partner experiences extreme panic and can sometimes feel physical pain if they are highly in tune with their pair's emotions."

That explained a lot about why he couldn't get control of his emotions tonight. Sure, he hadn't been in control much at all since Blaire arrived, but tonight broke him. He had no control over his body, and it terrified him. He sighed as he hung his head forward.

Kai added, "Sometimes the partner even dies from the effects of what they go through when their Korrena pair finally dies, depending on how closely bonded they are."

Lukas stiffened as Riley shouted.

"No, no, no!" She began to sob hard. "Blaire is not going to die. Please don't talk like that. She's going to be okay! She's going to be okay, right? Right?"

"You're absolutely right," Aiden said placatingly. "The professor and nurses said Blaire would be just fine. For now, though, we should all get some sleep because Blaire is going to need us tomorrow."

Lukas got up from the floor. He had stalled long enough. He took his clothes off before stepping into the shower to wash away the lifeblood of his one true reason for living.

After his shower, Lukas came out wrapped in a towel to find Kai and Mera gone, but Riley had made herself at home in Aiden's spare bed and was already asleep.

"Hey," Aiden said as he came out of his closet. "How are you holding up?"

Lukas shrugged. "I'm still alive."

Aiden sighed as he nodded, choosing not to push, which Lukas felt grateful for.

"Riley packed you some clothes in that bag over there." Aiden pointed toward a black duffel on the desk. "But she didn't get anything to sleep in… so I figured you'd want something comfortable." He held out a stack of clothes, passing them to Lukas.

"Yeah, thanks…" Lukas said quietly, his energy completely gone after what happened between him and Blaire before his meeting, and then this. He shuddered and tried to move his mind away from his swirling thoughts before he fell victim to another panic attack.

Nodding toward Aiden's spare bed, Lukas asked, "So… what's up with that?"

Aiden chuckled and crossed his arms, looking at Riley, who was snoring softly. "She missed sleeping near her big brother."

Lukas raised an eyebrow at him, and Aiden started laughing.

"No man, she didn't want to be alone tonight, and I don't blame her, so when she asked me if she could stay, I caved. She might be a pain in the ass sometimes, but she's my little sister, and I'm going to be there for her when I can." Aiden shrugged. "You go ahead and get changed and I'll go bag up your clothes so the professor can dispose of them tomorrow where other students can't get their hands on them. You can take my bed tonight and I'll take the floor."

"What? No…"

"It's fine. You need to rest, and the floor doesn't bother me."

Aiden went into the bathroom, not giving Lukas the chance to protest.

Lukas quickly changed in the middle of the room, since Riley lay turned away from him, already asleep. Climbing onto Aiden's bed, he lay back and sighed, staring at the ceiling. He wasn't going to be able to sleep tonight.

"You can have this bed if you want it," Lukas said as Aiden came out of the bathroom without a bag of clothes. He assumed Aiden kept them in the bathroom to keep the scent away from him, to avoid riling him up again. It was a good idea, honestly. "I'm not going to be able to sleep, anyway."

Aiden shook his head. "No." He stepped into his closet and came back with blankets in his arms and laid them out on the floor before pointing at Lukas. "You need to rest, because Blaire is going to need you tomorrow."

Lukas sighed as Aiden turned off the bedside lamp and moved to the floor.

"I'm sorry…" Lukas whispered in the dark.

"What for?"

"For thinking you wanted to take Blaire away from me."

After a brief silence, Aiden chuckled. "While I do care for her and would have been happy to be her partner, her heart belongs to you and your heart belongs to her. I would never ruin that, or our friendship."

Lukas said nothing in response as he stared up into the blackness of the room. He listened to Aiden shuffle as he settled in.

Aiden spoke the truth, and it took a lot for him to be honest about the fact that he did care about Blaire. Honestly, it would have pissed Lukas off more if Aiden had said he didn't care about her that way after claiming he did, but his friend was not that wishy-washy. Lukas trusted him, and right now, he needed him more than he ever had since they were children.

30

The Order

Muffled voices filtered through the haze of Blaire's mind as she found her way back to consciousness. A severe migraine pounded like someone had taken a sledgehammer to the side of her head, and her body ached, particularly her arm.

With a pained groan, Blaire peeled open her eyes and stared at the ceiling. She willed the room to come into focus, but she was having difficulty with the overwhelming feeling of being underwater. She felt sick.

Blaire turned her head and saw Professor Velastra smiling at her, sitting next to her bed in a desk chair. Confused, Blaire sat up, but lay back down as a wave of dizziness washed over her. She placed a hand on her head, covering her eyes.

"Oh, thank fuck. Are you alright?" Aiden asked as he rushed to her side of the bed, kneeling.

What was he doing here? What was going on?

The professor placed a hand on Blaire's shoulder. "Take it easy. You've lost quite a lot of blood and may be weak for quite a while, despite the transfusion."

Blood? She wasn't sure she heard the professor correctly, and then the rest of what she'd said dawned on her. Blaire panicked and tried to sit up again, but Aiden put a hand out to stop her.

Blaire looked down at her aching arm and followed the IV line up to the drip stand holding a red-stained bag. Her head spun. She looked away and spotted Riley, Mera, and Kai also in the room, looking at her with concern. Where was Lukas? Was he okay? Nausea gripped her stomach.

"What… are you talking about?" she finally asked with a hoarse voice, her heart rate kicking up a notch as her voice wavered.

Lukas burst into the room with a bottle of orange juice and a bag of cookies in his hands. He rushed to Blaire's bedside and dropped to his knees, setting everything down quickly onto the nightstand before he reached out to her with shaking hands, grasping hers. She had no idea what was going on. Why was he acting like this? Why was the room filled with people?

"Are you okay?" Lukas whispered as he stared at her, his forehead wrinkled in concern.

Heavy bags sat dark beneath his bloodshot eyes. He looked as if he had been crying. Something felt very wrong.

After looking around at everyone's faces in confusion, she whispered, "What's going on?"

Lukas, clearly not able to take anymore, got up and put his knee on the bed to climb in with her.

"W-w-what are you doing?" she stammered, flustered that not only was he getting in her bed again, reminding her of last night before his meeting, but he did it right in front of everyone. Blaire tried pulling away from him, but pain shot up her arm, so she stopped, having nowhere to go.

Before she protested, Aiden spoke up. "Just… let him, okay? He's been a complete wreck ever since he found you near lifeless and covered in blood…" Aiden looked away, a pained look darkening his features as if it hurt him to even say the last part.

Still confused, but without the strength to fight it, Blaire sat up and allowed Lukas to crawl in behind her on the bed, putting his legs on each side of her body and pulling her back into his arms. She relaxed in his tight embrace as he lowered his face into her hair.

The professor explained what had happened the night before, and Blaire closed her eyes, trying to focus and grasp for any information in her memory.

She gasped.

"What? Did I hurt you?" Lukas tensed, his hold loosening as he looked at her with concern.

"No… I just remembered something. After you left last night, I went to bed, and I woke up later when I felt something pinch my arm." She looked down at her bruised arm and then at the white gauze wrapped around her forearm. "Someone wearing a robe was drawing blood from my arm with a needle… when I jerked away, it hurt like hell, but before I could do anything, they put some kind of cloth over my face. I don't remember anything after that."

"Chloroform, most likely." A woman stepped from the bathroom and walked over to the professor. "Whoever did this likely wanted her to remain unconscious and was prepared for a fight. I wouldn't be surprised if they used a drugging agent to keep her unconscious. I doubt they would have been able to take her flesh in that manner without her alerting the entire floor, unless they drugged her."

"What? Who are you?" Blaire tried to get to her senses, but her head felt foggy. Had someone really drugged her?

"I'm a nurse from the student health unit. You've had a good piece of your flesh removed from your arm and you've lost quite a bit of blood because they were sloppy." She gestured toward the bandage on Blaire's forearm. "There's no way you'd have been able to stay quiet without a bit of help, and whoever did this likely didn't have the ability to compel you. Though, compulsion wouldn't have kept you quiet, only compliant to their wishes."

The bruise covering a sizable portion of her arm, the bandage, and the tubing that remained attached to her backed the nurse's words with concrete proof, but the incident was still surreal to imagine. The idea she couldn't recall anything beyond the struggle with the hooded figure didn't sit well with her, and it made her feel even more ill than she already felt. She wanted to vomit.

Lukas squeezed her tightly, as if giving her any slack would cause her to float away.

"Whoever did this is a dead man walking," he whispered against her hair, and she shivered.

Aiden clenched his fists and nodded his agreement. "That goes without saying…"

The professor frowned and shook her head. "That is easier said than done."

"What do you mean?" Riley asked as everyone looked at the professor with varying degrees of confusion, disbelief, and frustration.

Professor Velastra stood and moved the desk chair out of the way, not offering an answer as the nurse began the process of unhooking the tubing from Blaire's arm and bandaging the small injection site before it had the chance to bleed. She packed away the used items in a bag marked for biohazardous materials.

Turning to Blaire, she said, "You are in the clear at this point. I have left materials in the bathroom to change your bandages. Please refrain from getting your stitches wet for the next forty-eight hours, but then you can clean them gently with soap and water twice a day."

"Stitches?" Blaire's voice rose as she sucked in a breath sharply.

"Well, yes. The wound is quite deep and sloppy. This helps avoid infection, avoids further bloodshed, and will minimize the scarring."

Riley looked at Blaire with sadness in her eyes. "She's going to scar?"

The nurse sighed. "Unfortunately, yes. There's no avoiding scarring due to the severity of the wound and her inability to heal like a Vasirian."

Blaire stared at the gauze on her arm.

"That said, please keep your stitches clean, and come to the medical department should you have any complications—redness, fever, infection, and the like. Should none of that arise, come by in two weeks and we will assess if it is time to remove them."

The nurse wheeled the IV stand to the door, carrying a large chest with a bag resting on top of it with her. "I'm sorry this happened to you." She left without another word.

Silence settled in the room. Blaire couldn't believe that in a place of education something so horrific could happen. But considering this wasn't a standard university filled with humans, it wasn't so far-fetched. She had relaxed since being attacked in the courtyard when she first arrived. With friends, other students warming up to her, and Lukas, she had been lulled into a false sense of security. Blackthorn wasn't much safer than the outside. The monsters were just different.

The professor locked the door behind the nurse when she left, then turned to address them all.

"I wanted to wait until she left, as I don't know who on staff we can trust with this next bit of information I wish to share with you all." Professor Velastra crossed the room back to Blaire's bedside. "I believe the Order may be behind this heinous act."

Lukas dropped his forehead to Blaire's shoulder, muttering, "Son of a bitch."

"Why can't we trust the staff?" Aiden asked, slumping down onto Lukas's bed, and running a hand through his hair.

"If the Order is behind this, it's quite possible they have others on staff who are aware of their motives. If they get wind we are suspicious of them, I fear what the consequences might be. You can trust the staff in general, but not with this information. It would be reckless to go around pointing fingers, in any case."

"Why would the administration do something like this?" Blaire asked.

The professor sighed, sitting down on the chair beside the bed.

"While they are Blackthorn administration, they are much more than that. The seven members who preside over the Order not only determine the fates of the students here within Blackthorn Academy and its branch locations, but they have strong connections to government officials"—she waved a hand—"and some other not-so-savory organizations."

Mera finally spoke up from her position against the wall next to the closet. "They also preside over Vasirian in both North and South America."

Nodding, the professor added, "Correct. Unfortunately, this information isn't in your guidebook, as it's something taught to our students from a young age. To give you a crash course lesson, two other councils oversee other Vasirian in the world the way the Order does for the Americas. A council located in Asia presides over the Asian region and Oceania, and a council located in Southern Africa oversees that region. Then, there's the king..."

"King?" Blaire asked.

"Yes. There isn't a council like the others located in Europe because the Blackthorn Clan themselves are located there. They have their own sub-council that oversees the affairs in the European region. But at the head of the Blackthorn Clan sits King Adrian Blackthorn, succeeding his father after his passing a few months ago."

The Vasirian world was much bigger than Blaire thought. With councils all over the world, the Vasirian population must be fairly large. How had no one ever discovered them? And they had a king? It was all a bit much with everything she'd just gone through.

"The Blackthorn Clan are the be-all and end-all for our kind," Mera added.

The professor nodded at her. "Yes, they are the quintessential element when determining the standard our race lives by. For centuries, they have set the rules and regulations that govern our kind."

Kai shook his head and spoke up, bringing the conversation back on topic. "Why would the Order want to take Blaire's blood, though? What value is her blood to them?"

"I suspect they wish to conduct experiments, considering this is the first time in known history that a human has manifested a Korrena mark."

"But I don't have a mark."

The professor looked at Blaire. "The mark doesn't permanently present itself until the bond is sealed, but in its early stages it can be seen on occasion by the other half of the pair."

Blaire shook her head and pursed her lips. "No, I've never seen a mark on Lukas."

"Is it possible humans aren't able to see the mark?" Aiden asked, rubbing his neck as if trying to calm himself.

"Well," the professor turned to look at Aiden. "That may be a possibility. But as it seems their mark is presenting itself on the side of the neck, Blaire may never have noticed it because of Lukas's long hair."

"Blaire did have her hair up on the first day I saw it."

"Have you seen it since then?" Riley asked.

Lukas looked up at the ceiling, closing his eyes in deep thought. He clenched his jaw and then sighed before nodding in confirmation.

Kai raised an eyebrow at him. "What's wrong?"

"Nothing," Lukas said, as he put his forehead on Blaire's shoulder.

"No, if there's something pertinent to our situation, Lukas, then you need to share." The professor tilted her head in his direction. "Have there been other developments?"

Lukas looked at the professor, the muscles in his jaw working overtime. Something seemed off, and Blaire wasn't sure what to make of his sudden change in behavior. He seemed nervous.

"I didn't see it for a while in the beginning, except I think once, but it was extremely faint… but recently I saw it like the day I saw her on the street." Lukas looked down at Blaire's bruised arm, not meeting the eyes of the others in the room.

The professor's brows knitted together in confusion. "Why was that something you felt you couldn't share with us?"

Kai cleared his throat as he looked at Lukas meaningfully. "Stimulating circumstances?" he asked as Lukas looked up at him, giving a firm nod.

They shared a look, something Blaire didn't understand.

"Interesting," the professor muttered under her breath as she stared between Lukas and Kai.

"What the hell does that mean?" Blaire asked in frustration. She was tired and in pain, and she didn't have the energy to figure out vague wordplay. What kind of circumstances would lead Lukas to see her mark when other times it wasn't there? Why would Kai know? She couldn't wrap her brain around any of this information, and it didn't do anything to soothe the floaty feeling she still had.

Professor Velastra looked at Lukas expectantly. "Yes. Can you share what these events were? It would help in understanding the progression of the bond between the two of you."

Lukas dropped his forehead onto Blaire's shoulder.

"What's wrong? Tell me what it means." Blaire turned her head and looked at him.

Lukas didn't say anything as he lifted his head. Then, catching her by surprise, he brought his hand up to rest on her jaw, dragging his fingers down the side of her neck to rest his fingertips against her pulse point. Her eyes fluttered closed, her heartbeat increasing in response to his touch. He pressed gently for only a moment before relaxing his touch against the side of her neck.

"This…" Lukas whispered, with a gravelly edge to his voice, into Blaire's ear as he pressed once more against her pulse point. "When I did this… I saw the mark just before I did this…"

Blaire's mind flashed to last night when she had been ready to give Lukas everything. The gentle pressure of his fingers got her attention. A simple act, but the touch burned her skin. The passion was hard to forget. She swallowed hard.

"And now?" she rasped. "Is it there now?"

"No…"

"It feels different," she whispered.

"How?" His voice fanned over her cheek from behind and she shivered.

"It doesn't feel hot… your fingers."

Aiden cleared his throat, and Kai smirked as Mera placed her hand over her mouth.

"Oh wow…" Riley said in awe, her mouth hanging open.

Blaire squirmed when Riley spoke, remembering others were there. The sexual tension in the room elevated and she was sure everyone could tell. She went to move, but Lukas dropped his arm to wrap around her. He didn't hurt her, but it was a clear command to stay still. His hands shook against her.

The professor clapped her hands. "Well then. I don't think we need more information regarding that. I suppose heightened sexual arousal would intensify the bond. But I find the sensation of heat associated with times of seeing the Korrena mark interesting. This is new. That said…" She stared at the way Lukas still held Blaire. "Lukas, it would seem you're still not over last night."

Lukas muttered under his breath, "In more ways than one…"

Blaire smiled despite her pain; he meant what had taken place between them on this very bed.

After several moments of awkward silence, Mera spoke up with a shake of her head, bringing the conversation back in a more stable direction. "I researched the phenomenon of humans having the Korrena mark when Blaire first arrived. I found texts in the old archives documenting Vasirian and human relationships, but there wasn't much there. Most of the pages had been ripped out, as if someone didn't want the information known."

"It is a possibility they found answers within the archives and wanted to destroy that evidence," the professor said with a frown.

This was information overload, and Blaire didn't know what to make of it. Some big group of somebodies in the Vasirian world wanted to know more about her? She wasn't anyone special. She was a regular human. The most remarkable thing she'd ever done was to appear on the news when she gave an interview after someone tried to rob the diner. Her humdrum life was the perfect example of why it made no sense she was somehow fated to this beautiful being who held her as if nothing else in the world mattered.

Kai crossed his arms and tilted his head in contemplation. "What purpose would that serve? It's our history, and if humans are a part of that history, then why erase it?"

"There is a strong chance that whatever those texts held carries the secret to what makes Blaire so special," the professor said.

Blaire sure didn't feel special. She felt more like a burden and an inconvenience. No matter where she went, she always caused problems for someone. Because of her ties to Caleb, her work life was under constant scrutiny. She couldn't have a social life because the Wilcox family bullied anyone who tried to be friends with her, so eventually, they ghosted her. She counted herself lucky Charlotte remained by her side, but she had heard the ways Caleb had tried to run her off too.

Forget about romance. It wasn't even on the table. Anytime someone tried to get close to her in the diner, as soon as Ricky got wind of it—which meant Caleb got wind of it—she'd soon find they were no longer customers, and she'd never see them again. Now, her existence was disrupting all their lives. It didn't matter as much when she thought she didn't want to be with Lukas, but now… she couldn't deny her feelings for him any longer. Being the first human in a Korrena pairing inconvenienced everyone around her.

"But that doesn't make any sense," Mera spoke up, shaking Blaire from her thoughts. "If they already know from the texts, then why is her blood so important?"

The professor sighed and folded her hands in her lap. "Unfortunately, I am in the dark as much as you all are. But I will say this much… considering how botched this job looks, they may come for her blood again."

Aiden growled. "That isn't happening."

Lukas pulled Blaire's body against his more firmly, and in turn, she reached up and placed her hand over his forearm, gripping lightly. He must sense her fear, as there was no way she could hide it. The idea this could happen again, even though she couldn't remember what happened, sent her mind into a panic. From the sounds of things, it nearly killed her this time. What if it happened again and they succeeded? She shuddered.

Riley asked, "What would they find in Blaire's blood? Why didn't they just ask her for a donation or something so they wouldn't risk killing her if it's just to find out something that will help everyone in the end?"

"That's simple." The professor waved a hand toward Lukas and Blaire. "They likely believed she wouldn't voluntarily give her blood for experimentation, since she has yet to share willingly with her own Korrena, so they took it by force." She sighed. "I am not sure what they will find in her blood—if anything at all. Again, this is completely unfamiliar territory for everyone, me included. Even the Oracle hasn't provided any insight as to what could be happening here."

"The Oracle?" Blaire had not heard that before, and she felt behind having to ask all these questions. Maybe she should have read the handbook more thoroughly, but so much had happened. She hadn't had the opportunity to fully finish it.

"The Oracle is a centuries-old Vasirian who sometimes gets prophetic visions which help guide the Order on the choices they make for the academy and all of Vasirian kind," the professor explained.

She turned in her chair, focusing her full attention on Lukas and Blaire, her expression severe. "You need to come to terms with your connection and fully seal the bond, because I strongly fear the Order will soon intervene. If your bond is not sealed, then there is no reason for Blaire to continue to stay at Blackthorn Academy." She leveled Lukas with an intense stare. "If there is no reason for her to be here, then they can't let a human live in the normal world with the knowledge of what we are. It's too much of a risk."

Lukas lifted his head and growled.

"Wait. Would they seriously just kill Blaire?" Riley shouted in a panic.

Aiden jumped up from the bed. "No way will I allow that to happen!"

Lukas once again tightened his hold on Blaire, his face seeking refuge in her hair as he whispered, "Never."

"I'm sorry, but if you do not claim Blaire in both body and blood soon, Lukas… then yes, the Order will most certainly terminate her contract, and in turn, her existence. Blaire is only here because she's fated to be your Korrena. If she doesn't fulfill her end of the contract, then there's no need for the contract to exist." She took a deep breath. "To put it bluntly, there would then be no reason for her to exist. Not in their eyes."

"Fuck that. Not happening," Lukas said.

Blaire turned to meet his gaze, his eyes holding such strong intensity she felt the conviction in them deep inside her bones.

Aiden dropped down onto the foot of the bed, holding his head in his hands, shaking it back and forth. "This can't be happening…"

Lukas shook his head. "It won't happen. I won't let them touch her."

"It's clear to everyone how you both feel about each other. Why won't you complete the bond?" Kai asked, his forehead wrinkled in confusion.

Blaire looked down at her bruised arm.

The professor filled in the silence. "It's understandable that Blaire is likely afraid. She's a human who has been thrown into our world.

She has been attacked more than once, so the idea of giving her blood to another must be frightening."

"Not to mention she's a virgin, and she has to do the… well, Lukas." Riley motioned toward Lukas with her hand, her face bright red in embarrassment from her indiscretion.

Aiden rolled his eyes. "Smooth, Riley, smooth."

The professor chuckled. "Well, yes, if that is a new thing for her as well, then it would add another element of fear for her."

Blaire pulled from Lukas's arms. "Please move."

"Blaire?" He looked at her, and the uncertainty on his face pulled at her, making her second-guess herself. But she couldn't do this.

"I need you to move," she said firmly.

Lukas slid from around her and sat next to Aiden while watching her with wary eyes.

"Y'all are talking about me like I'm not even in the room," Blaire said, her voice shaking, her Southern dialect coming through, her accent stronger in her upset. "I can't do this. I told you I just can't accept someone drinking my blood like it's not a big deal."

"But it is a big deal!" Lukas raised his voice, frustration evident.

"You don't mean it like I do. This isn't pretend. This is my life."

"It's my life too! You're my pair, Blaire! Do you not get how much I want this?"

Blaire stared at him with wide eyes before looking away. "I don't want to die…"

Professor Velastra pursed her lips. "This is why bonding is important. It can help protect you."

"No! He could kill me! Don't you understand that? If I almost died over having a piece of my arm removed, what do you think is gonna happen when he drinks me like I'm a Slurpee? I never asked for any of this!"

Blaire's eyes filled with tears, and she looked around the room at everyone staring at her with varying degrees of shock. No matter how her feelings for Lukas had shifted, she couldn't do it. Not only did she not want to die, but she had conflicting feelings about allowing another person to drink her blood. Just because she had a dream where she enjoyed it, didn't mean that in the waking light she would accept it. She used to read books like that all the time, but it didn't mean she wanted a vampire to turn her into an undead creature, either. She knew Vasirian weren't vampires, but the concept of drinking blood was still the same. But if she didn't do it, she would die. Her mind spun with confusion, and she started to hyperventilate, wrapping her arms around herself.

"Blaire… no." Lukas stood.

"Just s-stay back," Blaire stammered, tears slipping free.

The professor clapped her hands once more to bring attention to her and away from Blaire. "Blaire should rest, so everyone should leave for now." The professor stood from her seat. "She needs to process everything." She looked at Blaire pityingly. "There are risks with every decision we make in life, but now is not the time to be making hard and fast decisions when you've been through such an ordeal."

Aiden stood up from the bed and ran his fingers through his messy hair.

"I'll let Seth know what's happening. He didn't want to come this morning because he wasn't sure he could handle it if Blaire still had any active bleeding." Aiden then looked at Blaire. "He's sorry, but I know you'd understand. It's harder for some of us than others. But he was here last night. He helped."

Blaire bit her quivering lower lip and nodded, unable to meet his eyes.

Riley frowned, and they all moved to exit the room.

The professor stepped up and placed a hand on Lukas's shoulder.

"Keep an eye on her. Until we know who we can trust on these grounds, I'm relying on you to keep watch over her. Assigning protection in any other form would draw too much attention."

"I won't leave her side."

The professor smiled at Lukas before moving to the exit, leaving Blaire and Lukas alone in the room.

The silence that followed hung awkwardly in the air. Blaire didn't know what to say and Lukas wasn't volunteering to be social, which she was grateful for, for once. So often she wanted him to engage with her, but right now, all she wanted was to sleep and forget everything.

After several moments of silence, Lukas let out an unsteady breath.

"I can't believe I almost lost you..." he whispered, staring at her from his bed.

Blaire didn't know what to say. The entire dynamic between them had shifted further, but she also had a new reason to fear this new life she had fallen into. Would she even live long enough to see what this was between them? Her life was in danger again. Was this really any different from being under the Wilcox rule?

31

Let's Go Party

It had been two weeks since her attack, and Lukas hadn't left Blaire's side since she woke that morning.

She felt no lasting side effects to the loss of blood, for which she was thankful. When Blaire asked the nurse removing her stitches about why she didn't feel sick like before, the nurse informed her that blood transfusions were often used as a treatment for anemia, so she wouldn't experience the same ill effects she had with her heavy cycle.

Lukas remained withdrawn.

An uncomfortable tension lingered in the room after Blaire's declaration about not sharing blood with Lukas. She feared expressing to him what was taking place in her heart; the potential consequence of allowing him in was huge. She'd have to accept bonding with him, which meant allowing him to drink her blood—risking her life—and she wasn't prepared to do that. It wouldn't be fair to let him know the feelings in her heart when she couldn't commit to him the way his kind required.

On Friday afternoon, Lukas answered a knock on their door. Riley had visited after class every single day since the attack to check on Blaire and bring the classwork she missed. He got up from the desk where he sat doing homework and let Riley inside. He glanced back at Blaire sitting on her bed going through her little jewelry box, and then walked out the door with a nod to Riley.

Blaire figured Lukas needed a break from babysitting her. While she was afraid of what would happen if he left her alone, he probably didn't want to be with her every waking moment, especially with the rift between them. He protested going to class when Aiden forced him.

"How are you feeling?" Riley sat on Blaire's bed, dropping a large bag to the floor at her feet before picking up one of Blaire's bracelets and examining it.

Blaire looked up, smiling at her friend. "I'm feeling much better. I'm honestly ready to return to class on Monday."

Riley let out an exaggerated breath of relief. "It's about time. Between Lukas brooding about wanting to stay with you, and Aiden's worrying, I've been going stir-crazy! Like seriously, you would have thought those two were the ones injured with the whining they do."

Blaire giggled and shook her head. "I'm happy you're here."

"I'm like a pet you just can't—and don't want to—get rid of," Riley said with a cheeky grin.

Blaire laughed again. She wouldn't get rid of her. Riley had become her best friend. She missed Charlotte, but she had never connected with another girl the way she had with Riley.

"So would you be up for going into the valley tonight?"

"Tonight?" Blaire tapped her fingers on her lap, wary. "I don't know..." Even though the attack happened in her room, part of her wanted to stay in the cocoon of the dorm with Lukas as a watchdog.

"Yeah, there's this club we all used to go to regularly before you came to the academy that I think you'd like." Riley shrugged. "It would get you away from this place, the memories… and away from whoever did that to you." She motioned to Blaire's bandaged arm.

She had a point. Not a strong one, but a point.

Blaire frowned. "But what if they follow me?"

"Haven is run by Vasirian. But the clientele is a mix of both Vasirian and humans. I don't think the Order would cause a commotion there and expose us to the humans."

Another point.

Blaire had seen Haven on the edge of the plaza, a dark building with colorful spotlights illuminating the black brickwork. It stood out next to the sea of beige shops that made up Valley Center Plaza. Crowds lined up down the street on the weekends, but she had never gone inside.

Blaire chewed her lip. "I've never done the whole club thing. It's never been my scene. Caleb never let me go to anything like that when I was invited back in high school. Not to Haven, but other bars for teen nights."

Riley glared at nothing and set down the bracelet. "Caleb isn't here, so you're free to go. So yeah, you're going."

While her tone gave no room for argument, Blaire could refuse Riley if she wanted to. The freedom within their friendship encouraged her to take a chance.

She laughed again, nodding. "Sure, sure. I guess I can go."

"Damn right you can."

Riley crossed her arms in clear defiance of whatever she saw as a threat, and Blaire couldn't help but laugh at her. She needed the lighthearted laughter Riley brought her today. The tension in Lukas's presence had been stifling.

"It's totally different from typical clubs, though, so it's okay if clubs aren't exactly your 'scene.' It's this amazing gothic club with gorgeous lighting, furniture, and a huge dance floor. But there's more to do than just dance."

"Like?"

"Well, I only go to mostly dance…" Riley laughed. "But there are game rooms in the back with pool tables and stuff like that. And there's comfortable furniture so you can just sit and relax with a drink and socialize if that's more your thing."

"Drink?" Blaire asked flatly. Her lips twisted, and her brows knitted.

"Yep!"

Had Riley forgotten how old they were?

Riley bent down and grabbed her bag from the floor. "I knew you'd say yes, so I came prepared."

With a grin, Riley stood and set the large bag on the bed as Blaire eyed it curiously. A weird sense of dread washed over her. She wondered what Riley was up to when she took in the cheeky smile on her face.

Riley unzipped the bag and pulled out a completely black, strapless bodycon dress. Blaire widened her eyes in surprise.

"Just wait." Riley grinned ear to ear as she held the dress up to show off the details.

The dress had a steel-boned, transparent corset as its upper half, with a sweetheart neckline and satin over-bust cups with the same satin fabric as vertical strips that covered the corset boning. Between the boning on the corset, from the bottom of the cups down to the natural waist, and the entire back, lay a sheer black material. The corset was designed to close at the back with tight lacing that allowed the strings to hang free once cinched. The black form-fitting skirt of the dress started at the base of the ribs where the natural waist ended, which, judging by the length, should fall mid-thigh on Blaire.

It looked gorgeous, but the dress didn't suit her. She had long legs, but dresses like this suited curvy women with larger breasts than she had. She wasn't small. In fact, she was decently blessed in that department. Not Charlotte-levels of blessed, but a conservative C-cup. The dress looked like it fit someone with a D, at least.

Blaire shook her head at the weird analysis of herself. It had been a while since she had been overly critical of her appearance. She hadn't worked out at all since arriving at the academy. Without Caleb there to constantly drag her self-esteem down, she found herself not caring as much. She took care of herself, of course, but she didn't feel like she had to overwork to avoid consequences for not achieving perfection. There would always be a new bar to reach.

Blaire shook her head quickly, ridding herself of the thoughts that threatened to encroach on her good mood like kudzu vines suffocating everything in their path.

"There's absolutely no way I would look good in that," she finally said with a self-deprecating laugh.

Riley gave her a look like she was insane. "You would look sexy as hell in this dress, and Lukas is going to love it!"

Blaire's cheeks warmed, but Riley wasn't paying attention, digging around into the bag again and pulling out a pair of black suede heels. They matched the dress nicely, but Blaire couldn't dress like this.

"Riley..." Blaire shifted uncomfortably.

"Relax! Everyone dresses up for the club, and you'll look fantastic. If anything, wearing jeans and one of your pretty tops will make you stand out like a sore thumb."

A knock sounded at the door before Blaire had the opportunity to protest further.

"That's Mera."

"How do you know?"

Riley grinned sheepishly. "Well… I already knew you'd agree to go out, so I told Mera to get ready and meet us here."

Blaire blinked at Riley as she started laughing and walked to the door, letting Mera inside.

Mera had dressed for a gothic nightclub. She wore a black miniskirt embellished with chains linking small D-rings that were sewn to the skirt like a belt low on her hips. She also wore a black leather over-bust corset with chains linking together wrapping around the ribcage. Beneath her corset, a black fishnet top covered her arms all the way to her fingers with her thumbs sticking out through holes. She styled this with a pair of chunky platform boots that buckled up the sides and matching fishnet stockings with rips in various places.

"Damn, Mera, you look badass," Riley said as she walked back over to Blaire's bedside. "We still have to get ready."

Mera shrugged and glanced around awkwardly, clearly not comfortable with compliments. "That's fine, but Kai, Lukas, and Seth are at Aiden's dorm getting ready, and they said they'd meet us in the courtyard in fifteen minutes. That was"—she checked her phone—"five minutes ago, according to my last text with Kai."

"Fifteen minutes?" Riley tossed her hands in the air. "There's no way we'll be ready. Call Kai and let him know to give us thirty from now, and we'll hurry." Riley began digging in her bag again. "We gotta get moving."

Mera sat on the edge of Lukas's bed, tapping on the screen of her phone.

Blaire picked up the dress on the bed with a sigh. "Do I have a choice?"

Riley grinned. "Nope. Get your sweet cheeks up and get ready to put on a show."

Mera looked up from her phone, rolling her eyes at Riley.

This was going to be a disaster. They scrambled to get ready.

Mera helped Blaire with her makeup, giving her a black smoky eye with a sharp winged liner and only a gloss to accent her naturally pink lips. Mera said using a nude or natural shade on the lips, when paired with dramatic eye makeup, drew more attention to the eyes, creating drama. Blaire wasn't going to argue. She didn't fool around enough with makeup to know the ins and outs of it all.

Mera also teased and fluffed Blaire's hair, spraying it with so much hairspray it sent her into a coughing fit. It gave Blaire's long, blonde hair a wild and windswept look.

Riley finished getting ready and pulled out a pair of black rhinestone studded earrings, passing them to Blaire. "Put these on."

Blaire put them in her ears, surprised her holes hadn't closed. Caleb made her take her earrings out six months ago and stop wearing them because they were too flashy, saying that's why one guy asked for her number at the diner. It was stupid; he was just looking for an excuse to control her. She'd had pierced ears since she was a child. But she stopped wearing earrings rather than battle for something that small.

Blaire couldn't believe what she had tolerated. Working with Professor Sinclair had made her see how much she had fallen into compliance with Caleb's demands even before the threats on her life. Her efforts were intended to bring back the good stepbrother she once knew and cared for—still seeking approval. She had rationalized his behavior would change if she gave in. These were all trauma responses to abuse; the professor told her. She wasn't magically healed, but she wasn't wearing blinders anymore. She worked on healing one step at a time. Allowing herself moments like this—where she did things she would have been forbidden to do before—gave her power back.

Once Blaire finished, Riley opened her closet door. "Come check it out."

With a sigh of resignation, Blaire crossed to the full-length mirror, trying not to trip on the new area rug with the heels she wore. As she took in her reflection, she gasped. She didn't know what to say. She still looked like herself but amplified. The torture of allowing Mera and Riley to pull the lacing tight shaped her torso nicely, and her judgment about the bust had been wrong; she nearly spilled out of it.

"You look like sex in heels." Riley grinned like she'd been given a thousand birthday gifts all at once. "Lukas is going to lose his mind."

Mera crossed her arms, shaking her head. "Hasn't he been doing enough of that lately?"

"Well, at least this time it'll be for good reasons," Riley said with a laugh.

Blaire fidgeted and tugged on the bust of the corset to try to pull it up higher; the tops of her breasts were very much on display.

Riley looked at her and giggled. "Yeah, not happening. We've locked that corset down tight."

Looking down at her phone, Mera said, "Kai says they're waiting in the courtyard now, so we need to go."

Riley grabbed her cropped leather jacket and bag off Blaire's bed as they headed for the door to meet up with the guys.

It was surprisingly easy to walk in the heels Riley brought her. Blaire hadn't worn heels since her high school graduation, but these block-style heels provided better balance.

Mera exited the dorm building first, followed by Riley as she swished her black skirt with a hot pink tutu beneath it back and forth. She reminded Blaire of a child sometimes, but it wasn't a bad thing.

Blaire stepped out into the courtyard behind them and glanced toward the trio of young men waiting. Lukas wore his signature tight black jeans with a couple of chains hanging at his hip and what looked like a black Henley beneath his leather jacket.

"Well, at least someone was allowed to dress in their usual clothes," Blaire muttered.

Riley shrugged. "Yeah, but his natural look works for the club."

"I thought there was, like, a gothic dress code or something. He's definitely not gothic. Nor Aiden, for that matter; he's wearing a pair of black jeans and a black t-shirt. That's definitely not dressing up. The way you were acting…"

"Well, not exactly, but he looks like a badass, so he fits," Riley said, as if that was the most obvious conclusion. "Aiden does what he wants. That's as gothic as it gets for him."

Mera laughed. "Well, Kai obviously looks the part, and even Seth looks nice with the black slacks and black button-down."

Riley fidgeted with the safety pins clipped on her shirt, not responding.

As they approached the guys, Blaire heard Kai say, "The gothic look suits her." Suits who? She was the only one who had never dressed like this before. She straightened her spine self-consciously, and now Lukas looked at her strangely. Did she mess up wearing this?

She swallowed hard as Lukas raked his eyes up her legs and over the dress. His gaze lingered at the way too exposed bustline before moving to her neck and then stopping on her face. Her eyes widened at the intense flash of hunger lingering there. She allowed the quick flash of a smile; maybe she didn't look completely awful.

"She looks hot, right?" Riley said proudly, as if she did all the work.

Aiden rubbed the back of his neck and Seth rolled his eyes at her.

Lukas cleared his throat as Blaire closed her eyes, her cheeks and neck flaring with heat. He growled low in his throat. Her eyes flew open to see his gaze focused on her neck, his eyes glowing subtly around the edges of his iris. He ran his tongue over his lower lip. She shivered, biting down on her shiny bottom lip as she watched him. The air between them crackled, and she overheated in the cool spring air.

Aiden nudged Lukas forward and he stumbled toward Blaire.

Lukas cleared his throat. "Y-yeah, yeah, she looks great."

"And I'm sure that's the PG version of what's going on in his head," Aiden said with a smirk.

Seth laughed, then looked at Riley and fell silent. She looked at him and then away just as quickly.

Blaire looked down and fidgeted with the hem of her dress before Riley perked back up.

"I can't wait for you to see the inside of Haven. Every weekend they have a different color theme. Everything from the accent lights to the throw pillows on the lounging couches, and even the signature drinks are colored to fit the theme," Riley rambled so quickly it was hard to keep up. "It's really crazy sometimes, because with the fabric draping from the ceiling reflecting the accent lights, and the smoke the fog machines make, it can sometimes look like a scene straight out of a horror movie when the theme is red or black." She giggled and clapped her hands.

Aiden chuckled. "Breathe, Riley."

Kai wrapped his arm around Mera's lower back, pulling her to his side. "There's always black in Haven."

"Yeah, but the one weekend I went where they actually chose that as the color theme, the entire place felt like an abandoned castle." Riley turned back to Blaire. "Just wait, you're going to love it. The bartenders don't even ID us for drinks!"

Blaire's forehead wrinkled in concern. "Won't we get in trouble?"

"We go all the time. They're Vasirian. They never card academy students," Aiden said with a shrug.

"Privileged brats," Blaire muttered in jest, rolling her eyes.

Kai shrugged. "It does have its perks on occasion."

Mera looked at her phone, checking the time. "We should get going." She took Kai's hand and started walking toward the gates, followed by Seth and Aiden.

"This is going to be awesome!" Riley exclaimed, grinning so big Blaire wondered if it made her face hurt. Riley ran after the others, her safety pins and buckles making all sorts of noise as she called out for Seth to slow down.

Lukas hadn't said anything the entire time, just stood watching Blaire. She finally looked up to meet his eyes.

"Do you really think I look okay, or is it too much? I'm not used to this sort of thing…" She pinched the ends of her hair, stiff from all the hairspray.

Lukas cleared his throat again and ran a hand through his hair before whispering, "If you only knew."

"What do you mean?"

He stepped toward her until they were toe-to-toe, then looked down at her. Blaire didn't have to tilt her head far back to look up at him with the heels on, but despite being closer to his height, intimidating intensity radiated off him like heat. He wasn't keeping his distance anymore—she certainly had his attention now.

Lukas lifted a hand and ran his fingertips over her jawline, and then slowly down the side of her neck, over the wildly beating pulse point. He lingered there as his breathing became deeper. He gently pressed against her pulse, never removing his eyes from hers. An increasing warmth where his fingers rested sent an unfamiliar jolt through her body.

He resumed his exploration by dragging his hand down the front of her throat, then just his fingertips over her sternum until he moved farther down to the top edge of her dress, lightly caressing the top of her exposed breasts. Blaire's breath hitched.

"Lukas…" she whispered, closing her eyes as he leaned his head down toward her. He was going to kiss her again. The anticipation shot straight to her core, and she had to clench her thighs together.

"Are you guys coming or what?" Riley shouted from halfway down the path where everyone had stopped and looked back.

Lukas raked a hand through his hair and groaned in frustration, stepping back as Blaire opened her eyes. He swore under his breath as he turned away and clenched his fist.

He stalked away, leaving Blaire trying to catch her breath. This was becoming difficult. She couldn't even control the way she responded to him out in the open like this.

She was a mess.

32

Haven

Walking into Haven felt like stepping into another world. Blue and purple lights saturated the room, reflecting off the sheer fabrics draping from the ceiling, creating an eerie atmosphere when combined with the fog that cloaked the air from hidden machines.

A set of descending, black stairs, lit on either side by blue strip lights, and black candles on wrought iron candelabras, led guests down into the club and through a lounge area where black leather booths and tables with various candles atop their surfaces surrounded the massive dance floor in the center of the club.

Above the dance floor sat an elevated stage for live performances, with a DJ booth situated above that. The far back wall of the club on the other side of the dance floor and lounge area, where the back door to the alleyway and bathrooms were located, held a huge bar with purple underbar lights and black, leather cushioned stools lining the front.

Several bartenders filled drinks from the many alcoholic choices available on display on the mirror wall behind the bar.

Blaire breathed in the strong incense mixed with the scents of the alcohol being consumed by the bodies that moved to the mix of metal, some form of rock electronica, and sensual beats.

"It's blurple!" Riley said in excitement as they reached a table at the side of the dance floor.

Aiden looked at her like she was crazy. "What?"

"The color themes! See all the blue and purple? Blurple!"

"That is the most ridiculous name ever," he said with a shake of his head.

Kai looked at Blaire. "What would you like to drink? I know everyone else's preferences."

"Oh, um. I haven't really—how about a Bahama Mama?" Blaire said quickly, remembering the name of a pretty drink she saw in one of Charlotte's vacation pictures from when she went to Hawaii with her moms. She didn't drink, so she had no idea what she liked, but she didn't want to look silly.

Kai nodded and walked toward the bar to get everyone drinks.

Lukas climbed into the booth, scooting in, giving Blaire the outside seat. Mera slid in on the other side and Aiden took the seat across from Blaire.

"Come on!" Riley shouted at Seth, grabbing his arm, and dragging him toward the dance floor.

Blaire hid a smile at Seth's "please no" expression, even while he willingly followed Riley.

Mera tilted her head as she watched Blaire. "How are you feeling now?"

"I'm fine," she sighed. "There's no reason for everyone to worry."

Blaire placed her hand on top of the large bruise and smaller bandage the nurse told her to leave on for another five days to protect the sensitive skin. It remained an angry reminder of that horrible Monday night that forced her to miss two weeks of classes. She would have been fine to return after the first week, but the professor wasn't having it. Concerned about Blaire's mental state after being attacked, she advised her to take a break.

Lukas growled under his breath when she covered her arm and reached for her, but Kai returned with a tray of drinks.

Blaire got up and started helping remove the drinks, passing them to who they belonged based on his instructions. Sometimes old habits died hard. She really had spent way too long as a waitress.

Aiden got up and let Kai slide in next to Mera before sitting back down and taking a sip of his whiskey sour.

Blaire sat back down and took a long pull from the straw in her drink, her eyes lighting up at the dance of tropical flavors over her tongue, both tart and sweet. "This is delicious!"

Aiden chuckled. "Never had it before?"

She shook her head quickly as she took another sip.

"I thought it was something you liked," Kai said as he took a drink from his beer.

"Oh. Well, no. I saw a picture of it before. It looked like it might taste good, so I figured I'd try it." Blaire squirmed in her seat.

Seth returned, taking the attention away from her. "That girl is fucking insatiable!" He threw his hands up in the air.

Aiden laughed and got up, patting Seth on the back as he slid into the booth next to Kai. Seth took a long drink of his beer and lay his head back against the booth as Riley rushed up and grabbed hold of Blaire's good arm, surprising her.

"Come dance with me!"

Blaire laughed and shook her head. "I'm not very good."

"Whatever. Just shake your ass and you'll be fine. Come dance with me." Riley pouted and flashed her best puppy dog eyes, looking ridiculous.

Blaire laughed again and held up a hand. "Okay, okay. If you'll stop looking at me like that, I'll come." She took another long drink of the delicious blend of pineapple, orange, and coconut bliss before sitting it down on the table. She hopped up and straightened her dress before disappearing into the crowd with Riley onto the dance floor.

It took a few measures of the song for Blaire to warm up on the dance floor, but thanks to the comfortable buzz from the rum in her drink, she began to get into the music. They danced together like no one was watching, giggling, and tossing their hair around to the wild beat. Blaire was having the time of her life, when the lights suddenly dimmed further, and a sensual song began to play, a quarter of the bodies on the dance floor leaving.

Riley leaned in, talking loudly enough to be heard. "I'm going to the bathroom. I'll be right back."

Blaire shrugged as she swayed her body, her long hair cascading down her back. She glanced toward their table, able to see everyone now that bodies had moved. Everyone was talking, but Lukas. He stared at her with narrowed eyes as she continued to move. His intense gaze made delicious shivers pass through her body, and she liked knowing his entire focus was on her. After taking a sip of his drink, he ran his tongue across his lower lip and Blaire felt the sensation on her own lip, recalling their last kiss.

Bodies moved between them, blocking her vision, and she breathed out the knot that had worked itself up in her chest. The song changed, but the sensual rhythm continued. Blaire was completely caught up in the music and the haze of alcohol over her mind. She lifted her arms into the air, losing herself in the beat as she swayed her hips with her eyes closed until she felt a body move up behind her, hands landing on her hips.

She smiled. "Lukas," she breathed out, hanging her head back against his chest. Knowing that watching her dance pushed him to join her made her feel powerful. Knowing that he desired her. She slowly opened her eyes when he didn't say anything, looking up into the face of not Lukas, but Caleb.

She tensed in horror. She should have known it wasn't Lukas by scent alone—the drink must have clouded her head too much to realize. Immediately, she sobered. She pulled away from him, but Caleb gripped her hips tight enough there would be bruises later.

"W-what are you doing here?" she stammered, frozen in his grasp.

Caleb leaned down to her neck, smelling her, and she shuddered in disgust. He moved to her ear and whispered, "Ricky saw you, and those academy brats, in the line outside earlier, and called me. Aren't you glad? Aren't you happy to see me? I'm happy to see you."

"N-no, I'm not. P-please, let me go." She couldn't believe he had reduced her to a stuttering mess so fast.

Caleb laughed, running one hand down to rest on her thigh, hitching up the edge of her dress. He ran the other hand up her side to graze the side of her breast.

"Did you dress up for that long-haired asshole I saw you with before?" He gripped her tighter and jerked her ass against his groin.

Blaire whimpered and shook her head quickly in an effort not to anger him as she tried not to cry right there on the dance floor in front of the other dancers. They all likely assumed she and Caleb were just a couple dancing close together. Her eyes filled with tears that threatened to spill.

Caleb spoke through gritted teeth. "You've had your fun, and now it's time for you to come home where you belong."

Her spine stiffened as her temper flared. She fought too hard to get away from him, and her counseling sessions were helping her close away that part of her life and move on, and here Caleb was threatening to reverse all the progress she'd made. That couldn't happen. She looked toward where their table was, but the dance floor had filled with more dancers when the song changed to something faster. She couldn't see Lukas. She needed to get to him before it was too late.

When Blaire jerked away from Caleb and stepped forward to leave, he grabbed her by the back of her hair, wrapped it around his hand, and pulled her back to his chest. She yelped at the sharp sting on her scalp, and a few dancers glanced over at them, but then turned away. He tightened his grip.

"Don't make a scene," he hissed into her ear. He stayed behind her and guided her off the dance floor to the back doorway that led into the alley.

It was over. She would never see Lukas again. Never see Riley, Aiden, or the others. Tears fell over her cheeks as he pushed her through the doorway.

Out in the alley, Caleb pushed her back up against the brick wall and slapped her across the face.

"Where did you get the fucking nerve to even think you could just run off and join some preppy little academy and leave me?"

"I-I-I-I'm sorry," Blaire sobbed as she bent forward, wrapping her arms around her body to protect herself.

Caleb moved in on her, forcing her to stand as he pressed himself against her body on the brick wall. She wanted the ground to open and swallow her at that moment. Her worst nightmare was coming true. He was going to take her back, and this time she'd never escape. It was all over.

A sickening feeling washed over her as she stared into his dead hazel eyes, as if he'd lost any rational side of himself and had given in to his twisted mind. No traces of the stepbrother she once knew long ago remained. Would he take her to his grandparents? Would they make good on their promise to make her disappear? Blaire trembled uncontrollably as the reality hit her that she might not see the sunrise. Her tears wouldn't stop as they streaked down her face, ruining the beautiful makeup job Mera did for her.

The back-alley door banged open again, but Blaire was too caught up in her fear to care who was there. No one would stop Caleb. She was alone.

"You'll definitely be sorry when you get home. I'm tired of waiting, Blaire. It's time you fulfilled all the duties of a wife. My wife. Did you seriously think having an affair with someone like your preppy rich boyfriend was better than being with me?" Caleb stepped forward and backhanded her again when she failed to respond, choking on her tears. "You will answer me when I'm fucking talking to you!"

Blaire collapsed from the force, but muscular arms caught her before she could hit the ground—Aiden. He wrapped her in a tight embrace as an inhuman sound sent a chill down her spine. She looked up as Caleb startled, turning.

Then Caleb slammed into the brick wall, and it cracked, pieces of brick falling behind him, blood spluttering from his mouth from the force of the impact. Lukas held him against the wall, snarling at him. It all happened so fast; she didn't have the opportunity to process it at first.

He looked absolutely feral.

He'd come for her.

"What the fuck is your problem?" Caleb shouted as he jerked against Lukas.

Mera, Kai, Riley, and Seth finally piled out the back door. Lukas and Aiden must have run out ahead of them.

When Caleb pulled only slightly from his hold, Lukas again slammed him against the wall with more force than Blaire realized he was capable of using. Caleb coughed up more blood, and it ran down his chin and neck. Blaire shrieked when he hit the wall, and Aiden pulled her close to his body, pressing her face to his chest to keep her from seeing what was happening as she sobbed.

"It's alright…" he whispered as she clung to him, unable to stand on her own anymore. She was shaking so badly. He smoothed her hair with his hand to comfort her.

Blaire could hear the sounds of a struggle. Caleb's screams of pain and cries for help. Lukas's growls and snarls as he took out his rage on her long-time abuser. She tried to pull away from Aiden, but he tightened his hold and whispered over the top of her head, "No. You don't want to see this…" Would Lukas kill Caleb? She wasn't sure she wanted him to stop.

Everything went quiet after a few moments, and Blaire pushed against Aiden. He relented, which allowed her to lift her head. He still held her firmly, and it was a good thing, because the scene that met her eyes chilled her to the bone. Caleb lay in an unmoving heap on the ground. His body was covered in blood, and bone pierced his pant leg where it had been broken in half in a way that bent his leg at an impossible angle. It was hard to make out his face. It had been beaten so badly, beginning to swell.

Blaire's legs gave out, and Aiden clutched her to his body in support as she began to breathe quickly and deeply, growing lightheaded.

Caleb groaned on the ground and Lukas lifted him, but Caleb wasn't able to stand on his own anymore. Lukas was drawing out his torture. He didn't look like he was enjoying it, but he could have long since ended this. She sensed he wanted Caleb to suffer. Lukas forced him back against the wall and Caleb spit out a tooth as he wheezed, trying to take in air but having difficulty. One arm hung limply at his side, useless. Lukas wrapped his hand around Caleb's throat and squeezed, making his eyes bulge as he gasped for air that Lukas denied him.

"I promised… that I would… kill you…" Lukas seethed, his voice vibrating with his rage. He sounded as if he'd swallowed glass.

Blaire knew it was going to happen, and while everything in her screamed to look away, she couldn't force herself to look away from her tormentor as he stood on the edge of his end.

Lukas snarled and moved his hand in preparation for the final move, and Caleb blubbered, barely able to form words as he struggled to breathe.

"What… are… you?" he rasped, coughing up blood.

Blaire looked away from the broken man to Lukas. His fangs had descended, and his eyes glowed a bright green that reminded her of bioluminescent seas.

"Nothing you will live long enough to worry about." Lukas snarled and lunged for Caleb's throat, mouth wide.

Caleb screamed in terror as Blaire turned away, unable to watch the final act.

"What the fuck?" Lukas bellowed from further away.

Blaire looked back to find him being held by several members dressed like Blackthorn Academy security, two others holding Caleb against the wall unconscious.

Professor Velastra stepped from the shadows of the alley and took in the scene, frowning at Lukas, who struggled against the guards.

"What's going on?" Aiden asked as the others finally drew closer.

"Lukas Virtanen, control yourself at once," the professor snapped. Her voice was cold as ice, in control. "You were mere seconds away from committing an act that would have you exiled to Cresbel Asylum."

Blaire looked up at Aiden in confusion and he leaned down to whisper in her ear, "Those who commit crimes in the Vasirian world, like killing humans, are sent there as punishment. Like your prisons… but worse."

"But he needs to die for what he's done!" Lukas snapped.

The professor walked over to Caleb, who hung limply in the large arms of their security team.

"He's not dead. Yet. But you need to get a hold of yourself, Lukas. If you are sent away, who will look at for Blaire against…" She looked around at the security team. "Other threats."

Lukas stiffened and looked at Blaire in Aiden's arms. The anger still burned in his eyes, but the glow had become less consuming.

"I hear sirens!" Seth shouted as he glanced down the alley.

Kai followed his line of sight. "Someone likely heard the commotion and called the cops."

"The police are coming," the professor said. "When the staff informed us of what was happening here, they noted that someone saw Blaire being dragged out the back door in tears and reported a domestic situation."

She looked at everyone gathered in the alley. "Get back to the academy, and we will handle cleaning up this mess."

"What do you mean? What are you going to do?" Aiden asked.

"He knows too much. Lukas, in his loss of control, exposed our secret. He can't be let go like this… Furthermore, his condition is critical."

"What's going to happen to him?" Mera asked the question likely on everyone's mind.

"His mind must be dealt with. That said, to ensure no further complications like this happen again, we will handle the situation regarding Miss Wilcox."

Lukas growled.

"Blaire," she corrected in exasperation. "Lukas, you need to calm down and focus on protecting your pair."

"I'll take care of Lukas," Aiden whispered, looking down at Blaire as he wiped tears from her cheeks with his thumbs before gently passing her over to Mera and Riley, who wrapped their arms around her.

Aiden approached the security team, who still hadn't released Lukas. "We need to get you out of here." The men let go, and Aiden put a hand on Lukas's shoulder, steering him toward the alley's exit, away from his kill.

They all ran down the alley, moving swiftly across the courtyard and back toward the academy. The dorm building that housed Kai and Mera's room was closest to the courtyard, so they all ended up there.

Lukas stormed into the room ahead of everyone, jerking off his leather jacket and throwing it across the room before dropping onto the middle of the queen-sized bed on his back, rubbing his face with his hands, smearing blood on his skin.

"Dude… really?" Seth said as he picked up an animal's skull from the dresser. "Your aesthetic is really screwed up, bro."

Riley and Mera led Blaire into the bathroom, where Mera used cleanser to clean away the ruined makeup. "I don't know what to say…" Riley whispered as she dabbed at the cut on Blaire's cheek with the cool cloth.

Blaire winced. She didn't know Caleb broke the skin when he hit her, but it hurt more than the time he knocked her out. "There's nothing you can say… it's done now, right?"

Mera hummed. "If the professor intends to utilize the academy's resources to compel him, they can make him believe anything happened. And take away any memory they so choose."

Blaire still couldn't wrap her mind around an ability like that. To be able to force someone not to move, to use the power of suggestion to bend them to your will, and to take away their actual memories? It was unnerving.

"I'm sorry I left you…"

Blaire stared at Riley in surprise. "What are you talking about?"

"If I hadn't gone to the bathroom. If I'd just gotten someone else to come on the dance floor before I did…" She hiccupped and moisture hung in her eyes, her lashes damp. "Maybe… maybe this wouldn't have happened."

"Stop that. You didn't know. I didn't know. With everything that has happened recently, I wasn't even thinking of my stepbrother."

Blaire had become too relaxed in her new life and the safety Blackthorn had given her away from the Wilcox family. With only seeing her stepbrother at the diner that one day, she'd gone so long without his interference that she didn't think of him. That he would show up at a nightclub at all wasn't in his nature, but she hadn't considered someone else telling him she was there.

"I know… I'm just… I'm sorry. Please don't hate me," Riley mumbled.

Blaire pulled Riley into her arms. "I could never hate you. Lukas saw me moments before it happened. It happened so fast…" She sighed. "But you came for me… you all came for me."

Riley nodded and Mera moved to the door, saying, "We should check on Lukas."

Once back in the main room with everyone, Mera moved to sit with Kai at the foot of their bed. Their room certainly matched their fashion sense with a black iron headboard made of ornate flourishes, black bedding, and a sheer, black canopy attached to the ceiling. The same sheer fabric framed their window. To the right of their bed on the left wall sat a desk with black candles, animal skulls, and incense that filled the room with its aromatic scent. A small lamp with a sheer, black scarf over the top, cast the room in darker lighting.

A large, black dresser sat on the right wall covered in makeup, loose jewelry like spiked collars and bracelets, and lots of black candles. Positioned behind the dresser on the wall, was a large mirror draped in beads and scarves.

The room was cluttered with boots, heels, creepy stuffed plushies, and black clothing in various materials all over the hardwood floor. Every wall was covered in photographs of the two of them, metal band posters, gothic artwork in ornate frames, and other occult oddities. The layout was the same as the rest of their dorms, but it was completely different visually. It was certainly shocking.

Aiden ran his hands through his hair and sat down on the desk chair, staring as Riley led Blaire over to the head of the bed next to Lukas and pushed the pillows back so they could sit next to one another. Riley clung to Blaire's side, and she wasn't about to object. She found comfort in her friend's nearness.

Lukas bobbed his knee up and down, shaking the bed.

"What's wrong, man?" Aiden asked as he watched Lukas.

Kai shifted on the bed and put his elbows on his knees. "It's probably the blood. Not only is Blaire bleeding, but he's got that disgusting animal's blood all over his hands."

Lukas growled low in his throat, not able to speak words at the moment.

A tear slid down Blaire's cheek as she reached a hand to his chest, seeking to soothe him, but not knowing how.

"You need to fight back," Seth said to Blaire, breaking the silence that had fallen upon the room. "Show the same fucking backbone you did with Lukas when you got here."

"Shut the fuck up. She won't be alone with that piece of shit again," Lukas grated out from his position on the bed. He placed his hand over Blaire's on his chest. "It was the one and only time."

Mera looked over at Lukas and sighed, before turning her attention to Seth.

"Despite the fact that Blaire is strong-willed, like we all know her to be, someone who's been through the kind of abuse and trauma she has, tends to freeze up with their abuser, even when they know they can be safe."

Blaire dropped her head and began to sob uncontrollably. The shame was too much for her to take. The memories of what happened to her hit her like a gunshot to the chest. Tonight could have ended very differently if not for her friends, who were now witnessing her breakdown.

Riley pulled Blaire into her arms.

"I'm sorry. I'm so, so sorry," Blaire whispered over and over.

"Stop," Aiden growled out. "It's not your fault. It's the fault of that creepy ass stepbrother who thought you'd be married to him."

Lukas sat up abruptly, dropping Blaire's hand. "There's no way in hell I'll ever allow that to happen!" He gritted his teeth as he snarled out, "I will fucking kill him before I let that happen. I won't stop next time. I really will turn him into red mist."

Aiden said, "It's not going to be a problem anymore. The school is taking care of it. He likely won't even remember Blaire, or at least his obsession with her, by the time they finish with him,"

Blaire trembled in Riley's arms, hugging herself and leaning away from the reminder of the feral version of Lukas.

"Fuck, Blaire." Aiden looked over at her. "I can see you shaking from here. What's wrong?"

"She's scared," Lukas said through his clenched teeth.

Seth furrowed his brow. "How do you know?"

"I can fucking feel it!" Lukas shouted again and Blaire jumped, clinging onto Riley.

"Shit. Man, she's afraid of you," Aiden said, standing up.

Lukas jerked his head to look at Blaire, his eyes going wide. "What? No. Why would she be afraid of me?" He paused and reached out toward Blaire, his voice softening, confusion, and anxiety laced his tone. "Blaire?"

Blaire flinched and pulled tightly into Riley's embrace to get away from him, not able to get control of her shaking. She didn't want to be afraid of Lukas, but she still saw his descended fangs, his glowing eyes, Caleb's bloody and broken body under his hands, his monster looming large and threatening in that alley—

"No..." Lukas ran his hands through his hair, squeezing the strands at the back of his neck. "Fuck! I would never hurt you! Fuck! Don't you get how I feel about you?"

Blaire knew intellectually he wouldn't hurt her, but something was wrong with her. The events of tonight. Everything that had happened since she arrived. It all came crashing down around her. All she could do was cry; she couldn't even tell Lukas she was sorry for being afraid.

"You need to go wash the blood from your hands and calm down. You are of no use to Blaire in the state you are in right now," Kai said calmly, but with an authoritative edge to his voice.

Lukas jumped up from the bed and stalked to the bathroom, slamming the door.

Kai stood. "Perhaps a movie would do good to ease everyone's tension." He pulled a random movie from his collection and put it in the player, turning the lights out before returning to the bed and settling in with Mera. Aiden sat back down in the chair, rubbing his face. Seth joined him, sitting on the floor next to his feet.

After fifteen minutes, Lukas came out of the bathroom much more docile. He moved to sit on the floor in front of the bed where Blaire now lay on her side, softly crying in Riley's lap as everyone watched the movie in silence.

Once the movie ended, Kai turned the light on, and everyone got up to leave. Riley started to wake Blaire, who had fallen asleep curled up in her lap, but Lukas held out a hand.

"Don't. I'll carry her home. She's been through enough and just needs to rest."

"Are you sure you're okay to do that?" Riley questioned, squinting at him as she eyed him warily.

Lukas sighed. "I'm good now." He pulled on his leather jacket.

Riley nodded and sat back to allow Lukas to lift Blaire into his arms.

"It's best we don't mention this to anyone unless the police come calling," Aiden said as he looked around at everyone, and they nodded in agreement.

The walk back to the dorm was torture. In the silence, Lukas faced the fact that the person who had become the most important thing in his world was now afraid of him. He had to fix this. Blaire had suffered so much, and all he wanted to do was protect her from everything.

Tonight, he wanted to kill someone for the first time in his life, really kill them. Sure, he'd wanted whoever had taken Blaire's blood dead, but he hadn't felt this murderous tension. The need to destroy. If it erased Blaire's trauma, he would do it without hesitation. Had he not played around with Caleb, taking pleasure in making the monster suffer for everything he'd put Blaire through, and instead ended his pathetic existence swiftly, he wouldn't have regretted it for a second. But if he had done that, he'd have been taken away to Cresbel Asylum, and he'd never see Blaire again. It was a twisted silver lining to the storm cloud of their night out.

Once he entered the dorm room and kicked the door closed with his foot lightly, he walked Blaire over to her bed, laying her down on her stomach. He unlaced the corset of her dress, before turning her over, and slipping the garment from her body. She wore only a pair of black lace panties underneath, but desire for her body submerged beneath his worry. Too upset with what happened, he just wanted to take care of her.

Lukas lifted her into his arms as she fell limply against him and slipped one of his t-shirts over her head. He rested her back against her pillow, lifting her arms to work them through the sleeves, before pulling the shirt down to cover her body. He pulled the covers up over her, then kissed her forehead, before getting up and turning off the bedside lamp.

Tomorrow he had to do damage control.

33

Attack

Blaire, screaming his name, startled Lukas awake. He bolted upright and looked around, disoriented, in the night-dark room. The smll of Blaire's blood filled the air. Moonlight from the window illuminated the two figures over Blaire, holding her down. They were cloaked, obviously minions of the Order, as they would never do their own dirty work.

"Lukas!" Blaire cried again as she struggled against her captors.

Lukas flew out of the bed and grabbed one of the assailants as the other made a run for the door. Blaire shrank back into the corner of her bed as he took the hooded figure to the floor. He wasn't going to let them get away, but Blaire's terror kept him from striking with his fangs. He didn't know if she was afraid of him, or them, but he had to protect her—even from himself. He wrestled with the person on the floor trying to get away from him, before he got a good hold on them, pinning them down. He wanted answers.

"What the fuck do you want with her?"

The figure said nothing, and Lukas couldn't see their face in the depths of their cloak, especially with the room as dark as it was. The figure twisted, and pushed away enough to scramble to their feet, bolting out the door. Lukas growled and sprang up to give chase.

"Lukas..." Blaire called to him in a meek voice.

He glanced back at her as he panted heavily.

"Please don't leave me alone."

Lukas raked a hand through his hair. "Fuck." He walked to the door and closed it, trying to calm down as he made his way back to Blaire, grabbing his cell phone from the nightstand and turning on the lamp. She looked okay, if pallid and shaky.

He punched in Aiden's number as Blaire slid to the edge of the bed, grabbing hold of Lukas's arm, and clinging to it where it hung at his side, burying her face against him. She was trembling all over.

Aiden finally answered the call with a groggy voice.

"The Order came again," Lukas said with barely repressed rage.

That woke Aiden. He yelled through the phone, "Did they take her blood again?"

"Yeah, they got what they wanted."

Lukas couldn't see her arm, but he could smell the blood; he knew they had taken it again. "I couldn't chase them because Blaire needs someone with her, but there were two of them."

"I'll be there soon. Want me to call Professor Velastra?"

"Yeah... I need to take care of Blaire."

Lukas disconnected the call without a response and pulled from Blaire's hold to sit on the bed beside her. He pulled her into his arms and held out her arm, which had a thin trail of blood running down it but had stopped actively bleeding. He inspected to see if they botched it like before. It wasn't that bad, but... he swallowed hard as he stared at the blood.

Lukas tightened his grip and shuddered. He felt so pathetic. He was having a hard time controlling the urge.

"Does it hurt?" Blaire whispered.

Lukas looked up at her face with a raised brow. "What are you talking about?"

"I was told that being around me… not tasting my blood… could potentially hurt you," she whispered, biting her lower lip.

He ran a hand through his hair and closed his eyes. He didn't know how to address this with her. He shook his head.

"No, I'm fine."

Blaire glared at him, and he knew she saw right through him.

"I can tell you're struggling. Stop being such an asshole all the time."

Lukas looked at her with wide eyes, shocked she called him out like that. He sighed and stared into her eyes. "It's not hurting…"

When she opened her mouth in protest, he held his hand up.

"It's not hurting, but it is extremely difficult to be around you like… this." He held Blaire's arm up to make his point, before lowering it back down and looking away, ashamed of what he was in that moment. Why couldn't he control himself?

They sat in silence before she shifted.

"You can clean the wound," she whispered softly.

"Fuck no. I'm not even about to entertain that idea." Lukas stood abruptly, letting go of her arm.

Blaire reached out and grabbed him by the shirt, pulling him back down to sit again.

"There's no reason to waste something you want, and besides… it's already there, so it's not like you're biting me, just… cleaning me," she rationalized, shrugging as if it were no big deal.

All Lukas could do was stare at Blaire's face in shock. His entire body heated, and his fangs descended as he looked down at her arm, his breathing unsteady and ragged. He had wanted to bite her so badly earlier when he saw her in the courtyard dressed for the club. He had wanted to bring her back to their dorm and claim her right then.

Lukas's head swam from the heady scent of her blood mixing with his desire for her. He looked down at her arm, at the glistening dark trail that ran down her arm to her wrist, and he swallowed hard. To have her consent to him, to consent to share her blood with him finally… even if it wasn't biting her. He was having a tough time keeping it together.

Lukas looked back up at Blaire's face. "Are you sure?"

Blaire nodded, not saying a word.

"No. I need to hear the words, Blaire."

She looked down and bit softly into her lower lip before holding out her arm.

"I want you to clean my arm," she said before shaking her head. "No, I… I want you to…" Blaire swallowed and looked away in embarrassment as she whispered, "taste me…"

"Fuck. Me," he rasped out, his throat dry.

He slowly leaned down to Blaire's arm, never taking his eyes off her face as he slowly moved his tongue across her wrist, causing her to gasp. The taste of her blood exploded on his tongue, and he shuddered. He had never tasted anything so delicious in his life, and he wanted more. He closed his eyes as he trailed his tongue up the inside of her forearm, above the bandage, along the trail of blood until he reached the puncture wound at the crook of her elbow. She whimpered.

He slowly looked up at her. Her heavy breathing filled the silence of the room. He never thought she would be excited by the idea of him taking her lifeblood, but her blown pupils, rapid heartbeat, and unstable breathing said she was.

"Blaire..." Lukas whispered her name as he leaned in to claim her lips, slowly at first, savoring a kiss that wasn't the result of the chaotic mess that had been their lives lately.

He coaxed her mouth open, and she willingly parted her lips as he slipped his tongue into her mouth. Groaning into the kiss, he started laying her back on the bed. He wanted her badly. His desire for her was reaching a fever pitch. He needed to take her.

The door flew open, and Aiden rushed in. Lukas jerked away from Blaire, sitting up. Something always interrupted them. He ran a hand through his hair, and Blaire sat up, adjusting her t-shirt, her lips swollen and blood-stained. His lips burned to taste more.

"I... uh... I'm sorry for interrupting. I thought something had gone down." Aiden looked around awkwardly, rubbing the back of his neck.

Lukas shook his head. "Yeah, something went down alright. That's why I called you."

Aiden looked back their way and motioned toward them. "You, uh, might want to clean your mouths off."

Blaire blushed, reaching up to wipe her mouth where Lukas had left traces of her blood.

Lukas licked his lips clean slowly, never taking his eyes off Blaire. She looked down at her lap, clearly embarrassed by Aiden catching them in the moment.

"So, what the hell happened?" Aiden asked as he moved to sit on Lukas's bed across from them. "Are you okay?"

"Yeah, I feel alright. I'm just a little dizzy, so they must not have been able to take as much, because I woke up during the act and Lukas stopped them."

"Then we're lucky Lukas was here this time." Aiden speared his fingers through his hair. "We need to get to the bottom of this. Blaire is clearly in danger, and she can't handle them trying to drain her this frequently."

Lukas clenched his bruised fists that hadn't healed yet. "She shouldn't have to get used to them trying to fucking drain her at all."

Aiden sighed. "That's a given. But I spoke to the professor, and she said if Blaire is fine, there's no reason to meet tonight. The perpetrators are likely long gone, and it'll just stir up the school and shine a bigger spotlight on her, which I'm sure she doesn't want."

"I really would like to have one normal week go by," Blaire muttered.

Aiden grinned and shook his head. "Now that you're in our world, normal is relative."

Blaire sighed and rolled her eyes.

"But she also said she wants to meet with us in the morning to discuss things."

Lukas said, "I appreciate you coming, even though she's alright, because I couldn't be sure if they'd come back and if there wouldn't be more of them now that they're aware she isn't alone tonight like she was before."

"There's no reason to thank me. I'll always be there for you, and for Blaire."

Lukas nodded and Aiden got up, heading to the door.

"I'll call the others and let them know what happened. We can all meet with the professor tomorrow." He locked the door from the inside before exiting the dorm room.

Lukas glanced over at Blaire, his eyes falling to her lips. She bit down on her lower lip again and he sighed.

"You're going to need rest to recover your strength."

"Will you stay with me?" she whispered, looking uncertain about her request.

Lukas stood and stretched. "Of course, I'm not leaving the room for anything. I don't plan to go back to sleep, so I can watch over you. You'll be safe tonight."

He moved toward his bed, but stopped when she tugged on his shirt, preventing him from crossing the room. He moved his eyes up from her hand to her face and found her blushing.

Blaire looked down, whispering, "I mean, I want you to stay in the bed with me." She jerked her gaze up to meet his, adding, "Just in case… well, in case they come back. And then you could actually sleep?" She nodded to herself as if confirming something.

Lukas raised an eyebrow. That was as good an excuse as any.

He turned and got into her bed, climbing over her body, and settling in with his back toward the wall before wrapping his arms around her, pulling her into his chest. Blaire buried her face into his bare chest, snuggling up to him. He was in heaven. He reached down and pulled the covers over them both before reaching out and turning off the lamp, settling in and holding her close.

"You're safe now. They won't come back tonight," he whispered into her hair. "I'm here. I'll always be here."

They lay in silence and darkness until her breathing changed as she slipped into sleep. He put his nose into her hair and breathed in the scent of her shampoo, swallowing the lump in his throat before whispering, "I love you… I won't let anything happen to you."

He couldn't imagine existing without her anymore.

He sighed.

He only hoped one day she'd love him as well.

34

Fears

Blaire woke to the sound of rain pattering against the window, feeling unusually warm. Her arm still hurt from what happened two weeks ago, but last night added a dull ache at the crook of her elbow. She never did like having her blood drawn.

She shifted and felt a warm body against her back, and it all came back to her. Lukas was in her bed with his arms wrapped around her from behind. Blaire squirmed to change her position, but she froze when Lukas released a groan in response to her movements.

This was bad. While she had been ready for him weeks ago, she had been running on pure desire. Lukas had her so aroused at the time, she would have done just about anything in that moment. Except give him her blood. She felt more clear-headed this morning, and she wasn't sure she was ready, not with everything that had gone down recently. Her desire for him wasn't gone, but her head was a mess.

Blaire tried getting up from the bed, but Lukas tightened his hold. He moved his hand to her hip, and slowly rolled his hips against her backside once, before relaxing his hold. She bit down on her lower lip, and after giving it a moment to make sure he wasn't going to move again, she slowly turned over, so she faced him and wasn't pressed up against his obvious erection.

Breathing in his spicy apple scent, Blaire snuggled her upper body close to his, burying her face into his chest, closing her eyes, and listening to his heartbeat.

Lukas shifted, and his hand moved. She opened her eyes in time to see him reach down and slip his hand into his sweatpants. On her quick inhale, he froze, his hand still down his pants, gripping himself. The visual of him touching himself stirred something inside her. Maybe she wasn't as messed up in the head as she originally thought.

Lukas looked up, realizing she was awake. "It's not what it looks like. I wasn't doing anything. Just adjusting morning wood."

Blaire laughed softly and met Lukas's eyes. "I know. I've been awake for a while."

Lukas raised a brow at her, pulling his hand from his pants. "Why didn't you say anything?"

"I didn't want to wake you. And… I was comfortable. Did you bring me home last night?"

Lukas nodded, before resting his forehead against hers. Blaire closed her eyes. He caressed her cheek gently, moving his fingertips across her jaw, before running a finger over her lower lip. She parted her lips as he pulled his touch away.

"Blaire," he whispered. He leaned in to kiss her softly once, then pulled back to look into her eyes.

Blaire swallowed audibly and Lukas leaned back in to kiss her once more, deepening the kiss as he pulled her body against his with the arm wrapped beneath her. He trailed his other hand down her side and over her hip. She moaned into his mouth as he lifted her leg over his hip, pulling her lower half flush against his hardness with a firm grasp. Her breath hitched.

Lukas kissed down her jawline to her neck before biting gently, not with his fangs, just a gentle nibble with his normal teeth. Blaire gasped, laying her head back in silent invitation. He leaned in and sucked on the delicate skin on the side of her neck near her pulse point.

Blaire ground her hips against him, not realizing what she was doing anymore, lost in the moment as she panted, clinging to Lukas's body. He lapped at the abused flesh of her neck, groaning at her movements before dragging his lips to her ear.

"If you don't stop now, I won't be able to control myself from claiming you right here and now," Lukas whispered with a rasp, growling low in his throat into Blaire's ear.

She shuddered and moaned, then snapped her gaze up to meet Lukas's eyes, which were glowing dimly. She could still feel the warmth of his need against her throbbing core, making it difficult to focus, but she wasn't ready for this. Claiming involved him taking her blood. While she let him clean her arm, she wasn't ready for more. Wasn't ready to be bitten. The panic building inside her made her freeze and look away.

Lukas's face fell. He kissed the top of her head before whispering, "I understand. When you're ready, I'm here."

Blaire slowly looked up to meet his eyes as she lowered her leg. "I'm sorry…"

"You have nothing to be sorry for," Lukas said, the strain still obvious in his voice. "I won't lie and say I don't want you,"—he motioned to his obvious problem—"but I would never take what isn't mine to take."

Lukas closed his eyes. Clearly, it pained him to say that right after he told her she was his. "I would never force anything on you," he added with conviction.

Blaire looked at him with pinched brows, but she believed him. He'd had more than enough opportunity if he wanted to force himself on her. He was not Caleb. She rested her forehead against his chest, sighing before pulling back.

"I'm going to take a shower," she said quietly as she sat up. "We probably need to go see the professor soon."

Blaire was still a mess from the club. Her hair looked like a couple of badgers got into it and had a fight. She wore a large t-shirt she assumed was Lukas's. He must have put it on for her when he brought her back to the dorm.

Lukas nodded. "Take your time. I'll call Aiden and get the others ready."

Blaire climbed out of bed and padded across the floor to the bathroom to shower as Lukas reached for his cell phone on the nightstand.

Clean again, she came out wrapped in a fluffy black towel. Lukas paused mid-sentence, lying still, holding his phone to his ear, staring at her. He sat up quickly on the bed as he ended the phone call.

Blaire blushed and disappeared into the closet to find her clothes and shoes. She decided to go casual; she couldn't be bothered to do much else, picking a pair of dark wash jeans and a long-sleeved mint hoodie. She didn't feel like putting in the effort after everything that happened, and the hoodie would protect her from the rain. She didn't even bother hiding the ugly bruise on her cheek from what Caleb did. Everyone knew what happened. There was no reason to hide, and she was honestly tired of hiding all the time. She left the closet after changing and carried a pair of socks and sneakers to the bed. She sat down and waited for Lukas to finish showering.

When Lukas stepped from the bathroom wrapped in a towel low on his hips, Blaire's mouth went dry. He had tied the towel low enough that his well-defined V showed with a faint dusting of brown hair leading down into the towel. She swallowed hard as she took her fill. He was gorgeous.

She averted her eyes, tucking her wet hair behind her ear as warmth crawled up her neck and over her face. She needed to focus on things other than his body. What was wrong with her?

"Pull your hair back."

Blaire looked up at Lukas and wrinkled her brow in confusion, caught out by the sudden seriousness of his tone. "What?"

Lukas knelt on the floor in front of her. She gasped and looked down at his half-naked body as her heartbeat raced. The heady scent of his body wash was more potent fresh out of the shower and with no clothes on. He reached up and moved Blaire's hair away from her neck.

"I thought so. It's faint, but it's there."

Lukas trailed his finger over the side of her neck. His fingers lingered over the minor bruise left from when he had his way with her neck earlier.

"What is it?" Blaire whispered, her eyes fluttering closed at his touch.

"I can see my mark again." He pulled his hand away, looking up into her eyes as she opened them again.

Blaire lifted her hand to touch her neck, and then Lukas turned his head to expose the same side of his neck, moving his long hair away from his skin. She gasped and covered her mouth. The mark on Lukas's neck looked similar to the moon glyphs for Blood and

Will she'd seen on a poster in Charlotte's bedroom, but like they'd combined into one unique symbol. She didn't know what any of it meant—if it was a real thing, or just some New Age, mystical stuff like Charlotte's family gravitated toward, but she remembered the poster because she found the art interesting.

Lukas clenched his jaw as he took in her reaction.

Blaire ran her fingers down the side of his neck over the faint marking, and he shuddered at her touch, his eyes falling closed.

When her hand fell away, he stared into her eyes, taking her hands in his.

"It's not a mistake…" he whispered, swallowing hard. "I was so fucking foolish to ever act like it was. I'm sorry. I'm so fucking sorry."

Blaire looked down at Lukas. This was so unreal. Something tangible lay between them, something more than this bond. To see concrete proof of it, physical evidence, overwhelmed her. She got up from the bed and rushed into the bathroom. She needed to see what it looked like on her skin.

Once dressed, Lukas came to the bathroom door she left open and stopped, watching her look at her neck in the mirror. She strained to find the right angle.

"We should grab breakfast on the way over from the canteen, since we missed the weekend breakfast service already. You need something to replenish your strength after last night."

Blaire turned from the mirror with a sigh.

"What's wrong?"

"I can't see it," she whispered, and then looked at Lukas as he ran a hand through his hair, exposing his neck. She frowned. "It's gone…"

Sighing, Lukas nodded. "Until we bond fully, it won't show permanently like it does on other Korrena pairs, like Kai and Mera. And you won't be able to see it on yourself until that happens, either."

"You mean until we have sex, and you drink my blood," Blaire muttered, pushing past him into the bedroom.

"…and you drink mine."

Blaire gasped and rounded on Lukas, horrified.

"Did you miss that in the handbook?" He ran both hands through his hair, looking at her with concern as he leaned on the doorjamb.

Blaire fidgeted with the string of her hood. "I… I thought it was only because it was two Vasirian. I thought you just had to drink my blood only."

"Yeah, I already asked Professor Velastra about that, because I wasn't sure either." Lukas sighed and looked anywhere but at Blaire's face. "And yeah, we have to share lifeblood to fully connect."

She shook her head. "I don't know if I can do that."

"Then what?" Lukas stepped away from the doorjamb, his voice rising. "First, you don't want me to bite you, then you don't even want to have sex with me—which I'm finding really hard to fucking believe considering the way you were wrapped around me this morning, practically begging for it."

Blaire's mouth dropped open. She couldn't believe he was speaking to her that way after everything they'd been through. She finally thought they had worked out their differences and she was finally seeing the true him, but here he was acting like an asshole yet again.

"What? It's true. I know you want me as much as I want you." He raked his fingers through his hair and swung his hand down in frustration. "I'm dying to claim you, and it's not because I want to get laid. I want you. I want everything about you!"

Blaire wrapped her arms around herself and turned away from him to stare out the window at the falling rain that cast the entire academy grounds in a depressing gloom, reflecting her mood.

"Look, I know this is something you've never done before, but I would never fucking hurt you. How many times do I have to say that before you'll believe me?"

Blaire shook her head. "It's not that…"

"What? Is it because I'm a monster?" Pain threaded Lukas's voice as he spoke the words.

Blaire turned and glared at him. "That's not fair."

"I don't know anymore, Blaire. I don't know if you believe it or not. One minute you act like you want me, and the next you act like you're afraid of me."

Lukas once again dragged his hand through his hair. He did that when frustrated, and the more agitated he got, the more he did it. It made her want to glue his hands together and trap him in the silky strands.

"I don't think you're a monster… I'm scared," Blaire whispered. "Yes, I'm scared of my first time, but it's more than that. What if you can't stop when you do bite me? They said my blood would be addictive to you because you're my Korrena. What if you drain me dry? What if I die?"

That was the real fear. The real thing that held her back from accepting bonding with him. Fear of sex, considering that prior to Lukas, any real-life experience with things of a sexual nature involved abuse, was something she could eventually move past. But he could kill her when she shared her blood with him, and she was helpless to prevent that. That was what she couldn't get past, and the reality was there was much more to the bonding than she realized.

She took a breath and looked into Lukas's sea-glass eyes, whispering, "And now this? Having to drink blood too… I'm not a Vasirian, Lukas. I don't want to drink someone's blood."

Lukas dropped onto his bed and hung his head. "I would never do anything that would put you at risk of dying. I will be able to stop."

Blaire sighed.

"As far as everything else? I'd be gentle with you, but I won't force you into this. I'd never force you to be with me, and I certainly wouldn't force you to have sex with me."

"I know… Can we just drop the subject? We need to go anyway." Blaire sat on the edge of the bed and pulled on her socks before slipping on a pair of sneakers.

Lukas cursed under his breath and ran a hand over his face as he stood, grabbing his leather jacket. "It's fine. Let's go."

35

Vasirian Business

Everyone was waiting outside when they reached the office. Riley rushed to Blaire and wrapped her in a tight hug before pulling back and grabbing her arm, holding it up.

"Are you okay?"

"Yeah, I'm fine. Just a bit shook up, but Lukas has been with me the entire time." Blaire shrugged and rolled up the sleeve of her hoodie, showing the faded bruise from before, but no major damage this time.

Aiden frowned at her arm and shook his head. "The professor said to wait inside, so we should head in."

Once inside, Blaire sat on one of the leather chairs and started eating the sausage, egg, and cheese biscuit she picked up from the canteen as Riley plopped down on the chair next to her.

Blaire looked around at everyone and wrinkled her brow. "Where's Lukas?"

"He's having breakfast." Riley pointed back to the door, where

Lukas leaned against the wall. Blaire could see his lower legs, but the shadows of the room obscured his upper body.

Kai cleared his throat. "I assume he's trying to be discreet about it, for your sake."

Blaire looked down. Likely because of this morning. "I'm sorry..."

"Don't worry about it. It'll just take getting used to," Aiden said with a shrug. He didn't know what had gone down with them this morning. He didn't know she told Lukas of her fears about the blood.

Moments later, the door opened, and the professor stepped inside carrying a large, well-worn tome. She walked around the desk and dropped it with a thud before leaning over the desk, inspecting Blaire's face as she sat drinking her juice.

"You look much better compared to the last time," she said with a satisfied nod.

"Yeah, Lukas stopped them before anything could happen."

"Something happened. I wasn't fast enough. It wasn't enough," Lukas grumbled.

Blaire looked back as Lukas stepped forward from the shadows, having thrown out the empty packet, looking every bit the predator. She swallowed hard as anticipation shivered through her. Anticipation for what she didn't know, but the mystery was thrilling.

She shook her head, chasing away the wayward thoughts, and frowned. "There's no way you could have predicted they would have been there in the night."

Lukas gritted out between clenched teeth, "I could have been in the bed. I should have been. I should have sensed something was wrong. I did last time before I even came into the room."

The professor folded her arms and then reached up to tap her chin. "The last time, Blaire was nearly dead, so it isn't a surprise you would have sensed her from a distance like that. That said, the Order probably used up the sample they took from before, which is odd considering how much I suspect they took the first time."

Lukas dragged a hand through his hair. "What the hell can we do? Because if this shit continues, Blaire is going to die."

Aiden crossed his arms as he leaned against a bookcase. "She may not survive the next attempt."

"I completely agree," the professor said with a nod.

Blaire hung her head and sighed as she drank her orange juice in silence.

"Shouldn't the Order give them more time to bond before trying to kill Blaire?" Kai asked.

Mera placed her hand on his shoulder. "At this point, it's not a matter of them killing Blaire because she hasn't bonded with Lukas yet. Aiden is right. If they keep trying to take her blood and botch it up like before, then she might not survive, even if we are with her. Because if Lukas hadn't found her the first time, she wouldn't even be here now."

Again, they were talking about her like she wasn't sitting right there. Talking about her death. Was she going to die? Was this really how it would happen when she had tried so hard for years to live? To escape and be free. Blaire shut her eyes to fight back the tears that threatened to fall.

Lukas paced the room, and the professor sighed, placing her hand on the black tome before looking at Blaire, then at Lukas.

"There is one possible way they may stop pursuing Blaire, or at least if they continue, it won't result in her death."

Lukas spun to face the professor and snapped, "Tell us what it is!"

The professor crossed her arms, meeting his stare. "Turn her into one of us."

As if it was the simplest thing in the world.

Blaire bolted up out of her chair, spilling her juice and dropping the last few bites of her biscuit. "No way! Stop talking about me like I'm not here! Y'all keep doing it!" She threw her hands up and then jabbed a finger at her own chest. "I'm the one in charge of my life, and I'm not gonna just let Lukas drink my blood to lay some 'claim' to me and risk killing me." She clenched her hands into fists as they shook, lowering her voice. "I'm certainly not gonna let you do whatever crazy thing is needed to become a Vasirian! That ain't happening! I'm human!" Her chest rose and fell rapidly as she sucked in gulps of air to avoid spiraling into an anxiety attack. She had been told they didn't turn humans into Vasirian. What in the hell was the professor talking about? She felt completely blindsided.

Everyone was looking at her like she'd told them the world was going to end in twenty-four hours. Lukas looked stricken, his mouth hanging open and his eyes wide.

Aiden pushed off the bookcase and took a step toward Blaire with his hand out, as if approaching a skittish animal. "Calm down…"

Riley reached out to touch Blaire's arm. "It's okay. No one is going to do anything you don't want."

Blaire's hands trembled as she repeatedly clenched and unclenched her fists, her fight-or-flight instinct telling her to run. Run and never look back.

Riley looked up at her with pleading eyes. "Please sit down? For me?"

Blaire didn't say anything, collapsing back into the seat and putting her hands over her face, hanging her head back against the seat. She wanted to scream.

The professor sighed, looking toward the ceiling as if seeking guidance. "Becoming a Vasirian would be the quickest and most efficient way to avoid death due to blood loss… that is, if Lukas can pull it off."

Lukas's brow furrowed in confusion. "What the hell are you talking about?"

Tapping the tome again, the professor said, "It's not without its risks. I've done research in anticipation of both of you desiring to change Blaire after you complete the bond; and while it's unorthodox for a Vasirian to turn a human… a taboo, really…" She waved a hand dismissively. "It is not completely unknown, or there wouldn't be documented details on how to turn a human." She once again tapped the surface of the old tome.

"How do we do it?" Lukas said, his eyes narrowed as he clenched his fists.

Blaire turned in her chair, yelling at Lukas, "I can't believe you're serious about entertaining the idea, because it is not going to happen!"

"Fuck! Why are you so difficult?" Lukas threw up his hands and resumed pacing.

The professor ignored their bickering. "We are ordered by King Blackthorn to bring no harm to humans—a rule that has been enforced since King Adrian's father, the late King Luciano Blackthorn, took the throne. Before his reign, it is not known how humans and Vasirian interacted. The old texts from King Rosendo Blackthorn's reign have either been lost or destroyed with time."

Blaire glared at the professor. "Oh goodie, I'm once again the exception to the rule? I'm just all kinds of lucky. First, I'm the first human to have some strange connection with a Vasirian, and now? I get to be the first human 'approved' to be changed into some other being entirely!" Her voice rose at the end, on the borderline of hysterics.

Riley put a hand on her arm and squeezed reassuringly, looking at her with concern.

Professor Velastra crossed her arms. "This is merely a suggestion to possibly save your life."

"So, how does he do it?" Kai spoke up from his place on the wall.

The professor looked around the room at the others, and Blaire couldn't help but notice how she avoided making eye contact with her. "A Vasirian must drink the blood of a human to the point of near death, their heart almost stopping, before sharing their blood with them. This is why no one speaks of this, and why it isn't done."

Blaire was as white as a sheet, staring at the professor as she continued.

"The human is usually too weak to stay conscious after consuming the Vasirian's blood, so they go into a deep sleep, like a coma, during their transition. After which, they awaken as a Vasirian themselves. It is risky to turn a human because drinking enough blood to bring a human to near death can cause a frenzy, and when that happens, it is difficult for a Vasirian to stop when they have consumed so much, which is why it is considered taboo. And in this case,"—she motioned between Lukas and Blaire—"it would be a Korrena pair, making it more difficult due to the addictive nature of Blaire's blood to Lukas."

Blaire gripped the edge of her chair, knuckles white. She was having one long nightmare she couldn't wake up from. The professor just confirmed all the fears she had voiced to Lukas earlier.

"I told Blaire I could stop, that we could complete our bond without me killing her."

The professor sighed. "Perhaps that part is true, but to turn Blaire, to take so much of her blood to nearly kill her… that's not as simple as the intimate sharing of blood in the bonding ritual."

Blaire held her head in her hands. "No… No way… I can't… I won't…"

Sitting in her chair on the other side of the desk, the professor said, "You don't have to. It is simply an option and the easiest way."

Blaire looked up at her. "You said they might still pursue me anyway, so what's the point? What benefit is there to becoming another being entirely? To risk my life?"

"At least it would keep you from bleeding to death," Riley tried to add helpfully.

Kai crossed his arms and nodded his agreement. "Riley has a point; one I believe you should strongly consider if you're going to follow through with bonding with Lukas."

"Yes, but only if he can stop himself," the professor added. "If you become a Vasirian, you wouldn't die if the Order did come again. Your bonding would likely be more stable than it has been thus far. Beyond that, I am unsure how transitioning will affect you as a human beyond obtaining the same abilities and physical benefits we have—for example, accelerated healing." She waved at Blaire's covered arm.

This was too much. How could they be talking about this so casually? Don't they understand she's been a human her entire life and to just throw that away wasn't as easy as deciding to change your clothes?

Blaire jumped up from the chair. "I can't do this. I just can't."

She looked at Lukas with tears in her eyes before rushing from the room, though she still heard the professor speak as the door remained open.

"You may need to convince her, as it may be her only fighting chance at survival."

Aiden said, "Until we get it sorted, we'll protect her."

Blaire bolted down the hall.

Blaire sat in the corner of her bed against the wall with her arms wrapped around her legs when Lukas entered the room, Aiden and

Riley following close behind. She didn't want to see any of them. They wanted her to give up who she was. It didn't make sense to her. While her heart had changed, and she couldn't deny she was falling for Lukas, she was not okay with losing her humanity forever when she didn't trust that he would be hers forever.

Lukas sat on the side of his bed, running a hand through his hair before holding his head in his hands.

Riley flopped down onto Blaire's bed. "Don't worry about it. Being a Vasirian isn't so bad, really. I've been one my whole life!" she tried to lighten the mood, but Blaire didn't feel like laughing.

Lukas rolled his eyes and shook his head in his hands.

"Besides, one of the perks of it all is you won't get old for a really, really long time," Riley continued, nodding. "Despite how it looks, Professor Velastra is actually seventy-four."

Blaire stared at her blankly, her expression slack.

"No one told you about how we age?"

"No… Only that you live a long time."

Riley sat up on the bed. "Well, we actually slow down aging in our twenties, and by the time we reach our seventies, we don't look older than a human does in their early thirties. Cool, right?" She didn't give Blaire a chance to respond. "And what's really awesome is when we reach that age, our body's aging slows down again, so we only look about forty when we reach one hundred years old! We actually stop aging entirely when we turn one hundred fifty years old."

"How old do you look when you stop aging?" Blaire asked, her curiosity piqued.

Riley grinned. "Sixty in human years."

"So, wait a minute… how do you get away with it?"

"Get away with what?" Riley tilted her head.

"Well, working… being around humans when you never age. I

mean, eventually, someone is going to notice."

Riley laughed and shook her head. "See, usually we just look like we age gracefully for a while, but at some point, we have to transfer to different locations if we're working with humans. Many of our kind work in jobs that are run by Vasirian or travel a lot and do business with several people, so it makes it easier." She crossed her ankles beneath her and began picking at the buckles on her boots. "But it's easier just to lie about our age and use fake documents. That way, we can prolong how long we can be in the fields of our choosing without question. It also allows us to work different types of jobs, because we can spend twenty years doing one thing, and then move on to something different starting over at whatever age we look like then. Rinse and repeat for centuries."

Blaire shook her head rapidly. "This is insane…"

"It really isn't that bad. Like the professor said, you'd have no problems healing quickly, so your bruising problem would be a thing of the past."

"Shut the hell up," Aiden said with a sigh.

"What?" Riley looked at her brother.

"You're not helping the situation at all." Aiden walked over and handed Blaire a beautiful ornate knife in silver and black, with rubies inlaid down the sides.

She looked up at him and raised a brow. "What's this for?"

He shrugged. "Kai had it in his room for decoration, but he always kept it sharpened. I figured it could prove useful for protection."

Blaire held the dagger in her hand, inspecting it before setting it on her nightstand. "Thank you," she whispered.

Aiden sighed and sat on the bed next to Lukas, who was staring at Blaire.

She didn't like the idea of having to be in a position where she needed a weapon to protect herself. Even against Caleb, the idea of using an actual weapon to fight back made her uneasy. She didn't know if she'd be capable of inflicting harm on another person, even to save her own life. She didn't feel strong enough to face this. Of all the things that had happened to her starting from the time her mother married Caleb's father, this was by far the most challenging. How did anyone expect her to do any of this?

"I am going to do whatever it takes to make you safe," Lukas said before dragging his fingers through his hair, resting his hand on the back of his neck as he hung his head, mumbling, "...even if you don't want the bond with me."

Blaire jerked her head up and stared at Lukas. That was the furthest thing from reality. It scared her how badly she wanted this with him. How badly she needed him. Just because she was afraid of everything, and had reservations about the blood—dying, drinking his blood. And just because she didn't want to be a Vasirian, didn't mean she didn't want him. Her words, when she was upset, may have sent the wrong message. She opened her mouth to say something, but Riley cut her off.

"It's obvious Blaire wants the bond, you idiot. You're blind to think otherwise." Riley crossed her arms over her chest.

"Yeah, I was starting to think so too, but this morning... and that meeting in the office..." Lukas clenched his jaw. "I just don't know anymore."

Blaire hung her head, not able to say anything.

"This morning?" Riley asked.

"It's nothing. Just leave it."

Aiden shifted the conversation, sensing the tension rising in the room. "If Blaire doesn't want to be a Vasirian, she doesn't have to be. But what in the hell can we do to protect her as things are now?" He motioned up and down at Blaire's obvious human state.

"For one, I'm not going to leave her side going forward. I'll sleep with her every night until this issue is resolved," Lukas said, gripping his fists tight.

"You mean once they finally kill me?"

Lukas jumped up. "No!"

Blaire flinched, looking up at him with wide eyes.

He leaned toward her, resolve clear on his face. "That will never happen."

Blaire tugged on her long hair, twisting the ends. "I'm sorry. You can't blame me for feeling this way when twice in two weeks they've attacked me. Between that and what happened with Caleb all in such quick succession… I'm just so tired and fed up with all of it." She closed her eyes. "All I wanted to do was escape my stepbrother and the future he planned for me, but now I may not even get a future with the way things are going."

Aiden clenched his fists tight, cursing under his breath.

Lukas dropped back down onto the bed, gripping his hair in frustration.

Riley said, "We know a lot has happened recently, but we'll protect you, and you'll never have to be with your stepbrother again. Besides, the school took care of him." She placed her hand on Blaire's arm.

Blaire didn't know if what she dealt with living with Caleb would be better than this. She should have just stayed. Served apple pie for the rest of her life in a greasy diner. Caleb might have been abusive, and she might have had to endure marrying him and being the mother of his children, but she wouldn't be dead. Was that better than death, though? It was its own special death.

As her thoughts descended to a dark place where nothing constructive would come of them, she sought out the one thing that kept her grounded lately. She brought her gaze up to stare at Lukas, and her heart beat faster when she considered what life would be like married to him, being the mother to his children someday.

Lukas lifted his head and met her eyes, as if sensing her. He said nothing, but his eyes spoke volumes. She couldn't tell what was going through his head, but the intensity she found in those striking green depths chilled her to the bone.

The group remained silent for a while longer before Aiden sighed loudly, standing. "We need to get off campus to get away from everything."

Riley looked up at him. "What do you have in mind?"

"We could go to the movies again and then check out this new Mexican restaurant that opened up in Valley Center Plaza recently."

"What about Caleb?" Blaire looked at Aiden and chewed on the inside of her cheek.

"That's a non-point now. We'll have to talk with the professor to find out what they did to his mind, but they said the situation between you both was going to be handled to avoid any further incidents."

Blaire sighed. "As long as we don't go back to Ricky's Diner, I'll go. I don't want to see my old boss, knowing he had a hand in all this."

Lukas shrugged his acceptance, still staring at Blaire.

Riley got off the bed and stretched. "I need to go get a packet, because I skipped breakfast, but then I'll be ready."

"I'll let everyone else know, and we can all meet in the courtyard in fifteen," Aiden said as he walked to the door. "Call my cell if anything happens."

Once they left the room, Lukas sighed and moved from his bed to sit next to Blaire on the edge of her bed with his back to her.

"I meant every word I said about not letting them kill you," Lukas whispered.

Blaire dropped her head to rest against his back. He startled, then closed his eyes, and when she breathed in his scent to calm herself, he relaxed beneath her.

They sat in silence for several minutes. Everything was catching up to Blaire, and all she wanted to do was crawl under her covers and sleep until it was all over.

"I'm just so tired, Lukas… I hate that everyone is getting dragged into this mess because of me."

Lukas scratched at his palm and sighed. "You haven't forced anyone into anything. Besides, you couldn't keep Riley away if you tried."

Blaire laughed softly and Lukas stood from the bed, holding his hand out to her. "I'm hungry for actual food. We should get going. Everyone is probably already waiting for us."

She reached out and took his hand, and he pulled her up before leading her out the door to meet everyone.

36

Running

The rest of the weekend, and the following three weeks, passed smoothly. Blaire returned to classes without incident. The only real difficulty had been waking every morning to Lukas pressed against her backside. She'd spent her teen years not caring about things like that, unlike others her age, and then avoiding it with Caleb, but during the months spent at Blackthorn, she'd had a sexual awakening. That long-haired Vasirian set her body aflame.

On Friday, Riley finally talked Blaire into leaving Blackthorn to visit the Valley Center Plaza to go shopping at the store she had mentioned last month. Blaire was apprehensive to go, even though she'd been assured by Professor Velastra that the Wilcox family would no longer be a problem. She was still fighting an internal war with herself about bonding with Lukas and the suggestion to give up her humanity to protect herself. But leaving the school's grounds got her away from the administration, and things had been going so well, that she gave in without much pressure from Riley.

She wasn't sure she could afford anything the upscale store had, but the outfits were gorgeous, definitely the kind of thing one would wear clubbing. She picked up a pair of wedges, turning them over to see the price. Yeah, she definitely couldn't afford anything here, even with the allowance the academy gave her.

Riley huffed. "You know, if I don't ace the makeup final next week, I'm going to be in such shit."

"That bad?"

"Oh yeah, and once again, Mera and Kai ranked in the top five of the class." Riley rolled her eyes.

Blaire put the shoe down and stepped far away from it. "Do they always score that way? Couldn't they help you study?"

Riley laughed. "Oh hell no. The last time I tried to get Mera to help me study, I wanted to pour bleach into my eyes. She had me start after class and not stop until sunrise on the morning of the test. My brain was complete mush! And Kai? Well, if Mera knew I asked him, she'd help."

"Oh… wow." Blaire frowned as she looked through the racks of clothing. She did well on her final, after Aiden's help with all of her catch-up work, and was ready for July's summer break. "What about Seth? You share a lot of classes together, and Aiden said he's pretty smart."

Riley froze, holding a dress in front of her on its hangar, her face turning pink.

"Are you okay?"

"Y-yeah. I'm fine. But no, I can't ask him."

Blaire raised her eyebrow and tilted her head. "Why not?"

"I just can't. That's all there is to it."

The finality in her voice said Blaire shouldn't push. Riley always got flustered around Seth, and he acted as hot and cold with Riley as Lukas had been with her. They were obviously attracted to each other, but why wouldn't they act on it? It wasn't as if they had the issue of being another species in the way.

"Anyway, they always score that high because Mera is basically a genius, and Kai is always competing with her, so he has no issue keeping up anymore. I really don't understand what's so fun about the competition, but whatever gets him off."

Blaire burst out laughing as Riley held up a black dress in front of her.

"You should try this on."

"Oh no, I can't afford anything here. Especially now that I don't have a job anymore. The allowance the school gives me covers my basic needs, but nothing on the scale this store offers."

Riley waved a hand dismissively. "My parents are loaded, and since I'm the baby, they won't care if I spend money on my best friend."

Blaire shook her head. Big surprise, Riley's parents were loaded. All Blackthorn Academy students came from families with money, one of the perks of coming from long family lines that had amassed wealth over centuries. Some more than others. But she was happy to know Riley saw her as her best friend, too. Moments like this made her hang on to whatever she could and not completely abandon everything.

"Fine, fine, but only because you said something sweet." Blaire took the dress and disappeared into the dressing room.

"I did?"

Blaire laughed as she took her clothes off. "So, is it just you and Aiden?"

"Oh no, I'm the baby of four children. My older sister Heather, who's thirty-four, and my brother Brandon, who's twenty-nine, have already left the academy and are working elsewhere."

"Really? What do they do?" Blaire asked as she pulled on the mini dress.

"Well, Brandon works as a chef in Korea. He's got a bunch of restaurants and his own cooking show in Seoul. And Heather works for a pharmaceutical company. She lives in New York City near my dad."

Blaire fought with the zipper on the dress, but finally managed to get hold of it. "What's he do? Do you have a mom around?"

"Yeah, but all anyone knows is he works in the Mayor's Office for International Affairs in Manhattan. We don't even know the details of what he does." She laughed. "Mom works in one of the branch locations of Blackthorn Academy, though."

"What, really?"

"Oh, yeah. She's a teacher in the high school branch. I'll introduce you sometime."

It must be nice to have a mother so close. Blaire swallowed hard to get her emotions in check as she adjusted the dress and stared at herself in the mirror.

It was another black bodycon dress, but it had a halter top with the back cut out, the material ruched at the waist and down the thighs where a slit up the front stopped close to the juncture where her thigh met her pelvis. She was definitely too tall for this to feel comfortable.

"Uh, Riley? This isn't going to work," she called from the dressing room.

"What? No way. It's the same size as the other dress. Let me see."

Blaire huffed a sigh and stepped out of the dressing room and held her hands out, motioning toward the long span of leg on display.

Riley whistled. "Wow. That's…"

"See! It's comically short for someone my height."

"No. It's hot, that's what it is." Riley lifted her phone and snapped a photo, and then tapped at her screen rapidly before looking up at Blaire. "There. All done."

"You're ridiculous. What are you doing?"

She shrugged, looking impish. "Oh, I just sent the photo to Lukas."

Blaire's eyes went wide. "No, oh no, you shouldn't have done that."

"Why not? You look smokin' hot."

Blaire muttered under her breath and retreated into the dressing room, changing back into her jeans and flowy black blouse with a chain accent at the neckline.

"So, have you had any more dreams like before? Do you think it's your bond?" Riley called from outside the dressing room.

Blaire sighed and sat down on the seat in the dressing room, slipping on her black flats before coming out. "I haven't had any dreams like that since all this started happening with the Order and my stepbrother. As far as the bond… I don't know, Riley."

"It could just be the stress that's keeping you from having the good dreams." Riley snatched the dress out of Blaire's hands and walked toward the register. "This dress will be perfect to wear to Haven when we go again."

"I'm not sure I want to go back there again, honestly." Blaire trailed after her.

Riley turned and frowned at her. "Look, Caleb isn't going to show up there anymore. You can't run from every place where something bad happens. Soon there'll be no place left for you to enjoy your life."

She knew that. It wasn't something she liked to dwell on. The ghosts of negative events were one of the reasons she originally planned to leave Rosebrook Valley.

"Blaire?"

Blaire froze at the familiar male voice behind her. Riley spun around and stepped closer to her side. Swallowing hard, Blaire turned around.

He looked terrible, sitting in a wheelchair with a busted and bruised face, with a cast that went up to his thigh and another on his arm. An older man stood behind him, likely a worker assisting him.

"Caleb…" she croaked.

"Let's go," Riley said, tugging on her arm.

"Hey, wait. What's wrong?" Caleb asked, looking genuinely concerned.

Did he not remember? Had the professor been right? She had to know for sure. This would be the only way she'd ever feel comfortable in Rosebrook. She needed to know if she could truly trust their words.

Blaire shook her head, pulling her arm from Riley. "What happened to you?"

Caleb grinned sheepishly and rubbed the back of his head with his good hand. "Car accident. I was going too fast coming back from Atlanta and… yeah, it wasn't pretty."

Blaire nodded tightly.

"I'm so glad I saw you when we were passing the store from the street. I was just going to get some last things I need before tomorrow."

"Tomorrow?"

"Yeah, I wanted to be able to see you before I left, but I didn't think it was going to be possible with my hospital stay. It's hard enough being out like this, but business waits for no one." He sighed. "I'm sorry, Blaire, but we're not going to be able to meet on Sundays for brunch anymore."

Riley gaped like a fish and Blaire had to compose herself. He sounded nothing like the Caleb she knew.

"W-why not?" she hedged.

"There's a new branch opening in Seattle. Grandpa wants to extend the business to the West Coast and wants me to head the entire operation. I leave tomorrow."

This was too good to be true. He didn't know anything. Professor Velastra told her the memories of his attraction and his intentions to be with her were taken away, as well as his grandparents' knowledge of that. She said they'd even wiped Ricky's memory of Caleb's bribery to keep tabs on her. The vibes coming off Caleb felt completely different—as though he were a just a classmate.

"I see," she said quietly, not sure what to say to the news. It was hard to pretend he hadn't been the big bad who made the last two years a living hell.

Caleb glanced around and grimaced. "So, I need to get going. Won't be long before I need more pain medicine, and I still need to buy new suitcases." He motioned toward the door, and the older gentleman took hold of the back of his wheelchair. "Maybe I'll see you next time I'm in town, if you haven't already graduated Blackthorn and moved off into the world." He offered her a bright smile.

"Yeah, you… take care of that."

As the man wheeled Caleb away from them, Blaire stood speechless.

The professor had told Blaire that while she would have much preferred to wipe their memories of Blaire's existence entirely, they didn't go that far or plant suggestions beyond what was needed to make Caleb view her as only a stepsister. So, the Wilcox family still hated her for where she came from, but she didn't care. They would leave her alone now that they didn't believe she was bringing down their grandson. Seeing Caleb behave this way assured her the professor had told the truth. Blaire was finally free from them. She'd never have to deal with the Wilcox family again. With Caleb moving three thousand miles away, she'd never see him and be reminded of a past she would much rather lay to rest.

Riley whistled. "I've actually never seen the effects of compulsion, but that's something else… just… wow."

Wow was right.

Riley didn't say anything more as she completed her purchase of the dress Blaire tried on, as well as several other items of clothing she picked for herself. As they left the store, Blaire changed the subject.

"You know, the way you and Seth were dancing at Haven… is something going on between you two?" Not only was the topic a good distraction from the complete mind-screw of her whole interaction with new Caleb, but she wanted to get Riley to talk about Seth, curious why she seemed so bothered by him.

Riley turned red. "He's basically Aiden's little brother. There's absolutely no way something could happen with my brother."

"But he's not actually your brother," Blaire argued with a grin, swinging the shopping bag with the dangerous black dress inside.

They chattered about nonsense the rest of the way home, even the weather—anything but boys. Oh yes, Riley had it bad for Seth if she avoided the topic altogether.

As they neared the dorms, Riley turned serious.

"Have you thought any more about becoming one of us?" she said quietly.

Blaire sighed. She had dreaded someone bringing this up again. She still didn't have the answers they wanted to hear, and she hated disappointing them, but they didn't understand. She shook her head. "I just can't do it… It's not that I have something against Vasirian, but I can't wrap my head around giving up my humanity and the whole thing about drinking blood."

"I feel so sorry for Lukas…" Riley whispered.

Blaire looked over at her in confusion.

"Even if you complete the bond, if you stay human, Lukas is going to have to watch you grow old and die when he'll have barely aged a decade. Then he'll have to live possibly centuries without you."

Blaire stopped walking. "Just how long do Vasirian live?"

"Well, the oldest known Vasirian is the Oracle. She's just over four hundred years old." Riley sighed. "Look, just think about it. I don't want to see Lukas alone, and I don't want to be left alone either..."

Riley turned away toward her dorm with glossy eyes, leaving Blaire alone. She didn't think her presence affected Riley like that. She was screwing up with everyone.

Blaire walked to her dorm room and went inside. Lukas was gone, so she hung the dress in the closet. She looked down at the worn duffel bag on the floor and closed her eyes. She couldn't do this anymore. Not after hearing the stakes were even higher. She wouldn't do that to him.

She grabbed the bag and put it on her bed. She didn't know where she was going to go, but she didn't have to worry about the Wilcox family stopping her. In the short term, she would go to Charlotte and take her up on her offer of shelter now that it was safe for her family. Pulling her clothes from their hangers, she packed what would fit inside the duffel tightly, zipping the bag. She left it on the foot of the bed as she stepped out to meet Riley before her last dinner service at Blackthorn.

Lukas entered the dorm, searching for Blaire to go with her down to dinner, stopping short when he saw her duffel bag on the foot of her bed. He checked their closet and saw most of her clothes gone. Fear gripped him. Stepping back into the room, he glanced around and saw the photo of Blaire and her mother missing from the nightstand. Only the ornate knife that Aiden had given her sat there on its surface.

Blaire couldn't be thinking of doing what he suspected. Things were going well since they'd stopped talking about her becoming a Vasirian, and the Order hadn't made another move, so he couldn't understand what had changed. He thought things had gone back to normal.

Lukas unzipped the duffel and saw it was packed tight with clothes, the picture lying on top. He picked up the frame and held it in his shaking hands.

She was leaving him.

He sunk to the floor and stared at the young teen Blaire, surrounded by sunflowers and warmth. She was his light, and she was leaving. All he could think of was everything she meant to him, every encounter they had.

Blaire laughing at Riley's stupid jokes. Blaire getting angry at him because he acted like an ass. How her Southern accent got thicker, and her dialect changed when she got frustrated. Blaire twisting her hair when nervous. Blaire biting her bottom lip when she was uncertain. Blaire stuffing her face in the cafeteria with all sorts of foods she loved, carefree.

Blaire sleeping.

Blaire whispering his name in her sleep when he struggled to sleep and sat near her. Blaire snuggling close when he lay next to her with his arms around her. The scent of her.

Blaire talking to herself as she sat on her bed doing homework, a quirk of hers—she talked aloud to herself. He had taken it so personally at first, but it was one of the many qualities he'd grown to love about her.

His mind reeled with all the memories of the months she'd spent in the academy. He couldn't imagine spending another day without her. His greatest fear was becoming a reality, and he didn't know how to stop it. He'd be alone.

Lukas pulled himself from the floor and put the picture back in the duffel, zipping it closed. He ran a hand down his face, wiping away the uninvited tears.

At a knock, he rushed to the door, throwing it open.

"Whoa. Hey, man." Aiden stood in the doorway. He furrowed his brow. "You alright?"

Lukas cleared his throat. "Yeah, why?"

"I dunno… your eyes are red. Did something happen?"

"No. It's fine."

Aiden tried to look in the room, but Lukas stepped forward into the hall, closing the door. He couldn't tell Aiden what he suspected until he knew for sure. He had to figure out how to stop her without help.

"You ready for dinner? Blaire and Riley just left my place for the cafeteria."

"Yeah…"

"Seriously, man. Are you sure you're alright?"

Lukas ran a hand through his hair as they walked down the corridor. "I don't know. Just leave it. I can't talk about it. Not right now."

"You know I'll listen if you need me…"

"I know," he said quietly. His friend would be there for him. But he wasn't quite sure what anyone could do for him right now. This rift between him and Blaire was something he needed to fix.

They didn't say another word until they were in the cafeteria. Blaire was already at their table with Riley and Seth. Aiden took his usual seat across from Blaire, and Lukas settled in next to her.

She wouldn't even look at him, just stared at her barely eaten plate of shrimp scampi. No way would she put off eating one of her favorite foods. Another sign something was wrong.

She had started opening up more with him—talking to him and even joking around—but now she wouldn't even make eye contact. It was all the confirmation he needed that she was planning something she didn't want to share.

Lukas swallowed hard and tightened his fists on his lap. It took every ounce of his willpower not to confront her in front of everyone.

"Do you want to go to Haven next weekend?" Riley asked, as she took a bite of her rice pilaf. Her casual tone belied an ulterior motive and gave him another clue.

Lukas glanced between the two girls. Riley didn't know about the packed duffel if she was asking about next weekend. Blaire never hid anything from Riley. What was going on?

Blaire snapped her gaze up from her plate. "Oh. Um… I don't know, maybe?"

Riley's brows pinched together. "What's wrong?"

"Nothing!" Blaire protested too loudly.

Everyone stared at her.

"You both are acting weird tonight," Aiden said with a frown.

Seth laughed. "As opposed to when? They always act weird."

Riley sniped at him. "Well, aren't you sweet?" She rolled her eyes.

Blaire glanced at Lukas, and when their eyes met, she looked away. "I'm fine," she murmured, pushing the shrimp around on her plate.

That was a lie. Lukas could feel her tension and pain. It killed him not to soothe her discomfort.

Riley frowned. "Well, just let me know about going to Haven…" She gave Aiden a look and he shook his head at her.

"Where's Mera and Kai?" Blaire asked Aiden, changing the subject.

"They had a meeting with one of the professors about next year's coursework."

An awkward silence fell over the table again.

Lukas didn't know what to say, but he had to stop Blaire before she did anything stupid. He didn't want her to leave. In the beginning, this would be amazing news, but not now. Not now that she had wormed her way into his very being.

He needed her.

He might not be good enough for her, but he would spend his life trying to be what she needed. His eyes felt hot behind his closed eyelids. It was all he could do to ward off the tears. He didn't want everyone to see him break down again. They'd seen enough of his dramatics lately to last a lifetime, he was sure.

Everyone ate in silence, other than the occasional verbal sparring between Seth and Riley.

Blaire finally stood from the table, picking up her full tray. "I'm not very hungry. I think I'm going to lie down."

Lukas tensed. She was going to make a run for it, and he had to stop her.

She looked at everyone at the table quietly, her eyes stopping on Lukas. So much pain filled her green eyes that he felt it in his soul. She stared at him, as if she were memorizing his face, before turning away and leaving the cafeteria after throwing out her food.

"What was that all about?" Riley asked.

Lukas stood and glanced at Aiden, and he nodded. His best friend knew something was wrong, but he didn't push.

Aiden turned his attention to Riley to distract her as Lukas left their table. "Dunno. You wanna go to Happy Panda tomorrow?"

Lukas ran down the hallway, knocking into a few students as he rushed down the stairs to the deserted courtyard. Everyone was either at dinner or already in their dorms for the night.

Fencing around the edge of school grounds left only one way out of Blackthorn, and he hoped Blaire didn't have any tricks up her sleeve as he ran as fast as he could to the gate to wait for her.

He wasn't going to let her go without a fight.

He loved her.

His heart belonged to her, and he needed her to know that.

37

Desperation

Shifting her duffel bag higher on her shoulder, Blaire made her way across the darkened courtyard quickly, stopping as she reached the top of the winding road that led away from Blackthorn Academy toward the gates.

She couldn't do it. She couldn't accept becoming a Vasirian, and she didn't want to force Lukas to complete the bond with her, only to watch her grow old and die. If the emerging bond between them already caused them difficulty and pain, then what would happen to Lukas when they were irrevocably tied together? She wouldn't do that to him.

Blaire sighed heavily and moved to one of the benches that lined the flower beds around the courtyard, sitting down on the hard surface and dropping her bag at her feet. The adrenaline she had been running on when she fled the cafeteria gave out, replaced with a hollowness deep within.

Blaire didn't want to leave Lukas. He might not understand it now, but in the long run, he would be okay. He would be able to find someone compatible—someone like him. Someone he could one day marry and have children with. She put her hand on her stomach as a wave of nausea washed over her at the thought of the loss of that future with him. He could find someone the Order approved of. Someone who could spend hundreds of years with him and wouldn't die in the next sixty to eighty years.

She breathed in the scent of blooming hydrangeas and closed her eyes, trying to make sense of her scattered thoughts.

How did she expect Lukas to understand her feelings when she didn't understand them herself? Only recently had she uncovered the true reason why she hesitated so much to complete the bond with Lukas, because she did want him. She had fallen completely for him, but she didn't trust that he could stop when it came time to exchange blood. How much did he need to take? How much did she have to take from him? She'd pushed back so hard against the idea of consuming blood she failed to ask the important questions.

Then, there was the question of becoming a Vasirian. She didn't want to do that. She understood the benefits. Understood what it would bring her with Lukas and the future, but she was caught up on the whole throwing away her humanity bit. What would become of her soul? She wasn't sure if that was really a thing, but if it were, would that be lost forever if she became another being? Did Vasirian have souls? Drinking blood daily to survive didn't exactly appeal to her either, but would that change once she was turned? That was if she survived the transition. Which was another thing she feared, given her weakness when her tissue samples had been stolen in the night.

Blaire stared down the road to the tall black gates standing between her and freedom. But was it freedom, or was she just running away from another place where something bad happened, as Riley had put it? She couldn't run away her whole life. That wasn't freedom, that was fear. Her entire problem circled back to fear. Fear of the unknown. But what did she know for sure?

She had friends here who cared about her, and she cared about them.

She had the opportunity to get a degree toward an amazing career and give back to others who had suffered as she had, so they didn't grow up trapped in their trauma.

She had Lukas.

Despite what she thought before, and his rough behavior at times, he cared for her. What was she going to do now? She couldn't leave him, and it wasn't because he would follow her. She couldn't abandon him. Her heart wouldn't allow it.

Thunder rumbled in the distance, and she lay her head back, wrapping her arms around herself as she took a shuddering breath.

She loved Lukas.

Her chest tightened as she suffocated on the reality of her situation. She was a fool, making the biggest mistake of her life.

The door opened to the dorm room, and Lukas stepped inside, his face weary and his eyes rimmed red. Blaire watched him from her bed, where she sat with her bag next to her.

Lukas closed the door and thunked his forehead against it before releasing the handle and turning toward the room. He looked up and froze, staring at Blaire as if he'd seen a ghost.

"You're here..." His voice sounded raw. "Please, don't leave."

Blaire looked at the bag beside her and shook her head. "I couldn't do it."

He took hesitant steps toward her and then dropped to his knees in front of her. Her eyes widened at the tears running down his cheeks. His beautiful green eyes swam with emotion, and several of those emotions passed over his face, but the strongest of all, hitting her deep in her stomach, was relief.

Blaire's heart jumped. "Why aren't you angry? This isn't like you."

Lukas looked up at her with pure desperation on his face, his eyes glazed over. "This was always me. It was always there." He closed his eyes as his tears spilled down his cheeks.

She had seen him vulnerable, but not like this. His sorrow washed through her, drowning the defensive speech she'd been rehearsing for the past half hour since returning to their room.

It was time to face this like an adult. To put into action everything she'd been learning with Professor Sinclair, to claim the life that had now become available to her with Caleb out of the picture.

She nudged him with one foot until he opened his eyes. "We need to talk, and it's better if we're not next to each other, so we know whose feelings are whose. Can you…?"

Taking a deep breath, he wiped his face and stood, moving to his bed to sit across from her, giving her space. "I waited for you at the gate." Swallowing hard, he wrung his hands together. "But you never came, so I thought I was too late."

"I didn't make it that far."

"Why?" Lukas looked up from his hands to meet her eyes, and his swam with more unshed tears.

"I couldn't leave you."

He made an odd noise in his throat, half sob, half laugh, his face a mask of tragedy. It broke her heart.

Taking a deep breath, she said, "I'm afraid, Lukas. I'm terrified of dying."

"I said I wouldn't let that happen."

She held up her hand to stop him. "Let me talk… please."

Lukas mashed his lips together and nodded.

"I want to be with you. The idea of having sex with you both excites me and scares me. I know it's normal to be afraid, but you need to understand that before you, I've only associated sexual acts with something traumatic."

Lukas nodded quietly, not interrupting but acknowledging he was listening.

"Couple that with the fact I have to let you bite me and drink my blood… I don't know if you can stop. The idea of it already sounds off-putting—especially drinking blood myself—if I'm being honest with you. But even if I could get around that, knowing you might kill me has made me put on the brakes. It's what has held me back for a long time. I know you said you could stop, but you can't make that promise. This is new for you, too."

Lukas closed his eyes and sighed, and when Blaire didn't say more, he looked at her and said, "You're right… but I need you to trust me. Blaire, you're not the only one who's afraid."

"What are you afraid of?" she asked, studying his face.

"All those times I stopped myself when I felt you give in to me… I couldn't do it. I knew you were afraid of me. Of what I am. That's not the way I want to complete our pairing. I don't want to be like your stepbrother and force my desires on you."

Blaire shook her head and looked at him incredulously. "You're nothing like Caleb."

"I would feel like it, and that's enough. I would feel like you were coerced into it because you were aroused, not because you wanted it in your heart, in your mind. As long as you respond to what I am in fear, then you're not ready for it. I told you I would wait, and I meant that. I'll wait forever for you if you'll allow me to."

"I'm not afraid of what you are. I'm afraid of what you're capable of doing to me. I don't think that fear will ever go away. Without experiencing it firsthand, I'll never know if you have restraint, and without proof of that, I'll always be apprehensive."

Lukas sighed heavily. "The only way to prove it is to do it."

She nibbled her lower lip. "I've been thinking about that. How much do you have to take? How much do I have to drink?"

Lukas frowned, looking thoughtful. "I don't know exactly. I talked to Professor Velastra, and she told me the main stipulation was it had to happen when we both freely gave ourselves to each other. Drinking blood alone is not enough, having sex is not enough. There has to be that emotional connection—it's spiritual. That's another reason I won't do it while you're afraid. It wouldn't even work." He fiddled with one of his bracelets. "But she said she doesn't know the amount needed, because pairs generally get caught up in sharing blood in those moments and probably take more than necessary. It's not like it's measured," he mumbled, looking away.

Blaire licked her lips. "There's also the Order and becoming a Vasirian. I can't give up my humanity. Will I ever be able to do that? I… don't know. I can't promise you that. I won't say never, because I don't know what the future holds, but right now, I can't accept that concept. And if you can't accept my refusal, then I'm sorry, but…" She glanced over at her bag.

Lukas got up and moved in front of her, kneeling on the floor at her feet again, resting his hands on her thighs and looking up at her face. "I'm not going to make you do that. It was only Professor Velastra's suggestion to help against the Order, but I don't need that. All I need is you. If you'll have me."

Blaire shook her head. "When I packed to leave tonight, I thought that if I left now, then the bond doesn't complete, and you won't have to suffer when I grow old and die."

Lukas's eyes widened. He looked stricken.

Blaire looked away from him, unable to handle the pain on his face. Feeling it pouring off him in waves was hard enough. His relief from before was buried under a nauseating fear.

"If I leave you alone now, it'll hurt less," she whispered, staring at his lap as he knelt before her, unable to meet his eyes.

"That's not how it works, Blaire..." Lukas took his finger and gently lifted her chin until their eyes met. "No matter where you go, no matter how you age, my heart will always belong to you. Even if we don't complete the bond and you leave me tonight, that won't stop the hurt. I'd rather spend the rest of your life loving you the way you are, and live the remainder of my days after that knowing I had the pleasure of experiencing that with you, than walk away now, and spend the rest of my days not knowing what I could have had."

He brushed his hand over her cheek as tears dripped from her chin.

"Please just stay with me, and we can figure out this thing with the Order—without changing who you are. I'll let you go if I have to... but I'm begging you not to choose that path. I don't want to live without you anymore."

Things weren't perfect. Lukas had his moments. But if she waited for perfection and held him to a standard even she couldn't meet, then she'd never be happy. She needed to trust him. He hadn't given her a reason not to. Maybe it was time to trust in this. Trust that he'd respect her wishes about not becoming a Vasirian, at least not yet. Understand her fear of the bonding process.

Blaire closed her eyes as she leaned into the hand that still rested on her cheek. "I don't know how I could have thought leaving was a good idea..."

Lukas sucked in a breath. "Does that mean…?"

Blaire nodded against his palm.

Lukas stood and twined his hands in hers, gazing into her eyes. Her heart filled with the hope rolling off him in waves. He tugged her to her feet beside him, then lowered his lips to hers in the softest of kisses. Not demanding, not begging, not taking more than giving or descending into the fiery passion that had dominated their interactions for months, simply thanking, cherishing, and loving. Tears spilled from her eyes at the contrast.

He ended the kiss and picked up her bag, taking it to the closet with purposeful steps, where he dropped it on the floor before collapsing onto his bed with a grin.

She would unpack it tomorrow; she couldn't think of doing it tonight. After everything that happened, she didn't have the desire to deal with it. She wiped her cheeks and entered the closet to get her pajamas.

Once she had changed into her nightshirt, she came out of the bathroom into their now darkened room and padded quietly over to her bed. As she adjusted the covers, Lukas was still moving around the room, and she heard him unzip his jeans and drop them to the floor before footsteps moved in her direction and stopped beside her bed.

"I told you I wouldn't leave you alone… and I need you right now."

Blaire hesitated for a moment, alarmed he meant sex, but her sensitivity to his emotional state said that wasn't his intent. He needed reassurance. She slid over to allow him in, her chest swelling with contentment.

Lukas pulled back the covers and climbed into the bed with her. Reaching out and wrapping his arm around her waist, putting his other arm above her head on the pillow, he pulled her flush against his body and let out a shuddered breath as spooning with her brought him relief.

She needed Lukas as much as he needed her in that moment.

He buried his nose in her hair and closed his eyes as they both fell asleep in the silence of the room.

Blaire stirred in the darkness; her sleep disturbed. The sound of rain hitting the window as a late June storm raged outside had woken her up. The room suddenly illuminated as lightning flashed outside, followed by a loud clap of thunder that made her yelp.

"Blaire?" Lukas questioned groggily.

"It's nothing. Sleep," she whispered shakily, and pressed her back tightly against him, clinging to the arm wrapped around her from behind.

Another loud crash of thunder shook the window and Blaire flinched, covering her mouth.

Lukas lifted himself on his elbow, peering down at her. She could barely make his face out in the dark.

"We need to fix this," he said quietly.

"What are you talking about?"

Lukas leaned down and kissed her forehead. "You associate storms with the disturbing things you went through, right? Maybe if you had something better to replace that memory…"

He lifted himself on the bed and Blaire rolled onto her back, looking up at him as another flash of lightning illuminated his body and she jerked.

"I need you to see me…" He reached across her and turned the lamp on, filling the room with light, offsetting the eerie atmosphere the lightning flashes brought to the room. "I want you to focus on me, not on what's happening out there. Can you do that?"

Blaire nodded quietly and Lukas smiled at her, leaning in to kiss her softly like before. A tendril of want uncoiled inside her as she sank into his warmth. When he pulled away, breaking the kiss all too soon, he grinned at her frown. He slid down her body and ran his hands up her outer thighs until he reached the hem of her t-shirt, looking into her eyes, silently asking for permission. She nodded, and he smiled at her. Seeing him smile at her, feeling how relaxed he was, distracted her from the raging storm outside. He had never been like this before, tender, questing, and in good humor.

Maybe it was the relief at having decided she wasn't leaving. Maybe it was the proximity of his being in bed with her. She didn't know. But the same carefree feeling suffused her from the inside.

Lukas pushed her t-shirt up above her hips and rested on his haunches, staring down at her body. She squirmed under his appraisal, and he shook his head. "Shh. It's okay… You're beautiful." he whispered, looping his fingers under the waistband of her panties. Blaire lifted her hips, allowing him to slide them from her body and toss them to the floor. "Absolutely beautiful."

Her face heated.

Lukas lowered himself and positioned himself on his stomach with his head between her legs. Blaire gasped when his breath tickled against her warm center. When the flat of his tongue dragged up her core, a low moan left her throat. "Oh, God…"

He chuckled against her, and the vibration caused her to jerk. He wrapped his arms around the tops of her thighs to hold her still as he leaned in and began to lap greedily at her wet slit.

He treated her body as his own personal buffet, and when he sucked her clit into his mouth tightly, she gasped at the foreign sensation and began grinding her hips reflexively against his face.

Lukas lifted his head quickly in surprise, staring at her.

"Blaire..." he whispered. His eyes were glowing that beautiful, bioluminescent, pale green.

She swallowed hard, face burning from the embarrassment of her shamelessness. "Sorry..."

Lukas grinned wickedly. "Don't you dare be." He went back down and dragged his tongue over her slit slowly.

Her mind sank into that place where she didn't know up from down, but she didn't want to stop falling. Her thighs trembled beneath the hands that held onto her legs as she tried to buck away from him, overwhelmed by the new sensations. He removed one hand from her thigh and brought it around to slowly tease her entrance with the tip of his finger. She sucked in a breath.

He whispered against her center, "Do you trust me?" He moved over to kiss her inner thigh softly as he waited for her response, lazily swirling the tip of his finger over her dampness.

Blaire looked down at him, and his glowing eyes caught hers as she nodded.

"I need the words, beautiful..."

Blaire whimpered and squirmed, and when he ran his tongue over the skin of her thigh, pulling his finger away, she breathed out, "Yes... completely."

Lukas groaned low in his throat, and he sucked on the bundle of nerves again tightly as he slid one finger into her. He had her so aroused his finger slid in easily.

Blaire laid her head back and moaned, her body instinctively rocking against the intrusion while he lapped at her swollen core. He worked another finger inside and she arched her back, gripping the covers on each side of her body.

He played her body like an instrument, sucking on the little nub that brought her to new heights of pleasure she didn't know she could experience. She thrashed her head from side to side as she practically mewled for him. She had absolutely no control over what her body did anymore.

"Lukas… it's… it's too much…" she panted, squirming against him. She'd given herself an orgasm before, but this sensation building was like nothing she had ever felt, and it made her entire body tingle and overheat.

Just as she felt like she was going to cry from how sensitive she felt, Lukas stopped and got up on his knees in front of her, staring down at her and dragging his hand across his mouth to wipe the glistening juices from his face. That act alone had her aching for more. Blaire bit her lower lip as Lukas reached for the bottom of her shirt, sliding it up her body. He kissed over her hip and stomach before pulling her shirt completely over her head and tossing it to the floor.

Blaire stared at him breathlessly, but this was far from over. She was more than ready for where this was leading.

Lukas leaned down to kiss her breasts gently before sucking on her hardened nipples, his fangs grazing the tender skin. She whimpered at the sensation, but he didn't stop. He lifted himself to his knees, staring down into her eyes, unable to tear his gaze away from her. The intensity in his eyes made her full body shudder, his unique scent permeating the room and making the haze in her head worse.

"Lukas…" She reached up to run her hand down his chest. Her hand moved over his abs, and they tightened as she passed over them.

Lukas groaned and closed his eyes. "You have no idea how long I have wanted you to touch me like this," he rasped.

Blaire swallowed hard and moved to where her fingertips grazed over the front of his boxers, passing over his straining arousal. She gasped. She knew he was big. She had felt him pressed against her in the mornings, but she never felt it firsthand like this. She pushed the waistband away with curious fingers, wanting to see it. At the sight of his erection, a small wave of fear washed over her, thrilling like the first drop on a roller coaster.

"Shh, it's alright," he whispered, no doubt sensing her fear, as he climbed off the bed and pulled his boxers off, digging around in the nightstand, before returning.

Lukas knelt between her thighs again, stroking himself slowly while she watched. He stared down at her with a silent question. Her breath hitched at the intensity she found in his eyes.

"I'm ready…" she whispered, but she couldn't hide her apprehension when he could sense her every emotion. She was ready, but the uncertainty of whether she would make it through this tried to intrude on her blissful place.

Lukas laid his head back, closing his eyes as his breathing suddenly became more ragged. They both knew it was time, and they both had longed for this moment.

He growled low and tore open a small packet with his teeth before proceeding to roll a condom down his length. Blaire watched him with rapt fascination. Lukas reached down and dragged his hand up her slippery folds as she moaned, laying her head back. She was ready for him. He stroked himself a couple of times to lubricate his shaft and then positioned himself at her entrance before slowly pushing into her.

Blaire gasped when he got the head inside as another wave of fear swept over her and she started to sweat, squirming at the tight, stretching, alien sensation. She sucked in a breath, and he placed his hand on her stomach, stopping his movements and sliding out.

"Look at me," he whispered in a strained voice. His neck muscles were taut, and she could tell he was having a hard time with stopping.

She stared up into his eyes, glowing, green, and fierce again.

"I told you I wouldn't hurt you, but I need you to relax. If you're not relaxed, it's going to hurt. If you relax, it won't hurt… not with what we've already done."

Her brow furrowed.

"I…" He clenched his jaw. "I did what I needed to do to prepare you… to make this easier for you."

Blaire smiled and reached for his hand. He took it and laced his fingers through hers.

"It's not easy for me either. I want to make sure I do it right. Make it good for you. I had to… do some research." A flush overtook his cheeks and neck. He hadn't had a girlfriend before, but she didn't assume he'd never… She squeezed his hand tightly and he looked back at her face.

"I'm ready," she whispered again, reassuring him.

Lukas bent forward and captured her lips with his as he slowly slid into the heat of her body, and she arched into him, moaning into his mouth. The sensation was incredible. Letting go, in more ways than one, made everything different. The stretch he caused still burned because she'd never had anything that large inside her before, but it still couldn't beat the intoxicating pleasure his being inside her brought forth. He didn't move once he was all the way inside, letting her get used to the feeling—and getting used to it himself—as he stroked the inside of her mouth with his tongue.

When he trembled against her, aching with wonder, she pulled from his kiss.

"You can move…" she whispered.

Lukas ran his tongue over his bottom lip and slowly pulled back, almost pulling all the way out of her, but keeping the head inside. Then he slowly slid himself back in and shivered. His entire body was tense as he held himself back, until she reached up, and grabbed his forearms that held the covers in a death grip on each side of her body, rocking her hips against him to encourage him. She needed him to know she wasn't afraid anymore. That she wanted this. He groaned.

Her body molded to his so well. They truly were made for each other.

Getting the hint, Lukas raked his gaze down her body, over her breasts, and down to where they were connected. He licked his lips again and lifted her upper body up toward him, wrapping his arms around her back as he pulled her flush to his skin.

Sitting back on his heels, with her straddling his waist, he kissed her like a man starved. She tightened around him, whimpering into his mouth before he released her lips. The sensations rolling off him melded with those from inside herself. Their empathic connection was madness.

Blaire wrapped her arms around Lukas's neck and buried her face into the hair plastered to his shoulders with sweat. He pulled her closer with his hands, gripping her ass in a bruising grip as he thrusted up into her at a quicker pace. He found places inside her she didn't even know existed and dragged out the most delicious feelings.

She writhed against him, whimpering, and moaning her approval of what he did to her, her entire body trembling as she held on for dear life while he took her body without caution. Blaire could feel the same sensation building deep in her stomach from earlier and she dug her nails into his shoulder blades, chasing after it this time; she wasn't letting it slip past her again.

"Fuck, Blaire… so good. So fucking good," he groaned.

It was so close, so close to happening. "Lukas. I'm gonna…"

Lukas quickly dropped forward on the bed with her, holding himself deep inside her, not moving. She whined in protest at the sudden loss of his movements as he unwrapped his arms from behind her.

Reaching over to the nightstand, he grabbed Aiden's knife.

Blaire gasped and stared up at him. "What are you doing with the knife?"

Still seated inside her, Lukas moved his hair that was damp from sweat away from his shoulder. He winced as he slid the knife slowly across the skin where his shoulder and neck met.

Blaire realized what was happening then, and as she watched the blood ooze from the knife wound, she tensed as anxiety warred within her, threatening to close off her connection with him.

He leaned over and set the knife down before covering her again and looking down at her. Thunder rumbled outside, the first she had noticed since they began their carnal embrace.

"It's time," he said, his voice trembling despite the serious and composed facial expression he held. He stared down at her as his blood ran from his wound down his chest.

Blaire's heart pounded in her ears like the beat of hundreds of tribal drums.

"I'm scared…" she whispered

He reached down to caress her face. "Please don't fear me… I'd rather die than hurt you. I promise I'll stop."

She trusted him. She needed him. Needed this. She still didn't relish the idea of drinking blood or having her blood taken, but if it would cement them together as one, then she was ready. He would take care of her.

Lukas hovered over her, placing his hands on each side of her head again, his forearms straining.

"I love you, Blaire… I can't live without you, and I won't let you go," he whispered.

He claimed her lips in an agonizingly slow kiss, rocking his body inside her again. As the ache built again, sensations clawing for release, he moved over to her neck, dragging his fangs down the side to the soft flesh at the corresponding spot to where he cut himself.

"Please..." he whispered, his voice raspy, straining for control.

Blaire slowly tilted her head. "I'm yours, Lukas," she whispered.

It was true, she was his, but he belonged to her, needed her as much as she needed him, and that knowledge made all the difference.

Lukas shuddered and growled before burying his fangs deep into Blaire's skin as she cried out, her body trembling in his arms as pleasure like she hadn't known before rolled through her. The bite wasn't painful at all, instead, only bliss.

He pulled away from her neck enough to snarl, "Now!" before returning to drinking from her as she clung to him.

Without giving herself time to second guess the move, Blaire placed her mouth over the open knife wound and licked it once. Her eyes rolled back in her head, and she drew lightly at the wound. The taste was anything but revolting. It was extremely intoxicating, better than that sweet drink she had at Haven. She had no idea why she waited so long. Was this what they meant by the blood of your pair was addictive? She was a human, and even she could see herself becoming enthralled by the taste.

Blaire started to suck on the wound more greedily and again felt that familiar wave cresting low in her stomach. Lukas groaned into her neck, no longer drinking from her as he pounded into her body, his movements becoming jerky as he lost his control.

When she fell over the edge finally, she broke away from sucking on Lukas's skin and threw her head back, shouting his name, his blood running from her mouth, as Lukas snapped his hips a few final times before letting go, his body convulsing over hers with grunts of satisfaction.

They stayed locked together, their heavy breathing the only sound in the room before Lukas slowly extracted himself from her body. He left the bed to remove the used condom and dispose of it before coming back to her arms. Collapsing beside her, he pulled her to his chest and kissed the top of her head.

"I love you so much… Gods, I love you," Lukas whispered.

Blaire put her head to his heart and laughed in embarrassment. "This was way better than any of the dreams I've had." Laughing at his confused expression, she leaned in and gently kissed him before whispering over his lips, "I love you… I've loved you for a while now, but I've just been too afraid of what it meant for my future. But I couldn't run from you in my dreams."

38

CLAIMED

The next morning, Lukas and Blaire walked into the cafeteria together for breakfast, meeting up with everyone. Lukas felt exhausted, but he welcomed it. It was the first time the exhaustion that gripped his body was for something good.

Riley squealed immediately when she saw Blaire.

"What's wrong?" Blaire said, taking a step back in surprise.

Jumping up and down, Riley pointed at Blaire's neck, clearly visible since she had worn her hair in a ponytail. The mark stood out clear and crisp, like a new black tattoo.

Blaire blushed and put her hand over the mark. Lukas wrapped his arm around her shoulder as they took their seats.

He was so happy he couldn't even put it into words. She was his officially. She had told him she loved him, and he knew she accepted him for what he was. Now their mark told the world.

"That's amazing, man. I'm happy for you both." Aiden smiled at them. It was genuine.

Lukas knew Aiden was attracted to Blaire still, but his best friend wouldn't try anything, and neither would Blaire. He trusted them both.

Kai grinned. "Yes, it's about time this happened."

"What he means to say is congratulations," Mera said as she gave Kai a withering glance. He shrugged.

Riley sighed dreamily. "I can't wait until I find my pair."

Rolling his eyes, Seth said, "No one is going to put up with you long enough to complete a bon—ow!" He rubbed his arm where Riley punched him.

"I will kill you and help them look for your body."

"You wouldn't…" Seth glared at her.

Riley shrugged. "Try me. Do you honestly think they'd suspect me? I'll even lead the search team."

"Considering you're admitting your intentions of killing me in front of everyone? Yeah."

Riley rolled her eyes.

Everyone laughed and made plans for the rest of the weekend before Mera spoke up, causing the mood to shift.

"Have you decided if you'll allow Lukas to turn you, since you've accepted the bond?"

Lukas tensed and ran a hand through his hair. He wasn't wanting to deal with this yet, not with how good things were going. Couldn't he have one day of peace and happiness with Blaire before everything fell apart? He looked over at her warily.

Blaire shook her head, but Lukas didn't sense the usual knee-jerk angst at the question. "No, I'm not ready for that, and honestly, I don't know if I'll ever be, but I'm not going to run from the Order, or Lukas. I'm not going anywhere. I tried that already, and I realized before I even made it anywhere, it would be the biggest mistake of my life if I did. The idea almost cost me everything that mattered to me." She looked up into Lukas's eyes and he leaned down, kissing her lips softly.

"Aw, it's so sweet!" Riley squealed.

Seth covered his face with his hand and shook his head, annoyed with her outbursts.

Kai raised an eyebrow. "What do you mean, Blaire?"

"I was going to leave Blackthorn, but I decided that wasn't the path I wanted to take anymore."

Lukas gripped her shoulder. Being able to touch her soothed so much of his insecurities; feeling her body made everything better.

Riley gasped. "No! You can't leave!"

"I know," Blaire said, nodding. "I acted impulsively on fear and didn't think things through. Things just overwhelmed me, and I ran away, but I would never be happy with that decision, especially with how I feel for Lukas."

Seth shook his head. "So, you actually do like him?"

Blaire looked down and murmured, "I've known for a while I was in love with Lukas, but I tried to convince myself it was for the best to let him go."

Lukas reached out and pulled her close, burying his head into the side of her neck, kissing over the mark there.

Aiden rubbed the back of his neck. "I'm glad you both got your heads out of the sand and shared your feelings with each other, because it was honestly getting difficult to watch."

Riley laughed. "Yeah, you can say that again."

Aiden sighed. "And we will protect her from the Order, no matter what, so that's a moot point."

Seeing his friends expressing their desire to be there for his pair warmed Lukas inside. Having friends dedicated to protecting the one person made for him in this world was everything. He spent so long keeping his distance from others, and now he had a support system he wouldn't trade for the world.

"Hopefully, now that they have completed their bond, the Order will see no reason to continue to experiment on Blaire," Kai said, sitting back in his seat and crossing his arms.

Lukas sure hoped so. Without her willingness to become like him, she was at high risk. He wanted to convince her, but at the same time, he wanted to respect her wishes. It was difficult. He loved her so much, and the idea she was so fragile was hard to swallow.

Mera shook her head. "It's doubtful, because if Professor Velastra is correct, the whole reason for their behavior is because they want to see why a human can be a Korrena, not because they wanted to force the pairing."

The table fell silent for several minutes, no one quite knowing what to say. Lukas grew agitated. Blaire rested her hand on his thigh, and he tucked his head into her neck again. She could feel him, and it was the most wonderful feeling to know she sensed him.

"Whatever the reason is, they won't make it easy for them," Seth said.

Lukas nodded. "You're absolutely right, but I will spend my life protecting Blaire no matter what it takes."

If he had to go up against the Order, he would do it. Nothing would stop him from protecting the keeper of his heart.

Walking away from the window on the highest floor of the administrative building, the Oracle crossed over to stand before the seven robed council members. They sat on high-backed chairs resembling thrones of black stained wood, with burgundy upholstery, positioned at the top of several steps in front of a large, red stained-glass window.

"The human has been claimed and now bears the boy's mark," she said, her voice soft but firm as she stared forward.

One of the cloaked men jumped to his feet, face twisted. "We will be unable to determine what is so special about her blood now!" He threw his hands into the air. "This is a disaster!"

The one in the middle of the group raised his hand to call forth silence. "Sit down and calm yourself Kirill," the man said in a thick Italian accent.

The man fell into his seat as he cursed in Russian beneath his breath.

The middle council member continued calmly, "Now, as long as she remains human, we can continue to conduct our experiments on her blood. The bond should not change anything about the makeup of her blood or genealogy." He looked to the Oracle for confirmation.

She nodded once, then smoothed her hands down the front of her robe. "The girl is still very much human, and as long as she remains that way, there should be no change."

"Excellent." The middle council member clapped his hands.

The Oracle lifted her hand to stop his premature celebration. "But I have seen the indecision within the child. She is wavering in accepting the Dark Kiss. It will not be long before she relents and accepts it."

The seven members began whispering and cursing among themselves as she walked to the window again that overlooked the courtyard.

"We have very little time left to discover the anomaly."

39

Message

Blaire sat on the bed reading the last few pages of the novel she started on when she arrived at Blackthorn Academy, finally done with her schoolwork and ready to relax for the brief summer break.

The door opened, and Lukas entered the room. And when his eyes found her, he smiled. She would never tire of seeing that reaction to her. With all the fears laid bare, and the bond completed, he had settled down. She felt at greater peace within herself as well. She no longer felt this constant pull to act without knowing what action she was supposed to take.

"This was on the door for you," Lukas said as he sat next to her on the bed, passing her a cream envelope with her name in stylish black calligraphy on the front and sealed with a burgundy wax seal of a feather on the back.

Blaire looked at him with furrowed brows as she popped open the seal. "I wonder what it is."

Inside the envelope was a delicate parchment with the same intricate calligraphy. Lukas looked over her shoulder as they both read the message inside.

There is more to your blood than a lover's bond eternal.
A long ago buried secret,
An unknown history stained crimson,
A balance broken to hold control and power.
The stars have aligned;
Your awakening is nigh.
The Dark Kiss is the key,
But the consequences are shrouded.
A child born of a love tested and won
holds the key to salvation for a king bound.

Lukas sat back and ran a hand through his hair. "What the hell does that mean?"

"I don't know… did you see who left the note on the door?"

He shook his head. "No. It wasn't there when I went to the canteen, but when I came back it was just taped there."

Blaire read over the cryptic message again. The first line seemed fairly obvious. She had deduced something was different about her blood; it seemed to be the general assumption among everyone around. The "different" element remained up for debate. And the "lover's bond eternal" had to be the Korrena bond. But the rest of the message lost her.

"Maybe we should show it to Professor Velastra?" Lukas asked.

Blaire folded the message and put it back in the envelope. "There's not really anyone else we can talk to about this kind of thing. We still don't know who on staff we can trust."

Lukas wrapped his arms around Blaire and pulled her close.

The Order hadn't made another move since the night everything went down with Caleb, but that still didn't mean they weren't watching her and Lukas. It didn't mean they wouldn't come again for her blood. Unless they had found what they were looking for, she was still at risk of being attacked again.

Joining Blackthorn Academy had been the best decision of her life. At the time, she didn't know it would be that way. The fight to get to this point had made her question everything from her sanity to her own self-worth, whether her choices were valid; but she came out on the other side stronger. She remained true to herself and was rewarded with a bond with someone from whom she would never walk away. With Caleb and the Wilcox family out of her life, Blaire could move forward with Lukas and try to find happiness.

But a dark shadow still loomed over their heads. Until they got to the bottom of what the Order wanted with her for sure, or until they discovered for themselves why human Blaire was destined to become a Korrena pair to a Vasirian, this peaceful reprieve would only be temporary.

One thing she knew for certain, though…

Lukas would be by her side through whatever storms were to come.

Newsletter

Sign up for Stephanie's Newsletter to keep up to date on the latest news around the Blackthorn world and future series and get special sneak peeks at the writing process and chapter previews for future books.

http://eepurl.com/h_N5uP

or visit my website

www.stephaniedenneauthor.com to sign up.About the Author

About the Author

Stephanie Denne is an author of Paranormal Romance and Dark Fantasy for new adults and adults. First in a long saga, Mark of the Vasirian is her debut in the writing world.

Inspired by art and music, she felt the need to give life to characters that had been rolling around in her mind for 12 years. Never having written anything before, when she sat down and started drafting, she discovered she had a passion for the craft and the story naturally grew into something much bigger than she could fit into one book—much less a few, or even one series!

Born in the United States of America in the Southeast, Stephanie has now called Ontario, Canada her home since 2011. When not writing, she can be found reading her favorite stories, playing video games with her husband, painting with watercolor, or cuddling with her two Golden Retrievers. But not the cat—the cat has her own agenda.

ACKNOWLEDGMENTS

I want to first thank my wonderful husband, who listened to me ramble constantly as my story shaped in my head. Without your critical thinking, I might have gone off track a few times. Pointing out potential plot holes, and even helping me settle on the initial title for Mark of the Vasirian when I was deciding between a few, made the process flow a lot easier. The hard work you do each day allowed me to focus on this project, and it has truly warmed my heart. I can never thank you enough. I love you.

To my editor Kelly, you are an angel for putting up with a rookie like me. From late-night messages about everything from psychology to human menstrual cycles, and vampiric races (oh boy!), you listened and helped me find my voice. This series would have had a very different start if not for your guidance and patience, and I'm very grateful as you helped bring out what I really wanted to say, and who I really wanted Lukas and Blaire to be.

I also want to give my appreciation to those who helped me in different ways through the process.

Satyros Phil Brucato, an amazing author with a backlog spanning many years, provided reassurance when I wasn't sure I was doing okay. Knowing that even some of the best authors have faced the "Red Pen of Death" made me not want to throw in the towel at the first sample edit. Your blog entries and writing guides were an asset in my process, your wisdom invaluable.

Kat, from KatChatsFinnish on YouTube. Thank you so much for your guidance in ensuring I used the correct words in Finnish for Lukas's mother to convey what I wanted her to say.

Rick, or Revarick. Your Moon Glyphs were the perfect inspiration for Lukas and Blaire's mark. A stylistic combination of two glyphs to make it unique—as many have found inspiration in your creation—that fit their character perfectly. Thank you for your creativity!

To my in-laws, thank you for being the support both my husband and I needed through the pandemic so that we could pursue the careers that we both wanted without added stress. I'll never forget it. This book would not have happened had I not been given this opportunity.

And to every reader who has made it this far, I can't begin to express my gratitude that you picked up (or downloaded) my book and completed it. I hope you loved it as much as I loved creating it and that you will stick around through the saga to come. I appreciate each and every one of you. Thank you from the bottom of my heart.

Printed in Great Britain
by Amazon

36648217R00280